THE TREE OF SOULS

Also By Katrina Archer

UNTALENTED

THE TREE OF SOULS

KATRINA ARCHER

A Ganache Media Book
Vancouver

The Tree of Souls is a work of fiction. Names, characters, places, and incidents either are the product of the author's imagination, or are used fictitiously. Any resemblance to actual persons, living or dead, events, or locales is entirely coincidental.

2016 Ganache Media print edition

ISBN 978-0-9880512-7-0

Cover design by Heather McDougal

www.ganachemedia.com

For Guylain

NOW

I wish I could remember why I hate myself.

Mud from the riverbank welled up between my fingers like blood. I clawed my way up the slippery, crumbling bank.

The mouthful of water I choked out tasted bitter. *Like guilt.*

My head ... Stray thoughts fluttered within me like wounded birds, fragile yet uncatchable. *Focus.*

The night breeze draped ribbons of cold across my naked back. I shivered. I could barely feel my toes. Water sluiced from my hair, trickled down my neck and between my breasts, then fell with a soft plop into the mud. I felt a treacherous desire to slide back with it, and let the river carry me away into oblivion. But that wasn't an option. Not for me. Important. I had to ...

What? Fates help me. Have to what?

I collapsed at the top of the bank, rolled over onto my back. Each blade of grass cut into my tender skin like stinging nettles. Closing my eyes, I watched the colors waver behind my lids. The moonlight did nothing to warm me.

Where am I?

I tried to let the past pour in.

Wind tearing at my limbs. Black water rushing up. My skin

sizzling like a red-hot iron rod quenched in ice water.

Drowning. Safe on land now, but drowning still. Drowning in the cloying smell of night jasmine, in air that flowed too thick to breathe, in the chorus of frog calls that washed across my ears in a gabbling torrent. No wonder infants fresh from the womb squalled, if the world assaulted them this way.

I focused on calming my ragged breathing, stilling the trembling in my limbs. After a few moments I adjusted, the sensory deluge becoming simply a strong current. My eyelids snapped open. The night lay unchanged before me. Over my head swayed the fronds of a giant plant, its leaves at least a pace across.

Off in the distance a man shouted. The soft thud of hooves in the grass intruded into my exhaustion.

With the sharpening of my awareness, I felt something else. A presence, questing.

Hide.

But where? The terrain sloped gently away from the river up to a line of towering cypress trees. A worn path followed the bank itself, and I could already make out the riders. If I raced to the trees across the moon-washed expanse, they were sure to spot me. I questioned whether I could sprint at all. So, hoping the movement wouldn't give me away, I pushed myself into a crouch and reached up, grabbing one of the enormous leaves to use as a screen.

Except the stem bit me. Its thorns stabbed into my already inflamed skin, and I yelped. I snatched at the leaf instead, but its rough surface, while thornless, felt like crushed glass against the pads of my fingers. I whimpered, but brought the frond down anyway. I held my breath as the mounts approached. The hoofbeats ceased when they drew even with my improvised shelter. I heard the soft creak of leather as a rider shifted. I willed him away. And yet …

Somewhere, not too far away, something else hunted me. I didn't know how I knew. But it meant me harm.

Wait. No. I fought to hold onto the thought. *She* meant me harm.

A velvety nose nuzzled the edge of the leaf, blowing warm exhalation of horse across my face. Boots crunched to the ground and a hand swept aside the frond. A man loomed over me. A torch guttered in his hand. His eyes widened as he took me in.

I squinted in the torchlight at the other riders behind him. Not a woman among them.

With nowhere to run, perhaps safety lay in numbers.

"Are you just going to stare at me or do you have a cloak I could borrow?" I said with more bravado than I felt. My voice sounded strange in my ears, wrong somehow, like an echo cast back at me from distant mountains.

He unclasped his cloak and draped it across me, snugging it about my neck. I stifled a scream as the scratchy wool set my skin afire. I would have flung the cloak from me but for the eyes watching me from the edge of the ring of light the torch cast.

The man spoke to someone behind him. "Take the men and wait for me down the trail." I heard a horse snort and the sound of several animals trotting off into the darkness. A hard nugget of fear lodged in my throat. What did he not want them to see him do?

I struggled upright and concentrated on the remaining man,

taking in the fine cut of his clothes, the confident stance. No brigand, this, yet I stayed wary. Eyes of palest green appraised me, and I tugged the cloak up against my chest. Nothing evoked any recognition in me. Not the house colors he wore, slate grey slashed with blue. Not the feathers of chestnut hair falling across his eyes. Not even his voice, deep but with a hint of gravel. I breathed in his scent. He smelled of suspicion and worry, but I sensed openness as well, like a warm summer breeze with a hint of fennel.

Overwhelmed, my nose twitched, and I sneezed.

A cloud passed in front of the moon and I flinched. Instead of feeling less exposed by the absence of light, I felt more so—as if the darkness and the shadows created pathways the being that hunted me traveled with impunity. Pathways unsafe for me to be found on.

But I had nothing to offer this man in exchange for shelter. If indeed his intentions were at all honorable.

He leaned in, moving the cloak aside to touch my throat. Not honorable then. My skin tingled where his fingers traced the outline of a small circle below my collarbone.

He has no right to touch you.

I almost laughed at the errant thought, but the fear nugget grew into a stone. I couldn't force a sound up my throat past it. No right? As if in my weakened state I could do anything about it. I slapped his hand away, knowing it would do no good.

"How did you come by it?" he asked.

Air whooshed out of my nostrils. I'd been holding my breath. "I—what?"

I must have looked as confused as I felt. He repeated the

question, and pointed at my chest.

Looking down, I gasped. A circular brand, the size of a large coin, puckered the skin below my collarbone. I needed a mirror to properly see it and the pattern burned into my skin.

He brushed his thumb against the brand and this time I let him. At his touch, the probing presence manifested itself as a crawling along the skin of my temples. I felt like the most vulnerable kind of prey. Like a rabbit hunted by an eagle, a mouse by an owl. Or a departed soul, hunted by the daemons that fed on a soul's essence. I needed to convince this man to take me with him or let me flee.

"Who are you?" I asked.

"I am Fayne Grey. Tenth Elder of Clan Grey, son of Garrith. And you?" His polite tone seemed at odds with his challenging stare.

I opened my mouth to tell him, but stopped, tense and dizzy. *Who am I?*

Again I avoided his question with another question. "How did you find me?"

"Chance. There are marauders about. I was just returning with a patrol from checking on the intentions of a ... less than friendly neighbor. Now—your name?"

My throat tightened again, as if to keep the words from spilling out. "My Lord, I cannot give you my name."

"Cannot or will not?"

"Cannot. I ... seem to have forgotten it." Fates! That sounded vacuous. The emptiness of my past yawned before me. "Among other things."

"Do you remember how you wound up in the river?"

I shook my head, recalled only flickers of memory: a woman's face, startled—no, angry? Both. A fall from a large height. Clinging to a log until my frozen fingers lost their grip. The river spat me onto the bank just as the last of my strength ebbed.

Lord Grey still stared at my brand. "You don't have the look of any Clan. Yet you bear the Mark of the Clans."

Maybe I did have something to trade after all.

"Until I find out who you are and how you got it, you will stay at the keep. Come. I can't leave you here." He gazed up the trail as the wind gusted. "It's a night fit only for shades."

I shuddered. His words echoed my fear. He might not trust me, but a fortified keep sounded better than spending the night underneath my plant. Yet instead of relief, the offer of shelter induced a sense of unease. Staying in one place made me too easy to track. I might be better off remaining mobile.

I rejected the thought. I was in no state to run. I needed clothes, and my strength back before I could consider anything else. And if I could pry out of this Fayne what this mark meant, maybe it would help solve the mystery of me. "Lead the way."

"What shall we call you in the meantime?" Fayne asked.

Only then did I fathom the loneliness in the lack of a name. My shadow, opaque and impenetrable, flickered and danced in the torchlight. The guilt that weighted me as I hauled myself out of the river washed over me again. Maybe whatever I fled from wasn't the only creature of darkness that walked these paths. Maybe I walked them too.

"Umbra," I said. It seemed somehow appropriate.

Then

Jezarel slashed at the grass stalks with her riding crop, decapitating several in an explosion of seed heads. Her cheeks burned still. She didn't know who angered her more, her father, or that idiot boy Osif. She clutched the glowing ember of her humiliation to her heart, nursing its hot core until her disappointment at Osif's rejection threatened to spill over in a mess of tears.

"But your father will kill me, Jezarel," she mimicked Osif's whining tone, giving it an extra edge of sniveling cowardice. Except that she couldn't be sure Osif's fear of her father's wrath made him pull away when she offered him her lips. What if he just hadn't wanted her?

Was she not desirable? How could she ever hope to make a good match for the tribe if no boy would look at her? She could just hear the other girls laughing in triumph—the Izir's daughter, last to be kissed.

Jezarel paused in the tall grasses at the edge of the old watering hole. Someone else beat her there. Hidden from view, she admired the tanned back of the youth, his muscles rippling across his shoulders as he dunked his shirt in the shallow pool.

Jezarel smiled. Here was a boy her father couldn't keep her from talking to. Her father's stodginess drove her mad. She would *not* be the last of her friends to know a man's lips. She set her shawl lower, baring her shoulders, and stepped forward.

Then changed her mind. What if this boy laughed at her? What if he sent her back to her father with her tail between her legs, like Osif? The thought mortified her. Twice in one day—could she bear it? She nearly melted back into the steppe grass. But no. An Izir's daughter never ran from a challenge.

An Izir's daughter … Jezarel heard her mother's voice in her head. An Izir's daughter behaved with decorum. Put the tribe's honor first.

But the tribe's honor hinged on Jezarel's marriageability. She'd heard the whispers. Cousin Lailaz didn't even bother whispering her jabs. "Prude. Who'd want that stuck up face?"

Jezarel contemplated the shepherd boy. If she could just get that one first kiss, then maybe some cloak that masked her womanhood would fall away. Suitable men would ask her father's permission to court her. The tribe's currency would rise. Lailaz would shut up.

The snickers of the girls if she failed, though, echoed, in her imagination. Someone would find out, somehow. Then it came to her—she knew just the trick to nudge this shepherd boy in the right direction. Today started in humiliation, but it wouldn't end that way.

Jezarel tugged at the pouch hanging from her waist and poured a little pink quartz dust into her palm. What had the peddler woman said, again? Oh, yes. Glamour was all about planting the right suggestion. Keep a light touch on the soul.

Jezarel tossed the dust into the air before her, hummed three notes in a minor key, then blew the dust towards the youth.

She waited five heartbeats. Nothing happened. She'd almost given up when the boy tilted his head, as if listening to something. She walked out of the grass towards the pond, swinging her hips, hoping her gait looked alluring as opposed to ridiculous. She tamped down her nervousness—the glamour should obscure her awkwardness.

He turned towards her. Success! Except—she saw not a boy, but a man. Jezarel drew up short. She cursed the sunshine and soothing breeze for lulling her. Something that had seemed like a flirty game now felt different. Riskier. Not as explainable to her parents. She stumbled to the left away from him, bumped into a palm tree. She spun but he cut off her escape: trapped!

"Mmm, mmm, mmm. Fresh lamb," said the man.

Her heart took off like a startled dove. The enormity of her mistake dawned on her. From behind, Jezarel had taken him for a handsome young shepherd. Up close, skin creased from years in the steppe sun gave the lie to her initial estimate of his age. The breeze shifted and a miasma of onions, sheep dung, and old sweat wafted over her.

She'd put too much into snaring him. She darted past him, but he grabbed her wrist.

"Don't hurt me!" She flung the words out like a shield. "My father—" Her words cut off. Pointless, she knew. He was too fixated on getting what he thought he wanted.

He laughed and tossed her to the ground. Her head cracked against the hard earth. She tasted blood on her lip. Jezarel clawed at his face, but he batted her hands away. The oasis's palms and willows loomed over her, silent, watchful sentinels that rendered no aid.

It wasn't supposed to happen this way! She'd cast a simple glamour—just a little something to pique his interest. How could it go this wrong? Fates! All for a kiss.

Jezarel didn't even think to scream. There was no one to hear. Her walk took her too far from camp. His harsh panting drowned out all other noise—the sound of the gurgling brook, the chattering parrots, the zinging crickets—leaving nothing but his fetid wheeze. That and the slap of her fists pummeling uselessly against his chest.

He grinned at her struggles, so she grew still. Why did she listen to the peddler woman? The hag lied to her about the spell. Stupid, stupid! Jezarel began to cry. If she escaped, she swore she'd never leave herself unprepared and exposed again.

"I thought to take your purse," the man said, "but maybe I'll take something more."

Jezarel flinched. Disgust swamped her. He would *not* defile her. She scrabbled at the pouch at her hip. Maybe it contained some leftover powder. She didn't know how to undo her handiwork, but maybe she could disable him with another spell. May the Fates help her focus.

A hair-raising wail erupted from the high grasses that surrounded the oasis. Jezarel's attacker froze. A shadow fell across his face. He leapt up and fled.

Jezarel tilted her head back. From her upside-down vantage, she saw a tall, slim silhouette limned by the sun. That, and the glint of a sword.

Jezarel sniffled and wiped the tears from her cheeks. She

wouldn't die today, or lose her maidenhood. Suddenly her embarrassment at Osif's hands seemed petty. She'd almost brought an even greater shame to her family—all because of her own pride. Yet … even though she'd cast a questionable spell, surely the shepherd's response seemed all out of proportion. Jezarel silently thanked the Fates for saving her. Shivers rippled through her limbs, filling the void left by her fear.

The newcomer said nothing. Had she traded one evil for another?

Jezarel risked rolling over. She got to her feet and studied her rescuer.

Black baggy breeches. Black tunic. Pale grey eyes scrutinized her from behind the shroud of a black scarf.

"Thank you," Jezarel said. She tried to quiet her breathing, recoup some of her lost dignity. Her heart fluttered still, as if unsure if she needed to run.

Still the newcomer said nothing.

Jezarel shifted from foot to foot under the weight of that stare. Could it see the trembling in her hands? The stranger's eyes lingered on her torn blouse. She snatched up her silk shawl from where it lay trampled in the dust, gave it a shake, and wrapped it about her shoulders. She drew herself up to her full height, making the most of her willowy stature. Maybe if she acted like the Izir's daughter she supposedly was—"I hope you don't think you're next."

The stranger guffawed, gripped the scarf, and untwisted its lengths from the face it concealed. A cascade of wavy ebony hair fell out into the sunlight. A girl!

"I don't play kissing games. And you should be more careful

11

who you pick for yours."

Jezarel flushed. Had she seen the whole sorry thing? What else might she suspect? Best to change the subject. She looked at the sword. "Do you know how to use that?"

"Yes. But I didn't need to." The stranger sheathed her weapon.

"What's your name?"

"You may call me Kairiya."

"I'm Jezarel." This girl, who looked to be her own age, fascinated her. She wore breeches like the women of the western desert trading caravans, but lacked their distinctive drawl. "Where do you come from?"

"Around."

"Where's your family?"

"I take care of myself."

Jezarel mulled this over. Finally she put her finger on what puzzled her about Kairiya: the paleness of her eyes, and her skin. "You're not Gherza!"

Kairiya glowered. "I was raised here on the steppe."

"You don't look like it." Jezarel stared pointedly at the breeches, then put her forearm alongside Kairiya's. Jezarel's olive skin glowed next to Kairiya's pearly coloring. Jezarel fingered Kairiya's curly locks, but the girl shrugged her away. "No Gherza woman comes by waves naturally."

It was Kairiya's turn to flush. "A barbarian defiled my mother."

The men across the eastern mountains. Having come uncomfortably close to suffering a similar fate, Jezarel resolved to overlook this mark against her new friend. Because she had decided to make Kairiya her friend. Kairiya—her savior today—might save her in other ways. She offered the perfect antidote to the isolation of being the Izir's daughter. A girl who didn't play kissing games wouldn't laugh at Jezarel's lack of suitors, either. If Jezarel could convince her to stay for a while, the rest of summer might just get more tolerable.

The unfortunate incident with the shepherd bore fruit after all. "Come meet my father. He'll reward you for your trouble."

NOW

I awoke in a cozy feather bed, my head aching. Thirst parched my throat, but my skin felt less sensitive. Wriggling upright against the pillow, I reached for a goblet of water I found on the nightstand, but knocked it over. I felt too big for my body.

I frowned and studied the chamber, looking for something I could use to soak up the mess.

Square room. Plain windowless walls. Nondescript canopy bed. Oak door. Except the very fact of a room and a bed leached wrongness through the fuzziness in my head. The stonework looked much finer than a typical croft's. I cast about for anything familiar.

I remembered the painful trip from the river, every movement of the horse causing my raw skin to rub against the borrowed wool cloak. Lord Grey questioned me along the way. His barrage left me confused and exhausted. How old was I? How long had I floated in the river? Did I remember where I fell in? Had I been herding? Riding? Log driving?

Over and over I sang the same refrain: "I don't know." The last question I didn't understand at all. How did one drive logs? His eyes narrowed more with each new query, and I wondered if he'd just abandon me at the side of the trail in frustration.

My own attempts to break the barrier in my mind felt almost tactile, like digging away at a dyke of mud. A mud I sensed I should know, could I only scoop it up and touch it to my tongue, or smell its loam. A mud composed of rich clay, which I could work back into the shape of me, if only. If only … Somehow I knew that *if* wasn't buried as deeply as everything else. I just needed to dig in the right spot, and the sculpture of my intact mind would emerge from the muck.

I spied a pile of clothes on top of a chest in the corner of the room. Swinging my legs over the edge of the bed and trying to stand, I stumbled. It wasn't so much lingering weakness but that I'd misjudged where the floor should be. I felt as though my skin was a coat several sizes too small. I clutched at my knee where I'd skinned it. Yet even while I gritted my teeth at the sting, wonder and elation coursed through me. *You're alive.*

According to Fayne, by all rights I should be dead. With the late-winter rains, the river raged at its highest level in years. Two local crofters drowned the previous week trying to save their sheep from the flooding. He took me for one such victim until he spied my brand.

I shook out the robe I found on the chest. Of simple cut, the soft wool was dyed a deep sky blue. My clumsy fingers fumbled with the lacings. Hoping to coax out a shy memory by not looking too closely, I let my mind wander. I dropped a washcloth I found next to the pile of clothes onto the water spill by the bed. While my own history hid somewhere in my murky head, a sense of familiarity lingered about the Clans. Clan Grey was unknown to me, but other names swam up from the depths: Orell … Dayr.

I went back to the chest and examined the brand in the looking glass. A whorled pattern marred the skin just below my collarbone. I traced it carefully with my fingers. Nothing. No sense of heat as when Lord Fayne touched it. Absentmindedly, I hummed a note. Without thought, my voice slid down through two more harmonic tones.

The brand pulsed, almost pushed against my fingertip. The tingling burst across my temples. The presence I'd been studiously not thinking about swooped down on top of me. I ducked as though it readied to pounce on me from the rafters. Watcher's eyes! Had I given myself away that easily?

I whipped my finger away from the brand. A small tendril of smoke trailed along in its wake. Sorcery?

And what was that noise? A vibration permeated my body. The brand throbbed in resonance—to me! My throat still emitted that deep hum. The note kept building upon itself within me, as though I'd struck a deep well and the water gushed forth.

Be quiet!

The inner shriek yanked me out of my trance. With a squeak that ruined the resonance, I cut off the hum. The tingling faded. With it gone the room felt empty again.

So. Investigating the brand too naïvely meant danger. I shivered. Fates help me if I was somehow embroiled with the dark arts. My voice sang treacherous songs. I put aside the thought. I'd leave the brand alone for now. Only a fool would go down that path with a head empty of knowledge.

I picked up a linen scarf and tied it about my throat, obeying Lord Fayne's order to hide the Clan mark from inquisitive eyes. Show it to no one, he'd said. He'd explained no further, but his silence and this new misadventure strengthened my intuition. Find out what tied me to the mark and I'd learn more about myself. This Fayne knew more than he was telling me.

I eased my feet into some leather slippers lying next to the chest. I frowned down at my dainty toes, perfectly enveloped by the tiny shoes. *Don't you look the lady.*

I tried the door. It gave way without protest, surprising me. So they hadn't locked me in. Either I wasn't a prisoner or Lord Grey felt I didn't pose much threat. I poked my head out and found a slight woman staring up at me from her seat opposite the door. A burly guard stood at attention a few paces down a hallway that stretched improbably into the distance. So. Not enough of a threat to lock up but they still wanted to keep an eye on me.

The woman stood and laid her needlework on the rush seat of her chair, smoothing silk skirts as she rose. *Silk? These Clansmen have come up in the world.* I shook off my inner voice. Silks shouldn't surprise me so when I couldn't even remember my own name.

The woman, not much more than a girl, really, smiled from behind a wave of auburn hair.

"Umbra. I'm Errith Grey. You must be hungry." Fayne's wife? Sister? Cousin? She clasped my wrist in slender fingers and led me off down the hall, the guard following a few paces behind.

Food. Oh, yes. I felt faint at the thought, but priorities warred in my head. My little experiment with the brand might have attracted the wrong kind of attention. But how to ask Errith without arousing concern?

"I can't imagine what you went through. I can't even swim! The river frightens me so," Errith said.

"It would frighten me too if I remembered much of it."

Errith giggled. "The only advantage to forgetting! How I wish sometimes I could put away my own troubles like that."

"What troubles are those, My Lady?"

Errith ignored my question, but her charming smile fled. "My brother's wrong." Not wife, then. I wondered if there was a lady of the castle. "You can't possibly be a crofter. You don't sound at all like one."

An opening. "Has anyone come looking for me?"

"No. But the watch know to find us if so."

Watchmen. Good. Cold comfort if I was up against sorcery, but I might get enough warning to run. I risked a bit more. "What of any—unusual—occurrences?"

In Errith's quick glance I caught a glimpse of a keen mind hiding beneath the girlish façade. "Such as?"

"Lord Grey mentioned marauders."

"You think they attacked you?"

Aside from the brand, there wasn't a mark on me. I turned the few facts over in my head. I'd fallen, naked, into the river. Had I jumped to flee an attack? Or did someone—the woman whose face I'd seen—push me? I toyed with the most innocent explanation—simple accident. Could the hunted feeling be an artifact of my imagination? A consequence of shock? Or even worse, a trick of a mind unwilling to face a shameful scandal? Maybe no danger existed at all, only embarrassment. Maybe I'd flung myself off a cliff over a broken heart.

No. The trials and tribulations of local farm girls didn't interest Clan lords. The questing presence might all be in my head, but my experience with the brand reeked of sorcery.

I could be in league with these marauders. Might the brand

mark me as a member of a faction allied against the Greys?
Subtle of them to offer me a bed and a meal if so. Lull me with
kindness to establish trust and extract my secrets, then slide in the
knife.

I let out a deep breath. Errith watched me, waiting for an
answer. "It's possible, Errith. But I really don't know."

We strolled down a hallway illuminated by flickering torches
set in intricate iron sconces, the guard always following a discreet
distance behind. *Fayne Grey doesn't trust you with his sister.* No. And
I'd do well not to trust the Greys.

Every so often, sunlight fought its way in through slits in the
walls. Errith led me down a spiraling stone staircase. This was no
rude guard tower. Where my instincts told me I should see
thatched outbuildings of wattle and daub, instead, through the
arrow slits, I glimpsed thick stone battlements, solid masonry and
a courtyard surrounded by several multistoried wings and turrets.
The scale of the buildings felt enormous—everything several
sizes bigger than I anticipated.

The interior defied my expectations as well. Rich tapestries
hung from the walls, and here and there stood a marble statue of
the finest workmanship. We entered a small room—Errith called
it a solar—with a plush carpet instead of rushes on the floor.
Cloth drapes embroidered with thread of gold framed the large
window inset with panes of actual glass. A fire tossed and
flickered in the hearth. A master carpenter must have built the
delicate chairs surrounding the table; they seemed too fragile to
sit upon yet when I did so, the wood gave no complaint.

You're the only thing that doesn't belong.

I murmured thanks for the Greys' apparent wealth when I

spied the table laden with food. Errith offered me slices of pear and pushed a bowl of plump red grapes my way. "It's not the season, I know, but Fayne brings them in from the coast. Sheep cheese?" She held out the cheese board. I sank a knife into a hard block. I popped the hunk of cheese into my mouth and the mild flavor burst across my tongue and and through my nose; it was like learning to eat for the first time. I groaned. Errith gave me a strange look.

When did I last take such pleasure in food? I didn't care. I ate like someone rescued after years on a barren island, even though the way my body filled out my robe told me I was anything but a victim of famine. My curves might not be lush but I'd wager the feast in front of me that Lord Fayne noted them. I'd recognized a certain look in his eyes.

Even if there isn't a lady of the castle, do you really think he'd see someone like you as anything more than a brief distraction? The bitterness in the thought interrupted my chewing.

I sighed. Bitter or not, it served no purpose to starve myself. I piled my plate with dried apricots, nuts, three boiled eggs, and a half-dozen rashers of peppered sausage. "Boar?" I asked between mouthfuls. Errith nodded. I could tell she found my manners uncouth, but Fates be damned, I was hungry. Errith filled my wine cup and waited while I ate my fill. She didn't bother talking to me. She probably thought I'd choke on any reply.

Sated, my strength returned. Yet I felt ill at ease, almost guilty. The inner voice I was learning to dislike hissed, *All prosperity comes at a cost. On whose backs did the Clans clamber to achieve this?* I worried at the edges of that question a little more. The Greys' wealth left me unsettled. Was it just them? The thought of other rich Clans pushed me even more off kilter. I felt like the only person not in on some jest.

Time, then, to stop playing the fool. My ignorance left me too vulnerable to my mysterious stalker.

"Errith, will you show me around?" A tour would give me a much-needed reprieve from my thoughts, together with opportunities to press Errith for information. We set out to explore my host's home, our ever-present guard trailing us. I glanced at him, and chose the blunt approach.

"Am I a prisoner here, then?"

Errith nodded, her body betraying her lie. "No, no, Fayne says we are to treat you as our guest."

"A guest who can leave anytime?"

Errith's tact outweighed mine. "You need to get your strength back first, and some clue of who you are. We'd be remiss if we let you wander helpless outside the castle, with no idea of where to go, who might be looking for you. The world turns dangerous, of a sudden." I couldn't disagree, yet I sensed my best interests did not lie foremost in her thoughts. She fingered a black woolen braid she wore twisted about her wrist. In my self-preoccupation, I'd not noticed it until now. Someone close to her died. Not long ago.

Better late than incorrigibly rude. I offered her the formal condolence. "May the Fates comfort you in your loss and speed your loved one's journey."

"Yes, may Father arrive swiftly at the Far Gates. I thank you."
The Gates forbidden to you.

I stumbled. What did that mean? Something inside me, a part of myself I could not enter at will, knew things the rest of me did not. I wondered if I should beat against that locked compartment in my head to break it open or flee while I could still avoid the answers and their consequences.

Forbidden. The Fates didn't bar access to the Far Gates of death for minor crimes. I fought down a wave of nausea. Just what had I done to leave me, stripped of everything else, with only a deep and sure knowledge I deserved the ultimate punishment?

Errith caught my arm and led me on through the castle. "Maybe something you see will help you remember: who you are, where you fit." My station in life, Errith meant. She didn't know how to treat me without proof that I was low-born. While falling short of giving me the full respect due a noble, she extended me most courtesies, which suited me fine. Perhaps I needed to thank the mark on my neck for that small favor.

I didn't sense within me an urge to treat Errith with particular deference, or feel inferior to her in any way. But without a name or a Clan to claim me, best to keep my head down and humility high. Errith didn't make me uncomfortable, the keep itself did. I couldn't shake the idea I would be more at home in a tent.

Errith showed me the kitchens, but even after such a large meal the bustle and noise of the cooking stimulated nothing in me but a rumble in my belly. Not a cook, then, although I suspected I could manage to feed myself if it came to that. Cooking felt like a necessity as opposed to a calling.

With the keep's steward, we cobbled together a wardrobe for me from items the Greys and their guests discarded over the years. Errith perked up when I insisted on appropriating a few breeches and men's tunics. "The women who work the logs and the wagon trains often dress that way," she said. "Yet you lack the rough hands or manner of speech to match." I shrugged. Should the need or opportunity arise, I couldn't picture myself escaping a castle and hiking overland in embroidered skirts.

Which reminded me. "Will you take me to the garrison? Maybe one of your men has seen me before." I wanted to assess what stood between me and the unknown.

Errith didn't object to my pretext and took me to visit the watch. The breeze carried the loamy scent of new spring growth into the courtyard. With my face turned to the sun like those sprouts in the field, I felt just as new.

None of the soldiers remembered seeing me about the castle, or the crofts they patrolled. I couldn't help wondering if Errith introduced me only so they'd know me when I went near the keep's gate. So they could prevent me from leaving.

No matter. What kept me from freedom also kept out my hunter. Despite my certainty that the experiment with the brand gave me away, warmed a trail gone cold, the guards reported no requests for entry by any strangers.

Yet as Errith moved away from the gate, I couldn't help looking over my shoulder at the empty fields outside.

Soldiers can't fight sorcery. I swallowed. The first line of defense was knowing what I fought against. The wrong question would associate me with magic in Errith's mind, but I needed her confidence to learn what I needed.

Better to draw her out more about the black mourning flags and banners fluttering from the ramparts and windows. Was it a hunting accident, or just old age? But my curiosity threatened the fragile rapport I'd established with Errith. She cast me a distrustful glance.

"It's bad luck for you to mention Father so often. You might distract him from his journey. Don't tempt the Fates—if the Listener hears you, he might set the Watcher's eyes upon him in the middle realm too early. He doesn't deserve to wander lost forever outside the Gates. Or worse. He deserves his chance to stand before the Judge. Why are you so interested in my family's grief?"

I nearly countered that she seemed awfully intent on hiding something from me but thought better of it. The journey from this realm to the far one was fraught with obstacles. I'd never get into Errith's good graces if she thought my words kept her father's soul too near, easy prey for daemons. Or worse, if he attracted the Fates' attention before the appointed time.

Errith obviously believed the cautionary tales of twisted shades: that they set upon the foolish soul tarrying to get a last glimpse of its loved ones through the veil between planes. Yet I couldn't shake the sense that Errith acted overly sensitively to questions regarding the manner of her father's death.

In the sewing and weaving atelier, I met Errith's ladies, the wives, daughters, and cousins of the lesser branches of Clan Grey. They chatted over their needle and tapestry work, casting curious stares in my direction. I examined my crooked stitches. Competent enough to mend a tear, but manipulating the finer cloth felt awkward to me, even though the silk soothed like a balm on my fingers. I persevered, though; the sewing afforded me access to the castle gossip. I caught an exchange between two younger cousins while they worked at laying out a small tapestry.

"It's so sad—Lord Garrith's life tapestry cut short like this. It might not go the length of the hall."

"It feels like just yesterday we finished the hangings for the wedding."

"We'll reuse those when Errith marries into Clan Dayr instead."

"Yes, but Rhinn and Fayne made the better match. I'm not so sure Errith was best pleased that Fayne gave her to Niall. Dayr marrying into Grey—so much better for Grey, don't you think?"

"How could such a joyful occasion turn to such tragedy? Poor Rhinn. I think Lord Fayne blames himself."

"Maybe that's why he took in our guest. He couldn't save the one so feels he must save the other."

The elder girl noticed my interest and hushed her partner. They spoke of inconsequentials for the remainder of my time in the atelier.

Now I considered yet another mystery. Errith never mentioned a girl or a wedding. Was she too ashamed of something? From the sound of it, at best the wedding was off and at worst the bride dead. An honor killing? The little I'd overheard lacked the tone of outrage I associated with a family's wounded honor. *What do you know of honor?* Surely the families wouldn't agree to a substitute marriage arrangement with either family's honor impugned.

My frustration grew. No one in the keep recognized me. I saw nothing more of Lord Fayne. Errith said he'd gone to scout the borders of Clan Grey territory. I could tell her brother had warned her not to trust me, as she did not elaborate, fending off my questions. There was another brother as well, but he toured the Grey holdings checking on crofters.

What if I wasn't a noble? If I borrowed a horse, I could visit the local crofts and see for myself if anyone knew my face.

I weighed the idea. Even if the watch let me out, exploring the area by myself left me exposed. But it might be worth the risk. The sun would stay up for a few hours yet. I might run into someone along the river who'd seen something. I tried to remember if the Greys found me up- or downstream from here. Up. Which meant a longer trek before I came across anything useful.

Errith sent the guard away, tired of his constant oversight and deciding I posed a minimal threat. But she kept me close to her women, so I hadn't yet seen the stables. She excused herself to make water. *No time like the present.* If nothing else, I'd learn just how freely the Greys would let me move around.

I got up, stretched and made a show of yawning. Pleading fatigue at my ordeal to the ladies, I slipped out and hurried to my room. With luck, by the time Errith came to check on me, I'd be beyond the gate.

I replaced the linen around my neck with a black scarf more comfortable for riding, tugging it up to cover the brand. I shed the wool dress that satisfied the ladies' sensibilities and donned leather riding breeches, which would be more practical than a skirt even if they still chafed my skin somewhat. I crossed the keep and entered the stable yard.

The barn dog shot up from his lazy snooze, snarling at me, hackles raised. My calves tensed—if he lunged, only a swift kick would save me from a bite. I stared him down. He suddenly whimpered, tucked his tail between his legs, and slunk into the barn.

"Never seen him do that. Not to a woman." The groom eyed me once then refused to look at me.

I shrugged, but the dog unnerved me. Its dislike resonated against my own self-contempt, which lingered, festering like an abscess. If even a barn dog hated me, did I have good reason to feel so uncomfortable in my own skin? The discomfort warred with the almost childlike wonder I experienced each time my physical senses brought the world around me into exquisite focus. Shame might lurk in my past, but my gratitude at being alive filled every breath I drew into my body. "May I borrow a horse?"

"'Fraid not, my lady. You're to stay in the castle. Lord Fayne's orders."

May he be damned in the Watcher's eyes! I spun on my heels, annoyed. My restlessness grew as I bumped up against the bars of my gilded cage. I wandered around the keep's courtyard, until the clang of weapons caught my ear and I located the practice yard.

Two men practiced with blunted swords. I watched the interplay between them. Both were accomplished sword fighters. The elder, with grey-flecked hair, appeared to be the keep's master-at-arms, judging from the patch on his shoulder. The younger man was giving him a spot of trouble. Both men breathed hard, but the younger, pressing, had backed the master-at-arms into a corner of the yard. A handful of watching soldiers shouted encouragement.

Anticipating the bout would soon end in victory for the younger man, I sauntered over to where several practice swords leaned up against the wall.

I trailed my fingers over the sword hilts. Why did they draw me so? I gripped the hilt of the second-to-last sword, raised and hefted it. The leather grip fit securely beneath my fingertips. The balance felt right. I slashed the air, testing.

"The lady thinks she can fight."

I turned at the mocking tone. The younger man had indeed defeated the master-at-arms. Now he smirked at me, the sandy locks falling across his forehead concealing neither the healing cut above his eyebrow, nor his skepticism.

"I can certainly fight you," I said without thinking. And I knew. Knew in my bones I could take him on and win.

"You must still be weak from your ordeal."

Offering me a face-saving way out? "Maybe that just evens the odds in your favor."

One of the watching soldiers chuckled. "Give 'er what she wants, Lian!"

Lian. Lord Fayne's younger brother. Not the best way to meet, but to the Fates with it. So much for humility. I raised my sword and settled into my stance.

Lian didn't hesitate. He struck before I could blink. Our swords clashed, and for an instant, I worried I'd misjudged badly. I was still weak. And he was very good. I barely parried his blow while my first thrust fell far short of touching him. Lian's quick feints tested my defenses to get a feel for my skill level. My own form felt off—I kept misreading the distance between us, my blows never quite landing.

Lian's sword crossed with mine, our hilts locked together. His dark green gaze bored into my own. He stepped in, to try to throw me off balance, then raised a hand and placed it on my chest, as if to push me back. The tips of his fingers slipped beneath the scarf and touched the edge of my brand. A strong buzzing sensation radiated out from the brand over my skin. A door in my mind cracked open.

The courtyard disappeared, replaced by a vision of a stand of silver birch next to a crossroads. The afternoon sunshine faded to the muted greys of either dusk or dawn. In my mind's eye, I now looked up at Lian. He loomed huge and threatening over me and a man lying on the ground beside me. Lian scowled down at us, blood dripping from his sword and welling from a small slash above his eye. The man flinched and clutched his stomach, his life ebbing away through a wound in his belly.

I blinked and the scene vanished, the courtyard coming back into focus. I couldn't worry if the vision represented a true memory or something else, not if I wanted to win this duel. Lian's sword slashed at my torso, and I barely jumped back in time.

Lian's next hard thrust sent me reeling into the far corner of the courtyard. The soldiers laughed.

So did Lian. "Had enough?"

Hot anger flashed through me. I ignored it and focused on Lian. Why would my mind place me with him somewhere else? Did he know me? If he did, why not admit as much? Was this battle more than just a friendly duel?

This time, I circled him, taking his full measure. I spotted a weakness in his footwork. He moved in to attack. I parried his thrust, stepped aside, and tapped him on the arm as he hurtled by. First hit.

He spun around. I stopped thinking and let my muscles take over. Our swords flashed in the sunlight, the ringing of each blow echoing off the keep walls. Blades connected, my breathing grew harsh. Neither of us gave any quarter. I ducked a roundhouse, and shifted my weight into Lian, forcing a misstep that I pounced on. I faked a thrust, parried his answering blow. I knocked him off balance. He tried to regain his footing but my sword knifed through the air. I halted it a hair's breadth from his jugular.

"Now who's had enough?" I said.

Lian's pine green eyes hardened, but after he regained his footing he had the grace to bow. "You've just humbled the second-best swordsman at Castle Grey, my lady. Would you care to take on the best?" He jerked his chin towards someone behind me.

Fayne sat astride his big stallion. Concentrating so hard on Lian, I hadn't even noticed his scouting party arrive. From the look on his face, he'd noticed my newly found skill.

Despite my quivering elation at besting Lian and learning something of myself, I let the grin stretching my cheeks ebb. I wouldn't be too happy either if I discovered a skilled swordswoman in the midst of my family instead of the waif I'd taken in. I'd misjudged by showing my hand, no matter how inadvertently and how rewarding to finally find something at which I excelled. Mysterious might work in my favor, but any perception I might be dangerous as well would get me killed and thrown to the Judge's mercy for my trouble.

A mystery connected me to Lian. To solve it, I needed to stay close to the Greys. And for that I needed Fayne Grey's interest in me and my brand to outweigh his concerns.

"I'm afraid I will plead fatigue this time," I said.

"And I've had a long ride. Another day, perhaps." Fayne shot his brother an irritated glance. "Why are you here? Did you finish warning the crofters?"

Lian shrugged. "They'll still be there tomorrow."

"We need them alert to any strangers now. You've wasted a day. We'll continue the rounds tomorrow." Fayne turned his mount towards the stables.

"My Lord," I interjected, "may I go with you? One of the crofters might know my face."

"Can you sit a horse?"

"I think so."

"I guess we'll find out in the morning. Meet at the stables at dawn."

THEN

"No. It is not appropriate. She is a half-breed."

Jezarel pouted at this pronouncement from her father. She glanced at her new friend. Kairiya took the Izir's words in stride. Insults were nothing new to her, and too much depended on this introduction to get upset over a little name-calling. Jezarel pressed her case. "But Father, she saved my life."

"Which would not have needed saving if you stayed nearby as I bade you. What were you doing at that old watering hole anyway?"

Kairiya thought even brave men might quail beneath the Izir's piercing stare but Jezarel obviously honed her resistance to its demands over the course of years. "Father, she has nowhere else to go. Besides, you always say I need someone to keep me out of trouble."

"I'm not sure a stranger is the one to do so." He gave Kairiya an appraising stare. "You happened along at just the right moment. What brought you to us?"

Kairiya told him the story she'd rehearsed so carefully. Everything her parents had ordered her to do rested on him believing the lie. "My mother left our tribe when I was very young. We've traveled with the trading caravans ever since. I wished to learn more about my family. So I parted ways with the traders the last time they crossed the sands, and seek out the Inarra. I wanted to refill my waterskin for my next leg when I saw that man attacking Jezarel."

"A barbarian raid wiped out the Inarra ul-Gherza early this spring."

Kairiya blinked. He'd given her the excuse to stay, as her mother said he would, but he mustn't see her satisfaction. "That news never reached the caravans. Mother will grieve."

"And you will not?"

Kairiya's jaw tightened at the rebuke.

"It is difficult to grieve for people you do not remember or never met," Kairiya said. "I hoped to know them better, and for them to know me. Now I've lost that opportunity. But if you are worried about your own daughter, I may be useful. I learned much from the caravan guards about how to deal with raiders."

Kairiya was counting on the fact that as summer drew to a close, the tribe would move to the more sheltered plateau grazing lands. The trip came with risks, passing as close as they did to the mountain passes. The Izir might welcome another pair of skilled fighting hands to protect the herd from raiders. Without the herd, the tribe's prosperity died. And if she didn't worm her way into Jezarel's confidence, Kairiya's future died as well.

Kairiya's father never forgave failure.

The Izir sighed and Jezarel waggled her fingers at Kairiya in victory. "Very well," the Izir said. He turned to Kairiya. "The Zaghril ul-Gherza tribe welcomes you." To Jezarel, he added, "But she stays out of the family quarters and dines with the *nazeem*. One of these days you will have to give up this habit of picking up strays. A husband will not tolerate such nonsense."

Kairiya exhaled in relief when Jezarel left with these concessions before her father could change his mind. Kairiya dipped her head in respect to the Izir as they exited the tent.

Jezarel nudged Kairiya with an elbow. "Is it hard living with skin so pale you can't hide a blush? I thought you might throttle him at one point. *That* would have been entertaining." Jezarel skipped off down the lane of trampled steppe grass between the camp's multitude of tents before Kairiya could respond. A goat scampered out of her way.

Three girls lazed in the shade of a tent. One of them grinned and pointed at the goat, then Jezarel.

"Who's that?" Kairiya asked.

"My cousin, Lailaz."

As Jezarel and Kairiya walked past, Lailaz puckered her mouth into a kiss and made smooching noises. "Can't even get the bucks to stick around for you, Jezarel?"

Lailaz's friends snickered. Jezarel glared at them, but neither spoke.

"At least my face doesn't attract them—unlike some," Jezarel flung back.

The three girls jangled their bracelets at Jezarel in scorn.

Kairiya halted in the lane between the tents. Jezarel stopped when she realized Kairiya no longer followed her.

"I am not a minder of children," Kairiya said.

"And I am not a child."

"No?" Kairiya tilted her head towards Lailaz's tent.

"They just get under my skin."

"Then you need to thicken it."

"They know only Lailaz can get away with the insults, and just stay for the show."

Ah yes, Kairiya thought. The Izirina's speaking privilege—no talking back unless spoken to first. Her mother told her about this convention, that it didn't apply to family. Kairiya just ignored it, assuming Jezarel would mention it if Kairiya's forthrightness bothered her.

Kairiya looked back at Lailaz, who smirked with pleasure at successfully annoying Jezarel. Kairiya knew that kind of smirk well, having been its target more times than she could count. *Half-breed. Blood traitor. Bastard.* She'd learned to live with the slurs, for lack of any way to stop them. Kairiya studied Jezarel and Lailaz. Unlike Kairiya, Jezarel was no powerless outsider. Maybe it was bad counsel to tell Jezarel to ignore Lailaz.

"You're not mad about eating with the *nazeem?*" Jezarel asked.

"I'm happy to. A stranger's what I am, after all. My mother taught me enough to know that only a member of the tribe eats with the Izir."

"Come on. Let's find the camp supply master and get you a tent."

Jezarel headed off toward the stores but when they interrupted the supply master's apprentice counting inventory, the boy directed them to the bazaar, keeping his gaze downcast the entire time. Jezarel sniffed. "Fates."

"What?"

"My father has even the ones too young for me properly cowed."

After the episode with the shepherd, Kairiya didn't doubt that the man kept a close eye on his daughter. Jezarel's penchant for trouble suited Kairiya just fine.

The bazaar lay on the other side of the main oasis from camp. The sweet water made this spot a center for trade. Gherza tribes from across the steppe congregated to sell their wares here at the last oasis before the steppe turned to desert. The Gherza had never extracted from the caravan people the secret route across, and Kairiya suspected Jezarel's father let her stay partly to see what she knew of it.

"You know," Jezarel said, "we used to run the bazaar at the smaller oasis where you … found me, but when the water soured up there, the market moved with it."

"What drew you there?" Kairiya spent days studying Jezarel's movements, so knew Jezarel spent an unusual amount of time there, but not her reasons.

"It's a place to be someone other than the Izir's daughter for a while." Jezarel sighed. "My brother and I used to hunt for treasure—glass buttons, a chipped clay vase. Once, we even found a horseshoe! A caravan dray horse must have thrown it—the tribe doesn't have a smithy."

Jezarel skipped across the source of the small rill that fed the current watering hole. When Kairiya joined her Jezarel grabbed her hand. Though she disliked being touched, Kairiya did not draw away.

Jezarel rewarded her with a smile. "It's so good to have a friend in camp who doesn't bow their eyes or brush their lips with fingertips to ask permission to speak to me." Jezarel laughed up at the great swath of sky that capped the plains.

Off to the east Kairiya imagined the faint purple smudge of

the foothills, even though they rose up too far away to really see. In between the girls and the bazaar, nothing but the vast sea of grasses moved in the wind.

They found the supply master shouting at a date seller. He refused to pay for spoiled fruit. He gave Jezarel a chit to take back to his apprentice at the supply tent, where she and Kairiya commandeered a small tent with an old floor rug, and two boys to erect the structure. Jezarel led them back to a large, red-and-white striped tent, and told them to put up the shelter next to it. Once they started building Kairiya's tent, Jezarel dragged her friend into its colorful neighbor.

"This one's mine. You'll sleep next to me."

"I thought I wasn't to enter the family quarters."

"Father meant the shared quarters. This is my place and I say who comes and goes. And don't worry about that *nazeem* business. You're my friend. Father never eats with the hired servants, but he's not a fanatic for protocol like some. Even he enjoys the occasional dinner with acquaintances from outside. And I'm not talking about formal occasions between tribes either. You'll be eating with us in no time. Just give him the chance to get used to you."

Jezarel plopped down on the silk cushions next to her bed. She fumbled around underneath the straw mattress pad and withdrew a long package wrapped in oilcloth. She unwrapped the folded covering to reveal the gleaming curved sword within. "I want you to teach me how to use this," Jezarel said.

Kairiya lifted the sword out of its wrapping and inspected the blade. "A strong weapon. Where did you get it?"

"It was my brother's." Jezarel read the question in Kairiya's eyes. "A barbarian killed him."

"We both owe the barbarians a blood debt," Kairiya said.

"Will you teach me then?"

"It's hard work—not like finger dancing and learning the tea rituals. You will hate me before long."

"I reserve my hate for the pale men of the east."

"Then we're agreed. But if you don't take the training seriously, I will leave and you will never see me again."

Kairiya held her breath. Did she overdo it?

"I was stupid today, but I learn from my mistakes. I never want to be defenseless again. We'll train at the old oasis until the tribe moves to the foothills for the winter," Jezarel said. "No sense annoying my father."

Kairiya allowed herself a smile. She was in. Now to make herself as indispensable as possible.

NOW

We crested the knoll above the valley, the rising sun burning off the morning mists. It couldn't do much, though, about the column of black smoke we'd spotted while we trotted along a shepherd's track towards the croft. My hope that traveling in a group would keep the entity hunting me at bay eroded. Fayne heeled his horse down the slope.

Arriving at the croft, I stared at the destruction. The attack had torched the thatched hut; its rafters still smoked. The animal shelter reeked of burned mutton. Only silence and the occasional pop of a hot ember greeted us. Fayne swore then rounded on Lian.

"Had you done as I told you, they might have had warning," Fayne said.

"Would they have stood a better chance out in the hills?" Lian retorted.

I'd given Lian a wide berth since our little skirmish the previous day. Despite the promising sign that my memories might not be lost forever, the vision I'd had frightened me. I'd lain awake staring at the shadowed rafters of my room, because I feared the dying man I'd seen must be Garrith Grey. While my role and Lian's in the tableau remained unclear, I could not escape the fact that I might have witnessed his death.

It made a twisted sort of sense: traumatized, I'd escaped the same attack that killed the Grey patriarch, but couldn't remember it due to the shock of my near drowning. The half-healed state of the small cut above Lian's eye matched the timeline of events.

The memory fragment raised uncomfortable questions. If I was complicit, I couldn't understand why Lian still pretended not to know me. *Unless he's involved.* The blood on Lian's sword hadn't been mine. It could belong to an attacker Lian bested. Or it could have spilled from his father. I hoped my predrowning self hadn't backed the wrong horse in a succession battle.

Did Fayne know of my presence there as well or was Lian hiding this from him? I'd do well to not assume innocence on the part of any of the Greys. *As you assume your own innocence?* I swallowed. That Fates-damned guilty conscience again. I shook my head. How did I know the vision even represented something real? My mind could just be playing tricks on me.

I dismounted while the brothers argued. The sweet smell of death hung in the air. The attackers struck while the crofters slept. The fire showed no mercy. A trail of churned earth indicated the direction the invaders fled. I puzzled over the mix of shod and unshod hoof prints. I wondered anew what Fayne kept from me.

I walked around the ruin of the hovel, an intuition just beyond my senses pulling me towards the rear of the croft. The structure backed onto a cote for sheep. The gate swung open—only one animal huddled in a corner. The ewe took one look at me, bleated in fear, and scampered through the opening before bounding away.

Behind the pen, the slope rose back up the other side of the valley, its scrubby late-winter grass strewn with lichen-covered boulders and a few scraggly lavender shrubs. Olive trees dotted the slopes, but the press fell victim to the fire, though the grindstone looked salvageable. A boulder larger than most marked one corner of the sheep enclosure.

A movement behind the edge of the stone confirmed my suspicion. I drew the sword Fayne Grey had grudgingly given me, in case the crofter mistook me for a returning marauder and defended himself. I stepped around the rock, sword raised. The sight that greeted me froze me in my tracks.

An elderly woman sat on the ground, cradling a small child. The crone's lank, grizzled hair brushed the child's cheeks as the woman bent over him, rocking and sobbing. The sword clattered to the ground at my feet. I sank to my knees.

Burns covered the boy, and I could see that even though he still lived, his wounds were mortal. His shallow, labored breathing captivated me. He opened his eyes and stared into mine. His eyes widened, terror turning to resignation.

"You've come for me," he said. The crone looked up from his body, startled. I cupped his cheek in my hand. The life leaked from him, evaporating between my fingers. I sensed the insistent tug of death, and his resistance, the burning tenacity of his youth to cling to this world. *It is always hardest for the very young.*

"Shhh. You're going on a journey, where no one can hurt you anymore." I pointed up the hill.

A last breath sighed out of him. I passed my hand in front of his face, feeling his silky essence whisper through me on its way beyond, to begin its pilgrimage to the Gates and the Fates' judgment. The brand at my throat pulsed with heat. I glanced to my right, and saw the boy standing there. He took one last look at his lifeless body. "Go on now. You can't stay any longer," I said, though I couldn't say how I knew.

He walked up to the crest of the hill and waved at me before vanishing from my sight in the rays of the sun.

The crone choked out a sob, but didn't take her eyes off me. Fear made her voice tremble. "What are you?" I tried to calm her, but she shoved me away, hunching over the boy's body. She clasped him to her chest, still hoping to shelter him from his fate. "What have you done? He's not ready to face the shades! Did you damn him to those daemons?"

"Umbra! What's this?" Lord Fayne appeared from behind the boulder, Lian crowding behind him.

"She killed him! The witch killed my grandson!" the crone cried. Lian's expression flickered to something that looked almost like gratification.

I shook my head in denial. "There was nothing I could do. He was dying."

"She laid hands on him and cast a spell on him! I heard her!"

I shrugged. "She's raving. It must be the grief. I told him no one would hurt him anymore. Just words of comfort. If that's a spell, I'm a donkey."

Pressing my hands against my thighs to hide their shaking, I stood up. I'd felt it. Felt his soul leave his body. Touched its numinous grace. I wanted to scream. It smacked of necromancy, of evil knowledge a normal person shouldn't possess. Yet the emotion running through me didn't feel twisted or vile. I wanted only to help him, ease his passage, protect him at this important moment of his existence. His beautiful little soul gave off a scent of sun-warmed little-boy hair and anise. His pain was over, and I somehow knew he'd be cared for on his journey to face the Fates. Finding out why I knew that took on even more importance than understanding my link to Lian.

I walked back to my horse, ignoring the woman's increasingly hysterical yammering. After speaking to her for a moment, Fayne followed me around to the front of the croft. He reached for my wrist. I pulled away, even though the heat of his fingers felt good against my skin. The simple warmth of life. So different from the touch of the boy's dying soul.

"You saw his burns. It's amazing he survived this long," I said.

"Myra may be old but she's not senile. I've never known her to act fanciful."

I looked Fayne right in the eye. "I didn't kill him. Is it a crime to offer kind words to the dying?"

"No. But that child will need more than kind words to survive the middle realm. May his soul journey swiftly."

"That's all I did—wish him fast travels. Please believe me." I couldn't look at Fayne as I said it. "I don't know who I am, but I wouldn't kill a child."

Ever so gently, he took my hand in his, like a person soothing a frightened puppy. "I know, Umbra. When you're ready, when you remember … whatever it is … recall that I believed you in this moment."

I shot him a glance. Why was he being so … understanding?

Fayne released my hand, then told Lian and one of the soldiers who'd accompanied us to deal with Myra and her dead grandson. I didn't like the glance Lian cast me as he left. I'd

43

almost call it happy, and I couldn't understand it.

Despite Fayne's words, I could smell his distrust. Though it felt important now that I not disappoint him, I couldn't blame him.

What are you? Myra had asked. Indeed.

What was I that I could see the dead?

THEN

Kairiya grinned, and ignored the mute plea in Jezarel's eyes. "Just a bit longer," Kairiya said.

Jezarel groaned. By now, if Kairiya remembered anything at all from her own training, every muscle in Jezarel's body should be screaming from exhaustion. Kairiya had to hand it to her, though. So far, Jezarel had not complained. She'd made a promise and seemed determined to keep it. No matter how many forms and exercises Kairiya insisted she master before Kairiya let her touch a sword.

"I can feel every Fates-damned pebble through the soles of my feet!" Jezarel said through gritted teeth.

Her thigh muscle shuddered visibly as she balanced on one leg with her other foot pressed against the inside of her thigh. The two buckets of water hanging from the yoke around her neck wobbled. The liquid sloshed dangerously against the rims of the containers. If one drop spilled, Kairiya would make her start all over again.

A drop of sweat trickled down the side of Jezarel's nose. Kairiya smiled, watching Jezarel struggle not to give in to the need to brush it away. How it must tickle! Not a breath of wind stirred the palm fronds. Summer, saving all its warmth for the end, draped its heat over the grasses of the steppe. Shimmering mirages hovered beyond the oasis. Soon the northern *siratha* winds would howl across the grasses, bringing the bite of winter with them, and the tribe would seek the shelter of the plateau forest. If all went well, Kairiya would make the journey with them.

But today, Jezarel and Kairiya sweltered.

"That's enough for now," Kairiya said. No need to be cruel.

Jezarel exhaled and shrugged off the yoke. "Fates! I've never worked so hard in my life."

Kairiya snorted. "I'm sure."

"I'm not as pampered as you seem to think. I do camp chores all the time."

"It takes more than chores to get the muscles needed for good swordplay." Kairiya reached out and squeezed Jezarel's upper arm, gone wiry and rock hard in the three weeks since Kairiya began the training. "Yours are coming along nicely."

"It's not like I'm completely unskilled with weapons. I'm a decent markswoman."

"Ever shot a man?"

"No. But I bagged a steppe wolf that raided the herd last summer."

Kairiya nodded, impressed. "Still think this is more fun than finger dancing?" Kairiya asked.

Jezarel passed one hand in front of her face, fingers flowing in a beguiling pattern in front of her fluttering eyelashes. "You and I met because of a finger dance gone wrong."

"Why would you throw yourself on a wastrel like that?"

Kairiya asked the question despite knowing the answer. She'd counted on Jezarel's lovesickness when she'd hired the shepherd.

"You don't understand what it's like being the daughter of the Izir."

"Try me." Kairiya suppressed a physical urge to grab Jezarel and shake her out of her privileged complacency. How could she even begin to believe her life was at all difficult? Especially when compared to Kairiya's own scrabbling struggle just to be seen as a person within her Clan. Jezarel knew nothing about hardship. But Kairiya couldn't really offer up that contrast to Jezarel, now, could she? Not without betraying the cause her parents set for her.

Despite herself, despite Jezarel's complaints, Kairiya was coming to like the Izir's daughter. She confided in Kairiya, treated her as friend. Friends were no easy thing to come by in Kairiya's world. But no friendship would survive the successful completion of Kairiya's mission. Jezarel was just a pawn in a game she didn't yet know she played. Kairiya's parents had warned her that game wouldn't truly begin until the tribe moved to the plateau. They wanted her well and truly ensconced within the tribe by then. Kairiya couldn't quite meet Jezarel's eyes.

As if Kairiya's demeanor reminded her of it, Jezarel said, "None of the boys will even raise their eyes to my face. They're too afraid of offending my father." Jezarel kicked over one of the buckets. "He won't even betroth me to anyone. Saving the precious flower of his loins for an important match. How else was I supposed to get my first kiss? I didn't mean it to go any further than that. But that man wouldn't stop ..." Jezarel broke off.

Kairiya wondered how far Jezarel went to get that kiss.

Kairiya'd felt a telltale resonance in the air from her position hidden near the watering hole. As a precaution, she'd put extra oomph into her courage-stealing wail despite the fact she supposedly had an agreement with the shepherd. Good thing too —the wail broke his abnormal fixation, one with magical overtones. She'd wanted Jezarel scared, not hurt. She hadn't counted on her target's own foolishness. Magic always left Kairiya feeling grimy; she preferred to rely on the clean rules of swordplay.

Kairiya followed Jezarel's gaze to the sword she kept strapped to her waist. "You're not ready for this yet. Soon, though. Your balance is coming along. Get that figured out and we'll start on the forms."

"We leave for the mountain meadows tomorrow," Jezarel announced. "There won't be time to train during the trek."

So soon. Kairiya wished the grazing location of the herds wasn't so tied to the seasons. The day suddenly seemed colder. Kairiya shook her head. She should be happy. Instead, she felt vaguely sick.

NOW

The trail the invaders left grew fresher, so we muffled the
metal on our bridles and saddles to give the force ahead of us less
warning of our presence. Fayne's tracker estimated the group
numbered half a dozen, enough to overpower unarmed crofters,
but no match for Fayne's larger group of well-trained armsmen.
Fayne rode beside me, grim faced, as we approached the third
burned-out croft. He raised his arm to signal a halt and pointed at
a copse of pine and scrub. Hoof marks churned a line of earth
leading straight to the trees.

With quick hand gestures, Fayne directed his men to surround
the thicket, motioning me to stay put. All the soldiers reached
their positions, and Fayne twice whistled the call of a warrelbird.
Half of the men surrounding the grove charged into the trees.
The others remained behind to cut down any stragglers escaping
the initial rush.

I heard shouts and the clang of metal on metal. My brand
pulsed at my throat. Death stalked the copse. Someone screamed.
A man dressed in flowing black robes stumbled from the trees.
He stared around, confused. I turned to Fayne's tracker, whom
Fayne had left with me. He still didn't trust I wouldn't run away,

though I didn't understand his interest in keeping me close.

"Shall we finish him off?" I asked.

"Finish who?" The tracker gave me an odd look.

A chill flooded through me. The man in the black robes was already dead.

Four more robed men, some in black, some in dusty tan, emerged from the vegetation. None of Fayne's rear guard moved. I watched as the robed men disappeared one by one. I could never quite make out the exact moment I lost sight of them, but I knew I wouldn't see any of them again.

I shuddered. So the boy wasn't just a one-time thing. I could see the dead just before they crossed to the middle realm. What I didn't understand was why. Part of me wanted to claw my eyes out. Another oddly empathetic part of me wanted only to help the deceased on their journey. I examined that feeling, trying to tease meaning from it.

Fayne returned, looking satisfied.

"Gherza raiding party. They've been getting bolder, but maybe we taught them a lesson."

"You knew what we'd find," I said.

"I heard they came through Moongate Pass not long after my father's death. Since they seemed content to pass through Clan Arneth and Clan Dayr's holdings peacefully, I assumed they wanted to speak with the Clan Elders. But my scouting trip confirmed the raids and my worst fears. I worry they plot something bigger."

Something stirred in me at mention of the Gherza, but only quick impressions emerged from the locked corners of my mind. Tent panels flapping in the winds of the high steppes. The braying of a mule, reluctantly climbing to the alpine plateau of the Barrier Range. The tinkling song of a gold-bangled wrist, sorting dates harvested from a palm on the fringes of the steppe near the western wastes. The Gherza. Nomads and traders. Fayne thought that they now had designs on the Clan territories.

A shriek pierced the air and we all spun to face the copse. A dark shape hurtled towards us from the shade, curved scimitar raised. Fayne darted to the side, and in one lightning motion sent the attacker sprawling. He rolled onto his back but Fayne's sword flashed to the man's neck before he could rise.

"Filthy lowlander. Why attack us?" The Gherza said, grunting when Fayne's boot pinned his chest to the ground.

"For murdering my crofters as they slept, you coward," Fayne answered.

"Never! We are not barbarians."

"Then why have your people crossed the pass?"

"The witch's power grows, and what do you treekillers do? Nothing. We come to right the balance." The Gherza spit on Fayne's boot.

Fayne's sword quivered. "Watch your tongue. I have little love for that hag."

"You tolerate the witch in your midst. Our quarrel is with her, but her presence also taints you."

Myra had called me a witch at her grandson's death. But the Gherza didn't seem to care about me, even though I stood out as the lone woman among a pack of men. The power that searched me out the night the river coughed me up—that had seemed witch-like. I shivered. At the thought, I suddenly felt watched again. I peered around me but didn't see anyone but this Gherza and Fayne's men.

Though I didn't want an association between me and witches in Fayne's head, I spoke up. I needed answers. "What witch?"

"That unfriendly neighbor I spoke of when I pulled you from the river," Fayne answered. Before I could press him further, he returned his attention to the Gherza. "If you didn't slaughter my crofters, who did?"

"Look to your own. It is barbarian work, not Gherza."

Instead of killing him, Fayne removed his boot from the man's chest. The Gherza stood up.

"Are you a leader among your people?" Fayne asked.

"No. Just a scout. The Izir stayed back at camp."

"Take this message back to your Izir," Fayne said. "Clan Grey wishes a truce with the Gherza." Behind me I heard Lian hiss. Fayne continued. "This witch of yours brings trouble to all of us. The Gherza and the Clans will be stronger if we search her out together."

The Gherza's black gaze remained inscrutable. He nodded, and I got the impression he'd accepted Fayne's offer. He reached for his belt.

Something thrummed past my ear. The Gherza jerked. His hand reached up to the arrow protruding from his chest before he slumped to the ground.

Fayne whirled. I looked back—Lian lowered his bow. Fayne snatched the bow from Lian's hands and tossed it to the ground.

"What were you thinking?" Fayne shouted.

"He drew his throwing knife."

"He did no such thing."

"Sorry for saving your skin."

"We needed him."

Lian shrugged. "No one needs those savages."

Savages. That's what bothered me about the Gherza. I peered at his body. His tattered robe fluttered in the wind. His black hair hung lank and unwashed. I remembered the Gherza as fierce and proud. They loved to decorate their bodies and swords with chased gold and jewels, but the scimitar lying on the ground was plain. Suddenly Errith's idea that I might be part of the crew of a traveling wagon train gained currency; why otherwise would I know of these people?

I gazed after Lian, recognizing the slow burn in my stomach as an echo of Fayne's anger. The Gherza didn't deserve to die. The more I saw of Lian, the more I hoped that I hadn't purposely aligned myself with him at some point in the past. I would need to confront him about knowing me. Just not now. Lian seemed the type of person to tangle with from a position of strength.

We abandoned the body, although as we left the copse I still couldn't shake the feeling of eyes on my back. I turned at a small noise. Was that movement in the trees someone shifting to hide behind a trunk? Or just shadow play? I shook my head. The men had already searched the stand of trees thoroughly. I told myself there was no one there. I was safe, with a sword at my hip and surrounded by armed men.

Continuing on, we came upon an unharmed shepherd tending his flock. Fayne sent him off to warn his neighbors to seek shelter at the keep. We returned to the keep, with Fayne reassured that the crofters would activate their family networks and spread word of the marauders, and the Gherza.

Fayne seemed inclined to take what the Gherza said at face value, and leave the question of who killed his crofters open for now, much to Lian's chagrin. The mix of shod and unshod hoofprints we found lent credence to the Gherza claim. Since the Gherza didn't shoe their horses, to whom had the shod horses belonged?

The sight of me would cause news of a mysterious woman stranger to flash across Fayne's holdings. Would I regret the decision to announce my presence? I'd washed up on that riverbank knowing very little, but somehow convinced that a woman meant me harm. This witch? I doubted she held honorable intentions. Especially if my own abilities tended towards the witchy. Witches didn't have a reputation for tolerating competition, if that's what my seeing the dead made me.

Back in my small chamber, I sluiced the day's grime off my skin, squeezing excess water from the washcloth back into the basin. I stared at the Clan mark in the looking glass. I traced the whorled outline against my skin, the ridged scar tissue rough under my fingers. This time, no answering tingle pulsed beneath my collarbone. Why had I felt anything when Fayne touched it? Did it only respond to the touch of others? Its warming seemed to signal death. Perhaps it was some sorcery tied to the brand that allowed me to see the dead.

Knuckles rapped against the door—a page summoning me to Lord Fayne's library. I arrived to find Fayne pacing in front of a crackling fire.

"Tell me, Umbra, did anything that occurred today jog your memory?"

"I wish it had, but in truth, I'm more confused than anything else."

He came to a stop in front of me, his eyes going to the scarf around my throat. "Still no idea how you obtained the brand?"

I shook my head. This close, that hint of fennel in his smell distracted me. It invoked a deep sense of safety in me. An inappropriate urge to step even closer and breathe it in enveloped me. A small, sensible part of me held back. While he'd rescued me, I didn't know if my interests aligned with his. He could still throw me out on my ear, or worse, if he thought me a danger to his family.

His question brought another to mind. "Is the Clan mark uncommon?" Maybe the brush with magic led me down the wrong path, and the mark was one of honor. It might explain why the Greys treated me so well.

"I've never seen it on a person," Fayne said. "It's only used as a sigil on flags. And other objects of Clan significance." He turned away, so I couldn't quite make out his expression. "Oh, to the Fates with it, there's no point beating around the bush—"

Lian and Errith burst into the room, Lian clutching a rolled parchment, its seal broken. They crowded around Fayne, so I backed towards the door. But instead of leaving, I leaned against one of the shelves near the door, and made myself as discreet as possible.

"Braith of Dayr has summoned the Conclave," Lian said.

"For what reason?" Fayne asked.

"According to this, 'Clan Grey must answer to the Conclave for the murder of Rhinn of Dayr, and the loss of the staff.'"

So. The Rhinn I'd overheard Errith's ladies speaking of died a violent death. If everything—Rhinn and Garrith's killings, and the loss of this staff—happened at the same time, the puzzle made sense: Fayne's father, perishing to defend a daughter-to-be. Maybe I'd been too hard on Lian, and my vision showed nothing sinister. Only a son, frantic after fending off an attack, devastated he couldn't save his father. Maybe.

"The Council summons us. The Conclave meets at Darmid Tor, with or without Clan Grey. With, if we 'value our honor.'" Lian tossed the parchment on the writing desk. "As if there's anything left of our honor without the staff."

"We'll get it back." Fayne glanced at me. Fates! I'd been gleaning such interesting if incomprehensible tidbits that I'd thought he'd forgotten about me. I wracked my meager list of memories. The item meant nothing to me. Yet unless I'd misinterpreted his look, Fayne thought me involved. Did something connect me to this staff?

"The staff, though, will have to wait," Fayne said. "You can bet that Lord Braith is already ahead of us if his messenger just got here. We leave for the tor at first light and you're all coming with me."

Lian grimaced. "I don't see why—"

"The family must present a united front. I can't be everywhere at once. We'll worry about getting the staff back later. You'll canvass our allies and drum up support, because Braith will already be at them by the time we get there. It's time to tell the Clan Elders about my theory behind the raids."

"The Clans will never believe you," Lian said.

"They followed our father, and I am Elder now." Fayne replied. "They respect Clan Grey."

"Because we mill the best timber. Because he held the staff."

"And who lost it for us?"

Lian's jaw clenched. "My opinion matters just as much as yours. I say the Gherza raid us."

"You saw the tracks. There are non-Gherza among them. It could be anyone."

"Who else would attack Grey crofters?"

"Lian, think! The witch is the best suspect."

"She couldn't mount raids like we've seen. She keeps no garrison."

"Are you so sure? You of all people should know what she's capable of after Rhinn. What if she corrupted one of our own? Rhinn of Dayr died on our watch. Lord Braith blames us for his daughter's death with good reason."

"For Fates' sake—if you're that desperate to find a culprit within the Clans, look to that bitch at Arneth."

Fayne took a step towards his brother. His right hand twitched upward and I thought he might strike Lian. "You will not speak of Lady Shirra in that manner. Father's refusal of her offer in favor of Rhinn offended her, but I can't see her starting a feud. Not with her position already so precarious. It makes no sense that the Gherza attack us."

"You'll never convince the Conclave of Elders without the staff."

"That's enough, Lian. Umbra, you showed restraint and a clear head today." Fayne shot a glance at Lian, and I could tell that whatever Fayne thought about my possible connection to this staff, he didn't want Lian involved.

To discover what tied me to Lian without asking him directly, I'd do well to gain the rest of the family's trust. I might have no memories of a staff, but it held importance to the Clan power hierarchy. Based on a flicker of a look, could I risk following a mere hunch that Fayne thought I might get him closer to retrieving it? If it meant he might be loathe to lose sight of me, yes.

"Would Errith appreciate a female companion?" I flourished an imaginary sword. "I could double as a bodyguard."

Fayne's lips quirked. I got the distinct impression he saw right through me. *Maybe you should ask him what he saw.* But I'd given him what I thought he wanted—an excuse to keep me nearby. Accompanying the Greys got me away from my hunter, as well. "A fine idea. The Conclave will know if anyone's gone missing from their Clans. Someone might recognize your face."

Fayne left, not giving his brother a chance to argue. Lian threw a disgusted glance my way before following suit, leaving me alone with Errith.

"He'll sunder the Clans over this," Errith said.

"Who, Fayne?"

Errith nodded. "Lian's right. Without the staff, Clan Grey is just another voice at the table, instead of the chosen of the Judge. And Fayne's not Father. He's as yet unproven. He can't just walk into the Conclave accusing random Clans of treachery. The Elders will read that into his refusal to implicate the Gherza." Errith gave herself a little shake. Did I see guilt flit across her face? "Forgive me," she said. "I've spoken of things that should remain within the Clan."

If those things stayed there they wouldn't help me. "What happened to your father?"

Errith's lip trembled. "He was murdered. He died defending

the staff."

"I'm sorry, Errith, why did they risk their lives for a staff?"

"Not *a* staff. *The* staff." She looked at me like I was a simpleton. "It marks us as the rightful owners of our lands. Losing it brings us great dishonor, within the Clans, and before the Fates. Without it to unite us, without a single voice to speak for the Judge, if the Clans go back to their old warring ways, most will blame us. Father brought it to honor Rhinn of Dayr on her betrothal procession to Grey. Lian couldn't protect them, or Rhinn. Lian won't forgive himself. At least, Fayne won't let him."

"They fought for this staff against whom?"

Errith jerked upright, eyes wide with fear. "A witch most foul."

THEN

Kairiya watched the tribe break camp. How quickly they struck the tents, packed away the pillows, rugs, and braziers, loaded up the shaggy ponies and prodded the herds into readiness! Every man, woman, and child knew their task, and wasted no movement. The easy teamwork came as a revelation after so much time alone.

Jezarel was not what Kairiya expected. Yes, in many ways she acted soft and spoiled, but she surprised Kairiya over and over again by how little she complained, whatever the task Kairiya set her.

Kairiya moved aside as the Izir rode past on a black gelding. The animal's tasseled bridle winked and gleamed with topaz and emeralds embedded in the leather. She'd grown attached to the camp over the last few weeks and the less of the Izir's notice she attracted, the better. He'd kick her out without a second thought if he caught any inkling of what she was doing with his daughter. And she had to stay. Her mother would kill her if she provided the Izir any reason to give her the boot.

Kairiya still couldn't believe that the Izir bought her story about learning the sword from caravan guards. Her thoughts turned to those first brutal lessons from the man her mother shared a bed with.

"Again!" he shouted as the wooden sword whacked her arm. She cried out at the sting. "Stop sniveling. You'd have worse than a welt if this was the real thing." He swung at her, and she raised her own weapon to block, but not in time to prevent another hard smack. "Bah! Has the Listener stoppered your ears? How many times do I have to repeat this? I don't have time to teach an incompetent."

One of her father's armsmen laughed. "Why are you wasting your time, Orrith? I thought you were sending her to the Sisters of the Fates, anyway."

"Her mother thinks a merchant caravan might take her."

Kairiya set her jaw. Cloistered with the Sisters? Why hadn't her mother told her? "Please, Father, one more time." She might not get another opportunity to prove herself.

This time, though the impact traveled down the weapon and numbed her fingers gripping the hilt, she managed to block. Her father narrowed his eyes at her. "Well, well. Maybe you *can* learn. Still, better improve, and fast, or you'll force me to sell you to the flesh trader once you're old enough." He cast an eye the other man. "Who knows? Maybe that's worth even more coin."

Kairiya's thoughts skittered in panic through her skull, like rats trying in vain to escape a trap. Given her embarrassing breeding, she knew he didn't want her working the local fields, her presence a constant reminder of his indiscretions. Honest work within the Clans would also be difficult to come by, given how no one trusted anything touched by a half-breed. She and her mother thought the sword might let her find work with one of the merchant caravans, and take her out of his sight. But the flesh traders! Surely her mother wouldn't allow it. Kairiya tried to swallow, but the truth dried her mouth. Her mother wouldn't care, even if she did have the power to do anything about it, which Kairiya knew she didn't.

Kairiya gave her father the only reason she thought might sway him. "I'll be worth more if you teach me this, and maybe you'll be rid of me sooner. I can also send part of my wages back to you if I remain free, but if you sell me to the flesh trader ..." She let the thought hang there.

She'd reached the age where it galled her that she bore the punishment for her mother's sins, but the awareness that no easy way out existed haunted her every waking minute. She often wondered what crime she'd committed in a previous life that had angered the Fates enough to give her this one, but the priest at the shrine had been no help—he wouldn't even deign to talk to a half-breed.

She awaited her father's judgment with eyes lowered, sword hanging from her still tingling fingers. She doubted she'd feel more nervous if she were facing a pronouncement straight from the mouth of the Judge.

Her father jerked his head at the armsman. "Go see him. If he thinks you're teachable, then better you waste his time than mine."

And so Kairiya's feet started down the path that brought her to this day.

The torcs on the Izir's arms flashed a warning in the sunlight. Kairiya ducked as the Izir's gold-handled riding crop whizzed past her cheek. He rode on as though he'd just swatted at a fly. It didn't matter: her own people treated her the same way. Like something in the way. Not a real person. No one they wanted to know or love.

This trek to the mountains would challenge her. She had managed to stay clear of the Izir and his wife via the simple expedient of staying away from camp during the day. The long days of walking and riding would leave her no choice but to mingle with the tribe. She knew the Izira saw her as a bad influence on Jezarel. What mother wouldn't? But Kairiya had become fond of her new friend, and resolved to show her family that she was not the undesirable that they presumed, but simply something different. And useful.

The tribe moved away from the watering hole in a cloud of dust, neighing horses, maaing goats and sheep, and clanking pots and pans, the only sign left of its presence a large patch of flattened steppe grass. Soon the winds would erase even that.

NOW

Riding long days and changing horses regularly, we slogged through nasty weather to reach Darmid Tor. The monotony of the trip was broken only once, when one of Fayne's scouts gave a sudden shout, and fired an arrow into the trees. We all gathered our dripping mounts at the edge of the meadow we'd been crossing, awaiting the scout's return from pursuit. She emerged from the trees, holding up a patch of deep indigo cloth. "Someone was shadowing us."

"Gherza?" Lian asked, giving Fayne a pointed look.

"Couldn't tell. They were cloaked and hooded. Caught a piece of the cloak on my arrow tip, but whoever it was, they move fast, and I lost them. Mighta been a woman—very light on their feet."

"Any signs of others?" Fayne asked.

"No, just the one."

"The witch has been said to wear a cloak of that color," Fayne said.

I shivered as rain dripped from my nose.

"Then the staff is nearby. We should give chase!" Lian said.

"She's long gone by now," the scout said, "And the rain will wash away any trace of her."

"Let's push on," Fayne said. "If she's following us, maybe we can set a snare for her."

I had a lot to ponder during the rest of the trip. The rain played into my hands, its steady patter making it difficult for other people to overhear Errith and I talking as she rode alongside me.

"What makes this staff so important?" I asked. Errith peered doubtfully out at me from beneath the hood of her cloak. "Forgive my ignorance, Errith. My memory—it feels like I have holes in my head, and not always just to do with my own life. It's frustrating, but with your help …" I left the sentence hanging, hoping to appeal to her better instincts.

"The Clan that possesses the staff leads debates at Clan Conclaves, and has the right to decide issues that split the Clans at large. That Clan acts as the voice of the Judge."

I hid my confusion. Errith's comments indicated to me a Clan power structure more sophisticated and united than the fractiousness I'd somehow expected.

"But you say this witch stole the staff. What would she want with it?"

Errith shrugged. "To sow discord among us, what else? Rumors whisper she's more than just a witch—that she dabbles in necromancy."

What little I understood of witches and necromancers told me they usually didn't bother with political intrigue. Supposing my hunter was indeed this witch, if both I and the staff were her targets, what did it mean? Fates. What if the staff had another use, one known only to initiates of the dark arts? I swallowed. Did that make me an initiate of necromancy, or simply a witch's pawn?

I couldn't resolve the question on the ride, as I deemed it too risky to show interest in the topic. Were Garrith Grey and Rhinn Dayr accidental casualties of the raid that killed them, and the goal theft of the staff? Or was assassination the real motive, and the staff just a cover? Did someone not want Rhinn to marry Fayne?

I couldn't talk to Lian about it; something felt off about my vision of him and the wounded man. I wished to avoid any association with this witch everyone spoke of so warily. I held a weak position with the Greys, and until I understood what or who stalked me, keeping to myself my ability to see the dead seemed wise, and so did staying away from any whiff of the dark arts.

Errith struck me as my best source for information. I would court her attention more, and gradually draw out the information I needed from her. With luck, I'd unearth enough to defend myself when my stalker found me. Or even go after her myself.

We arrived at Darmid Tor soaked by the pouring rain, the scouts having seen no more sign of the person shadowing us, despite Lian's hopes of catching the witch with the staff. This gathering at the tor provided the perfect opportunity to study the Clans. From the number of horses and people milling about the site, most other Clans had already made camp. Fayne ordered our tents set up then went in search of the Elders of the Conclave. I explored the camp, perusing faces, looking for a smile of recognition or suspicious glare. I found neither.

The Clans set up the Conclave as a patchwork of family enclaves surrounding a central pavilion. Next to the pavilion, the carved stone block seats of an outdoor amphitheater terraced the hill. A small shrine to the Fates stood at the base of the path climbing the tor, a replica of the larger sacred building that capped the peak. I rode next to Fayne and Lian as we trotted past on arrival.

"What do you think, brother?" Fayne asked Lian. "If I make the pilgrimage, will the Fates see fit to hear me out and return the staff to Clan Grey?"

"That's your great plan for getting it back? We're in bigger trouble than I thought," Lian replied.

"No, I have something else in mind. But a little divine intervention couldn't hurt."

Lian snorted. This time, I didn't bother hiding my confusion. "Pilgrimage?" I asked.

Fayne said, "Only those with the most desperate pleas for the Listener's ears make that climb. It's said one can hear the voices of shades in the wind howling through the stones at the top." Fayne avoided looking up the path. "I'd go insane too if the Fates sentenced me to wander the middle realm for eternity."

Lian laughed. "I suspect you're too boring, brother, for the Fates to bar your soul's passage through the Far Gates."

"Then may I remain boring."

"It's your soul. You'd better be sure. If you go up that path as a supplicant, those shades will drive you mad if your heart isn't true." Lian peeled off to see to the supplies. Had I imagined it, or had his glance up to the peak leaned towards disconcerted?

Now I stared up the path and wondered if I dared climb it. Madness in exchange for my memories? I decided to explore other avenues before chancing it.

Errith told me each Clan supplied a caretaker to help maintain the site in between Conclaves. When the Clans met, a small market sprouted up in the far reaches of the hollow. With no coin of my own, I avoided its hawkers in favor of the pavilion.

Once again disorientation unnerved me. The reality I walked in presented a distorted mirror image of what I intuitively expected. The ceiling of the pavilion arched over my head, stone columns disappearing up into candlelit dimness. Huge timbers lofted the ceiling to impossible heights above me. Soft footsteps echoed on marble-tiled floors. But a part of me wanted to—thought I *should* see a low-slung longhouse of fieldstone, with a beaten-earth floor. I blinked, as though to clear a vision, but the pavilion remained. The world stubbornly refused to meet my expectations.

How could my instinctive perceptions of the Clans be so wrong? I could not bring to mind a single face that I might know, yet as a people I felt sure they should be a hardscrabble lot, feuding over their lands and meager resources. Instead, they lived in luxurious keeps, their temples grown to monuments, and they settled scores amongst themselves using a central system. Wherever they'd gotten this staff, they'd imbued it with enough significance for it to play an important role in the power structure uniting them.

It was as if the Judge dropped me in some far-off exotic land, one just familiar enough to trick me into thinking I might still be close to home, and not hopelessly lost. If only I could find a map.

I stared at an engraved row of Clan sigils. A perfect copy of the Clan mark at my throat stood out in the middle of the row, carved to the size of my head. I heard Fayne's voice, and the clear tones of a woman, approaching from an adjoining alcove.

"Have you reconsidered my offer?" the woman asked.

"My position remains the same."

"I hoped that after the unfortunate death of your father, you might change your mind."

"All the more important I honor his wishes now, don't you agree?"

"While I respect your filial loyalty, Fayne, you do both our Clans a disservice. Together we could rule the timber trade. And certainly manage it better than the Dayrs. But apart … If you won't listen to reason, will you at least listen to your heart?"

"It's too soon after Rhinn's death to enter into any new arrangement. Braith will take offense, no matter how I might have felt."

"'Felt'? Fayne, what are you saying?"

"It's a matter of trust, Shirra. Rhinn's death was a little too convenient for you, wouldn't you say?"

"How could you possibly think I had anything …"

She trailed off when she noticed me. I feigned total absorption in the Clan sigils.

"Umbra."

I jumped then reminded myself not to overdo it. "Lord Fayne! I hoped to …" *Eavesdrop on your conversation.* "… recognize a sigil here."

"May I present the Lady Shirra? The Lady is High Seat of Clan Arneth."

I curtsied, though I probably looked ridiculous, dressed still in my riding gear. Arneth. As I stared at her, I thought I might be sick. A musky whiff of blood filled my nostrils. But I must have imagined it, because I saw no hurts upon Shirra or Fayne. *Traitor.*

My body recognized the name Arneth even if I didn't. But why such a reaction now? The Greys mentioned the name before. Did Shirra herself provoke my reaction? Or her title?

Fayne went on. "Lady Shirra, this is Umbra, a recent … guest of Castle Grey."

"What Clan do you visit from?" she asked.

When I hesitated, Fayne stepped in to rescue me.

"Umbra suffered a bit of an accident, which affected her memory. We're trying to find her Clan."

Lady Shirra peered at me, one eyebrow raised. "Indeed! A blow to the head?"

"I don't know," I said. I hoped Fayne wouldn't add any more details. I didn't like the way she studied me. Like an owl stalking a mouse. Though she hadn't recognized me at first sight, her sudden interest indicated more than just a casual concern for my welfare.

"How sweet of Fayne to take you in. I'm afraid you're not of the Arneth. I would have heard if a pretty chit like you disappeared."

Chit? I stiffened, but before I could retort, Shirra went on.

"I'll leave you to your new project, Lord Fayne. It can be such a chore finding a home for strays." She sashayed back toward the pavilion's entrance.

Fayne chuckled at my open-mouthed expression.

"What did I do to deserve that?" I asked. Then I regretted the question. *A lot*, something told me. But then, if Shirra did know me, she was a very good actress.

"Shirra never misses a chance to skewer a rival."

"Rival?"

"How much did you hear?"

Lying would do nothing to shore up his trust. "You mean her offer to support …" I broke off, realizing my error.

Seeing my face, Fayne's mouth quirked. "Yes. She wants more than just a temporary alliance. She resents any new woman in my life. Especially beautiful ones. If you'll excuse me, I need to find Lord Padraig." He left in the opposite direction Shirra had gone.

Rival. Did he mean romantic rivalry? *You know better.* But he'd just called me beautiful. Heat flared across my cheeks. The moment he'd caressed my brand that first night flashed through my head, and what his palm had felt like after the little boy's death. Something in him drew me. *Don't be stupid.* I shook my head to clear it of this distracting fancy. It must have something to do with Clan politics instead. Had Shirra seen something that I had missed? Or was she drawing attention away from an area she didn't want me poking my nose into by setting me up as a rival?

I smiled to myself. That kind of thing would only make me more curious.

~*~

I visited the shrine of the Fates. I picked out a beeswax taper from the pile near the door and strode up to the flame in the ever-burning fire basin to light it. Kneeling before the obsidian slab at the head of the shrine, I bowed my head before the statues of the Watcher, the Listener, and the Judge. Their strange faces always discomfited me, one sculpted with only eyes, but no ears or mouth, the other with only ears, and the third with a stern-lipped mouth.

I tipped the candle over and dribbled enough hot wax to form a solid base, before wedging the candle upright into the cooling mass. I stared into the flame, stilling my mind, letting thoughts rise to the surface as they would.

Shirra claimed not to know me, but I was associated with Clan Arneth in some unpleasant manner—my body's reaction when I heard Shirra's name told me so. Lian also claimed ignorance of me, but if I'd recalled a true scene during our duel, he was almost certainly lying. Which made him dangerous. A man with something to hide could do desperate things. So could a woman wronged. A witch stalked the Clanholds and likely me as well. Though I'd managed to ease Fayne's suspicion, I could see things I shouldn't.

I needed to watch my step. I felt like a hunted animal in the dark, blind to the traps all around.

I bent my head and offered an entreaty to the Judge, to give me my life back. Better to know if evil lay in my past than to always wonder. But the faceless stone statues stayed mute, and my wish went unheard. *Nothing new there. The Fates don't love the undeserving.*

I could expect only madness if I attempted the greater pilgrimage up the tor, given my ignorance of my own heart.

I turned to go, but heard a scuffling noise in an alcove. The hairs on my neck rose at a sharp cry of pain. I drew my knife. Who would hurt a woman in a shrine? Unless … Had my stalker lain in wait here?

Fearing what I'd find, I swept back a heavy velvet drape. A handsome blond man spun around, unarmed. And behind him … I kicked myself. Nobody would hurt anyone in a shrine. But some might try to sanctify a tryst.

"Errith?"

She peered out from behind her lover's shoulder, hair tousled and lips puffy. She scrambled to lace up the front of her dress. I stared at her companion, words heard in the keep's sewing circle floating through my head.

"Niall of Dayr, I presume," I said.

"No, my lady. You take me for another." He brushed past me and disappeared up the aisle.

Errith grabbed my arm. "You mustn't say anything. Not to Fayne, not to Lian."

"Aren't you betrothed to Niall of Dayr?"

"Please, Umbra. Before Rhinn died, Fayne was the one to link our two Clans. But now it falls to me, even though my heart belongs to another. I just wanted to say goodbye."

"You're asking me, a guest in your brother's household, to keep secrets from him." Errith didn't need to know what secrets I already hid. But she'd given me a lever.

Errith looked as though she might die on the spot.

I shrugged. "Fine. But if I help you ..."

"Whatever you want, Umbra, just please don't tell my brother."

What was one more secret? Especially if, by giving me sway over Errith, it finally got me answers.

THEN

"These shade-cursed needle-flies," the Izira said, swatting at her neck as her horse plodded along. "The trader I bought that cream from cheated me! He promised me it would drive the flies away. Look at them!" The Izira slashed her crop through the cloud of bugs circling her head. "It's as if I'm wearing fly musk!"

Jezarel tuned out her mother's complaints. She'd heard a thousand times how the Izira couldn't abide the flies. She must really be irritated this time though to use an oath that strong. Jezarel wished she could tell her to stop—the constant moaning only reminded Jezarel of her own itchy bites. The faster they left the tall polegrass behind the better.

The tribe trudged along the trail through the canes before and behind her. The heat pressed down on Jezarel like a blanket she couldn't shrug off. The zinging insects drowned out all other sound, and the shifting parallax of the vertical stalks of polegrass tugged at her peripheral vision, hypnotizing her. The only saving grace was that the leafy canopy sheltered them all from the worst of the sun's rays. And that the Izir's scouts brought news that the plateau and its cool lake waters lay a half-day's ride ahead.

Jezarel twisted in the saddle to locate Kairiya and stifled a giggle. Kairiya fought a losing battle to stay awake in the warmth, her head nodding and drooping. If she didn't take care, she'd slide right off her mount.

Jezarel swiveled back to respond to a question from her mother, but Kairiya stiffened, wide awake in an instant. Jezarel followed Kairiya's gaze, fixated on something off to the right, hidden by the polegrass.

A wave of caterwauling savages burst from the polegrass, hacking at the caravan with rusty broadswords, pummeling people, goats, sheep, and horses alike with cudgels and maces.

Jezarel yanked on her mount's reins, bringing the animal to a skidding halt. Two small groups of men ganged up fifty paces in front of and behind her, cutting off the narrow trail and preventing the rest of the caravan from coming to the women's aid. The Izir battled to get back to her mother, but Jezarel knew that two or three of the raiders could hold the trail for much too long for rescue to arrive.

Kairiya, her sword already drawn, laid about her with quick, efficient slashes of the blade. Jezarel watched in horror as a man yanked one of her mother's women from her saddle and dragged her into the polegrass. More brutes quickly surrounded Jezarel. A filthy hand grabbed at her calf. She whacked at her attacker's face with her only weapon, her short riding crop. The stinking, sweaty smell of the barbarians filled her nostrils, and she gagged.

The riding crop was no match against the mass of men. Jezarel screamed—she tipped sideways from her saddle, and hit the ground with a thud. With the wind knocked out of her, she stared up into the pale face above her. The fairness of the eastern men beyond the mountains bleached his pasty skin as white as the belly of a dead eel. He grinned down at her helplessness, mouth full of gaps, the remaining teeth rotting. His tattered skins smelled of smoke and animal grease, and he wore a necklace strung from the bones of small creatures. Jezarel had time to think that she'd take her would-be ravisher at the oasis over this, any day. Then another image flashed through her head. Her mother, wailing over her brother's body. Was this the last thing Javeen saw before they bashed his head in?

Jezarel leapt to her feet, and assumed one of the stances Kairiya taught her. She felt naked without a weapon, but determined to avoid the fate that met her brother. A whistle pierced the shouting. Jezarel whipped her head around in time to catch the tall staff Kairiya threw at her. Her friend had hacked up a stalk of polegrass, a flimsy weapon, but a weapon nonetheless.

Jezarel whacked at the knee of the man in front of her. He went down in a heap. A hand ripped at her shoulder. Jezarel whirled, cracking the improvised staff into the temple of another barbarian. Her shoulder flared with pain as the blow connected. She stumbled, off balance, flailing to block any answering hit. But the man's eyes rolled back into his head. He keeled over. Beside her, Jezarel glimpsed Kairiya's flickering sword. Another attacker shrieked as it slashed him.

Jezarel got the hang of swinging her staff, but as quickly as it started, the fight ended. Finding the women not such easy prey, the barbarians cut their losses and melted back into the polegrass. At Kairiya's feet, one man lay writhing on the ground. Jezarel came up behind Kairiya.

"Kill him," Jezarel said. The barbarians showed her brother no mercy. She would return the favor. The muscles in Kairiya's face tightened. Reluctance? From a fighter such as her? "Just do it already."

Kairiya inhaled, gave Jezarel an indecipherable look. Then she plunged the point of her sword through the man's chest. "Happy now?"

Jezarel nodded, even though she wanted to be sick. She had never seen a man die. The dead, yes, many times. But the actual moment of death … So final. Just like that, gone. What used to be a person now merely an empty shell.

Jezarel didn't have as much faith as her father in the Fates' promise of a return to the Great Cycle. She'd never met anyone who claimed to have lived before. Her father tried to explain to her that it didn't work that way, but she always left the study of the lore to her brother. Javeen was to have taken up the mantle from her father, so she didn't pay much attention to his lectures. But with Javeen gone, the Izir expected more from her. She worried she couldn't summon that much belief.

Her father galloped up with several men from the front of the caravan.

"Are you all right?" the Izir asked.

Jezarel nodded. "Kairiya saved me again."

The Izir stared at the dead barbarian. "Yes, she will eat with the rest of us tonight."

Beside her, Jezarel sensed the tension leave Kairiya. Jezarel wondered again at her friend's hesitation then remembered how she didn't even raise her sword to Jezarel's attacker at the oasis. Was this some strange warrior code Jezarel hadn't learned yet?

The Izir sent a few men into the polegrass to hunt down the attackers and prevent further ambushes. As the caravan picked up the pieces and prepared to move out again, Jezarel overheard her mother arguing with her father.

"… against the treaty is one thing—but to send armed men to assassinate us? Are you sure you've made the right decision?" the Izira asked.

"It's best for the tribes." He tugged his mount's head around and the horse loped off to the head of the caravan. Her mother's brow creased in worry. Jezarel could have sworn her father was about to say more until he spotted her watching. Jezarel frowned. What treaty? And why hide it from her? Jezarel suddenly realized there might be more to taking Javeen's place than just learning the lore. And her parents did not consider her up to the task.

Now

The amphitheater thrummed with the conversations of hundreds of Clanspeople. From my seat next to Errith, I studied the crowd. No one appeared interested in me—no furtive glances suddenly directed elsewhere, no quick turns of the head feigning a newly found absorption in the sky or pebbles on the ground.

At a movement on the right side of the amphitheater stage, the crowd quieted. A man with walnut hair speckled with grey hopped onto the stage, surprisingly spry for his advancing years. I had no idea what I expected, but it wasn't what came next. He raised his arms, tilted his head back to the sky, and emitted a long, mournful wail that skittered up and down the octaves.

I shivered. The wail made me think of the humming noise that came from my own throat when I examined my brand. Yet I sensed no magic, and I doubted the Clan Elders were practitioners. I berated myself—my own worries made me read too much into every new thing I saw.

The note trailed off. The man brought his head back down, stared out at the crowd for a long second, then stamped his foot hard on the ground. The sound echoed round the bowl. He stamped his foot again.

The crowd followed suit, creating a slow, rhythmic cadence that reverberated against the stone tiers. The beat quickened. Eleven men and women filed onto the stage. They wore mantles marking them as Clan Elders. Each person took a seat on one of the stone blocks arranged in a semicircle on the stage, Fayne on the third from the end. The man in the center remained standing, a long rod of cypress held in his hands.

The pounding beat crescendoed into a chaotic rumble. The man raised the rod up high, then slammed its base down into the ground. All noise in the amphitheater ceased. In the thick, expectant quiet, the man with the rod stepped forward.

"I, Braith of Dayr, welcome the Clans. I call the Clan Conclave. Who brings the Staff of Binding?"

I flinched as if struck. Why should the deep bass voice of the dark mountain man on the dais cause my body to betray me when the sight of him didn't bother me at all? Something about the timbre of his voice felt familiar. And yet I was sure I didn't know him.

I made a mental note to ask Errith about the Dayrs, then refocused my attention on the unfamiliar ceremony. Staff of Binding. The ceremony, that name for the staff, all of it strove to emphasize Clan unity. Their wealth made sense if they truly were working together and not always at odds, scrabbling at each other's holdings. I still marveled that a simple token like this staff could eliminate old grievances. Another thing to ask Errith: where they obtained it.

Fayne stood up. "Clan Grey hears the Conclave's call."

The silence after Fayne's statement lengthened, and people in the crowd murmured. Fayne had not completed the formal

80

greeting.

"Who brings the Staff of Binding?" Clan Elder Braith repeated.

Fayne's mouth quirked with reluctance. "The witch stole the staff. Garrith Grey died defending it."

Shouts erupted throughout the audience. Beside me, Errith gripped her skirts. Lady Shirra shot to her feet, a look I couldn't decipher on her face. She reconsidered saying anything and sat back down. Braith banged his rod on the ground, and the crowd settled.

Braith's lips twisted, deepening the lines at the corner of his mouth and turning his stern countenance sour. "Dire news you bring us, Fayne. Without the staff, nothing binds us to each other, to the Fates, to this land, and the timber we paid for with Clan lives. We have broken the compact with all three Fates—Watcher, Listener, and Judge. You have opened us to their wrath. And with the Gherza crossing the pass—"

"I don't believe they are a threat. Not to us."

"My own scouts discovered a Gherza encampment in the foothills across the river from Dayr Keep."

Shirra stood up again, this time, to speak. "Across the river? Why does Braith scout Arneth's land?"

Braith waved a dismissive hand. "You should be grateful, Shirra, that Dayr watches both our lands."

Shirra raised a skeptical eyebrow, but sat down again.

Lian stood up from his seat next to Errith and shouted, "They mass on the borders of the Grey holdings. They use these raids to keep us too busy and distracted to defend their real target: the Aramar Plateau. They'll say that without the staff, we no longer have a right to it."

Once again, Elder Braith banged his staff to re-establish order. "With or without the staff, we shall defend the Clanholds."

"I propose we do nothing of the sort," Fayne said. The Clan Elders all frowned. Lian shook his head. Did he simply have a difference of opinion with his brother, or did he gain something by proving the marauders Gherza and not someone else? Fayne continued. "The Gherza's quarrel lies with another. They told me so."

"History says otherwise. They call us heretics for rightfully claiming the staff. They covet it. And holdings unparched by drought. To let them traipse across Clan land with impunity—sheer folly." Braith fixed Shirra with a pointed stare. "Clan Dayr brought the news of the Gherza to the Conclave when others dithered. A stronger, more vigilant hand might have repulsed them from the start."

"The same Clan Dayr that failed to seal its own border?" Fayne's barb scored. "No matter. Our fight is their fight. Against the evil that stole the staff," Fayne said.

"An alliance with the Gherza? They can't be trusted."

"The death of your daughter at the witch's hands didn't convince you, Braith? The only other way is all-out war."

"A war the Gherza provoked."

"No! Don't you see? Someone's duping us. Yes, raiders attacked my crofts. But the signs point away from the Gherza. Lian himself bears witness that the witch stole the staff."

"The legends speak of her Gherza past. She's in league with them."

"Those same legends say she fled them. She sows chaos to

hide her true aim. We can't afford a war. Neither can we afford to ignore the snake in our midst."

"Wrong. We can't allow the Gherza to think us so weak that they can just march in without a fight."

"If they really wanted to hurt us, they'd burn the forests on the Aramar Plateau. That's what we're goading them into if we go on the offensive. Without those trees, what happens to those mills you're so proud of? Those ships? You put our entire system of trade at risk by going after the wrong target. They say they only want the witch. Why wouldn't we give them a chance at her? They might even know how to defeat her—how better to go about getting back the staff."

I thought Elder Braith might reach out and strike Fayne. The tip of the rod in his clenched hands quivered, but instead he rapped it against the ground one last time. "The Conclave is suspended. The Clan Elders must confer."

The Elders, including Fayne, filed out of the amphitheater. Fayne's shoulders looked so rigid a knife might bounce off them. A growing chorus of indignation echoed around the bowl. My own internal chorus of confusion sang a counterpoint.

I could not remember anything personal about myself, yet I recognized the Clans, even though their culture seemed alien amidst its familiarity. I knew of Clans Arneth and Dayr. I knew of Darmid Tor but its structures looked different from how I thought they should. I kept turning corners anticipating to see some aspect of Clan life. And I would see it, even though it contradicted my expectations. Those expectations, regarding all aspects of the Clans, existed somewhere within me, percolating through the barrier separating me from my memories. They gave me hope that I might yet breach that barrier.

Yet the staff and the Conclave ceremony had taken me by surprise, my vague impressions not giving me an inkling of what I might see or hear. Given their obvious importance in Clan life, I puzzled over why they should mean nothing to me. Did I not remember them due to my amnesia, or because I never knew them in the first place?

Lian stood up and spit on the ground. "Fayne will bring Clan Grey to ruin."

Errith reached out to touch his wrist but held back. "He's the Elder, Lian. We must trust he knows what he's doing."

"No good will come of aligning ourselves with the Gherza. Nothing but timber thieves and witch doctors, the lot of them. And Braith has every right to want to avenge Rhinn's death. Fayne should too. She was to become a Grey, and her honor as much ours as Dayr's to defend. The Watcher will not look kindly upon our failure to do so."

"Lian, please."

As we left the amphitheater, few of the Clanspeople would look Errith or Lian in the eye.

Lady Shirra intercepted us, taking Errith's elbow and pulling her aside from the stream of people.

"Errith," Shirra said, "your brother's speech moved me."

"Spare me your flattery."

"Fayne needs all the friends he can get. I thought you might speak to him on my behalf, remind him of the advantages of joining our two families. A word in the right ear might sway the Elders to his position."

"As if you hold any sway. Clan Grey can do better than an

upstart."

"A pity you think that way. Maybe I should set my sights on Clan Dayr instead."

"Niall is already spoken for."

"Is he now? I didn't think elder sons took kindly to a cuckolding by their younger cousins. Speak to your brother. I would have thought you the one person sympathetic to Fayne's feelings for me. If not, how unfortunate if the wrong rumors came to Niall's attention."

Shirra moved on. Time to show Errith I stood on her side, that she could trust me. I touched her shoulder, felt her trembling. From fear or rage I couldn't say.

"How does she know? We've been so discreet," Errith said.

"Are you sure your lover didn't let something slip?" I asked.

"Jorry would never ..." Errith sighed. "It doesn't matter. Even if she has no proof, just a whiff of it—the Dayrs hold such prickly notions of honor. It's why Fayne gave me to Niall to begin with. Braith insisted upon Rhinn's death that our Clan needed to make good on a union. He wants assured access to our mill. Shirra's backed me into a right fine corner."

I refrained from voicing my own opinion that Errith did her own backing by not cutting off all contact with this Jorry. Even the least prickly notions of honor would deem her tryst a betrayal of the worst sort. Only the most delicate negotiations could unwind a betrothal without giving offense.

"Do you love him?" I asked.

"Who, Jorry? Of course I do."

"Then maybe you should tell your brother."

Errith cringed. "He'll be so disappointed in me."

"Better he hear it from you than from Shirra. Or worse, Niall. Even if it never comes out, would you prefer a life stuck in a miserable marriage until the end of your days?" *Love only gets people in trouble.* I shrugged the thought away. "Why is Shirra such a bad match for Fayne?"

Errith looked at me as though the answer was obvious. "Because she's not a true Arneth." She walked off, huddled into herself, before I could ask her what that meant. I didn't envy her the choice she faced.

By dinnertime, the Elders still had not emerged from their deliberations. I fetched Errith from her tent and we made our way to the pavilion, where long tables brimmed with food from the day's hunt. Carved bowls filled with grapes and cheeses punctuated the trays of steaming boar and venison. My mouth watered.

The press of people closed in around me and I took a few deep breaths. The room vibrated with life, the din of conversation reverberating off the walls, although an undercurrent of uneasiness flowed through the laughter. I took my plate to a quiet corner and watched the crowd. The darker mountain men stood like shadows next to the blond Clansmen of the coast. Given my own coloring it made sense to begin my search with the mountain Clans, like Dayr, Arneth, or Galraith.

The thought that I might not belong to any Clan niggled at me. Would I be better off Clanless? Emotions ran high at the Conclave and maybe it behooved me to keep my distance from the affairs of Clan Grey. I toyed with the idea of leaving with the clothes on my back. Wiser perhaps to simply start a new life somewhere. Did what lurked in my past really need confronting?

A part of me thought not.

Then again, did I really want to live without knowing myself? The mark on my throat tied me to the Clans somehow. Fayne wanted the staff. The witch possessed the staff, and wanted me, I felt more and more sure. Maybe Fayne and I had more in common than I believed. Tying my fortunes to his might get me the answers I needed.

I mopped up the juices on my plate with a piece of bread, and spotted Fayne talking to Shirra. I sidled closer, hoping to uncover something related to this supposed rivalry Shirra believed in.

"… you could have sent warning they'd breached your lands," Fayne was saying. They stood in a nook behind the food table.

"I had no idea. I was off visiting the shipyards."

"Dayr will imply you are weak, and not worthy of the Arneth title."

"He's just worried I'll convince the Conclave to adjust the lumber quota in my favor."

"So? Don't give him an excuse. Your position is shaky enough as it is."

"We need each other, Fayne. This distrust is unworthy of you."

"I don't want to believe you'd tip the witch off. But no one had more to gain."

Of course. If Shirra hoped to marry Fayne, she'd feel threatened by his betrothal to Rhinn. I could also see how if the Clans didn't view her as a "true Arneth," allying herself to the Clan with the staff shored up her position. In that case, though, it would be stupid to get involved in stealing the very thing that made her ally strong. Unless she hoped to play the savior by appearing to get it back?

Shirra went on. "Despite my regret at your father's choice, I hold you in too much regard. You should know that." A quartet struck up a tune and people congregated on the dance floor. Shirra inclined her head, placed a hand on Fayne's forearm. "Will you not dance with me? For old time's sake?"

They fell in with the revelers.

A voice slithered into my ear. "Perhaps we should join the fun."

I hadn't even noticed Lian approach. I demurred, but he grabbed my wrist and yanked me towards the floor. I barely managed to drop my plate onto a sideboard before he whirled me into a jig.

Lian gave me no chance to get my bearings. He spun and twirled me through the mass of dancers like I was a puppet. The music slowed, and he tugged me close. His hands explored areas I'd prefer remain unmapped.

"Now that I've finally got you to myself, are you going to tell me who you really are?" he breathed into my ear.

I pulled back but his arms held me fast.

"Come now, Umbra, nobody's buying your sorry tale of forgetfulness. I heard what that crazy hag said about you and her grandson. You can tell me the truth."

"Call me a liar again and I'll invoke the rite of the Fates." I'd already bested him once in single combat.

Lian threw back his head and laughed. "That old ritual? You won't find many takers for second. Unless some grandfather with no teeth still remembers the rules."

Why did Lian irritate me so? The rite of the Fates was no laughing matter. I shook free of his grip, but collided with another pair of dancers.

"Such grace with a sword but so little in dance. Come, Lian, it's my turn to show our guest how it's done."

Fayne. He handed off Lady Shirra to Lian then swept me away through the crowd. Shirra stared after us, trying to catch Fayne's eye. Each time he avoided her gaze, and I couldn't decide whether doubt or sadness shrouded his eyes. Despite his easy manner, he held himself stiffly, and I sensed his argument with Shirra had continued on into their dance.

"Have the Elders come to a decision?" I asked.

"Yes, but not in my favor. Let's not speak of this now."

He pressed his hand to my back and brought us closer together. Like Lian, he discomfited me, but for different reasons. He pulsed with vibrancy. I responded like a winter-frozen flower to sunlight. But knowing so little about myself, how could I allow any intimacy? Aside from any claim of Shirra's, I needed to also consider my unknown social status. What if I had a husband, children?

The mocking whisper, the part of me that knew itself through instinct rather than memory, laughed. *You haven't had a man in a very long time.* But how could I be sure? I wanted to trust myself. But that same whisper told me I'd be wiser not to.

When I mustered enough calm to look up at Fayne, I found him studying the room. I caught a glimpse of Shirra's face over Lian's shoulder.

Fayne reached up and fingered a long ebony lock of my hair. He drew his fingers down the entire length of the strand then let it float back over my shoulder. I knew Shirra'd not missed a thing. Fayne smiled as my cheeks heated. He bent down to whisper in my ear. Was he taunting Shirra now?

"There's something … exotic about you, Umbra. A certain dark allure. With those blue eyes and black hair, I'd almost say Gherza blood ran in your veins, but you're too pale. And too tiny."

Wonderful. His words snuffed out the tingling thrill that engulfed me at his touch. The last thing I needed was for the Clans to associate me with the Gherza at the opening of hostilities. But Fayne's comment forced me to widen my search for myself. He was right—not many Clanspeople sported raven hair like mine. A few dark chestnut, yes. But I did not see a single true black.

Perhaps I didn't belong to the Clans at all. But if it was obvious I didn't belong, then Fayne's motivations were definitely not altruistic. He had no reason to keep me close in such a political mess, unless he believed me involved. Which, unless I could disavow any ties to the Gherza or that witch, didn't bode well for me.

~*~

Fayne's horse ambled alongside mine, hooves thudding into the soft mulch. The Clans had organized a hunt while we all waited for the Conclave to reconvene. The boisterous shouts of the hunting party faded off into the distance, and I realized Fayne manipulated me into this ride alone with him.

"Did you recognize anyone at the Conclave?" he asked.

"No. No one seemed elated to see me, either." In fact, not a single face evinced any emotion at all at the sight of me. My

discomfort surrounding the Dayr and Arneth Clans didn't merit
mention. Plus I didn't want Fayne haring off to those Clans on
his own to ask about me. I feared both those names. For
unknown reasons. Better not to give myself away to either of
them in case they harbored the person who hunted me, if they
and the witch weren't one and the same.

"What about the brand?"

"I promised to keep it hidden and I did."

"Nothing here evoked how you came by it?"

"Was something supposed to?"

Fayne slapped his reins against his mount's neck. I'd had
enough of him keeping me in the dark.

"Why's the brand so important?" I asked.

"There's only one thing that could mark you that way."

One thing. That seared the Mark of the Clans into my skin. I
should have guessed.

"The staff," I breathed.

Everything became clear. Why he chose to shelter me. Why
he kept me on a short leash. Why he couldn't tell me anything
before the Conclave, at risk of triggering a memory that would
send me running to a rival Clan. I knew he thought me connected
to the staff, but not how. The brand made him sure I knew
something about the staff's theft.

"You're using me," I said. All those little comments, about me
being beautiful. Exotic. He said them just to seduce me into
trusting him. And I'd almost fallen for it. *Almost?* I'd *wanted* to fall
for it. Had he and Lian plotted this all along? One brother,
unfriendly and distrustful, purposely driving me into the other's
arms, luring me in with a safe haven so I'd reveal my secrets. And

I'd thought Errith the gullible one.

"You either possess the staff yourself and forgot where it is, or you know who has it. Others have killed for less advantage than that."

I searched within myself for an answering spark, some resonance to confirm the truth of his words. A whiff of burned flesh teased my nostrils, but my mind refused to release anything more to the light. Someone hated me enough to permanently scar me. What lurked in my past that I deserved such contempt?

We crossed a small meadow, where bees patrolled the clover, sunlight drenching the air in golden warmth. We neared the trees, where the deer trail entered the wood again—a missile flashed past my cheek.

My horse screamed, then reared up. I glimpsed an arrow quivering in the bole of a birch. I tumbled backward out of the saddle. Another arrow protruded from the animal's haunch. I whacked the ground hard on my back. Winded, instead of drawing breath, I choked out a desperate, harsh rale.

Fayne yanked his horse around. He drew his sword. Fates! Had my hunter found me at last? I rolled over onto all fours, and took a gasping breath. I looked up.

Men poured into the clearing. Gherza. Fayne charged.

I struggled upright. Fayne closed the gap between our attackers, and their arrows landed beyond him. They outnumbered him. Wait ... Was I the target, or Fayne? A witch wouldn't need to send a band of assassins.

I slid my sword from its scabbard and scrambled after Fayne. An arrow whizzed past my shoulder, but before the archer could let fly his next missile, I reached the fray. One bandit screamed as my blade parted his thigh. All conscious thought left me as I battled for my life and Fayne's, the forms flowing one into the other until I no longer knew where my sword started and I left off.

I sensed more than saw Fayne's horse go down. I fought my way past two large brutes with maces until I spotted Fayne. He'd leapt off the hapless horse and struggled to beat back the swarm pinning him down. I took up position protecting his rear. Fear froze my heart. Outmatched, unless reinforcements arrived, we'd be dead in minutes. I didn't claw my way out of the river to die here.

A masked man jumped in front of me, swinging a curved sword at my chest. I jumped back, but my foot caught on the hind leg of the downed horse, and I lost my balance. I tilted backwards. My attacker bashed the sword out of my grip.

My arm buzzed numb. I collapsed to the grass. The brand scalded my skin.

Time billowed and expanded, and I saw Fayne, blood dripping from a cut to his cheek, turn to come to my aid. Behind him, a dagger glinted in its inexorable arc toward his heart. I gazed up into the eyes of my executioner, the sword poised over his head for the killing blow.

I cried out, smelled clover and blood. So much life.

I felt the air part as the blade sliced downward.

To end.

Like this.

No.

The brand at my throat scythed icy cold.

No.

93

THEN

Kairiya poked her head out of her newly made up tent and inhaled deeply of the crisp mountain air. It smelled almost like home ground. The tribe set their camp up in a meadow, the goats and sheep already cropping at its lush grasses and the last of the summer wildflowers. It was a fine place to spend the winter, away from the harsh winds of the steppe. They wintered far enough south that little snow would bother them.

Jezarel said each of the Gherza tribes wintered in a meadow just like this one. She had pointed out the trail to the Inarra tribe's former camp on the way past, before apologizing as she remembered their supposed relationship to Kairiya.

The field sloped down to the waters of the Aramar Plateau's single large lake. Aside from the shoreline, the great plateau forest surrounded the meadow on all sides. Kairiya would only call it a plateau relative to the craggy peaks of the Barrier Range, for it was not flat. The trees covered a cascade of rolling hills, with ridges and valleys hiding who knew how many smaller ponds and rills. Some of these hills looked like mountains from the steppe.

Off in the distance the cloth of the forest creased into folds as the land wrinkled beneath it. The *siratha* winds broke themselves against the northern edge of this forest, but couldn't penetrate this far south.

The camp nestled on the western shore of the lake. To the southeast the lake jogged towards the great Barrier Range. It spilled its waters into the river that carved its will into the rock and created Moongate Pass, through which the barbarians came to raid. The winter snows made travel through the pass risky, so the tribes could soon cease to worry as much, but for now, a lookout stood guard to warn of trouble.

Thinking of the pass made Kairiya homesick.

Kairiya tamped down on the lingering misgivings that she woke with every morning since she killed the Clansman. She'd had to do it. Besides, his wounds were bad. She'd shown him mercy. But she shared his blood as well as the Gherza's. The Judge—no, The One Who Speaks; she needed to remember to always use the Gherza term—might still consider it killing family.

"Kairiya!"

Kairiya spotted Jezarel striding up the hill. She'd gone easy on Jezarel these last few days but she should resume the training. "Just the person I wanted to see. It's time we ..."

"Not today. There's something I want to show you first." Jezarel handed Kairiya a hip pouch. Opening it, Kairiya found a slab of hard sheep cheese and dried figs.

She debated arguing with Jezarel about frivolous outings but thought better of it. Jezarel might tolerate Kairiya's bossiness during weapons lessons but Kairiya still only remained here at her pleasure.

Kairiya followed Jezarel away from camp and they soon toiled along a narrow deer track. It wound its way around a low hill and within minutes they lost sight of the camp in the trees.

The trail climbed a low rise. Towards the crest the trees thinned out and the mountain breeze tugged at Kairiya's jerkin. Jezarel led her down into a small valley whose sides rose steeply beside them. The sun was approaching its zenith when the trail ended at the base of a wall of rock. Jezarel twisted sideways and disappeared into a cleft in the stone.

Kairiya touched the rock. A great feeling of weight and age settled over her. She shrugged off her misgivings and squeezed into the opening after Jezarel. Twilight engulfed her as the cliff obscured the sun. Moss and lichen lined the walls, and above Kairiya the faintest sliver of light stabbed through the rock. Ahead of her, the fissure jagged left and she could no longer see Jezarel. The rock pressed in all around her and Kairiya pushed back against the urge to flee.

Kairiya stepped around the jut of the cliff where Jezarel vanished and a new world opened before her. The cleft was a gateway into a tiny valley. The wall of rock circled the whole hollow, forty paces high all around. Tall pines and silver birch lined the cliff top like an audience looking upon a singer—the only way in the split in the wall. Toward the far end, a small waterfall cascaded into a deep, limpid pool. At the pool's edge, an elegant white tree spread its branches over the water. Jezarel waited for her beneath the tree.

Kairiya didn't dare to breathe. She stood rooted to the ground, just like the tree, immobile and silent. Jezarel couldn't have brought her here. This couldn't possibly be *the* Tree.

Jezarel's voice broke the spell. "Are you coming?"

Kairiya took a halting step forward, crossed the mossy open

area until she stood before Jezarel in the shade of the leaves.

"Isn't it beautiful?" Jezarel asked.

Kairiya nodded. She reached out, stroked the slim trunk. Ebony black bark wrapped half the bole in a warm embrace, but sloughed off the flesh of the Tree, exposing its pure white wood. Kairiya touched the wood, warm and as smooth as silk. The Tree's corkscrew silver-green leaves shivered above her as if recognizing her touch as a lover's.

Kairiya's mother told her tales of this tree. Of how the Gherza held it sacred. How they believed the steppes remained fertile because of this tree. How it brought life to the plains, and kept the western wastes at bay. How the tribe that guarded it passed down its location from family to family, hoarding their secret and protecting it even from other Gherza.

And so Kairiya cried out in shock as Jezarel scored a deep slash in the wood with a long knife. Golden amber sap welled from the wound. The blood of the very Fates?

"What are you doing?" Kairiya wailed. "She Who Sees will— she'll *see* us!"

"Of course She will. We bask in Her gaze. There's nothing to be afraid of—She would approve." Jezarel held out her hand before her and cut a gash into her own palm. She reached out for Kairiya's hand. "Come. We will be blood sisters."

The wonder of the Tree slowed Kairiya's thoughts. She didn't resist. Jezarel's knife slid across her skin, parting the flesh, releasing a thread of warm, stinging red. Jezarel clasped Kairiya's wounded palm in hers. Blood flowed around their fingers, filled the crevices and lines in their skin. Kairiya's cut pulsed and throbbed. She worried that she would no longer be able to hold her sword.

Jezarel stared into her eyes. "Blood sisters, sealed together forever," she said. Then she placed Kairiya's hand palm down over the scored tree, with her own next to it. The golden sap mingled with the ruby blood. Kairiya felt dizzy. Her awareness sought out every blade of grass, fluttering bird, singing cricket in the world as far as her mind could encompass. She was one with everything, her skin no longer a barrier between her and all the other living creatures of the earth. She gasped as Jezarel pulled their hands away from the Tree.

And saw that the Tree was whole once again. Her palm no longer ached. On Kairiya's skin, only a fine silver line revealed where the knife cut her.

"What have you done to me?" Kairiya tried to clear the wonder that made her muzzy, angry that she'd allowed this strange seduction. What had Jezarel encumbered her with? Would she forever now be pinned beneath She Who Sees' gaze? Would the Fates' blood running through her veins—was it really their blood, the sap?—leave her unable to escape their scrutiny? She'd spent her whole life trying to stay unnoticed, trying to avoid punishment from Fates and family both. Now this.

Kairiya shook her head in an effort to still her rising panic. She twisted her fingers into the sign of the warding eye behind her back.

"I lost my brother," Jezarel said. "Now I've gained a sister. The Tree ties us together, closer than family. Nothing but the Fates can break our bond now, maybe not even death."

"Why?" Kairiya asked.

"You saved my life, and with what you teach me, you will help me avenge my brother. It is fitting."

Kairiya inclined her head, hoping Jezarel would see it as humble acceptance. How could Kairiya accomplish her task— betray Jezarel for the glory of the Clans—if she was now blood sister to this woman?

NOW

Smoke poured in trails from my fingertips, fingers I couldn't feel anymore for the cold washing out of me. The trails split and twined, reaching, reaching for each of our attackers. I could only watch in shock as my own body secreted this … this … what?

The man about to decapitate Fayne batted away a tendril, but it curled around his neck and flooded across his face, covering his eyes, seeking out his nostrils and open mouth.

And then I touched them—I didn't know how—a dozen souls all pulsing with vibrant life at the end of each tendril, connected to me through the smoke. At my touch, the men shrieked. *Killers, all. No, not quite all.* I somehow retracted the stray whorl reaching out for Fayne. I closed my eyes and, in a flash of pure instinct ... twisted. The men's screams cut off in terrible choking gasps.

The silence was terrible. So deep it boomed throughout the clearing, reverberating through my skull.

I resisted opening my eyes. Lingered, hiding, behind my closed lids. Putting off this truth just a little longer. *Coward. You wanted to know. Now you do.* The smoke had felt like an extension of me. One that acted with a mind of its own. Or perhaps acted at the behest of that part of my mind shut off to me.

The brand still seared with cold. The presence I'd felt that first day at Castle Grey pushed at the edge of my mind. I sensed ... satisfaction from it. I shook my head, trying to dismiss it.

A hand clasped my wrist and yanked me to my feet, forcing me to let the world in. A cloaked figure stood beside the bole of a tree. When it saw me staring, it withdrew into the woods. Fayne stood next to me, his back to where the figure had been. All around us, our attackers lay in forlorn, crumpled heaps. All of them, dead.

Oh Fates. Oh Fates. A little wailing part of me scrabbled to crawl out of my own skin. To silence it, I said the first thing I thought might distract Fayne. And me. "I can't believe the Gherza would dare attack anyone so close to the Conclave."

Fayne looked shaken. I thought he'd challenge me on what just happened, but he bent down next to one of the bodies. "This man's hair wasn't originally black." Fayne twitched a lock aside to reveal a reddish strand beneath. He swiped a finger along the dead man's cheek, then held up the now-smudged tip for me to examine. "He darkened his skin to make him look Gherza as well."

"That's insane. Anyone could see through such a simple ruse."

"But from far away they'd look authentic. I don't think they expected to leave anyone behind." We both looked up at a rustling at the edge of the clearing. That figure, escaping? Fayne shook his head as I took a step forward to investigate. "This place isn't safe. More may come if we tarry."

Fayne struck off across the clearing, back to where my horse limped near the trees. He didn't wait for me. He didn't sheath his sword, either, and I wondered what scared him more: a new ambush, or me.

I walked slowly up to the horse, staying clear of Fayne, to keep either of them from spooking. I held firm to the bridle while Fayne dealt with the arrow in the animal's haunch.

"It didn't go too deep. She'll have to carry us," he said.

"So you're not angry, then?"

"I'm alive, aren't I?" I couldn't read the undertone in his voice. "Can we discuss this back at the Conclave? We're too exposed here."

He swung up into the saddle. I stared at his proffered hand. He was right. The attack left us vulnerable, and if I chose to part company with him now I'd be on my own, pursued in strange territory that just got stranger. While no longer as helpless as I'd thought myself, the new weapon in my arsenal horrified me.

If it horrified Fayne just as much, I'd commit an even bigger mistake by going back with him. I'd shown him direct evidence of sorcery. He said he wasn't upset, but his reaction felt off.

He flicked his outstretched hand, still staring at the edge of the clearing. He searched for the staff, and it had branded me. He knew more than he'd told me, but now I knew why he needed me. If that made him overlook certain abilities of mine, that gave me a lever to find out what else he'd not told me. I took his hand.

He scooped me up behind him, kicking the horse into a trot. A footpath connected with the deer trail, and we doubled back through the woods in the direction of Darmid Tor.

Fayne flinched whenever the horse's gait lurched and my hands clutched at his waist. Could I blame him? I wanted to recoil away from myself, but there was no escaping from what I'd done. Despite my desperate need to find myself, I wished I hadn't found this. I'd saved our lives, but it brought me little relief. I'd committed a sick and unnatural act. I wasn't even sure how, or even if I could repeat it, but the implications terrified me.

I wanted to cling to Fayne tightly, soak in his living warmth to dispel my awful chill, hear him tell me everything would be all right. But the taut set of his shoulders warned me off. With a simple tilt of my head, I could lean my cheek on the nape of his neck, yet I'd never felt so alone.

The hunting party was already back at camp, celebrating the bagging of a boar, when we arrived. They grew quiet, taking in our lame horse and bloody clothes. Lian came forward to grab the bridle. His eyes widened as he stared at me and I tugged my kerchief back up to hide the brand. He'd seen it though, I was sure of it.

"Gherza?" Lian asked.

"We were meant to think so, but no. Assassins." Fayne pushed me towards Lian. "Take her to the shrine, and guard her. I wish to speak with her in private when I get back."

"Where are you going?"

"To figure out who wants me dead. The horse pulled up too lame to carry both us and proof. I need to send someone after the bodies."

I wasn't so sure Fayne was the intended target. The attack could just as easily have been designed to kill or trap me. Fayne rounded up a group of armsmen and strode off to the horse pickets.

Since I first opened my eyes in the clearing, he'd not looked at me once.

~*~

I paced about in the shrine. I couldn't sit still. Lian placed a guard on the door then left to help Fayne.

I tried to dissociate myself from the killings in the meadow. But I couldn't shut out the evidence of my own body. My fingertips still tingled as though I'd just come into a warm room from a freezing blizzard. And I remembered. Remembered the cold tendrils of … something … emanating from me. Seeking out the blazing life nearby. Wrapping itself around the vital essence. Twisting. Until each essence separated from the vessel of its body and the coldness sent it fleeing into the void.

I shivered, then sagged against the wall, digging my fingernails into a wooden beam, as if the honest pain of splinters might drive out the deeper shadow in my own soul.

Whatever I did, I'd done it to save us both. What scared me more than this unexplained new power: I had enough control over it to not kill Fayne. This was something I was good at. Good at taking lives. Stealing souls.

I gagged. Was I really the kind of person who had worked to excel at this horror?

I took a seat in a corner of the room, and attempted to conjure up an explanation Fayne might find palatable. The long minutes slid away as my mind came up empty.

The latch at the entrance clicked and I shot to my feet. Fayne stood in the doorway. He sent the guard away then slammed the door shut behind him. He strode across the room.

"Lord Fayne, I—"

Fayne's hand moved so fast I had no time to react. He

grabbed me by the throat and shoved me up against the wall. The sharp prick of his dagger nicked the skin near my jugular.

"Did you think you could fool me?" he spit.

His crushing fingers cut off all my air. I could only shake my head slightly.

"Tell me why I shouldn't kill you where you stand."

His fingers squeezed harder. I scrabbled at the arm choking me. *Let me breathe, you bastard, and maybe we can discuss it.* Spots danced in front of my eyes. I started to pass out; the brand chilled again. What if I couldn't help killing him? I'd never escape the ensuing hue and cry.

Sweet air flooded into my chest. Fayne eased his grip, but kept the knife at my throat.

"I didn't mean to kill those men," I croaked. "I mean, I did, but not in that way."

"Just like you didn't mean to kill my father? And Rhinn?" The knife pressed harder. Warm blood trickled down my collarbone, its succulent perfume filling my nostrils. Such a fine line between death and life. The edge of a knife.

"What are you talking about?"

Fayne's knuckles gripping the knife brushed against my brand. "The memory loss, everything. All just a ruse, wasn't it, Umbra? Or should I say, Iril."

The name rang like a gong through my skull. Just as when I'd fought Lian, the room swirled and disappeared. A cloaked, hooded figure stood before me instead, smoke veiling the air between us. The figure raised its arms high over its head, a long rod clenched in its hands. Then it slammed the rod down and thrust it out at me. Searing, burning pain filled me. I flew back through the air.

The pain stabbed through my head. The vision cleared and I stood once again in front of Fayne. Confusion as to what brought the vision on warred with dismay at what little it revealed.

"I know that name," I said. "But it's not mine."

"Liar."

Maybe. I didn't feel like I belonged to the name, but I couldn't be sure. "I'm not this Iril," I said, and hoped I spoke truth.

"Who else but a necromancer kills like that? Myra wasn't lying. You saw her son after he died."

My mouth went dry. Necromancy did explain everything. But if I was the witch, who hunted me? "She killed your father?"

"You did."

"But I wasn't there!"

Or was I? The image of Lian standing over the wounded man flashed into my head. So it *was* real.

"I couldn't have killed him," I whispered, even though I knew I was lying to myself. I'd shown just how well I could kill, both with a sword and with my own fey power.

"You ambushed them. You stole the staff. Lian tried to stop you."

So the vision represented a true memory. But what little I remembered about the scene bothered me. If I'd been there, I must be Iril. But the man gave me the distinct impression he feared Lian, not me. And I felt no murder in my heart. At least, not for the man.

What was I doing there if I bore no responsibility for the ambush? Was I a cold-blooded murderer or did somebody misrepresent the event to Fayne? And if I'd stolen the staff, where did I hide it? Why would I need it?

And if I was the witch, who was the hooded figure who'd been shadowing us? Who, I was almost sure now, hunted me?

I feared that the guilty conscience plaguing me since I washed up on the riverbank had something to do with Fayne's accusations. With the brand on my neck tying me to the staff, I now understood why he'd kept me so close. I needed to tread carefully to convince him to withdraw the knife. Wouldn't I feel it, deep down in my core, if I was as evil as Fayne claimed? Guilty didn't necessarily equate to evil. And yet, I couldn't deny what I'd just done to those men.

"Why now?" I asked to buy myself time. "Didn't you know as soon as you saw me on the riverbank? Shouldn't Lian have known me?"

"No one's seen Iril. She takes pains to hide her face."

"I saved your life in the meadow," I said.

"You owe me two."

"Why would I want you alive if I'm Iril? Why would I leave Lian alive?"

The blade trembled against my skin.

"I swear I don't remember killing your family," I continued. "You have every right to vengeance if I did. But if I'm not who you say, you'll be just as guilty of murder as Iril. Let me find proof of who I am. Then you can decide what justice I should face. Besides, I can't help you find the staff if I'm dead." I held my breath.

Fayne's nostrils flared. But his hands dropped from my throat and he stepped back. I slumped against the wall.

"I'm sorry, Umbra. I'd started to think well of you, and then this ... thing you did in the meadow ..." The hand holding the dagger shook as he sheathed it, I sensed now from fear, not anger. Fear of me.

"I'm the one who's sorry," I whispered. "You have to believe that I wouldn't hurt you or yours."

"I've heard that from too many people lately. Some of them must be lying."

I pointed at my brand. "This connects us. I want answers just as much as you do."

His mouth set in a determined line. "Then we'll search out your past together," Fayne said. "Iril or not, you're my best hope to find the staff if I'm to convince the Clans to follow me regarding the Gherza."

"Did you find out anything about our attackers when you went back to the meadow?"

"The dead tell strange tales. Come see." Fayne led me from the shrine. He nodded and twenty men with bows aimed at the door lowered them. If I'd come out alone I'd have died in a hail of arrows.

I swallowed. I read him wrong in the meadow. His need for me hadn't caused him to turn a blind eye to what I'd done. He'd simply wanted to face me down where I couldn't flee. Yet he'd still faced me alone. Either extremely brave or foolhardy, he didn't want anyone else knowing what was said between us. Interesting. Perhaps I erred in thinking he and Lian worked together in a game of stick and carrot to gull me.

We stopped where Fayne's men dumped the fruits of their search. A single corpse, unmistakably Gherza. The fatal wound: a gash across the neck. I pulled Fayne away from his men, and spoke in low tones.

"I didn't kill this one. I didn't get in any throat cuts before …" Before I'd sucked the life from every attacker in that clearing. "Did you?"

"No. Now you understand why I called it strange."

So our proof of the Gherza's innocence in the attack had vanished, replaced with irrefutable evidence to the contrary. Because neither Fayne nor I could admit we hadn't killed this Gherza. The Elders would accuse me of witchcraft, and Fayne would lose his one lead to the staff. But killing Fayne and pinning it on the Gherza removed the last opposition to an attack on the Gherza. Who gained the most? I spotted Braith of Dayr approaching.

Fayne had confronted me alone. Without his brother. My next words came from nowhere, before I could take them back. "Your brother wants you dead."

Fayne didn't look back at me as he hardened himself to face Braith. "I'll thank you to get your own house in order, Umbra, before you accuse mine of perfidy."

But the brief widening of his eyes when I'd spoken told me that I'd shaken him.

THEN

Jezarel's feet danced across the stone path on the journey home from the Tree vale. She and Kairiya crested the hill above camp. Jezarel stopped dead as she spotted the group of riders coming down the trail from the mountain pass.

"Another tribe from the steppe?" Kairiya asked.

Jezarel frowned. "No, they've come from the east. It must be the men my father sent to spy on the barbarians."

Jezarel hurried down the path, eager for whatever news the arriving riders carried. Maybe they finally found the men who killed Javeen. She rushed into her father's tent, heedless of Kairiya, who followed more slowly. Jezarel's mother, with a few of her women, waited behind the canvas wall separating the Izir's reception room from the family quarters.

"Where have you been?" Her mother reached out to straighten Jezarel's disheveled robe. At a peremptory gesture from the Izira, another woman passed over an ornate beaded scarf. Her mother fussed with Jezarel's hair, wrapping it in the scarf and draping its folds over Jezarel's robe. "There. Now you are presentable. Your father asks for you."

"Why so formal, Mother?"

"Your father will tell you."

Jezarel and her mother entered the reception room to see her father just bidding farewell to the riders. He surprised her by raising his cup of wine in the toast of departure.

"May She Who Sees watch over your journey and speed your passage," the Izir said.

Surely they weren't leaving again so soon! The Izir confirmed Jezarel's suspicions when he pointed at a gilded box on the floor of the tent. Two of the riders hoisted it between them and the group exited the tent. With the flurry of departing legs gone, Jezarel noticed the second carved box, sitting alone on the rugs at her father's feet.

Jezarel looked doubtfully at the box. Adorned with carved designs unfamiliar to her, it lacked the gilding the steppe tribes so coveted. Its darkly oiled wood absorbed the dim light flickering from the braziers.

Her father beckoned her to him. He nodded at the box. "Open it," he said.

Jezarel touched the box, almost expecting it to burn her. With great reluctance she lifted the lid. Inside, she found a bolt of delicate cloth made from thousands of tiny knots in beautiful floral patterns. Despite herself, the intricacy of the work fascinated her.

"Your bride price," her father said. "Barbarian lace."

Jezarel heard the words. But it was as if her father spoke in code. She didn't understand.

The Izira approached and fingered the lace. "Finest quality. Only the best for my daughter."

Jezarel shook herself out of her stupor. "But Father, what

tribe would send such a thing to you? What of the wreath of grain? The entwined golden torcs?"

Her father's eyes held a truth she refused to see. But she could not deny the words. "You will do us great honor and bring peace between two peoples. You are to marry Murran, son of the Arneth tribe of the eastern Clans."

A barbarian.

He was marrying her off to a barbarian.

Jezarel screamed. And screamed.

NOW

Lian accosted me on my way back to my tent.

"What game are you playing at, Iril?" he hissed.

I shrugged free of his grip, and didn't answer. Did Fayne tell him his suspicions, or was this something else? His tone struck me as too familiar. What if ...

"You know the game," I ventured. I held my breath. I only knew the game smelled of danger. But his response here might just tell me volumes.

"You promised to show yourself to me at the right time. I thought, after the burned boy, it must be you ..."

Promised. My hunch proved right. Lian was in league with this Iril. Finally! An answer. I couldn't savor the satisfaction, though. I walked a fine line here. I didn't like Lian. But that didn't mean I wasn't Iril. *You don't have to like someone to use them.* Then again, if I was Iril, who stalked me?

Did Lian know my identity with certainty, because of my actions, or did he just suspect? If he thought we had some sort of agreement, he must know, unless Iril was so paranoid she didn't show herself even to allies.

I shivered and hoped Lian didn't notice. A necromancer. If it was true, why did it feel so wrong? Maybe the blow that stole my memory knocked a conscience into me. But until I knew for sure what plots, if any, I'd set in motion, I needed to tread carefully. I trusted Lian no more than I trusted my own cryptic memories. Regardless, I couldn't pass up the opportunity, however risky, to play both sides. It might get me what I needed to prove to Fayne his brother's treachery. Any misstep might do the opposite, though, and convince Fayne I really was Iril.

"I choose when and how to reveal myself, Lian."

"But why the secrecy?"

I couldn't explain my abilities in the absence of necromancy. And I couldn't prove anything to Fayne. Maybe I was still a witch. If so, I needed to start thinking like one. Maybe Iril and I were allies, or maybe we stood at odds. But that didn't make my reasons for necromancy any more noble than hers. *Oh, you could teach her a few things about venality.* Fine then. I'll give you venal.

"Lian, don't be a fool. I can't have others catching us out and coming to the wrong conclusion. It's better if we're only seen together on Grey family business." I thought of Errith. "Let them think you're meeting a discreet lover in secret."

"I'm still mourning Rhinn."

Rhinn again. She would have become a Grey if she lived. But the Dayrs promised her to Fayne. Had I misunderstood? A powerful Clan like Dayr would want their daughter married to the elder brother. Unless ... Again Errith popped into my head. *What of the lover left bereft by an arranged marriage?* If Fayne was to marry Lian's love, that would explain the bad blood I sensed between them. I almost laughed. The Fates seemed to have anything but their first loves in mind for the Grey children.

I said the only thing that came to mind that might keep Lian inveigled. "If people think you're over her, no one will suspect what we're doing." Which was what exactly? What kind of false hope had Iril given him?

"I don't like it."

"You don't have to like it. Just do it."

"I've done everything you asked. I set it up perfectly until you … interfered."

"I don't answer to you," I said. This confirmed my instinctive suspicion. Lian masterminded the attack in the glade. Interesting. I squirreled the fact away. I could use it to gain Fayne's trust. I risked doing just the opposite if I went about it the wrong way, though, as I'd done earlier. Assuming I wanted Fayne's trust. Right now, I needed to bolster Lian's. A witch worth her salt would be upset at him right now, wouldn't she? "What did you think you were doing, anyway? You almost killed me."

"I figured you could take care of yourself. Besides, Fayne's getting too close to the truth. With him out of the way, we both get what we want."

"Your timing leaves to be desired."

"It's the first time in weeks that he's left himself unguarded!"

"Now he's suspicious of me."

"It's your fault for not letting him die."

Think fast. "I did you a favor. Another Grey dead, and who stands to gain the most? You're too impetuous, Lian. The Elders would look straight to you for blame. And then where would we be?"

"Where's the staff?" Lian demanded.

"You're the last person I would tell." And I meant it. Lian

rubbed me the wrong way.

"You promised me."

"And I keep my promises. But now's not the time."

I marched away, hoping that would tide him over. I walked in uncharted territory and couldn't see the quicksand. I hoped I'd done the right thing. Two questions now seemed vital to answer: did Fayne and Lian act at odds, or in tandem to draw me out? And was I really this Iril? Without those answers, dust clouds obscured the horizon.

~*~

The Conclave reconvened at sunset. I sat in the amphitheater, wedged between Errith and Lian. When the Elders filed onto the dais, Fayne took a position apart from the rest of them. From the murmurs in the crowd, I could tell news of the attempt on his life had made the rounds.

"Clansmen," Elder Braith intoned, "we have chosen our path. We must rout the Gherza from the Clanholds. We cannot let them attack us with impunity. The Fates saw fit to favor the Clans over the Gherza. Let us not prove unworthy of that choice. My own daughter will not have died in vain. Gather the host. We leave at first light to drive them back across the pass and off the Aramar Plateau. Let them flee the might of the Clans united."

Fayne shook his head. "Clan Grey disagrees with Clan Dayr and the Council. The Gherza are not our enemies."

Braith snorted. "You speak on their behalf even after they attempted to take your life?"

"The Gherza did not try to kill me. Someone wants the Elders to think so."

"All the evidence points to the Gherza."

"Not the evidence I saw with my own eyes at the scene."

"The Conclave must put the proof brought before it over the word of even an Elder. The host will meet at the eastern border of the Dayr Clanhold. From there, we will find the Gherza and drive them out."

Elder Braith continued, relishing his next words. "We pray that the Watcher does not cast her eyes upon us before the return of the staff. For its role in the loss of the Staff of Binding, Clan Grey must relinquish its position in the Conclave of Elders."

Beside me, Lian punched his thigh. I hoped the bruise pained him. He *had* tried to kill me. Chinks showed in his alliance with Iril. Chinks that, as Iril I needed to fill in, or to exploit as someone else.

I nudged Errith. "Why do they call it the Staff of Binding?" "Binding" seemed like an odd choice of word, with possessive connotations as opposed to mutual unity.

"Because it binds the Clans together. We used to fight among ourselves all the time before we took it from the Gherza." She swept her arm around to indicate the Conclave. "Instead of fighting, we trade and build, our prosperity all bound in each other's fortunes."

I shook my head. It made sense, but I wondered. I bore the staff's mark. One branded animals one owned. When I'd touched the mark, I'd felt exposed to my hunter, almost as if she could see me. Did I delude myself that I could escape her? My newly found ability gave me an advantage now. Maybe it was time to stop running.

The Conclave dispersed, Clansmen scurrying to pack up their camps and gather what troops they could. Shirra sidled up to

Errith. "Perhaps now that we're almost equals, you'll reconsider my request," Shirra said.

Errith strode away with a grim look on her face. Shirra brushed her fingers along Lian's biceps, in plain view of Fayne. It struck me as an odd way to try to get back into Fayne's good graces. Lian didn't look like he minded at all, contrary to his prior profession of faithfulness to the departed Rhinn. He walked off with Shirra, the two of them deep in conversation. I thought I heard Shirra say the words "Niall of Dayr."

Uh oh. I ran after Errith to warn her.

~*~

I marched up the flank of Darmid Tor, following the mossy path. The Clan host wouldn't leave until morning, which gave me only a few hours to get to the top and back. I'd bid the Greys goodnight, pretended to go to sleep, then, when the bustle of the Conclave quieted, set out on my mission.

The Fates didn't answer me the other night in the small shrine. With the host setting out, I might never get another chance to make this pilgrimage. With more questions than answers, I didn't see another way of unraveling the mystery of me. They'd have to answer me in the temple at the top, wouldn't they?

The Fates don't have *to do anything.*

No. Fayne said only the most desperate went up to plead their case. Given the belief that the wrong action seen by the Watcher, or the wrong words heard by the Listener might consign one to harsh punishment by the Judge, it did seem foolhardy to confront the Fates directly. But I could kill people on a whim! I needed to understand this power, and if I couldn't control it, better maybe if I really did go mad and never returned from this expedition. At least then nobody else would die.

What if they drive you so insane the only thing left to you is killing? You're endangering people more!

I stopped dead in the trail, then steeled myself and continued on. I'd already fought this argument with myself while waiting for the camp to quiet down. I needed answers, whatever the risk.

A true heart, Lian said. I didn't know my own heart. But I was learning. I had to trust that my natural aversion both to Lian's casual venality and the act of necromancy meant something. The Fates would judge me at my eventual death—if I could postpone that death at either Fayne's or my hunter's hands by getting that judgment now instead, all the better.

Compared to the mountains of the Barrier Range, Darmid Tor rose up only a paltry height above the surrounding orchards and plains. Yet halfway up, the wind snuck up behind me then whipped around, plucking at my sleeves. I pressed on, each step that took me higher also angering the wind. Now it battered against me, a clear message to head back down the hillside if I knew what was good for me. I bowed my head and kept going.

I reached the top, where a veritable cacophony of howls and shrieks greeted me. The temple here, indeed the model for the smaller shrine below, moaned and thrummed as the wind tore through its columns and crannies. I expected masonry to start peeling and flying from its walls at any moment. I stumbled through the entryway, looking for relief from the gale.

And found none. The general volume of sound abated a bit, but the air still rushed through the great hall. At the far end of the temple, the three statues of the Fates stood sentry, immense and immutable, terrible and stern. Unlike the ones in the small shrine, these wore their identity through voids: the Watcher's empty eye sockets, the holes in place of the Listener's ears, the Judge's gaping mouth. The wind poured and whispered through those openings, and thralled the ears with bewitching murmurs, hisses, and sighs.

I quailed.

The wind muttered and gibbered. I thought I'd already gone insane, for I swore I heard my name. I wanted to flee, but instead set my feet upon the stones and advanced towards the statues. I stared for the space of three breaths into the face of each of the Fates, then prostrated myself on the floor in front of them.

Now I understood the stories told of this place, because the mind clutched at the gabble, trying to make sense of its sibilant whistles and bass groans. Perhaps only a madwoman could come to terms with it. Yet I lay there, and listened, and my fear slowly abated under the caress of the breeze on my hair and across my forearms. It was just wind. Just noise.

—*Watcher, see my pain. Listener, hear my prayer. Judge, speak to me only truth. Please tell me. I listen. Please.*

The wind burbled and hooted. And then...

... umbra ...

... search ...

... gherza ...

... father ...

The light of dawn stabbing me through the Watcher's empty eye sockets brought me back to myself. The temple lay still, quiet and expectant. I pushed myself to my feet, stiff from the cold stone floor. I backed away from the Fates, never taking my gaze from them. Once out the temple door, I spun and jogged for the head of the trail. My mind seemed intact, but best not to tempt them.

Did I dream it all? I didn't remember falling asleep, and if I heard anything, it was but a word here and there. But I now had a certainty that the Gherza held one of the keys I needed.

You are mad.

Maybe. A Gherza father. Where would I find one of those? And how would I know the right one?

I sighed. Nothing about Iril, or my power. I'd never convince Fayne to go hunting for Gherza first. He wanted Iril and the staff. This new clue might require traveling with the host all the way into the Gherza lands. Iril stalked the Clan side of the pass. It wouldn't hurt to dig into that lead before haring off after a clue I might simply have imagined.

But I would eventually seek out this Gherza father. If I didn't imagine them, I couldn't ignore the words of the Fates.

I smiled as another thought occurred to me. Did this mean my heart was true?

THEN

Kairiya sat cross-legged on a silk cushion in her tent and watched Jezarel throw everything she laid hands on around the room. Pillows and candlesticks flew into the tent walls, making muffled thumps as they hit first the fabric and then the soft rugs on the floor.

Whomp!

The box Kairiya used as a nightstand landed near her feet. None of the items belonged to her, and she did not care a whit if Jezarel damaged them. Damage to her person, however, was another matter. She conducted an internal debate as to when to rein in Jezarel, but her pupil quieted and dropped to the ground in front of her.

"They arrive next week," Jezarel said.

"Who does?"

Jezarel cackled, an unhappy sound. "My new family." She sobbed out the tale of her betrothal.

And so it begins, Kairiya thought. She hardened her heart against Jezarel's tears. There were worse things in life than an arranged marriage. She wondered if Jezarel had ever even heard of the flesh traders. Kairiya suppressed a shudder. She would *not* think about that. She'd avoided that fate, anyway.

Jezarel clutched Kairiya's hands. "Let's run away."

Kairiya shook her head. "Your father would hunt us down. And blame me."

"I won't marry a filthy barbarian."

"Yet you'll have me as a friend."

"It's not the same. You can't help who your father is."

"Neither can Murran."

Jezarel stiffened. "That's different." She tightened her grip on Kairiya's hands. "I'll kill him before I marry him. I'll stab him through the heart. How can Father dishonor Javeen's memory so?"

"If this Murran had nothing to do with your brother's death, and you kill him, you'll bring dishonor to your own father."

The look in Jezarel's eyes reminded Kairiya of that of a rabbit trapped in a snare. "I know. I'll witch him away."

"What?"

Jezarel got up and brought one of the braziers over. She rooted around in the deep pockets of her skirts and produced a small leather pouch. "If I could magic that sheepherder into wanting me so much I couldn't get him off of me, I can certainly make a barbarian go away."

Jezarel surprised Kairiya by finally admitting to using magic that day at the watering hole. Dabbling in the dark arts could lead to ostracism, or worse. Did Jezarel not know the dangers?

"You shouldn't play with things you don't understand," Kairiya said.

"Believe me, I'm not playing." Jezarel closed her eyes. She poured a small amount of dust out of the pouch and into the brazier. A small wisp of pink smoke rose from the bowl. The odor of overripe plums wafted across to Kairiya. "Come on, if you concentrate too, it will work better."

Kairiya snorted. "You're a child playing with her first flint."

"What do you know about it?"

"Enough to put a stop to this."

"Jezarel! Where are you? I'm supposed to be fitting you for your troth gown." Kairiya recognized the Izira's voice. Her impatience sliced through the tent walls.

Jezarel fluttered her hands over the smoking brazier. "Fates! She'll kill me if she smells this out." Her efforts succeeded only in spreading the scent throughout the tent. The wisp turned into a haze that obscured Jezarel. The Izira's footsteps crunched on the pebbles outside the tent. Jezarel picked up the brazier and darted left and right, searching for an opening to dispose of the incriminating item.

"It won't do you any good to toss it," Kairiya said. "Your emotions blaze so strongly right now that they're feeding the spell. If this is all the control you have then you really are in trouble."

"I can't help it! My grandfather expelled from the tribe the last person he caught using the arts."

"Then why did you risk it?"

Jezarel sagged. "I—"

The tent flap rustled. Jezarel squeaked and dropped the brazier.

Kairiya pursed her lips and whistled a short mournful note. The pink smoke from the brazier vanished.

"How—?"

The Izira poked her head into the tent. "There you are! Come, child, if we're to ready you in a week, there's no time to waste."

Kairiya almost laughed as Jezarel's expression turned from panic to well-feigned innocence. As Jezarel passed her to follow her mother out of the tent, Kairiya whispered, "Wait a few days. I may be able to help you with … other kinds of training. You'll just regret any spell you cast now."

Jezarel left in a huff.

Kairiya wondered what she herself would soon come to regret.

NOW

As the Clans filed away from Darmid Tor, Fayne ordered Lian to accompany Errith back to Castle Grey. Once there, Lian was to collect Clan Grey's garrison and meet up with the other Clans.

"As the Elder, you should be leading the men. You're shirking your obligations," Lian said.

"The higher duty is to the Clans as a whole, not just Grey." Fayne pointed at me. "I'm taking Umbra upriver to see if she'll recognize the place she fell in. It's our best hope to get back the staff." Fayne clasped his brother's shoulder. "Though I believe I'll prove you wrong about the Gherza, Lian, until then you're the best man to ready Clan Grey if there's to be a battle. So lead the men. But leave your mind open to proof should I find it."

"At least take some men with you," Lian surprised me by saying. Deflecting suspicion by appearing to care for his brother's welfare?

"No," Fayne answered. "It would anger the Elders to take men away from the host. Umbra and I can move faster alone. Besides, she's quite … effective in her own unique way. I'm not worried for our safety. We'll join you with the host as soon as we can."

As we saw off the Grey convoy, a group of riders trotted up.

"Lian!" Lady Shirra called from her mount. "I thought I would ride with you a ways. I must stop in at Lord Bothin's and negotiate a price for breeding his famous bull to my herd." Breeding a bull? At a time like this?

Fayne and Errith both frowned, seeming to share my incredulity, but Lian waved Shirra next to him. "I look forward to continuing yesterday's discussion," Lian said, and signaled the convoy to move out.

That did it. Shirra and Lian were definitely up to something. But it gave me an idea. I could turn the fact that Shirra wanted Fayne jealous to my advantage. Fayne played me like a river trout on a line before. If I could flip the game around, I could use the same rod to hook him.

"Fayne, where does Iril base herself?"

"Do you remember, that first night, I told you I was checking up on an unfriendly neighbor?"

"Yes."

"A long time ago, she took over a tower just to the north of my family's holdings. When Lian said she'd taken the staff, my men and I went after her."

"But you didn't find her there."

"No. I found you in the river."

"If I was Iril, why would I be in the river?"

"Our raid took you by surprise? With no other means of escape, you fled in a boat. Capsized in the current. Fell in. You said you clung to a log. What if it was the staff?"

"But that would mean the river carried the staff away." And left me with no way to prove my innocence.

127

"You might have hidden it."

I shook my head. "No. I don't remember hiding anything." I distinctly remembered holding nothing during my plunge into the river, and having nothing to hold onto except that large log as the current swept me along then dumped me on shore.

"That presumes I believe what you say."

I forced down an angry retort. Trust built slowly. I had to earn it. "Did you find anything when you searched the river bank?" Because he wasn't stupid. He must have searched.

"Nothing."

"Then you'd better pray to the Fates I'm not Iril, otherwise your staff is likely halfway to the ocean by now." Time to give him some information of my own. Maybe it would help break him of saying "Iril" and "you" in the same breath. "Fayne, I think we should go to her tower."

"I don't disagree. But I'd like to hear your reasoning."

"Me, my brand, the staff. Iril. We're all tied together. It's the logical place to start. There's something else you need to know." He looked up from his inspection of his saddlebag. "Someone's hunting me."

"So you *do* remember something."

"No. I can sense her. Magically. Ever since I came to on the riverbank."

"Magically."

"I know—more proof that I must be Iril. But what if Iril's the hunter? Maybe your theory's part right: what if I did wind up in the river attempting to escape someone? But what if that someone's Iril, and not you?"

"Then what would she want with you?" Good. He'd said

"she."

"Maybe it has to do with what I did during the ambush." He recoiled, just as I knew he would, but I'd moved past trying to sweep it under the rushes. "Look, with just the two of us, it will be difficult to maintain a watch. We're together in this now. You need to know what we might be up against."

"I know what I'm up against."

"I'm glad one of us does."

Our northerly route took us to the River Grell, where green water flowed past as the horses' hooves thudded softly on the grassy bank. Near sunset, we stopped in the shadow of a great willow tree. I left Fayne to tend to the horses while I found a quiet spot at the river's edge.

Here, a line of rocks jutted out into the river, and behind them, the waters collected in a quieter pool carved from the bank. Minnows nibbled at the reeds. I bent down, cupping some water in my hands and splashing the day's ride from my face. When the water stilled, I glanced down at my reflection, but my gaze flickered away again, to stare at the far shore. I feared to see what lurked behind my eyes, afraid of the truth.

Tugging off my boots, I stripped off my riding gear and waded out into the water. The icy shock of the spring melt numbed my limbs, but I kept going. I tilted my head back and the river closed over top of me. I tamped down a twinge of panic at the memory of my last experience with this river. I needed to learn to control my fear, though part of me hoped it might surface something from the depths of my mind.

The current slid across my skin. Holding my breath, I gazed through the rippling barrier between me and the world of air above, contemplating the fine line dividing death from life. I let the waves lap at the very tip of my nose, still not rising enough to catch a breath. Finally, the tension in my throat and chest overpowered me, and I broke through the surface, sipping at the air. I'd crossed this barrier once before, but this time, the water's embrace brought no answers. *Did you expect it to wash away your sins?*

Fayne studied me from the bank. Wondering if he should drown me? Or just admiring the view? "Exotic," he'd said while we danced at the Conclave. I could give him a better taste of that. A question occurred to me.

"Can you take me to anyone who knows Iril?"

"No one's ever seen her. Legend has it she's extremely old. I suspect the original Iril died long ago, and we're dealing with the last in a long line of apprentices. She cloaks herself and hides her face. Some say because she's horrible to look upon. Others, that her beauty would strike a man dead to behold."

So she could be anyone. "Well, you're looking at me and I don't see you keeling over."

He flushed at this not so subtle reminder of his discourtesy, but I didn't let him off the hook. He hadn't only asked me to dance the other night to goad Shirra. He'd been flirting. To make me think I could trust him, yes, but if a real spark of attraction lurked beneath his act, why waste it? If he wanted a look, I'd give him a good one. I surged out of the pool, water trailing behind me like a cloak. Then I took my time drying myself off and getting dressed again.

"Are you always this ... brazen?" Fayne asked.

"I don't know. Enjoy it while it lasts." My nakedness bothered me not a whit. He'd seen most of me that first night, anyway.

We ate a cold dinner and continued up the river in the morning, riding in silence. I didn't want to break the fragile peace between us. Towards noon I heard shouting up ahead. We rounded a bend in the river, approaching a cluster of small shacks huddled on the bank.

Just upstream from us the river narrowed, but here, a sudden widening calmed its flow. A man in the prow of a dory hooked a log, driving in a spike and attaching a rope. His partners at the oars turned the dory back towards shore, where a raft of logs was secured to the bank.

"What are they doing?" I asked Fayne.

"The logs bypass the rapids through a flume. The men collect them here for transport to the Grey mill farther downstream."

Flume? I ignored the unfamiliar term. "Your family owns a mill?" It was an uncommon occupation for a Clansman. The biggest trees in the Clanholds were the olive trees in their terraced groves, and the occasional juniper or cypress.

"All the river Clans own mills." Maybe not so uncommon. I hid my ignorance.

"My great-grandfather broke the Dayr and Arneth monopolies over the Aramar Plateau timber with that flume. He made his fortune selling to the coastal shipbuilding Clans."

Mills and now shipbuilding Clans. The veil to the world I thought I should know shredded, revealing something strange and exotic.

Upriver a sluice of water—the flume—detoured the churning white water of this narrower section of the river. It met the far riverbank at a stone-lined channel. As it rose away across the land it became a raised wooden aqueduct, and disappeared over a small rise. Log after log slid out of the flume into the river, and my mind boggled at the scale of the Grey operation. No wonder the keep looked so prosperous.

The part of me that remembered another world wondered: what happened to the Gherza's winter camps in the forest?

We moved on, and the river changed character, the gentle rolling banks thrusting up into cliffs, the water rushing and foaming over rocks midstream. I caught glimpses of the flume on the far bank, but its track diverged from the river's. With the path now too difficult for the horses, we diverted away from the water. We re-emerged out of the trees to find a promontory intruding into the river. A circular grey stone tower jutted up at its tip.

I stared up at the fortification, my heart thudding the beat of a slow dirge. "So this is the place?"

Fayne peered up the cliff. "Perfyd Tower. Some say it is cursed. Others that it is haunted. But they all agree Iril uses it when it pleases her."

The tower filled me with a lurking dread. It loomed over the surrounding countryside, perched like a crow at the top of the rock spur spiking out into the river. Its windows glowered at the surrounding knolls, brooding and baleful.

We'd discerned nothing of any pursuit on our travels. The feeling of eyes upon my back had faded. If Iril hunted me, she wouldn't expect me to walk right into her home, would she? If we hadn't managed to shake her en route, she'd be behind us. Unless she'd figured out our destination and beaten us here.

Fayne nudged his horse forward, but I balked. "How do we know she's not there?" Second thoughts skittered through my head. Did I have enough control over whatever power I possessed to confront a necromancer in her full prime?

"If you're her, that's not an issue, is it?" Fayne shrugged. "She must get cold like the rest of us. I don't see any smoke. Nobody's home."

Nevertheless, Fayne dismounted well away from the tower and made sure no prying eyes could see the horses from its vantage. The wind vane creaking atop the spire mocked me. Vacillating, it swung one way then the other—a hint of things to come? What if I found the answers I so needed? The wind vane seemed to croak, "Be careful what you wish for."

Spring had not taken hold here yet, and the dry winter grasses grabbed at my calves. "Don't go in," they murmured. The slitted windows on the tower face peered out at us, inscrutable, masking whatever lurked behind the dark basalt stone.

We approached on foot, alert to any sign of habitation. No one challenged us. The tower gate stood open and unbarred.

As we made our way up the circular stone staircase, my misgivings deepened. The higher we climbed, the more I felt I would find nothing I cared to know. Death clung to the stones. They stank of twisted, unnatural endings, not the clean departure of souls whose time had come. Where did it come from, my affinity for death? I could smell it, practically taste it. I must have cultivated it sometime in the past. Yet all I knew was that the person walking up these stairs didn't want it.

At the upper landing, a blackened door blocked our path. Malignancy throbbed behind it. Waves of darkness beat against my heart, hammering out a counterpoint to the pulsing life within me. It was all I could do to stand upright. An undertow snatched at me, and overwhelmed, I struggled not to drown in the necrotic tide surging from within the room.

"Are you all right?" Fayne, unaffected, looked concerned.

I gripped his hand. His warmth flooded through me and I felt less battered. "Whatever's behind this door ... I don't like it."

Fayne drew his sword. He eased the door open. We peered into a round room flooded with sunlight. And nothing else.

I stepped cautiously into the room. The feeling of darkness pounded at me, contrasting with what my physical senses told me. The circular room was empty. No threat skulked in the corners because no corners existed to hide in. A rough-edged, scorched circle marked the floor in the center. A wrongness permeated the room, as though the fabric of reality was torn.

I made my way lefthandwise around the room, glancing out each window until I came to the one directly across from the door. I looked out. The river flowed past the base of the cliffs, fifty paces below. A sudden dizziness engulfed me, and I grabbed the sill. I had fallen from this window. We stood at such a great height above the river, I marveled that the plunge hadn't killed me.

I turned back to the room. Fayne still stood in the doorway, watchful and at the ready. I crossed the room to him.

"Well, this is definitely where I—"

My feet entered the scorched circle, and the sunlight dimmed. Night swamped the room, eclipsing Fayne from view. What—?

A robed, hooded figure stood just outside the circle—no longer burned, but a mosaic inlaid into the floor. The figure chanted in a soft voice. A woman. I saw her through a haze. She held a long rod, its tip touching the edge of the mosaic.

I tensed, trying to understand what was happening. As the

scene unfolded, I took it at first for a vision, but something about it felt far too familiar. Was this a memory, then? A true one, a snippet of which I'd remembered when I first heard Fayne speak Iril's name?

In the memory, I wavered, gauzy, insubstantial. I tried to flee the circle, but an invisible force kept me trapped within the confines of the mosaic on the floor. Wisps of smoke rose from the floor, the color from each tile leaking up, tinting each wafting tendril. The woman's chanting intensified. The smoke spiraled in tight loops, trapping my essence and drawing me further away from escape.

Everything felt wrong. My presence, not just in the tower, but in the world. I had no body. Why was I here? Every fiber of my being screamed in protest.

The smoke thickened. I grew heavier. The haze coalesced into a recognizable shape, sucking me into the whirling vortex at its center.

The woman lifted her arms with the rod poised over her head. "Spirit guide to the far reaches of death, Iril commands you to take form!"

She brought the rod down, sweeping it out in front of her until its tip connected with the shifting haze. The smoke pulsed once. The end of the rod glowed incandescent red. And seared me into existence. My newly solid body flew backward from the confines of the circle. Smoke still whorled across the surface of my skin, blurring my outline and my vision.

The woman approached. I couldn't make out her features behind her hood. I reached my hand out, gathered my power— instinctively trying to defend against a daemon—but she held me at bay with the still-glowing rod. Her power gripped me, preventing me from unleashing my own assault.

"You will tell me your name."

Her hood fell away. Fear wormed into my gut. That face— one of the two faces that haunted my never-ending travels. I didn't understand what just happened, but giving her my name would be a colossal mistake. With the power she'd gained since last I'd seen her, she could exert absolute control over me. While she might not recognize me in this form, whatever evil purpose she'd brought me here for would pale in comparison to what she'd do to me once I gave her my name. She could compel it from me, too, using her dark powers.

If I couldn't defend myself against her, I'd remove what she wanted from her reach. I sprang up and launched myself out the window, speaking a single word, praying that my new corporeal form wouldn't weaken the spell.

Forget.

~*~

I looked down and found myself in the middle of the scorched circle, the mosaic invisible once again. Goose pimples dimpled my arms, and my knees and calves felt more like the branches of a shivering willow than a strong oak.

Fayne's voice startled me. "Are you back?"

"What?"

"You've been ... unreachable for almost an hour."

"I—this circle. It must have residual power."

"Do you know what happened here?"

"The circle gave me a ... vision." I tried to clear my head. My new memories clamored for attention, but I balked at letting

Fayne in on my "recovery." I needed to come to terms with them first.

"Iril?"

"She has your staff. You didn't tell me it was a token of magical power." And now I knew what it bound.

Fayne's eyes widened. So he hadn't known. "I don't know why she needed it. Just that she stole it. It is the symbol of the Clans, but as far as I know, its power lies only in its meaning to us."

"Iril doesn't intend to use it simply as a symbol."

Fayne shrugged. "Where is she?"

"That I can't tell you. We fought here. I lost." At least, she'd fought. I'd fled.

"I'm to take you at your word on that?"

I didn't see that he had much choice in the matter but I offered an olive branch. "I'm pretty sure she left here in a hurry. I may still be able to help you find the staff." I needed that staff almost as much as he did. Instinct told me I could not right the wrong done me without it, now that I understood its connection to me.

He stopped me as I headed for the door.

"If this is a trick, Umbra …"

I shook off his restraining hand. "I'm not Iril."

Now I knew for sure. I could barely hide my horror from Fayne. Standing in the burned circle triggered more than just my memory of what led up to my fall into the river. I figured I now had access to about half of my history. And wanted to throw myself out that window again. Better, perhaps, to lie and claim Iril's identity for my own.

The truth was even worse.

THEN

Jezarel was grateful for the extra training Kairiya put her through this week. Kairiya allowed her to hold a weapon and now Jezarel understood the delay. The forms had become so familiar that she almost did not need the wooden blade in her hand. It would have distracted her before. Now, it moved simply as an extension of her arm.

Jezarel and Kairiya practiced so much that Jezarel had no time to think about the approaching barbarians. The blows Kairiya landed bruised her, but Jezarel shouted in triumph when she finally managed to tap Kairiya's shoulder with her own blade.

"Yield!"

Kairiya shrugged. "In a real fight I'd have killed you thirty seconds ago."

"Maybe if you helped me with the other arts like you said, I wouldn't need to master the sword."

"The arts aren't play. They require discipline. Which you lack in spades. Or did you learn nothing from your mistakes the other day? Besides, you're the one who asked me to teach you weaponry."

"Before I knew you had other skills."

"I can leave if you're no longer interested."

"That's not what I meant, and you know it." Jezarel slashed at the dirt with the practice sword. She knew she sounded petulant, but Kairiya didn't realize how quickly her father backed Jezarel into a corner.

Shouts and the whinny of horses came from the valley. A large mounted party approached the camp. Jezarel shuddered. Her father's trap closed around her. The barbarians were arriving.

She and Kairiya stared in silence at the convoy. Unlike the sleek steppe horses, the barbarians' short, squat mounts grew scruffy coats. Almost no color adorned them—the horses' bridles bore none of the red and purple tassels so common with the tribes, and the people dressed in black, grey, or tan clothes. They wore no silks, only leather and coarse wool or linen. How could they live in such drabness?

"I have to go," Jezarel said to Kairiya. "Will you come with me? I don't think I can face them—him—alone." But she refused to shame her family by foregoing the traditional greetings.

"Will your father allow it?"

"If you stay in the background."

They arrived at the family tent, where Jezarel's mother wasted no time taking charge. Jezarel rued the formality required for today. The women added layer upon layer to her costume, constricting Jezarel more and more. Each length of silk draped and knotted around her frame like a snake wrapping its coils around her torso, sucking the air out of her lungs and the room. The silks, hiding and seducing all at once, emphasized her curves and revealed intriguing patches of skin.

Jezarel always looked forward to the moment when she would

wear these clothes and dazzle her betrothed, but now she would give anything for the full-body covering of a widow's cloak.

Her mother took the gilded and beaded hair covering and placed it over Jezarel's head, tucking in stray strands of hair and curling them round her fingers until they softly framed Jezarel's cheek. Jezarel's aunt threaded bangle after bangle over her hands until Jezarel couldn't move without jingling. Jezarel's cousins had all reveled in the sound, but Jezarel kept as still as possible, each charm-like note a reminder of what was about to happen.

Jezarel's jewelry and hair in place, her mother led her out to her father's reception room. "Do not embarrass your father," the Izira whispered. Kairiya followed a discreet distance behind and Jezarel breathed a sigh of relief when her friend took a seat next to one of the braziers.

Six barbarians stood in the room. Only one of them was a woman—her future mother-in-law, Jezarel presumed. The woman stared at Jezarel as if someone had just presented her with the scrawniest lamb in the flock.

Jezarel's gaze bored into her father's profile. She willed him to see her mute plea. It wasn't too late to tell her everything would be all right, he wouldn't force her to marry into the warmongering Clans who'd killed her brother. How could he betray the family honor in this manner? How could he throw her away like this? What had she done to deserve this shame?

But the Izir, focused on greeting his new guests, ignored his own daughter. She felt as though he had cast her to the great grey steppe wolves. She lowered her gaze to the floor. Perhaps the barbarians would go away if she refused to acknowledge their presence.

"Be welcome, Murran of Arneth," her father said. "May She Who Sees cast a kind eye on you and your family." The barbarians gasped at this, and one made a strange sign with his fingers. "I'm sorry, have I offended?" the Izir asked.

"We seek never to draw the Watcher's attention, lest the Fates take too much interest in our lives," Murran said. "But I understand the Gherza believe otherwise."

"Ah. My apologies. To us, if one lives life with honor, one need never fear to live openly before the Fates. Please, enjoy the bounty of the tribe." Her father's robes rustled and she knew he reached for a date, that he would take a bite from it before offering the other half to this Murran. If only it were truly poisoned.

Jezarel's mother left her side and knelt on the floor in front of the woman barbarian. She presented her with a pile of silks in hues of saffron, gold, and turquoise, then came back to Jezarel's side. She clasped Jezarel's wrist, then led her forward to stand in front of Murran.

The strangers had obviously learned something of tribal customs because one of them handed Murran a wreath braided from the steppe grasses. Though he placed it lightly on Jezarel's head, it weighed on her like the heaviest thing she had ever worn.

Jezarel brought her eyes from the floor to Murran's.

He was huge.

He towered over Jezarel. He had none of the litheness and wiry strength of the Gherza. The muscles of his arms and chest wanted nothing better than to escape the fetters of his tunic. His slate-grey eyes added to the effect that the Fates carved his jaw from some great block of stone—his face all hard edges and sharp corners. She was to marry this man? This brute?

Her mother prepared her all her life to make a good match for the tribe. Each time another tribe joined them at the oasis, Jezarel waited and wondered who her parents would choose. As time passed and no betrothal came, she'd wondered if rival tribes found something lacking in her. Hence her attempts to make herself more desirable. All for nothing. How Lailaz would laugh. The vaunted Jezarel, wanted only by undiscerning savages, given away to live far across the mountains, perhaps never to see home or family again.

Her appraisal of him discomfited him and he glanced away. Did his gaze linger overlong on Kairiya as he looked anywhere but at Jezarel? At this point, Jezarel would clutch at the flimsiest of straws.

Murran held out his hand to her. She looked at the rough, callused skin, the large, coarse fingers. They could never exhibit the grace necessary for a mutual finger dance. What would they feel like on her skin? An image of the shepherd Kairiya saved her from sprang to mind. Murran took her hand in his and it was all she could do not to jerk away. With surprising gentleness he eased a ring onto her finger.

"A token to keep until you are mine."

And then he was gone, his cloak whirling behind him and his family at his heels. Though it left no mark, the ring burned the skin around Jezarel's finger like a brand.

"Father, please don't do this to me."

"It is already done. The ring seals it. We consecrate the wedding under the auspices of the full moon."

"Father!"

"Peace with the barbarians will enrich us."

"Rich? They scrabble around in their skins and furs. What riches do they own that we could want? They are animals!"

"Enough! You will not insult a guest of mine while he partakes of our food and shelter."

Jezarel's parents left the tent. The weight of the hateful ring dragged at her hand. Kairiya put a hand on her shoulder.

"Perhaps he is a good man. You could grow to love him."

"A good man wouldn't care about other women in the same room as his bride." The germ of an idea sprouted in Jezarel's heart, warring with her loyalty to her father. "You have to help me. I saw the way he looked at you."

"Looked at me? He was just trying to figure out who I am—a half-breed in your father's tent. There's nothing there."

"Seduce him. Before the full moon. They'll call off the wedding."

Kairiya laughed. "Do I look like a temptress?"

"He's attracted to you."

"Don't jest."

"At least try."

Kairiya looked doubtful.

Jezarel pleaded. "If I marry him, I will kill him. And bring shame to my people. Maybe start a war. You're the one who trained me. Don't force me into this."

"Do you even know what you ask? What about how they wronged my mother?"

"Consider it poetic revenge."

"Jezarel. It's a stupid idea. Your father will kick me out if he catches me."

"Then we'll just have to take care he doesn't see anything."

"Murran won't want a half-breed anyway."

"You don't think? A hint of the exotic mingled with the comfort of the familiar?" Kairiya tilted her head and Jezarel saw she'd never thought of herself in that light. "I'm too strange to him. But you … You bridge the gap."

"Fine. But don't blame me if it doesn't work. He won't want to shame his people either."

"Let me show you a few tricks."

~*~

Jezarel paused at the side of the trail and placed her hand on the tall pine next to her.

"Why do you do that?" Kairiya asked. "Every time we come along here," which was as often as they had time for sword practice, "you stop and touch that tree."

"It's the last place I saw Javeen."

"Your brother."

Jezarel nodded. For a moment she couldn't speak.

The tree stood at a fork in the path. The leftward bend led to the small clearing Jezarel and Kairiya snuck to for their training sessions. The rightward looped around a small ridge then hugged the western edge of the lake. If Jezarel closed her eyes, she could almost hear the the hoofbeats of long-lost horses coming up the path, and her brother's hard laugh.

It had been almost exactly one year ago, the last time the tribe migrated to the plateau. She'd stood in the center of the trail, blocking Javeen's way. He'd reined in his horse, putting up a hand to halt the small group of men, most little more than boys, on mounts behind him. He'd laughed—laughed!—at her feeble attempt to stop him.

"Jezarel, get out of the way and let us do our duty," he said.

"Your duty is to Father."

"My duty is to the tribe. And the Tree."

"But Father forbid—"

"'Father said ... Father forbids!' Since when did you become his mouthpiece?" He looked over his shoulder at his little gang, grinning.

"Since you lost the sense in your head!" To her own ears, Jezarel sounded exactly like her mother giving a scolding. She tried to moderate her tone, knowing how much being treated like a child got her brother's back up. "Javeen—"

"What is the point of Father training me to defend the Tree if he won't let me do so when it's actually in danger? The barbarians are at the north end of the lake. Too close! We can't risk them getting any closer and finding the vale by accident."

"No one can find the vale if they don't know exactly where it is. You're just looking for an excuse to fight."

"What if I am?" He glanced back at his cronies again. "We're all tired of sitting on our hands and giving the barbarians the run of the plateau. Father can no longer hope that they will simply ignore us and let us be. They've proven otherwise one too many times. If no one stands up to them, they'll overrun us. And not some day in the distant future, but soon."

"You're not a fighter, Javeen. You're a shepherd."

"A shepherd with a sword!" He brandished his curved scimitar over his head. The boys behind him whooped.

"Just one shepherd. And a few friends. Father's right. At least wait for the winter gathering. Father hopes to persuade the tribes to unite against the threat. The Inarra will join us. And then maybe the others—"

"It will be too late by midwinter. The barbarians are raiding us now. We need to take action." He kicked his horse in the flanks and tried to swing it around her. Jezarel grabbed the bridle.

"Javeen. Don't be foolish. If you won't listen to Father, listen to me. It's too dangerous. I don't want to lose you."

Javeen leaned down from the saddle so his followers wouldn't hear. "It's all right, little Izirina. I will come back to you. I promise. But I need to do this. I will show She Who Sees by my actions that I am fit to defend the Tree. When I finally stand before The One Who Speaks I will have no regrets. But that won't be for a very, very long time."

And then he was gone, in a clatter of hooves and the shouts of his friends. Jezarel watched them disappear around a curve in the trail. She was still watching long after the dust had settled from their passage.

Jezarel blinked. Kairiya stood beside her, trying to see what so engrossed Jezarel up the trail.

"This is the last place I saw him, so to me, this is where I feel closest to him. He had no idea what he was getting into," Jezarel said. "They were fodder for shades. And now Father offers me up as the next sacrifice."

NOW

Umbra. Even wiped as clean as a slate I'd known. Known somewhere deep inside. Known enough to pick the only name that fit.

Long years had passed since last I'd lived.

My earliest memory now: standing before the Fates at the Far Gates of the middle realm. Receiving their judgment. Feeling their castigation. Opening myself to the Judge's reproof.

My mind could not contain the entire memory. A human mind probably never could.

:: you are found wanting ::

"But—" My voice, puny and weak. Had I really thought an appeal might sway them? These, the arbiters of the Great Cycle?

:: we bar you from the Cycle ::

I felt the words, more than I heard them. My eyes could not perceive the presence speaking them. Then I had a clear impression of other voices.

** irredeemable, brother? **

++ the damage is great ++

Silence, like the silence after a thunderclap.

:: she will atone here, as our guide ::

Then, a withdrawing. And my death truly began.

I was a shade. A creature of death, forbidden from the physical realm. But Iril found a way to bridge the divide between the planes. Iril—the mysterious presence trying to locate me, hunting that which had escaped her.

In my meddling with my own memory, I'd stripped myself of all knowledge of my existence between the planes—the truth about shades—which was why I'd felt so confused at my ability to see the dead. As far as I'd known, I was just a normal person with a strange ability. But I was anything but normal. I was a dead creature whose natural abilities, having nothing to do with necromancy, had been perverted in this plane.

The part of me that remembered being dead gloried in the sheer joy of life. Was I alive now? It certainly felt like it. Now I understood my misperceptions regarding the Clans. Their entire culture had changed and progressed since I'd last known them. But another part of me repressed a deep unease. I didn't understand the implications of this violation of the laws of death.

Even though a large piece of my personal puzzle just fell into place, my memory still gaped with holes. I knew what I was. My entire existence in the middle realm filled my head to bursting. But I could not remember who I was before I died. My name remained lost to me. And my history prior to becoming a shade.

Nausea filled my throat with bile. Now I understood the snide voice in my head, the one that challenged me every time I felt good about something, or twisted the knife deeper when I felt bad. For shades aren't born, they are made. Made from the essence of a man or woman upon their death. From a soul unworthy of returning to the Great Cycle of life. Made to serve and guide the dead on their journey across the planes, until such time as the Fates decreed the shade fit to rejoin the Cycle. If at all.

I'd done something very wrong, somewhere, somewhen. My core, my essence, couldn't deny it. Whether or not I could remember it, my crime wove itself into the fabric of my soul. And thus the ever-present guilt.

I leaned against the door frame, repressing a gag.

"Umbra, are you all right?" Fayne asked.

No. No I wasn't. Not unless he counted dead but present as "all right." The sheer volume of new memories in my head also made me dizzy. My head pounded. I squeezed my eyes shut, trying to impose order inside my mind. It was too much to take in all at once. I pressed a shaking hand to my stomach, took a deep gulp of air.

If Fayne distrusted me now, believing me to be a necromancer, what would he do if I told him the truth? Mothers used stories of mad shades come to steal away souls to frighten their children into bed. Did it matter that I knew these stories for falsehoods, distortions of the truth? Shades didn't steal souls, they protected them. The daemons of the middle realm preyed upon the newly dead. Without a shade to guide it, a fragile soul had no chance of standing before the Fates in judgment, to move into the next phase of the Cycle.

Now I understood why I felt so protective of the newly dead I saw here.

My function didn't make me foul or fearsome to the living, my crime did. But Fayne couldn't know that. He would only think of the terrible folk tales. With good reason after my performance in the meadow.

Would he be far wrong? One didn't have to be a daemon to be a monster. "Irredeemable," the Fates had mused. What *had* I done?

I clung to a tiny mote of hope. The Fates turned me into a shade. They didn't send me straight to oblivion. Maybe that meant they didn't consider me completely irredeemable. *Or maybe they think you deserve eternal punishment instead of an easy way out. In all your wanderings through the middle realm, did you ever hear of the Fates releasing a shade?* No. But I had to believe good lurked in me somewhere. Otherwise why not just let Fayne kill me and be done with it?

I almost laughed, thinking back to how worried I'd been going up Darmid Tor to be judged. The Fates had already judged me once. It seemed now the trick would be to convince them to judge me again. Apparently braving a simple hike up a hill wasn't enough to trigger redemption.

And what of Iril? She wanted an embodied shade, but I doubted she'd specifically conjured me. Except I knew her. From my human past, before my death. Against all reason she'd lived past her allotted time, some trick of necromancy. I'd recognized her as she threatened me. My new body must differ from the original, a consequence of the conjuring, for I'd seen no answering recognition in her eyes. And she, like I, went by another name now. Her former name stayed just as lost to me as my own. We shared a history from when I lived. One that meant she posed a terrible danger to me. One that caused me to tear my own memories from myself to prevent her from discovering our link.

Had I seen her at the Conclave? I pictured the face I'd glimpsed through the ring of smoke, the face I knew but couldn't name, but didn't remember seeing it among the Clan folk. Which made sense, if Lian could mistake me for her. Where was she now? She must be the shadowy figure I'd spotted several times, the one responsible for the feeling of eyes upon me. Iril should be searching as hard for me as I did for her.

Would she know what I looked like, given the smoke that still enveloped me when I dove out the window? I thanked the Fates that Fayne had made me hide the brand. She must possess some way of communicating with Lian if they were in league together. If she'd witnessed the deaths in the meadow, she'd know where to find her shade. Only time would tell if I had more to fear from Iril than she did from me.

But I needed her, too. She'd brought me here. She might be the only person who could send me back. If she even knew how. No matter how pleasant the physical realm felt compared to my natural habitat, I had to find a way back. I'd already shown myself dangerous to humans. My power, meant to defend humans from daemons, worked to kill humans here instead. If I killed any more, the Fates might deem their first punishment too lenient, and end me entirely.

Iril desired a shade. I could only deny her one by leaving. I could only leave by finding Iril and somehow coercing the way back out of her. Which risked giving her exactly what she wanted. An ugly paradox.

I wanted to flee this tower, find a quiet spot somewhere, and shiver and sob until I fell into an exhausted sleep. But Fayne would never understand. So instead, I stood up straight, willing strength into my shaking calves. I trotted down the stairs, Fayne at my heels.

"Umbra! If you're not Iril, then who are you? Where are you going?"

It was all I could to do keep my voice from cracking. "To find Iril. I thought that's what you wanted. Hurry!"

We'd passed several empty rooms on the way up, and I hoped that Iril left in such a hurry that she'd neglected to erase all traces of her presence. I drew aside the curtain to a sleeping chamber. Sure enough, the room appeared hastily abandoned. The doors of an armoire stood ajar, the clothes inside missing. Scraps of burned cloth lay strewn on the hearth. Iril took no chances, consigning to the fire what she could not take with her.

A large trunk sat against the far wall, two small boxes resting on top of it. Checking the boxes, I found herbs in one and a few crystals in the other. I lifted the lid of the trunk to check inside, and several loose stones clattered to the floor. Iril must have scattered them on the lid in her rush to pack what she needed. The trunk gaped empty, but the stones gave me an idea. I heaved against the trunk and slid it away from the wall.

And found my treasure. A pendant lay coiled where the wall met the stone floor. A small blue stone, teardrop-shaped, nested in the loops. *Don't touch it!* my inner voice hissed. I picked up the chain anyway.

"What do you hope to do with that?" Fayne asked me.

"The circle showed me. When Iril branded me with the staff, she … did something to me while holding power. I can use the residual echoes of her spell to establish a bond of sorts between her, the staff, and me. I think."

Helpless no longer. The adjustment to getting a large chunk of my memory back might take time, but at least I'd learned a few tricks across my decades as a shade. Relief penetrated the shock of learning I wasn't technically alive. I doubted shade lore applied in the physical world, but what if some of it followed similar principles to necromancy? The Fates frowned on necromancy— at its root, the dark magic's power stemmed from the control of the souls of others. To gain this control, a necromancer established a link between his or her soul, and the soul of another.

I also knew of the links between souls. Shades needed to be able to find their charges in case we got separated in the middle realm. From the moment I took a soul under my wing, I stayed lightly linked to it until I discharged my duty at the Gates to the far realm. Could I use the skill on this plane to find Iril? If I my luck held, she'd worn this pendant enough for traces of her essence to rub off. I could sense them in the way a dog smells a cat that rubbed against its master's clothing.

But how to create the link, here? In the middle realm, when I took on a new charge, the linking happened naturally, as soon as I came within proximity of the newly dead soul. Only rarely did a soul try to fight it, obliging me to impose my will. But here? Was there a way to force it? Iril wasn't dead.

I gazed within the stone, calming myself. A faintly etched pattern in the heart of the stone drew my eye—leaves? A tree? Even six inches away from my face, the stone evoked an itchy, unpleasant dissonance beneath my skin. My body recognized something inside it that it knew but rejected. Drawing upon my newly rediscovered trove of shade lore, I took a deep breath, closed my eyes and hummed, trying to find a resonance. Nothing.

"I don't like this, Umbra. Do you know what you're doing?"

Not really. "I have to try, Fayne. Do you have any other way to track Iril?"

He shook his head, staring doubtfully at the stone. "I don't have to like it, though."

—*Think.* The pendant on its own wasn't enough. Maybe the physical realm nullified my linking ability. I bit my lip. But my other power worked here. The one I'd used to kill those men. My mind skittered away from that thought. That power wasn't for killing people, and I didn't know what it meant that I'd used it, albeit unknowingly, in such a twisted way. Still, it proved my shade abilities had equivalents here. I just had to find a way to access linking.

The brand? The brand was the nexus that linked me, a denizen of the middle realm, to this plane, the staff, and Iril.

Not expecting much, I touched the stone to the circle of scarred skin at my collarbone.

A crawling sensation radiated out across my skin from the brand, like ants swarming my whole body. A singed citrusy odor filled the air. Fayne gasped but I ignored him, concentrating on not losing this new thread, and finding the resonance between the brand and the gem. I ran my voice up and down a sliding scale. If Iril never wore the pendant, my plan would fail. I focused in on the harmonic, the random crawling resolving into a low pulsing. I matched my breathing to the beat, my tone closing in on the pure pitch of the harmonic, then directed all my energy at the stone.

Fayne shouted. I opened my eyes—a faint wisp of smoke traveled between me and the stone. Fayne looked like he wanted to be anywhere but here.

His voice shook. "You were—not on fire, but—smoking. Covered in smoke. I—"

"Thought it was my ambush trick all over again? Don't worry. A leftover from Iril's spell." A small lie, but I doubted he'd find further explanation any more reassuring. I didn't. "Let's go."

"Did you succeed?"

I delved into the pendant with my thoughts. "One or both of Iril and the staff lie—Watcher take my eyes!"

"What?" Fayne asked.

"I'm right here." The voice at the door dripped with satisfaction, the pleasure of a trapper finding two rabbits in the snare.

I hid the pendant in my clenched fist, and faced Iril. Fayne followed my lead.

She stood in the doorway, one hand resting on the frame, the other holding the staff like a walking stick. She wore an indigo cloak, streaked with grey. It reminded me of something the Gherza called a widow's cloak. She hid her face deep in the shadow of a hood.

Fayne reached out to grab the staff. Iril whipped it up so quickly the end blurred.

"Don't try it," she said.

"Or you'll what?" Fayne retorted. "My mother frightened me all my life with stories of you. Yet that is all they seem to be. Just stories."

I admired Fayne's bravado but I held firsthand knowledge of just how much power she wielded. "Fayne." I put a restraining hand on his arm. He shrugged it off.

"No, Umbra. She's just a charlatan."

"Umbra, is it?" The hood tilted to one side as she considered me. I felt a dark thread of compulsion nosing at my temple. "Is that your real name?"

I wanted to stay silent but her will set my jaw working. "No."

She reached out and ripped the scarf from my throat.

"I suspected as much," she said when she saw the brand. "Tell me your real name."

Each word felt yanked from me but still I spoke. "I can't."

"Why not?"

"I don't remember." I started to sweat and tremble. I needed to resist, but I wanted so much to tell her my name, to satisfy her wish. I couldn't find the answer within me.

"Your name or why you can't tell it to me?"

"Her name, witch!" Fayne shouted. "She has no idea who she is!"

Iril kept her attention focused on me. "Interesting. Do you know what you are?"

I nodded.

"I enjoyed your little demonstration at the Conclave. At least I didn't bring you here in vain. Shall we see if you can do it again?"

"You can't control me." The words felt empty.

"Be like that then. Very well." She pointed at Fayne. "Kill the lordling."

Fayne whipped his sword up. "I'll escort you to the Far Gates myself before I let you take me." He stabbed at her torso.

Iril waved her hand before her face, as though brushing away a stray hair. Fayne emitted a choking sound. His sword clattered to the floor.

"How—?" he said.

"Sit," Iril ordered.

Fayne thudded down on the chest next to him, his limbs stiff. His sword hand made clasping motions, and the rest of his arm shook as though with some great effort.

"It's compulsion, Fayne," I said. "Stay strong. Focus on something, anything but her." I could feel Iril, trying to worm her way into my head. My thoughts grew fuzzy as she increased her grip on my soul.

"It's so—hard," he said through teeth clenched with the effort to get at his sword.

"I know. But there's two of us." My only hope lay in dividing her attention, diluting the strength she could wield against either of us. Could a necromancer compel a shade? I racked my brain for any hint of an advantage.

"She's going kill us," Fayne protested.

"Focus." A small nugget of hope floated out from the fog in my mind. "She can't make you kill yourself. Compulsion can never override your own will to live."

Iril laughed. "But I can make you kill him."

"Do your own murdering." Then I remembered Fayne's sword on the floor and regretted goading her.

"The point is to break you, my dear."

The compulsion built until my vision blurred. Beside me, Fayne's eyes glazed over; he'd succumb completely any moment. He was strong willed, but untrained. When he gave in, would she use him as a puppet to attack me? I somehow doubted it. She seemed to want me alive.

I ground my teeth together with the strain of fighting her, of fighting myself fighting her. And then I felt the absence of the cold knot at my core. I remembered a tidbit of shade lore picked up from one of the other shades I encountered from time to time in the middle realm.

"You can make me talk, Iril, but you'll need more than even your considerable power to force me to kill for you."

"And what would that be, pray tell?"

I kicked myself for not choosing my words more carefully. Now I'd have to answer.

"You need the instrument of my death."

"Which is?"

And I found myself grateful for only the second time that I'd stolen my own history. "I don't remember."

The staff quivered in Iril's hand. "That excuse wears thin. I cast a perfect spell. You should be too. In body. In mind. In all your fell power. You're useless to me like this. Why are you damaged?"

"I did it to myself. So you wouldn't know me." *Shut your Fates-damned mouth!* my inner voice wailed.

Iril stood stock still. "Know you ..." she whispered. "The Fates wouldn't possibly grant me this ..." Her concentration wavered, ever so briefly. I lashed out with the full force of my will. The pressure of compulsion lifted.

Fury overtook me. An icy wave built within me. My fingertips smoked. I reached out for Iril's soul. Twisted or not, this power was my only weapon against her. Her eyes widened. But unlike in the meadow, this time the power felt slippery, like holding on to a melting shard of ice. I struggled to form a smokey tendril to whip at Iril, but she whirled and fled the room, slamming the door in

158

our faces. A latch clattered into place on the far side of the door.

Without a target, the tendril dissipated, and the ice within me retreated. So. My power wasn't instantaneous. I'd need to react more quickly the next time I faced her.

For a second neither Fayne nor I moved. "Fates save us!" Fayne said.

"The Fates won't get us out of here. We've got to do it ourselves."

Easier said than done. Fayne battered at the door but only succeeded in giving himself a sore shoulder. We changed tactics, but it took a considerable amount of time to whittle a hole through the door large enough for us to tilt the latch off its catch. By the time we freed ourselves, Iril was long gone. Now we had a race: find Iril before she located the key to controlling me. I checked the pendant, clasping it around my neck.

"She's heading west." The bond within the pendant felt like a pressure against the back of my neck. It gave me nothing more useful than a vague impression of a direction to go in. But better than nothing. West. That way also lay the Gherza, and perhaps the clue—a Gherza father—the Fates gave me.

"She wanted you to kill me the same way you did those other men?" Fayne asked.

I nodded.

"She had me cold." He indicated his sword. "She could have just run me through. You—you're stronger than her, then?"

"I don't think so. Something I said surprised her, and she couldn't keep track of both of us at once anymore. Compulsion comes down to a contest of wills. She won't surprise me again."

"You seem to know an awful lot about it."

I deflected the question, although it puzzled me just as much as it did him. Compulsion wasn't in the arsenal of a shade, so did I know this from before? Like the swordplay, which felt like muscle memory? "We shouldn't let her get too much of a head start on us."

"And if we find her again? What then?"

"Forewarned is forearmed. I'll be ready next time." Fayne glanced down at my hands, then quickly away, but said nothing. I imagined at some point not long from now he'd work up the nerve to confront me. Though maybe he'd use any advantage over Iril to get back the staff. Even if that meant overlooking certain unpleasant truths.

When we reached the landing at the entrance to the tower, a twinge at the edge of my senses brought me up short. Though eager to leave this place and go after Iril, I forced myself to push open a small wooden door to the left of the tower entrance. A dank stairwell slithered into the ground. I lit a torch, and descended into the dim depths, Fayne following behind.

At the bottom, we found ourselves in a circular room, lime stains smearing the stone walls. Dark holes marked doorways carved into the rock—dungeons excavated inside the cliff. None of the portals had doors, though.

"A strange prison that has no gates," Fayne remarked.

I cast about me for what led me down here—a feeling of wrongness, less powerful than the one that pulled me to the top of the tower, but there nonetheless. I wandered over to one of the open archways on the right, thrusting my torch ahead of me.

And pulled back, retching.

"What is it?" Fayne asked. He peered around me into the low-ceilinged room on the other side of the arch. His own torch cast flickering pools of light onto the wall, illuminating the thing I'd rather not see again. A living corpse. As Fayne crouched nearer, he confirmed it. "He's alive!"

And that was the horror of it. Alive, yes. Emaciated. Breathing, barely. But only the barest trace of a soul, the essence mostly gone, sucked dry, the body empty of what animated it and gave it its uniqueness. Stolen by Iril.

I fled back up the stairs, and out the tower entrance, grateful for the soft caress of the breeze on my cheek, reassuring me that I still walked the world, and not a nightmare. The person in the dungeon was not a shade, but I wondered if Iril planned to do that to me as well. She must gain power by stealing souls, siphoning off their energy bit by bit, which was why the poor person in the dungeon still breathed. I'd never heard of a necromancer able to go that far. Simple control of a soul, yes. Stealing one was a far different matter. But what extra advantage could the soul of a shade possibly confer?

Fayne emerged from Perfyd Tower. "We can't just leave him here," he said.

"What would you have me do?"

"He'll die."

"He's dead already. Nothing will bring him back."

Fayne glanced back at the tower. "Then I pray the Fates protect his soul."

"They'll have to wrest it from Iril first." Appalled understanding crept into Fayne's expression. I went to find the horses. *Maybe you're the one the Fates want to do the wresting.*

~*~

161

The tug of the pendant at my neck led us ever westward. Fayne peppered me with questions as we rode.

"So you know Iril?"

"Apparently."

"From where?"

"I don't know."

"Perhaps you studied necromancy together."

I shifted in my saddle. It was entirely too possible. Then again, shade powers didn't equate to necromancy. One was purely defensive. The other, all about control.

"Was she your friend? Your enemy?"

I shrugged. I wasn't sure I wanted to know the answer to that question.

"Sometimes wronged friends become one's worst enemies."

"Fates take my future! Will you just leave it? I don't know!"

"I'm only trying to help, Umbra. A question might jog your memory."

My memory didn't need any helpful bumps at the moment. Any more revelations might send me over the edge. I held back from Fayne what I'd learned about myself at Perfyd Tower. His frustration at my evasiveness boiled over.

"When you feel like talking you can find me up ahead." Fayne heeled his mount forward and refused to ride with me in sight.

Our path intersected a main road. I stared at the churned earth that marked the passage of a caravan.

"Looks like we're going the same way."

Fayne grunted. He nudged the flanks of his horse and his mount loped off following the tracks.

The grunt was the most acknowledgment he'd given me in a

day. He kept a strict separation twenty paces ahead of my mount, stopping only if I signaled a change in direction from the lodestone at my throat. The longer we rode, the more familiar I became with the taut set of his shoulders, the way the muscles behind his jaw twitched whenever I forced him to acknowledge me.

But how could I tell him? Tell him that a creature of the darkness between worlds walked at his side, a being even the Fates likely considered beyond redemption. Every story he'd ever heard warned him that I should be mad at best, evil at worst. How could I convince him otherwise? The words of a supposedly crazy, twisted creature carried no weight.

Not to mention that I still didn't know *who* I was. I puzzled over that for a bit. Going back to the site of my embodiment had been enough to reverse at least part of the spell I'd cast on myself. But why not all of it? Why did I not know my true name? It was the strangest thing. My mind seemed to veer and swerve away from it every time I attempted to approach a memory of shade life that had me contemplating my punishment.

Was my spell still protecting me, or did the block on my memory have something to do with my death? Did one forget one's identity the further one got from life? But that didn't make sense. If I hadn't known my name to begin with, I wouldn't have cast the spell in the first place.

I must not be a very good spell caster, and in my overzealousness, I wiped out more than I meant to. The residual echoes of Iril's magic were enough to weaken my handiwork, but not enough to undo the core of the spell.

Most of what I could remember of my time as a shade would

not aid Iril in identifying me. Neither would it aid me in keeping Fayne as an ally. But, the mere fact that I could cast any spells indicated that before I'd died and become a shade, I must have studied magic and necromancy. Because shades didn't cast spells.

In my natural form, I could do little beyond escort a dying essence on its journey to completion of the Cycle. I possessed certain gifts to help me protect each soul from the daemons that wandered the middle realm. Gifts that let me extinguish daemons' manifestations. But embodied here on the physical plane, my powers seemed dangerous to people, not daemons.

I thought back to the lives I'd extinguished at the Conclave, searching my restored knowledge of my time in the middle realm. The act felt exactly like how I dispatched a daemon. As a shade, I never snatched a person's essence away and sent it who knew where. But when I destroyed daemons, I sent them into oblivion. I prayed to Watcher, Listener, and Judge that's not what I'd done to the men in the clearing, but I feared that I prayed in vain.

This new power—a twisting and corruption of my natural ability—was perhaps the reason Iril created me. This new power, which made me into a killer.

Weren't you already?

Monster. Whatever I'd done, I'd proven to the Fates I deserved that title.

I shivered as the shadows lengthened. Ahead of me, Fayne left the trail and halted his horse in a small meadow.

"We'll camp here for the night," he said.

We ate our dried strips of venison in uncomfortable silence while the campfire crackled and popped. I risked a question.

"Why didn't Lord Garrith want you to marry Shirra?"

"She's not of the blood."

"What?"

"Clan Arneth's line died out. The last heir perished from fever two winters ago. Shirra bought her title," Fayne explained.

An immense sadness draped itself over me on hearing of the end of Arneth. *Hypocrite. Don't play the innocent.* I pressed my fingers hard to my temple. To Fayne it might look like I thought hard, but really I just wanted the voice in my head to shut up. Maybe the stories of shade madness weren't far off.

"Which legally makes her a Clan Seat." Without knowing how long I'd roamed the netherworld as a shade, I couldn't tell what changed about Clan politics since my own death. The evidence to date told me "a lot."

"But relegates Arneth to secondary status until the Elders say otherwise. An alliance with a full-blooded Clan shortens the process."

"And your father ..."

"My father felt I could do better. Betrothing me to Rhinn secured our access to Dayr timber for our mills."

"But given the choice, you would have picked Shirra."

"A first son's duty is to his Clan."

"Now Errith's marriage secures the Clan's position. You could marry Shirra now. Don't you love her?" Even as I spoke the words, I questioned why I goaded him this way.

"How could I love anyone who might be involved in my father's death?"

He doesn't understand the lengths people will go to for love. I wondered at the depth of his feelings for Shirra. He'd been willing to renounce her in the name of filial duty. He didn't want to give her the benefit of the doubt before condemning her. *Once wounded, twice shy.*

Shirra gained the most by removing Rhinn from play. Yet I couldn't quite see a woman in her position angering a powerful Clan like Dayr. She needed allies, not enemies. Unless she wanted the staff out of Clan Grey's hands for another reason. A reason that trumped a potential marriage.

Fayne's eyes narrowed. "What is it?" he asked.

"Nothing. Just wondering how Iril discovered that the staff's an object of power."

"How should I know, Umbra? You won't even tell me what she did to you with it."

I flicked a twig into the fire. "It's called the Staff of Binding, right? Well, it doesn't just bind Clans together. I think she thinks it can bind people to her." That was as much as I was willing to give him. He didn't need to know it could also bind shades to the physical realm.

The puzzle pieces didn't quite fit. If Shirra did betray the betrothal party to Iril, then a three-way alliance existed between her, Iril, and Lian. Would Lian agree to a different Grey alliance with Arneth, knowing his brother's attraction to her? Shirra felt like a distraction to me. Lian knew the timing and the route of the betrothal party. And my trip to Iril's tower told me Lian was definitely a blood traitor.

I couldn't explain to Fayne, though, how I knew about Lian without also telling him about being a shade. Which meant keeping Lian's secret to myself.

Because I had been with Fayne's father Garrith at his death. Invisible to Lian, poised at the shifting boundary between the physical and middle realms, I cradled Garrith's head while his essence gathered itself for its final journey. And I witnessed Lian deliver the killing blow. Pick up the staff. Hand it to the hooded figure who emerged from the stand of silver birch trees at the side of the road.

A new thought occurred to me. Had Iril making me manifest, of all possible shades, not been a random accident? Did my proximity to the staff at Garrith's death have anything to do with it?

Fayne's stare penetrated my consciousness. His eyes looked almost silvery in the firelight.

"What does she want with you?" he asked.

I shrugged. A little bit of honesty wouldn't hurt. I was doing an awful job at getting closer to him. "You saw what I'm capable of. She covets control of it."

"How can you do such things if you're not a necromancer?"

I shook my head. I wondered if I should lie and tell him I was a necromancer after all, just not Iril. Two witches in the neighborhood might not enthuse him.

"What did you mean by her needing the instrument of your death?"

O, dangerous ground, don't crumble out from under me. The phrase made sense if one knew my nature—precisely what I wanted to keep from Fayne. Why could I not be more adept at quick lies? "'My death' is my power to kill. The magic in necromancy relies on the resonance between souls. She needs an object that induces that resonance in me to control me. She'll have a hard time finding it."

I stared at the incandescent campfire coals. Except for the

first bit about the meaning of "my death," I'd told him the truth. As a shade with the powers the Fates had gifted me, I could more easily resist the mortal powers of a necromancer. But if Iril found the item most closely associated with how I'd died so long ago, she could tune her soul to mine. And I'd be defenseless against her.

Fayne picked up on my doubts. "Can you fight her?"

"I don't know."

"Do you want to?" His eyes bored into mine.

"I'm not her toy." A plaything of the Fates, perhaps, but not Iril's lapdog.

Though a necromancer would prize a creature capable of mass slaughter with a mere thought. Fayne would be justified in cutting me down on the spot.

Despite the warm campfire, a chill slithered up the base of my neck. The guilt that pressed upon me had blinded me, making me assume that death might be the thing I deserved, and should expect mortals to deal to me. But if he killed me, I didn't know what would happen. The rules I knew might no longer apply. I might go back to being a regular shade, resuming my role as guide.

But what if it didn't work that way? Would I simply cease? Would I go back again to stand before the Fates, and if so, what could I do to change my future? Without knowing why they'd sentenced me, how could I hope to avoid the same mistake again? For all I knew, killing the men in the clearing had already sealed my destiny.

Oh, Fates. I was dead. Dead! And anybody here who found out would try to make me deader. I wanted nothing more than to curl up and hide from everyone, including myself. Curl up, shake, and cry.

Crying would get me nowhere. I needed to find that man the Fates had hinted at. The Gherza father. But I had no idea where to start.

Fayne shifted slightly. His gaze locked onto mine. "Umbra, though you won't talk to me or tell me of your troubles, do you realize the tales your face tells?"

I deflected his attempt to draw me out. "I'm sorry the Fates put such obstacles between you and Shirra."

"Maybe it would be easier to never trust one's love. To expect the pain of betrayal—then it wouldn't cut so much."

"You can't know what's in her heart." But now was the moment to find a way into his. I tamped down my fear and uncertainty. I needed to use his emotions as he had tried to use mine. I reached out, placed my hand on his chest. His heart thudded twice beneath my fingertips before I withdrew them.

Off in the brush, I heard the rustle of a small creature making itself scarce. The firelight flecked Fayne's eyes with silver questions. "What's in yours, Umbra?" All his frustration at me melted away, as though he could no longer hold onto it, replaced with the simple wish of one person to know another. He reached out and brushed a strand of hair away from my cheek. "Maybe someday you'll tell me what haunts you."

I flinched. I wanted exactly this: for Fayne to see a woman, not a killer. But his touch, so gentle, just like I'd hoped, made me want to howl with grief. He'd glimpsed in me something I didn't want to acknowledge. The specter of that ancient crime, the one that made me a shade.

~*~

A dust cloud drifted over the road, heralding the convoy we'd been following. Fayne laughed when he recognized the banners. "We've caught up to Lian."

Sure enough, I spotted Errith and Lian astride their horses. Shirra and her men mingled with Lian's. Since we'd all just arrived at a crossroads, Lian signaled a halt when he spotted us.

"Well met, brother! I didn't expect to see you until we rejoined the host." Lian clasped Fayne's forearm. "Do you return with us to Castle Grey?"

Fayne glanced at me and I shook my head. The left fork led in the direction of the Grey Clanhold. My pendant told me right. Fayne took the hint. "No, I plan to join the Clan host as soon as possible. We can discuss my news after we eat."

We settled down to a cold meal, though I noticed that Shirra kept herself apart from the group. She and Lian no longer acted as cozy as when we'd parted, her demeanor downright frosty. I prodded her a bit.

"Lady Shirra, will you accompany Lord Fayne and me to the rendezvous with the host?" I asked.

"No. I'm afraid I can't tarry until morning. I leave once we finish our meal."

"In the dark?"

"I have my men. We missed Lord Bothin at his keep. I hope to catch him before he reaches the host. With that and the need to rally the Arneth guard, it tempts the Fates to think I might join the host in time. So I must fly."

I didn't need the extra company, anyway, and I didn't see Fayne protesting either. It surprised me though, that she wouldn't take every opportunity to badger Fayne into a betrothal. But maybe now that the Council of Elders cast out Clan Grey she set her sights elsewhere. Her argument didn't quite make sense either. Fayne and I would only follow a few hours behind her. I shrugged.

Errith excused herself after dinner with barely a glance at Shirra, who made short shrift of her own meal then disappeared, I presumed to gather her men and depart. I collected my plates and went to the banks of a nearby rill to wash them off, leaving Fayne with Lian. We'd agreed to keep our hunt for Iril to ourselves. I withheld my true reason for this from Fayne: the off chance that I could string Lian along thinking I might really be Iril in order to extract details of what they plotted together.

In the deepening darkness, I sat beside the stream. The forest basked in an unnatural stillness, as if all the birds had fled. I heard none of their usual sunset serenades.

I steadied myself for my upcoming task. My broken reflection in the water distracted me. My image wavered, black in the waning light, just a paleness where my face emerged from its dark mantle of hair. But even if I saw it perfectly, what could it tell me? I wore a stranger's face, inhabited a stranger's body. I'd betrayed myself fully by casting that memory spell. Nothing about me looked familiar to one searching to find herself. That would teach me to cast a spell without preparing the means to undo it, grateful though I was to have what little history I knew back.

I was out of my element, but no longer completely helpless, if I could figure out how to repurpose my shade skills and control them properly.

I forced myself to explore the power I'd exhibited during the ambush, though the thought of doing so made me almost physically ill. The power to kill. I needed a defense against Iril— my sword would not be enough. My lack of control at Perfyd Tower worried me. I needed to learn if I could moderate it to only weaken a foe.

Whatever I was being punished for by my stay in the middle realm, I doubted the Fates looked on murder as a valid path to rehabilitation. Worse, a murder that likely removed the victim from the Great Cycle entirely. The only way to practice, though, meant risking a life.

I took a deep breath, and swallowed my misgivings. I *had* to learn how to control this, if only so I didn't kill an innocent by mistake. I started with a water bug skimming across the surface. But try as I might, I couldn't replicate the cold that seared my bones in the meadow, or at the tower. I took slow, deep breaths, closed my eyes and sent my thoughts seeking out around me for the essences I knew hid there. But I couldn't find them, and my brand stayed warm, no cold knives piercing me to the core.

The forest grew quiet around me. I heard the *hoo* of an owl off in the distance, but nothing fled the underbrush nearby. The dew dampened the grass around me, and I struggled to stay calm, frustration mounting within me. Could I not do it under controlled circumstances? Was it a reaction born of instinct, ungovernable? Something I could only do if I faced personal danger? I couldn't bear it if I killed someone by accident.

My anger at myself built until I quivered with a repressed scream. Into it, I funneled all my fear of Iril and the rage at what she'd done to me. Even though my living body felt like a gift, I knew she'd done me no favors and I'd eventually pay an enormous, unknown price. Instead of screaming, I directed all my pent-up terror at the sole outlet I could see: a trout swimming upstream.

The cold whipped through me like a gale. A wisp of smoke arrowed for the stream. The fish floated belly up past me.

I shivered. So I could kill if I grew angry or afraid enough. That wouldn't help me if Iril snuck up on me.

I returned with my "catch," full darkness blanketing the camp. Fayne sat alone beside the fire. Lian must have left to see his men settled for the night. Shirra and her men were long gone. Fayne got up when I approached and bid me good night. I wrapped my cloak around me and hunkered down for the evening, glad to forego making conversation.

I drowsed off, but shot awake to a man's shout thundering through the camp. Fayne's voice. I recognized the sound of shocked grief when I heard it. I leapt up and ran to find its source. A cluster of men gathered round a tent. I pushed my way through and looked inside. Fayne crouched on the ground, cradling Errith's head in his lap. Dark stains soaked her green travel dress, and a bloody dagger lay beside her, next to loops of hempen rope.

I knelt down next to Fayne and touched Errith's wrist. She was still warm, but her chest hardly rose and fell. Her essence still held on by a thread. She wasn't conscious.

"Errith, don't leave us," Fayne moaned. "Not you too. Not after Father." He brushed a strand of hair from her cheek but she didn't respond. At the door of the tent, a commotion signaled Lian's arrival.

"Fayne! What …" Lian's eyes widened. He barged into the tent, and kicked at the knife. "That bitch! I'll kill her."

Fayne and I both stared at Lian as if he'd gone mad. Finally I ventured, "Errith's not likely to recover, Lian."

"Not Errith! Shirra. It's Shirra's knife. She's murdered our sister!"

As he said it, I knew it for truth—Errith drew her last breath. Her essence gathered itself next to me for her final journey. But she shocked me—instead of simply wandering out of the tent and through the veil to find her waiting shade, her incorporeal form, visible only to me, flung itself at Lian, pummeling his chest with wraith-like hands. I knew he felt nothing. I gaped at the spectacle, and an involuntary "Errith?" escaped me.

She turned, already fading. In seconds even I wouldn't be able to see her. But just like Myra's boy, she recognized me for what I was. And before she vanished for good, her voice taut with grief and outrage, she left me her final secret.

"Shirra didn't kill me. Lian did."

THEN

Kairiya slipped out of the Gherza camp as a cloud veiled the new crescent moon. She avoided the sleeping Clansmen and threaded her way under the soft cover of darkness to the agreed-upon meeting place behind the ridge. The whole plan would fall apart should the wrong eyes see her now. Watching from behind the bole of a large pine, she saw her mother Asrar slink from the shadows surrounding the Clan encampment.

The woman dressed in the rough-spun woolens of the Clans, but everything else about her screamed Gherza. The rod-straight, ebony hair. The piercing blue eyes. Steppe-sky eyes, they called them here. So unlike Kairiya's own grey eyes, grey as the winter clouds of the Clanholds.

Kairiya sighed. Now she could no longer pretend she just played a game. Her mother would poke and prod at her until Kairiya fulfilled her role in Asrar's scheme of revenge against the tribe that exiled her.

"Your father claims you have the confidence of the Izir's daughter," Asrar said.

"I saved her from herself. She trusts me."

"Good."

"She wants me to seduce Murran."

"Convenient. It will allow you to get closer to him."

"It's not the part I'm supposed to play, Mother."

"There's nothing wrong with a little improvisation. We're here to start a war. A tryst can only sow more dissent."

Dissent, Kairiya thought. If only that were all she was here for.

As if hearing Kairiya's doubts, Asrar peered closely at Kairiya's face. "Don't let yourself get drawn in by these people, Kairiya. Remind yourself that if Jezarel's grandfather hadn't exiled me, I would be the wife of the Izir and you would be sitting in Jezarel's place right now. They wronged me. And so they wronged you. When this marriage is stopped, some of that wrong will be avenged."

"Really, Mother? They'll never take you back. You'll still be an exile. I don't see how killing Murran fixes anything." But now Jezarel had offered her another way of stopping the marriage without any killing.

"With Murran dead, Clan Arneth will no longer be ascendant. If the Clans think the Gherza killed him, this nonsense about trade alliances will die with Murran. The Clans will bring the Gherza low. I don't want to go back to the Gherza. But I will show them just how far I have come since they spurned me."

Asrar poked Kairiya in the chest. "You've finally been given an opportunity to prove your worth to the Clans. To your father. You know what awaits you if you fail. I cannot protect you from him then. But if you succeed, they will sing your praises throughout the Clanholds, and you will never need fear being sold again."

"I should never have had to fear it." The words, coming from her own mouth, startled Kairiya. But then, she'd been away from Asrar for weeks now. She'd tasted independence. The thought had even crossed her mind of slipping in with a caravan and disappearing. But she feared her parents would have ways to find her. And then she'd have no hope whatsoever of avoiding the flesh traders. Kairiya shuddered. "You're my mother. You could stop him if you wanted."

"You know that for falsehood, Kairiya. You know what he's like."

"So much for your arts, then. They're useless."

"Your father's not the only one to whom you need to prove your loyalty. I refuse to waste my arts on the ungrateful. If you'd paid more attention to what I taught you, you'd have the ability to save yourself."

Kairiya bit back an angry retort. She'd never won this argument with Asrar, and suspected she never would. "Jezarel plays at the dark arts."

Asrar could not mask the slight resonant tingle that the mere mention of magic invoked in her. It shivered the hair along Kairiya's forearm. The faint odor of rotting mulch stole into her nostrils. Asrar's magic always smelled off to Kairiya. To Asrar's constant annoyance, Kairiya preferred to practice her swordplay —she smelled only the clean scent of her own sweat. "Really? Perhaps we can use that. Bring her to me."

"How should I explain your presence?" Kairiya asked. Asrar would pay dearly for breaking her exile if the Izir spotted her.

"You told her of my 'defilement?'"

"Yes. She thinks we hail from the Inarra, and you still travel

177

with the trading caravans."

"Then I shall tell her I left them when I heard rumors the barbarians were crossing the pass once more. That I seek out your father now that my own tribe is no more. Convince her I can help her avenge not just her brother but the honor of a good Gherza woman."

~*~

Kairiya shook Jezarel awake, clapped a hand over her mouth so she wouldn't disturb the women in the next tent.

"Come, there's someone I want you to meet."

"Who?" Jezarel's voice husked breathlessly with excitement.

"Just come."

"Am I to finally learn the arts?"

"You'll see."

Kairiya led Jezarel back out beyond the ridge. A high wind shepherded the clouds away. The weak dappled moonlight revealed Asrar's hooded figure.

Jezarel clutched Kairiya's arm. "Who is this?"

"My mother, Asrar."

Kairiya read Jezarel's furrowed brow and forestalled her questions. "She has long searched for my father, and several months ago tracked him down. She followed him here with the Clansmen he guards. You mustn't tell anyone. Otherwise she'll never get the chance to confront him."

"Will she kill him?"

Asrar stepped forward. "Best you not know, child. But in exchange for your silence, I will teach you what you want to know. Kairiya tells me it may help you in your current predicament."

In silence, Kairiya watched her mother take Jezarel's hand. A small shoot of jealousy curled around her heart. Had her mother finally found the student—purebred at that—she always lacked in Kairiya? While she masked well her impatience with Kairiya's slow progress, and kept on tutoring her, Asrar ensured Kairiya became a well-rounded weapon by helping convince her father to teach her the sword. There at least, Kairiya did not disappoint.

Kairiya looked on with enforced detachment as Asrar ensnared Jezarel with promises of knowledge.

"Will you teach me glamours?" Jezarel asked. She proffered a small pouch to Asrar.

Asrar dipped her fingers in, took up a pinch of the last of Jezarel's pink dust, and sniffed at it. "Bah! What charlatan gave you this?" Asrar tossed the pouch aside. Jezarel gazed longingly after it but turned back when Asrar continued. "You'll learn the right way from me. Glamours, yes. But why stop there? I can show you thought entrapments—spells that fog a person's mind until they can think of nothing else but doing your bidding."

For now, Asrar avoided mention of the cost of this type of necromancy. Kairiya doubted Jezarel would listen so raptly if she knew these magics—and not a child borne of a hated barbarian —got Asrar exiled from the Gherza.

Asrar sat Jezarel on the ground in front of her. "Powder fragments the focus, scatters thought too widely. You need to concentrate, gather your target's thoughts to you. Once you master that, we can discuss using objects for amplification. Now, look at me, and breathe, thus—"

Kairiya pushed down her own misgivings. She often wondered if the quest for vindication truly drove her mother, or simply a thirst for vengeance. Whatever it was, Asrar's wiles now firmly gripped Jezarel, a pawn in her mother's private war against the Izir and his family. For Asrar was not of the Inarra. Asrar was the woman Jezarel mentioned in passing when she spoke of her grandfather exiling a practitioner of the arts from the Zaghril tribe. Would Jezarel be so eager to learn from Asrar if she knew? Kairiya long ago accepted her own role.

Asrar tended to gloss over the details, but as a younger woman she'd set her sights on the son of the old Zaghril Izir. Through her magic, she snared him until he became besotted with her. But the old man caught her in the act of renewing her spells one night. Asrar had been lucky to escape with her life. Kairiya shook her head. The only lesson Asrar took away from that episode was that secrecy was of the utmost importance when gathering power. Kairiya remembered the sessions in their croft, when her father was away.

"Focus, daughter." Asrar held a sparrow in her hand. Kairiya could see it, head still, eyes wide, chest fluttering with its tiny breaths, trapped within Asrar's encircling palms. "If you snare it, it won't fly away."

Kairiya had put her finger to the bird's breast, reached out with her heart, as her mother taught her, and felt the trembling life inside the tiny body, so small and fragile. Established a thread of a link, through which she could feel the animal's terror, its abject fear that it would die, eaten by these great beasts. So Kairiya soothed it, and when Asrar opened her hands, the sparrow sat quietly in her palm, staring back at Kairiya.

After, Kairiya roamed the hills and terraces around the croft, practicing the same trick with other small creatures: voles, mice, birds, and even a fox. She liked feeling their otherness, their animal minds small windows into different worlds. She also liked being away from the other children—the animals didn't mock her, or care whether she was Gherza or Clan. She always let the creatures go after a few minutes.

The day she caught the fox, she'd returned to the croft only to find her way blocked by Dellen, her worst tormentor among the local children. He was her father's legitimate son. She tried to step around him but he grabbed her tunic and laughed. "I heard half-breed eyes are supposed to be blue, but yours are grey." He looked over his shoulder at his two partners in crime. "Why don't I fix that for you?"

His fist connected with her face and Kairiya cried out. Her cheek exploded with pain. Dellen just laughed. She could tell he was winding himself up for a real beating and braced herself to run, when she heard his mother call him to dinner from up the hill. Dellen settled for poking Kairiya in the shoulder before he ran off to pad his stomach.

Asrar took one look at Kairiya's black eye when she entered the croft and snorted. "Haven't you taken anything I've taught you to heart? Use it to make your life easier, girl."

The next time Kairiya encountered Dellen, he was alone. This time when he grabbed her tunic she did as Asrar had taught her —she focused her intention and grabbed his wrist. She felt his pulse beating, and matched hers to his. They breathed in time together. Her mind squirmed away from the contempt for her in his, but she forced herself to remember Asrar's teachings.

And suddenly Dellen was nice to her. To the puzzlement and dismay of the other children, he started including her in their games and activities. He defended her from other bullies. For a week, Kairiya finally felt like she might become part of the Clan after all. Accepted.

But she kept having to renew the link with Dellen to refresh the spell. His original perceptions of her lurked beneath the suggestions she'd planted. And she knew, deep in her heart, that Dellen didn't really like her, would never like her. Any friendship he showed her now was a false mask she'd settled across his features. The more he defended her, the more the lie sickened her, until finally, one morning, she let the spell lapse.

The bullying resumed, but at least Kairiya felt clean again. The taunts, though painful, were honest.

Kairiya settled down with her back against a tree as Asrar began Jezarel's teaching. It would be a long night, and she wrapped her arms around herself for warmth. As Jezarel worked to produce her first real glamour, Kairiya closed her eyes. Watching would just feed the small voice of guilt whispering in her ear. Based on what she saw so far, Jezarel stayed only as innocent as any given situation demanded of her, anyway.

NOW

Fayne laid Errith's head gently down on the floor, brushed the hair from her cheek one last time, and left the tent without saying a word. Ignoring Lian's protests, he flung his saddle onto his horse and disappeared up the right fork of the road.

Lian made to follow but I clasped his elbow and dragged him after me into the forest. I didn't want anyone overhearing what I said. And I didn't want him following Fayne. Lian would kill Shirra to silence her protestations of innocence. I debated killing Lian myself, but then what would I tell Fayne? Not to mention the Fates. If I kept Lian focused on Fayne's original orders for him, it would buy me time to talk Fayne out of doing something he'd forever regret.

"Why? Why, Lian?"

"Don't ask me. Maybe Shirra wants to marry into Dayr now that she's given up on Grey."

With the heel of my palm, I punched him once, hard, in the chest. "Don't take me for a fool, Lian. You and I both know Shirra's not to blame for this."

"Don't touch me! You and I both also know you're not Iril."

Fates be damned. My role playing game was up. "Care to

stake your life on that, Lian?"

"Then that's some trick you pulled, traveling with my brother while at the same time ordering me to find a way to divert him and Shirra. Makes you pretty fickle, too."

"Did she also tell you how important I am to what she's planning?" I didn't need him thinking he could order me around. Maybe I could still convince him we conspired on the same side. Failing that, a threat might do the trick.

"You're the key."

Yes, but the key to what? I suspected Iril kept her plans close to her chest, and wouldn't tell a tool like Lian everything he needed to know. Which might work to my advantage in keeping him guessing where my own loyalties lay. "Then don't anger me with your lies. You know what I'm capable of."

I left my actual abilities to his imagination. Whether or not Iril had told him what I was, I'd proved myself just as dangerous as any necromancer. Maybe more so. When I killed Lian's men in the meadow, by forcibly taking their essences, it wasn't a normal death. If it was a manifestation of my shade power, they didn't return to the Great Cycle. Which was very bad. I hid my worry by snapping at Lian. "You're working with her against your own brother! Why?"

"You don't have any proof."

"I don't need any. I know the ways of death."

"What does it matter why? Iril ordered me to make trouble for Shirra. The witch is not a woman to cross."

So no three-way alliance existed, unless one went sour. "But to kill your own sister?"

"Errith dishonored the Clan. Shirra told me, and Errith didn't deny it when I confronted her. Her death takes care of two problems at once."

"Why pick on Shirra?" I asked.

"She's a blood traitor."

I shivered at the words. *Blood traitor. Sound familiar?*

Lian continued. "She kept saying how much she admired Fayne for his stance towards the Gherza. Stupid woman. I let her think I felt the same way."

"Shirra will deny everything, and when the truth comes out, you'll be of no use to Iril."

"She wouldn't have the staff if not for me. She won't betray me. I'll deal with Iril when I avenge Rhinn. Worry about your own skin."

So that sealed it. Lian had feelings for Rhinn of Dayr. I still didn't know how the staff figured into anything, but I doubted Lian did either. And if he thought he could somehow double-cross Iril, he underestimated her. "She can't help you if you're hanging from a noose. Idiot."

"They won't hang me. Fayne will kill Shirra on sight. No one will ever know what really happened."

Fayne had always shown a willingness to hear both sides of the story, but he'd consider himself twice betrayed by Shirra. I couldn't let him take vengeance on an innocent. I needed to go after Fayne *now*. But what to say to Lian to keep him thinking me aligned with Iril, so he wouldn't follow me?

It was so obvious, I nearly slapped myself. "Fine. I'll make sure Fayne takes care of Shirra."

"I'm coming with you."

"No! Take your sister's body back to Castle Grey and meet up with the host as your brother ordered. The farther away you stay from Shirra, the better. Less cause for suspicion."

Lian didn't look happy, but conceded the sense in the plan. At least he'd be out of my way.

I gathered my things and saddled the horse as quickly as possible, kicked it to a gallop and chased Fayne through the night. Lather flew off the animal's flanks. I hoped it wouldn't pull up lame. Somewhere ahead, Fayne pursued Shirra. I prayed to the Fates that I caught him before he overtook her.

The night was so black, I nearly smashed right into him. His horse drooped in the middle of the road, head down, chest heaving, completely blown. Fayne still sat astride the stallion, immobile. I reined up next to him.

"Fayne?"

He didn't acknowledge me. I dismounted and crossed the space between the horses. Touched his calf.

And realized he was crying. His leg jerked with each sob, made more wrenching by its utter silence.

I gently pried his fingers from the reins, and tugged at his hand until he slid from the saddle. We sank to the road, Fayne weeping into my shoulder. Uncertain, I stroked his back, his hair.

I was at a complete loss. A shade never comforted the living. I didn't know what to do with the grief of those left behind. I'd never stuck around long enough to even see it. I reserved my concern always for the dead, to ensure they didn't panic, that they made it to the safety of the far planes.

I stayed very still, letting Fayne's emotions run their course, acutely aware of how alive he felt in my arms. The smell of him, again that hint of fennel, filled my nostrils and I grew inappropriately warm. His head rested on my collarbone, one hand clutched at my shoulder blade, the other clenched in a fist on my thigh. His breathing slowed, the hand on my thigh relaxed. I thought he'd fallen asleep.

The shock when his lips found mine made my scalp tingle. His hand left my shoulder blade and caressed my neck, the pad of his thumb brushing against my brand. The scarred skin, recognizing something in his touch, throbbed like a cat purring. I gave into it, the physical contact after an eternity alone shooting jolts of pleasure straight down my spine. *I've died again …*

I pushed him away. Dead. Fayne had no future with a shade. I could try to convince myself this was just a game, a ruse to get him to trust me, but my body rejected it for a lie. I'd gone too far. No matter how much I wanted him to crush me against him, feel his warm lips on mine, it was wrong. Unnatural. *But it feels oh, so right …*

Fayne pressed his palm to my cheek, stared a question into my eyes, but didn't insist. Perhaps he'd come to his senses as well. A part of me wished he'd forget himself.

But the mood was broken. Fayne pushed himself up. "We can still catch her if we hurry."

"Fayne, why would Shirra kill Errith?"

"Eliminate a rival. Given her dashed prospects with Clan Grey, maybe she set her sights on a match with Dayr."

"Then why would she leave behind a dagger pointing straight to her? The Elders would find her guilty in an instant. Shirra is not stupid."

Fayne stared at me. "You're suggesting she's being framed."

"Yes."

"By Lian." Fayne wasn't stupid either. "Why would Lian kill Errith?"

—Because he's in league with Iril and already murdered your father, and what's one more murder after that? I wanted to scream it at him but I couldn't. Not without telling him what I was. Maybe he'd listen to a little bit of truth.

"Errith was in love with someone else. Not her betrothed. She confided in me at the Conclave. She must have told Lian. It was an honor killing."

Fayne laughed. "Clan Grey doesn't believe in honor killings. That custom died out long ago. Lian ..."

"Lian is playing a dangerous game of some kind. You've felt it as well. What if he was behind both ambushes?" I pushed a little harder. "Why is Lian alive and your father dead?"

"No. He's my own brother." Fayne strode up to his horse and grabbed the reins. "Could he commit fratricide over the leadership of Clan Grey? Our family's not perfect, and certainly not immune to a succession war. But this? It's monstrous, Umbra."

I planted myself in the road in front of the horse. Unless I could convince him, he'd kill Shirra when he found her. I didn't like Shirra much, but I didn't want her blood on my hands. I felt sure the Fates would blame me for letting her die for nothing. "Shirra's innocent, Fayne. You have to believe me."

"Why? Tell me, Umbra. Give me one good reason to believe you. So far, I've heard almost nothing but excuses or evasions from your mouth. He's my *brother*. And you're—I don't know what you are." He flipped the horse's reins over its head and shoved past me, leading it down the road.

—What am I? I couldn't tell him. I had to tell him. He didn't trust me now. Once he knew, how could he ever trust a shade? Either Shirra would die, tallying one more mark against me in the eyes of the Fates. Or I'd lose in Fayne my sole potential ally.

He was already twenty paces down the road. I could barely make him out in the dark. I yanked the words from my throat. "She told me, Fayne. Lian did it."

Silence. The horse had stopped. In the gloom, I couldn't tell if Fayne had turned around. Then his voice. "Shirra? Try again, Umbra. You couldn't possibly have spoken to her."

"I didn't. I spoke with Errith."

Now his pale face drew nearer through the gloom until his eyes, glittering like baleful stars, filled my vision. "You did not speak with Errith."

I reached for his hand. To feel its human warmth one last time, before the truth crashed down between us like a great fallen oak. "I did." I took a deep breath, like I might never get another one. "Errith told me Lian killed her."

"But—"

"I'm a shade, Fayne. I'm … not really alive, and by all that's natural I shouldn't be here. But while I'm here, I can see the dead, just before they leave for the middle realm."

Fayne snatched his hand from my fingers. "A soul eater? A night gobbler? It's just one preposterous story after another with you, isn't it, Umbra?"

Suddenly I was screaming at him. I was done with games. Done with lies. They'd gotten me nowhere. "Is it? Is it really that preposterous? You saw. I took them. Fates help me, I took those men's souls. I saved your Fates-damned life doing it. You wanted monstrous? Well, here it is."

My rage at his rejection of the only truth I had to give winked out as quickly as it exploded, leaving nothing but a gaping empty hole in my chest. "I'm dead, Fayne. Nothing you say will change that. Don't believe me? Then believe Iril. Necromancy, Fayne. She deals in nothing but death. And I'm the dead jewel in her black crown."

I sank to my knees, a horrible keening noise welling up from my core. My fingers pressed against the cool earth of the roadway as the sobs hitched in my throat. I waited for the sound of a sword leaving its sheath. Waited for the blast of cold with which my body would of its own volition answer the killing blow. Waited to be left alone by the road with Fayne's body and my guilt.

And waited. Cloth whispered against leather as Fayne shifted. His voice came as a sigh down at my level. I looked up and found him squatting on his heels before me. "Monsters don't cry," he said.

Don't they? I brushed at the tear tracks on my cheeks. I didn't trust myself to speak.

"It's quite a secret, Umbra. I can see why you'd be loathe to share it. Come. Let's get the bedrolls from the horses. I suspect you're just as drained as I am. We can discuss what comes next in the morning." Fayne stood up.

He held out his hand. Mine shook when I took it. He pulled me to my feet. Something strange and almost unrecognizable blossomed in my heart.

Hope.

~*~

I woke to a crackling campfire and the smell of salted meat frying. Fayne proffered the pan. I skewered a rasher with the point of my knife. I let the fat drip sizzling into the flames before tearing off a piece. Fayne seemed content to eat in silence for the moment. I kept quiet for fear of breaking the spell. Then I laughed. Maybe we were each treating the other like a feral animal we wished not to spook.

"What's so funny?" Fayne asked.

"Us. This. The picture of normal."

Fayne chuckled. His laughter was short-lived. "Shall we talk about the abnormal, then?"

So I told him everything stepping into the burned circle at Perfyd Tower revealed to me. What I was. How Iril bound me to the physical. What I'd seen of Garrith, Lian, and Errith. How Myra's grandson gave me one of the first clues, one I didn't know how to follow without my memories. Because my own tampering with those memories had erased all knowledge of the middle realm and the true afterlife from my mind.

"So you were alive, once?" he asked.

"Yes. But I lost those memories."

"Is that … commonplace for a shade?"

"No. What use is a punishment if you can't remember your crime?"

"The stories are true, then?"

"Yes and no. Daemons exist. They eat souls. But I don't. No shade does. We're like … shepherds. Guides. Made to fight the daemons." I held my breath. This went against everything Fayne's culture taught him to believe. To him, the middle realm was the last trial faced before attaining the Far Gates. Superstition and myth warped the truths of that journey. Half the stories designed to scare children into bed described shades as soul-sucking fiends. No one ever returned from the far realms to say otherwise. Or to say "thanks for the escort."

"But the men who ambushed us—"

"In the middle realm that's how I dispatch a daemon. I don't know why it works differently here. It's … not necromancy, although it looks similar to what necromancy might do taken to the extreme. Necromancy is all about control of the other, stealing the other's mind and soul for one's own purposes. I can't *do* anything with those souls. They're just … gone. What I do— it's just a shade's built-in defense mechanism: send the daemon to oblivion. Here, *people* are the threat, not daemons." Maybe it would work on anything that threatened me or mine.

"So you're not a monster."

I hesitated. "The Fates did judge me unfit to pass through the Far Gates. I probably wasn't a nice person, Fayne."

Fayne got up and kicked dirt over the fire. "I can only judge by what I see."

"And?"

"I see someone who is lost, willing to defend herself if necessary. But not an indiscriminate killer. Not evil. Otherwise, you would have killed me when I accused you of being Iril."

Now was probably not the time to tell him I almost had. It frightened me too much, the lack of control I still had over my power. He stared at me, not a flicker of disgust, pity, or condemnation in his expression.

I couldn't speak. He should have run screaming or struck me down the moment he heard the word "shade." Yet here he stood fast, treating me like a human being in need of comfort. I unraveled the knot of emotion tying up my tongue. "Thank you," I whispered.

"Don't thank me yet. I haven't quite decided you aren't simply insane."

"No matter how crazy everything else sounds, Lian killed Errith, Fayne."

Fayne stared off down the road, as if some beacon off in the distance might guide his path. He put his finger on my sternum, right on the brand. I ignored the answering tingle. His pale eyes bored into mine. "Fine. But so help me Umbra, if you're wrong, and Shirra really killed Errith, then she's a dead woman. And you'll take her life for me. See it as a lesson for making false accusations."

I swallowed. The sudden turn from empathy to cold consequences unnerved me. "I'm not your personal assassin."

He moved off to saddle the horses. "You prefer to be Iril's?"

"You know the answer to that." I didn't believe he had it in him to make me kill Shirra. He was too honest—when it came right down to it he'd enact retribution himself. "And if I prove to you Lian's the killer? Would you order me to kill him too?"

Fayne paused in his tightening of the saddle's girth. "No. If Lian killed Father and Errith, then his life is mine and no one else's to take. You will leave him to me. Swear it."

"I swear. So we're still going after Iril?"

Fayne nodded and swung up into his saddle. I joined him with relief. We rode in silence, the pendant leading us westward over the course of the next few days. My thoughts kept returning to the kiss. One moment I'd convinced myself it meant nothing, and the next I'd catch sight of his profile as we rode and my lips would tingle as though his still pressed against them.

As the ride wore on, Fayne looked more tense.

"What is it?" I asked.

"Our pursuit of Iril isn't counter to finding Shirra after all. She leads us to Clan Arneth lands. Castle Arneth lies just beyond those hills." And so did the Gherza host. And possibly the Gherza father I sought.

"We don't need to find Shirra."

Fayne didn't respond. A muscle jumped in his cheek.

"Fayne."

"You're asking me to put aside my blood right to justice."

"It's not justice to punish the wrong person."

Fayne reined his mount to a halt. "I only have your word on that. Admit it—it's a bit much to take in."

"This can't go on, Fayne. Iril's the only person who can send me back. I will find her. So I'm your best chance of finding your staff. I'd rather not face her alone, but I'm no longer willing to travel with someone who won't take me at my word. It means so much to me that you've not yet run screaming. But it's not that far from distrust to deciding I'm a rabid dog that needs putting down. If you turn on me …" I sighed. He needed to know the truth. "I might not be able to stop myself from killing you. Which is the last thing I want. Believe me or don't. But decide. Now."

Fayne sat rigid in his saddle. He refused to look at me.

"Why is it so hard to accept, Fayne?"

"Because of Rhinn."

Not the answer I expected. "What?"

"I knew Lian harbored feelings for her. I warned Father, but he said Clan Dayr would not accept a second son. He wouldn't break the betrothal. I tried everything, but he claimed my feelings for Shirra clouded my judgment, that Lian would come to accept the marriage. He was so angry when I refused to accompany the party that would escort Rhinn from Dayr. I threw my defiance in his face.

"So I wasn't there to protect him. Or Rhinn. I may not have wanted her as a wife but I had a duty to defend her and I didn't. But Lian ... If he loved her, how could he let Iril kill her?"

"Because he couldn't accept her belonging to another." It seemed so simple to me.

Especially since the kiss. No matter how much I tried to shrug it off, it weighed on me. It might mean nothing to him, but something in me wanted it to mean more. Something basic, something that dwelt at the core of the unremembered me.

But Fayne belonged to another. And I'd given him all the absolution he could want for her. "You should be happy," I said. "Nothing stands between you and Shirra, now."

"Nothing?" He faced me. Leaned forward. Cupped my chin in his hand. Feathered his lips against mine. I guided his fingers to my brand, reveling as it answered his touch with that resonant thrill. Like I was a harp that would sing only for him.

This time neither of us pulled away for a long, long time.

When we did, Fayne let his sea-green gaze wander over my features. I could have sat there soaking it in until the Fates came for me. But it was wrong.

"Now who's insane?" I asked him.

He sighed. "We're both haunted souls, Umbra. Maybe that's

what draws me. Maybe I don't deserve someone like Shirra."

"And you deserve a dead girl?"

"You're the wrong girl, at the wrong time. It *is* insane." He stared down at his mount's withers. When he looked up, the intensity in his stare pinned me. I couldn't turn away. "But denying how I feel has led only to grief. Tell me you feel nothing. Say it. I'll never touch you again."

And Fates forgive me, my voice failed.

Fayne nodded. "Then it's agreed. We all have daemons in our past. You and I will face ours together."

Together. The word frightened me and heartened me at the same time. I'd have to part with Fayne eventually. Where I ultimately traveled, he couldn't follow. In that place, I'd be alone again. Alone, and unable to feel much. The Fates gave shades one thing to make eternal solitude somewhat bearable: a blunting of emotion. Here, I felt again. Pain, anger, fear, yes, but when Fayne kissed me … I didn't want to let go of that searing joy. What harm could come from enjoying it while I could? *There's no harm in love until somebody dies.*

Unwilling to explore that sentiment further for the moment, I urged my mount after Fayne's.

Morning confirmed his intuition about Iril's destination. We stood beside our mounts studying Castle Arneth from the protection of a stand of stunted oak. The castle hunkered on a hill above the river. The road wound along the bank, intersecting a double line of tall cypresses that flanked a gate path ending at a dock in the river.

The castle itself looked somewhat worse for wear, with crumbling mortar, and broken stone from a few fallen crenellations at the base of the walls. For a woman trying to make Arneth a going concern once again, Shirra put keeping up with appearances low on her list of priorities. Then again, perhaps she'd spent all her coin buying into Arneth, and needed a good match to replenish the family coffers.

Nothing moved on the battlements or at the gatehouse, but the pendant told me Iril lurked nearby.

"You're sure she's in there?" Fayne asked.

I nodded. "What would bring her here?"

"Hard to say. Clan Arneth drove the Gherza from the Aramar Plateau years ago when the Gherza betrayed an alliance. It's what ultimately gave the Clanholds access to the timber there. Some folk tales say Iril's mother was a Gherza witch. Maybe she has it out for Arneth."

"But Shirra isn't an original Arneth. Besides, why would Iril wait this long?"

"Maybe she needed the staff first."

I wondered. Maybe it took Iril until now to strengthen the tendrils of her power, hone her skills in the dark arts enough to use the staff to obtain a shade. I didn't know the why of it yet, but she wanted my power to kill—and needed to control me in order to be able to use it.

How did Arneth factor into it? I didn't like how Iril ran off when she'd understood why I'd stolen my own memories. She couldn't possibly recognize me, but did I give her some hint, some reason to suspect my true identity? The name Arneth made me afraid when I'd been introduced to Shirra. What if I'd inadvertently told Iril where to find the instrument of my death?

"Shirra couldn't possibly be allied with Iril, could she?" I asked. Iril ordering Lian to frame Shirra made it less likely, but still I worried.

Fayne frowned. "I'd simply assumed Lady Shirra to be ambitious."

"I know she didn't kill Errith. The other doesn't necessarily follow."

Fayne pointed out the flag flapping in the breeze above the portcullis. "Shirra is not in residence at the moment. The flags display the Arneth arms, but not her personal sigil."

"So Iril forced or tricked her way in."

"Or Shirra left standing orders to permit her entry."

"There's only one way to find out."

We left the shelter of the trees, and a probing mental needle spiked at my temples. I felt a flash of triumph, then nothing. I swallowed.

"Iril knows we're here."

"We've done nothing to betray our presence."

"My presence is its own betrayal. I think that she can sense me. It probably works similarly to what I did with the pendant. She ... 'created' me, after all."

We approached the gate, Fayne with his shield held out in front of him, I with my senses alert for any strangeness in my brand, or essences recently loosened from the bonds of their bodies. In the gatehouse, a corpse slumped across the small table, mouth agape, eyes blackened around the edges as though seared from within.

"Guess that answers one question," Fayne whispered. Shirra's men hadn't willingly let Iril in.

"She's come looking for something, or someone. We need to

find her, and fast. Think, Fayne. She took one object of power: the staff. Does Castle Arneth hold another?"

I didn't want to think too hard about the other possibility: that this was a trap, waiting to spring on us.

"I know of nothing."

"You didn't know the staff had any power either. Is there anything similar, anything of significance to the Clans?"

Fayne closed his eyes, as though cataloguing relics behind his lids. He opened them and set out toward the main keep. I hurried after him. "What is it, Fayne?"

"The Aramar dagger. The one that killed Murran of Arneth." *Murran! What have I done?*

I put a hand to the wall to prevent from falling. Murran. I'd known this Murran, somehow, in my past. *Not somehow. You're the reason he's dead.*

I shook my head. This time I allowed myself an angry rebuttal to my inner voice. —*They're all dead. Everyone I've ever known. Murran of Arneth is long gone. Who's to say he'd have lived any longer but for me?*

I say. I know.

Why would Iril need this particular dagger? Fayne said it killed Murran, not a woman. *Daggers can kill more than once.* If I held myself responsible for this man's death, could I have killed myself with the same dagger afterwards, trying to expiate my guilt?

We crossed the inner courtyard. A half-dozen chickens sidled up, looking for grain handouts. Fayne nudged one gently away with a toe. I tried the same. The hen burst into screechy squawking, flapping its wings and even losing feathers in its haste to evade me. The others set up a similar racket. Fayne made shushing motions with his hands. "Did you have to set them off?" he whispered.

"I didn't do anything different than you."

Fayne frowned then shrugged. I followed him into the keep and up a stairway lined with hanging tapestries. He drew his sword. I supposed a familiar weapon in his hand made him feel better. I tugged at the edge of his breeches as his booted foot left the step in front of me.

"Fayne. Let me go first." He protested, I cut him off. "Look, we don't have time to argue. You can't fight Iril with that sword. Just tell me where to find the dagger." I'd have sent him to wait at the gatehouse, but I suspected he wouldn't let me face Iril alone.

I slid past him on the stairs. He brushed a hand against my flank, but said only, "Be careful."

We stepped out onto the first floor landing, and he pointed left. "It's kept in the ceremonial hall, unless Shirra moved it. The Arneths were fond of reminding everyone of how Murran died in service to the Clanholds and for the glory of the Fates."

We trod along the flagstones of the hall, minimizing with difficulty the click of our boot heels. The walls, bare of tapestries, launched even the slightest echo ahead of us to warn of our approach. I found myself wishing Shirra was a richer woman.

The door to the ceremonial hall stood ajar. I leaned to peer around it into the room when it flew open, knocking me back into Fayne. He hit the floor with a loud grunt as I landed on top of him.

"Ah! How convenient." The light-hearted voice belied the menace of the cloaked figure looming over me. Iril wore the same indigo robe with streaks of ash grey that she'd appeared in at her own tower. The staff was slung across her back, its tip protruding over one angular shoulder. In her left hand she held a dagger, and in her right, an ax. With a flick the dagger vanished up her sleeve.

Her hand grabbed my forearm and yanked me to my feet. Then she trailed her finger along my throat until it touched the pendant. "Silly me, so forgetful. Perhaps I'm losing my touch. But it brought you to me, so I shan't complain. Come, my love, there's no time to waste." *Love?*

I dug in my heels but the slim wrist protruding from the cloak pulled me onwards with a wiry strength. The flagstones offered me no purchase to resist. She shoved me ahead of her into the stairwell. Fayne shouted. Iril swung the ax in a wide arc, the flat of the blade cracking Fayne across his upper right arm. The blow sent him reeling into the wall, his head hitting the stones hard. He crumpled to the floor, stunned.

I reached within me for a shard of cold to stab at Iril's soul. She swapped the ax for the staff, prodded me with its end. My brand crackled like a wind vane struck in a lightning storm. The sizzling heat snuffed out my last chance at holding onto my power. I barely kept myself from tumbling down the stairs.

We emerged from the portcullis onto the cypress-lined gate path. I kept trying to force the cold from my center.

Iril pushed me up against the first cypress, holding me at bay with the staff. "Don't! Don't even think of it." She emphasized her point by pressing the end of the staff to my brand.

Smoke burst from every opening on my skin. My pores sizzled like the mouths of geysers boiling oil. I screamed. The world went dark for a moment as my grip on my body loosened.

Iril withdrew the staff and the world snapped back into focus.

"I'm sorry, my darling, it's for your own good. You'll understand soon."

"I'm not your Fates-damned darling! What do you want from me?" I choked out.

Iril cocked her hooded head. "That's no way to talk now that we're so close. We just have to solve the problem of this body, but that shouldn't be too difficult."

Behind Iril, Fayne stumbled through the portcullis. At the sound of his footsteps, she shook her head. "If he's in that much of a hurry to die, then I suppose it's a kindness to oblige him, no?" The knife she'd hidden in her sleeve materialized back in her hand. "Hold still. This won't hurt. Too much."

She pricked the tip of my finger with the knife. After all the smoke my body usually emitted, the blood welling across the knife surprised me. She pushed the bloody tip of the knife against the center of my brand. Hummed. A dissonant itch vibrated where the knife touched my skin. A filament of compulsion nudged at my will but I was ready for her. "Do it, Murran," Iril said.

"What?" Murran? Then I got it. With the knife at my throat, the instrument of Murran's death, she believed she held the means to controlling me. I knew better. But ... Iril had known Murran? Loved him? Just how old was she? How long ago had we lived?

"Kill the lordling," Iril said. "You're open to me now. It will be all right." She hummed again.

I leaned forward slightly, as though to offer my mouth for a kiss. At the movement the knife pricked my skin. I felt hot blood trickle between my breasts. "Iril, *my love*. After all your waiting ...

your anticipation … can't you feel it?"

Her hood brushed against my cheek. "Yes. I feel it … It's …"

I whipped up my hand, sweeping it in an arc against her forearm. The blow knocked the knife out of her grip. It tumbled on the soft mat of needles between the roots of the tree. In a nonmagical physical fight we were more evenly matched. I reached within me for the cold. "Nothing, Iril! You feel nothing. Where's the resonance? You of all people should know better. I'm not Murran." Which meant that knife held no magical power over me.

I hurled everything I had at her heart, but she grasped the staff and thrust it at my chest. "Bitch!" Iril shrieked. "I'll send you so far into oblivion the Fates will never find you." This time as the smoke sizzled across my skin, I feared I wouldn't survive it. The pain stopped—Iril withdrew the staff—and I found myself still leaning against the cypress tree, gasping. Fayne halted his advance just short of us, wary of Iril.

"Count yourself lucky I still need you to bring Murran back for me," Iril said. "You're going to give us both the means to recoup the time we lost together."

"Back?"

"From the dead."

Maybe I should kill her now, and risk the oblivion. At least I'd take her with me, and Fayne would get back the staff. Surely the Fates would see her as a deserving target. I gathered the power to me, but I still felt sluggish and disconnected. If I failed, Iril would kill Fayne. Could she also bring across another shade to do her dirty work? I didn't want to die for nothing.

My weak control over my power sputtered.

"You don't learn very quickly, do you?" Iril said. "You can't use that on me. I made you. The resonance between us is too strong for you to overcome."

I stared at Fayne behind Iril, where she couldn't see him. His eyes flicked down to the ground, back to my face. Magic wasn't my only weapon! I ducked down and snatched at the knife still lying on the ground.

Iril blocked my reach with the staff. She hooked the rod behind my knee and took my feet out from under me, throwing me to the ground at the base of the cypress. My attempt to get the knife stymied, I rolled away from the tree, desperate to get separation from Iril.

Fayne stepped between me and Iril. "I won't let you take her," he said. I appreciated the sentiment but Iril laughed.

"You won't *let* me? She's mine, and of no value to you." Iril bent down, watching us the whole time. She picked up the knife and beckoned to me. "Come, pet. The plan doesn't work without you."

I couldn't see Fayne's face but something in his expression amused Iril even more. "It's like that, is it? You poor, deluded man. Has she not told you what she is?"

"No creature deserves to be abandoned to you."

"No matter. Like it or not, she's coming with me."

A clatter of hooves echoed behind Iril: Shirra galloping up the gate path. She reined her mount to a skidding halt between us and Iril. Iril brought up the staff to defend herself. Shirra thrust her left hand out towards Iril, holding what looked like an orange rock.

"Get back, witch."

Iril retreated down the gate path so quickly it looked like she had been flung. With her back against the next cypress down the path, she glared at Shirra. Shirra eased her mount towards her, all the while holding out the object in her hand. "You know what this is."

"I'd give anything to know how it came into your possession."

"You will give me what belongs to Arneth. And that which belongs to all Clans."

I could see Iril sizing up Shirra, looking for a way around her, yet she backed away from us. The power in that little orange stone astonished me; it repelled Iril the way two like lodestones pushed each other apart. Shirra pressed her advantage.

Iril shrank from Shirra's outstretched hand, hissing as if burned. "Think again. That trinket protects you from me, yes." Iril's head swung back and forth between me, Shirra, and the stand of trees. She put more distance between herself and Shirra. "But perhaps you lack the experience to use it to compel." Iril exchanged the staff in her hands for the ax. When Shirra didn't react, Iril nodded. "I thought as much."

Shirra's horse tossed its head and pranced beneath her. While the uneasy standoff continued, I tested my own power against Iril now that she could no longer reach me with the staff. No matter how hard I focused, I couldn't hold onto the cold. Something granted her immunity from me. Despair overwhelmed me. How would I ever defeat her if my only weapon failed against her?

I couldn't see Iril's face beneath the hood but the way her knuckles whitened on the ax warned me I didn't want to be anywhere near it. We'd reached an impasse.

Iril singled out Fayne. "One last chance, lordling. Give me the girl."

"Never."

"So sure of yourself. Very well." Iril scraped the bloody knife along the head of the ax, thoroughly coating the edge of the blade with my blood. She opened her mouth and hummed an eerie four-note scale. "Blood of the guide, blade of the fall, call forth the scarab, the doom of them all."

I marveled at her belief that such a simple incantation might do harm, until Iril hefted the ax. She heaved it in a great arc, driving the blade deep into the heart of the cypress tree. The single chop reverberated down the gate path. The tree's branches shivered as though at a sudden breeze. Then she levered the weapon out of the trunk.

I saw only a small gash in the bark, revealing the pale wood within. Then the bark blackened and withered, the gap yawning wider as the trunk sagged around it. A foul, rotten-midden smell wafted out.

Iril smiled. "Come my darlings. Don't be shy."

Inside the wounded tree, something moved. Many somethings. A black scarab beetle crawled out onto the trunk. Purple and green iridescence shimmered across the insect's shell. Behind it, more beetles poured out of the tree. One of them crawled towards my toe, emitting a high-pitched chittering squeal. Beside me, Fayne hissed. I scrambled to my feet and moved away from the widening pool of insects at the base of the cypress, which now shed needles and looked less and less healthy by the second.

Iril bent low and slid the dagger underneath one of the bugs, scooping it up onto the flat of the blade. "Fly, my lovelies. To the feast."

The scarab's shell opened, and with a loud whirring noise, it took to the air, heading west towards the mountains. The rest followed in a black, swirling cloud. The noise of their flight buzzed down at the root of my jaw. More and more spilled out of the tree, a seething stream of shiny black bugs. Long minutes passed before the flow trickled off. The last beetle crawled out, and the tree collapsed in a shower of needles. Nothing remained of the body of the tree.

"Where did you send them?" Fayne sounded like he already knew.

"To the Aramar Plateau. Where they will do to the trees there what they did to this one," Iril answered. "If you want to save your timber, Clansman, give me the girl."

"Judge take you, witch. You think to coerce me with bugs?"

"What will your fellow Clansmen say? The scarabs endanger all of you. Do you think they'll value the life of one girl over the trade of an entire nation? Go play at being the lordling again. If you'd paid proper attention perhaps your sister would still live."

I clutched at Fayne's arm before he could go for her throat. "Don't, Fayne!" He trembled with the effort to stand still.

Iril stuck her fingers between her lips and blasted out a sharp whistle. A grey horse trotted out of the oak grove at her call. Keeping a wary eye on Shirra, Iril mounted and gathered up the reins. Her hooded face turned to me. "We need each other, you do realize?"

"I won't do your killing for you," I said.

Iril heeled her mount's flanks and it clattered off down the road.

Shirra slid off her horse and faced us. I held my breath. What would Fayne say?

"You have a knack for dramatic entrances and exits, My Lady," Fayne said. "I wish I had your resources." He nodded at the stone Shirra now made a point to put away.

Shirra thrust a finger at his nose. "I thank you not to imply I practice the same blasphemies as Iril. My talisman is only that—it keeps witches at bay but does little else. Don't ask me where I got it, either. Family secret."

Fayne pushed her hand away from his face. "Our thanks for such a timely rescue."

"I wish I arrived soon enough to prevent her from taking the Murran artifacts."

"I'm not sure you could have made any difference."

Shirra nudged a foot at the pile of already browning cypress needles. "What a disaster! With the trees gone—"

"Yes," Fayne interrupted. "The Clans will be living hand to mouth again."

Shirra shook her head. Had she been about to point out something different? But she didn't contradict Fayne. Instead, "Why do you insist on protecting this chit? You value her life above the entire livelihood of the Clans?"

"Shirra ..." Fayne shook his head. "Are you missing a dagger, My Lady?"

"I beg your pardon? What has that do with anything?"

"Answer the question."

"It so happens I am. I lost it on the journey."

"It's not lost, Shirra. We found it wedged in Errith's ribs."

Shirra gasped. "Is she ... ?"

208

"She died before she could name her killer."

"Fayne! I'm so sorry. For you to lose your sister so close on the heels of your father's death …" Shirra raised a trembling hand to her throat. "You must believe me, I had no reason to want your sister dead. Someone else committed this vile act. I still hold hopes of an alliance with Grey." Her babbling trailed off. "I didn't do this."

"First the betrothal party ambush, and now Errith. Some say you would murder to obtain that alliance, Shirra. Or to avenge the loss of it." Fayne glanced at me.

Shirra keyed off his look, and the venom she spit at me took me aback. "You *dare* accuse me? It will take more than unfounded lies to get me out of your way. I'll ship you off to Iril myself."

"A dagger with your name on it consists of solid foundation. If I took my evidence to the Council of Elders, they wouldn't begrudge me justice. Certainly that's what Lian intends to do," Fayne said. "Umbra is the only reason I've not killed you where you stand. She believes you're innocent."

Shirra looked at me as though I'd suddenly sprouted a third eye. "Why?"

I shrugged. Shirra wouldn't accept the real reason I knew. "I think Iril meant to distract us with Errith's death so we wouldn't interfere with her. If we'd waylaid you, we'd never have gotten here in time. We almost prevented her from claiming the ax and dagger."

"So Iril killed Errith."

"No. She ordered someone else to do it and frame you."

"Who? I won't let Arneth honor be impugned like this."

I shook my head. "That's between me and Fayne. For now."

Shirra pursed her lips, about to argue, but Fayne said, "Shirra, you would do me a great favor by letting me keep this within Clan Grey for now. I promise you, no matter what Lian says, I will clear your name with the Elders. As the Elder, it's my voice that matters. I'll deal with Lian myself. But I need time. Iril is our true enemy here, and anything else only a distraction."

"You can't just let one of her cohorts run around loose."

"At this point, I only have Umbra's word that another party's involved."

"But her word exonerates me?" Shirra glared at me. For Fates' sake, she should be happy for my help. But maybe my continued proximity to Fayne bothered her more.

"It's enough to buy me time to find proof of the other. We can't tarry. I must let the Elders know what Iril's done, and see if we can stop it."

"I'll see who Iril left alive here, then make haste for the host. Perhaps I'll see you with them."

"This isn't over, Shirra. Tread carefully, especially with Lian. He'll be demanding the Elders give him your head."

We left Shirra to round up what extra men she could find, while we retrieved our horses from the stunted oak grove and set off in the direction of the host's rallying point.

THEN

The next morning Jezarel insisted on visiting the Tree again. The hidden valley once more bathed Kairiya in a wash of calm such as she had rarely known. Stillness, yes, that she'd experienced —the stillness of a predator waiting for prey. But this peace differed, soothed. Bees hovered in the blossoms that burst through the Tree's foliage despite the lateness of the season. A songbird trilled a melody from high in the branches. Kairiya closed her eyes and breathed in the rich perfume of the creamy white flowers.

"You feel it too?" Jezarel asked. "My father claims that it's the peace of the Far Gates, that here, the veil between the realms thins."

"Because of the Tree?"

"My father brought my brother and me here to teach us. Three realms, three trees, each planted by one of the Fates. This one was planted by She Who Sees. It's why, when we became blood sisters, you could briefly see every living thing in the world. We became one with her."

Kairiya shuddered, but she didn't know how to express her fear to Jezarel. This business of *wanting* to be closer to the Fates was foreign. Gherza. She risked betraying her closeness to her barbarian roots if she told Jezarel of her objections. She'd been raised to do everything possible to avoid the notice of the Fates.

Jezarel pulled a silk-wrapped package from her belt pouch. She shook loose its folds, and Kairiya saw a gold chain nestled in the cloth Jezarel held in her palm. A teardrop-shaped blue stone glinted against the silk, steppe-sky blue just like Jezarel's eyes. Jezarel looped the pendant over a branch of the Tree.

"What's that?" Kairiya asked.

"A present for you. Patience—it's not ready yet."

"A present?" Kairiya was flummoxed. "What for?"

"Because you're teaching me how to be a warrior. Because you brought me to Asrar. Because you're my friend."

Kairiya stared at Jezarel and suddenly knew one thing. In this place, with the Tree as witness, Jezarel spoke from the truest depths of her heart. Jezarel called Kairiya friend.

Kairiya didn't know what to say. Guilt coated her tongue with a slick, sour film.

Such a seemingly simple thing, friendship. Yet no one ever named Kairiya friend before. Not of their own volition. The Clan children always shunned her, afraid of the Gherza witch's daughter. Her own stepsiblings—more wont to beat her into doing their chores than invite her to a game of chase-me-round. Jezarel treated Kairiya better than Kairiya's own people did. Then again, if Asrar told the truth, Jezarel was also one of Kairiya's people.

Asrar taught her to hate her Gherza heritage, drummed it into her until the contempt beat in time with the beat of her own heart, but Kairiya hadn't seen so much to hate for herself. Quite the opposite. Despite their nomadic lifestyle, everywhere the Gherza set their tents seemed like home to them, while Kairiya, who'd spent her whole life in a single rude hut, felt like an outsider even when surrounded by family. Kairiya envied Jezarel's easy sense of place.

For all Jezarel's intensity, and vengefulness, Kairiya liked the vulnerable girl she hid beneath her veneer of privilege. Jezarel was feisty. She knew what she wanted, and what she did not care for. She wanted Kairiya as a friend. And Kairiya must betray her. Betray her or face the wrath of her family, her Clan. Face a lifetime enslaved with the flesh traders.

Jezarel drew Kairiya's attention back to the pendant. "Watch, as the sun hits it."

The pendant swayed as a breeze shivered the boughs of the Tree. As the arc of shade slid away with the sun's path, the stone's blue depths brightened. Then a ray hit it head on, and Kairiya looked away, the light flashed so brightly. The scent of fresh lemons with a hint of vanilla filled the air. She could swear she heard a faint chime as the stone glowed, then dimmed.

Jezarel plucked the pendant from the branches and showed it to Kairiya. Merely a nicely cut gem before, now an image of the Tree lay etched within the stone's heart.

"For you," Jezarel said as she fastened it around Kairiya's neck.

For her. For a lie. If only Kairiya could wish away tears.

~*~

Kairiya moved her regular morning workout to a spot close to the Clansmen's horse picket. Anybody going out for a hunt couldn't miss her. Sure enough, before long Murran strode up to one of the horses. He stopped as he caught sight of her, limbs flowing into one slow pose after another while she focused on the forms.

"I've never seen a Gherza woman carry a sword," Murran said.

"How many Gherza women have you seen?" Kairiya replied.

Murran gave her a rueful grin. "Point taken. Still, you're different."

Kairiya shrugged. Couldn't he tell she was a half-breed, or did all Gherza look the same to him?

"Ride with me?" he asked.

Kairiya glanced back at the camp. She mustn't start rumors too early, before anything truly forbidden took place. Everyone continued about their business, so she decided to risk it. But she placed the horse Murran offered her between her and camp, just in case. Asrar assured her none of the Arneth men with Murran knew the Gherza half-breed. But maybe Asrar forgot over the years who knew of her. Only when they rounded the ridge did she mount.

"You are closest to my betrothed, yes?"

"We are friends." The word felt strange on Kairiya's lips.

"She opposes the marriage."

Kairiya mulled over what she knew of Murran. Her father sometimes spoke of Clan Arneth, but she had never met any of them. Murran had a reputation for fairness. But would this extend to understanding the fears of a foreign wife?

"She has no choice in the matter," Kairiya said carefully.

"Is it the lack of choice, or that I am a 'barbarian?'"

Silence seemed the most diplomatic answer to Kairiya. Then

she changed her mind. She was not here to be a diplomat. "A Clansman killed her brother."

"Charming. A wife who hates me from the beginning. Why do you call us barbarians, anyway? We're simply poor, we're not uncivilized."

Kairiya thought back to Asrar's rude hut near Orrith's roundhouse. The musky skins she slept in. Compared them to the silks and jewelry that lined Jezarel's life here. But to Murran she said, "You raid the tribes. You kill our people. And for what?"

Murran shook his head. "Fates damn those Dayrs," Kairiya caught him say under his breath. To her, he said, "Would you believe for trees? Trees for ships. Ships for trade."

"And you wonder why the Gherza call you barbarians. My Lord—" Kairiya almost kicked herself. She was not supposed to know Clan customs and honorifics. "Is this marriage the only road to peace between our peoples?"

"My father thinks so."

"And do you?"

Murran spurred his horse ahead instead of answering. "Are you any good with a bow? I've heard the wild goat in this area provides good sport. Perhaps if I brought her a hide, it might bridge the gap between us."

They eased the horses up the needle-carpeted trail, Murran riding a scruffy dun Clan mount, Kairiya a sleek chestnut steppe mare. Soon they left the meadow far behind, and the tall trees crowded in around them.

For most of the morning, they spotted no wildlife. Murran took the lead, but deferred to Kairiya's directions. Kairiya studied Murran's back as he swayed with the horse's gait. Her parents'

215

enemy. And so also hers. A handsome man; when he faced her, she admired the openness in his features. So different from the closed expression her father normally wore. Murran didn't look at her the same way as the Clan boys she grew up with. His eyes held no suspicion, his lips no leering sneer. Just an easy curiosity and genuine interest in what she told him about Jezarel and the Gherza.

She relaxed and let his charm draw her in. Jezarel wanted her to play this part after all, and she found it easier than expected. It didn't hurt that for now, Jezarel's goals aligned with her own—the more time she spent with Murran, the better.

Kairiya noticed the trees thinning. They emerged from behind a stone outcrop, the flank of the plateau falling away in a ragged escarpment to their left. Here, the plateau's high cliffs notched inwards towards the lake. Far off in the distance Kairiya spied the pale green of the steppe. Below, a chasm gaped, a silver rill winding at its bottom among the darker green polegrass. Murran halted his horse, and Kairiya peered around him to see why he'd stopped. A woolly goat stood in the middle of the trail, facing away from them, still unaware of their presence.

Ever so slowly, Murran reached behind him for his bow. But his horse shook its head, and the jingle of the bridle alerted the goat to its impending doom. The animal bounded off down the path, then leapt off the trail, climbing. Murran heeled his mount after it.

Kairiya followed with care. The trail sloped downward. The steep drop to the left made her dizzy. She tried to ignore the feeling of being sucked towards the void. A precursor to the fierce winter *siratha*, the downdraft that buffeted her, plucking at her jerkin, didn't help. She concentrated on watching Murran, trusting her horse to pick its way along better than she could. Another gust whipped her hair against her cheek. Distracted, she brushed it away.

Rocks rattled on the trail head. Kairiya snapped her attention back to Murran. His horse lost its footing on the loose shale, its hind legs scrabbling out to the left as the animal lurched right. The horse's haunches crashed to the edge of the path. The animal's forelegs kicked for purchase, the terrible clatter echoing off the wall of mountain. But the horse's hind legs found nothing but air. It slid screaming off the edge of the cliff and disappeared.

Kairiya couldn't draw breath for her own scream. It died in her throat as the impossible sight of Murran standing unhurt in the path finally registered. "Are you all right?" she shouted down to him.

He gave her a shaky grin. "I just ... stepped off. If I'd gotten stuck in the stirrups he would have taken me down with him, but I'm fine. Unlike my horse." He peered over the edge. "Fates. He was a good horse, too." A horse that had almost done Kairiya's job for her. Then again, an accident probably wouldn't have quite the explosive effect her parents hoped for.

"Murran! Don't move." Because Kairiya had spotted what caused Murran's horse to shy and fall—a golden cliff lion, perched on a rock not twenty paces from Murran. They weren't the only ones stalking goat today.

Kairiya drew her bow. The cat emitted a low, throbbing growl, tail swishing, muscles rippling beneath its tawny pelt as it tensed to leap. Kairiya nocked an arrow, inhaled deeply, and loosed the quarrel and her courage-stealing wail. The arrow hit the stone between the lion's paws. The lion gave Kairiya a long, yellow-eyed stare before it slunk off down the trail and vanished into a gully.

"You missed," Murran said.

Kairiya shrugged. "We're hunting goat, not cat. Do you want to keep going?" The loss of the horse presented her with an unexpected opportunity. Murran nodded. She gave Murran her hand and he swung up behind her on the horse. The horse ambled along the trail, and Kairiya relaxed her body into Murran's, letting his warmth take the edge off the cold gusts.

They saw no more of the cliff lion, but soon spotted goat spoor. Murran's arm tightened about Kairiya's waist and he pointed with his free hand. Kairiya nodded. White flashed against the rock: the goat, cornered in a gully. Murran slid off the horse and reached for his bow.

Kairiya felt a flash of sympathy for the goat. Sometimes it seemed her father had cornered her just as effectively. *Obey, be a good daughter. And maybe I won't send you to cloister with the Sisters of the Fates. Or to the fleshmongers.* Shut away, condemned to a vow of silence. Or her worst nightmare, a toy to be used by men.

He wouldn't marry her off, that Kairiya knew. No Clan Elder would accept a half-breed for a daughter-in-law. Even a lesser Clansman would insist on tripling her dowry to take her. *Do this for me and I'll give you a croft.* A place she could live in peace, far from the whispering and pointed fingers, yet still be free. Free, yet alone.

Murran grinned at her before loosing his arrow, and Kairiya allowed herself to savor the look he gave her. Let her imagination conjure him at her side, next to a warm fire, the prospect of a family in his eyes. A new thought occurred to her. Maybe she didn't need her father's help or approval to find happiness.

Then the goat squealed as the arrow pierced its neck. After helping Murran dress the goat, Kairiya crouched in the dirt, cleaning her blade. Out of the corner of her eye, she saw Murran admiring the stretch of fabric over her buttocks. Her heart thudded faster inside her ribcage. Neither Jezarel nor Murran seemed enthused by the prospect of their union. But Kairiya felt two-faced nonetheless. Kairiya's weapons had always been the sword and what little she'd learned from her mother. Using her own body in this way made her feel unclean.

But what if Murran turned into more than just a means to an end? What if he became the end itself? If he'd already considered Jezarel, he might not object to a half-breed. Except a half-breed did not carry the political advantages an Izir's daughter brought. Kairiya contemplated the dead goat. If she crossed her father, he would never rest until he punished her. There was no escape.

Murran slung their prize across the horse's haunches. Kairiya mounted and turned the horse's head back to camp, but Murran took a step the other way. "Give the goat to Jezarel with my compliments," he said.

"Where are you going?" Kairiya asked.

"I'll return before nightfall. I want a crack at that lion."

Kairiya hesitated. Should she tell him why she'd let it go? No. Asrar said the more dissent the better. Anyway, it wouldn't matter. The animal was long gone.

At dusk, Kairiya sat with the women, polishing her blade while they shelled the pods of the cloudpea bush for their silken lining. Murran appeared, a large bundle draped over his shoulders.

The happy chatter of the women ceased. The blanket falling away from the thing it concealed hissed loudly in the resulting hush.

"A gift for you," Murran said to Jezarel.

Kairiya looked in dismay at the golden pelt, the noble head that lolled in a parody of its former insouciance. Jezarel choked back a sob. Her mother gathered her in her arms, and the women hustled the pair off into one of the tents. Murran stared after them, nonplussed.

"I don't understand," he said.

"The Gherza consider the cliff lion sacred. Killing one is forbidden," Kairiya answered. "It's why I 'missed' when we saw it on the trail."

"You should have told me!"

"I didn't expect you to find it again." Rather, she'd hoped he wouldn't find it again, but she couldn't use that excuse to shake the blame for the animal's killing. Sowing dissent was one thing, murder quite another. Kairiya found she had less and less stomach for the latter. The cliff lion's clouded eyes bored accusingly into her back as she followed the women and left Murran to deal with the dead cat.

Kairiya entered the tent to find Jezarel ignoring her mother's pleas for calm.

"He insults our traditions! He cares nothing for our culture! You gave me to a savage!" Jezarel shouted.

The Izira ordered the other women to leave. She poured a steaming mug of jasmine tea and thrust it into Jezarel's hands.

"He doesn't know any better," the Izira said. She turned to Kairiya. "You are of their blood."

"I would never disgrace the Gherza as he did."

"I know. That is why you must teach him."

Jezarel snorted, but out of sight of her mother, Kairiya saw her sly smile.

The Izira continued. "You must bridge the gap between our two peoples. Show him what is proper. Make him worthy of my daughter."

And Kairiya knew that Jezarel had won. If the Izira commanded it, Kairiya would have to "educate" Murran. Giving her ample opportunity to seduce him on Jezarel's behalf. Kairiya now had a sanctioned excuse to spend more time with Murran.

Now

We forded the river a day west of Castle Arneth, and it wasn't long before we came across the tracks of the Clan host, a swath of mud churned up by the host's mounts and wagons.

"We're probably only a day or so's ride out," Fayne said. He pointed ahead, to a meadow, its grasses flattened from the host's passage. "We might as well stop here. It's getting dark."

I hobbled the horses while Fayne set up the cook fire.

"Do you have a plan once we arrive?" I asked Fayne, tossing our bedrolls to the ground just out of reach of flying sparks.

"Not really. I need to talk to Braith of Dayr."

I tensed. "He'll make you hand me over."

"He doesn't need to know you're Iril's price for dealing with the beetles. But he does need to know about Errith."

I stared at him. "You won't tell him about me? You can't keep it from the Elders forever. Shirra, for one ..."

"Shirra will stay quiet until she's fully exonerated in Errith's death."

"Fayne—"

"I won't give you to them. It's pointless. Do you really believe Iril will call off her beetles even if I did? If she needs your power

222

that much, I'd be a fool to just hand over her ideal weapon. Instead, I'll use the beetles to convince Braith it's Iril the Clans should concern themselves with, not the Gherza. She has the staff. She set the beetles upon us. She's our true enemy."

Fayne roasted up the last of a hare Shirra had gifted us with. After removing the cooked meat from the fire, Fayne planted the spit into the ground in front of the small log he was seated upon. The length of the log obliged me to sit almost touching him so we could both pluck meat from the carcass.

We ate without speaking, the silence lengthening until it felt like a taught bowstring between us. Out here, at times I could pretend we were just two people on a journey. But once we rejoined the host, Fayne became Lord Grey, and I, a hunted shade. We might not get another night alone ...

I shook my head, trying to shed the fantasy like a dog sheds water. We couldn't be together, and wishing otherwise was unfair to both of us.

"What?" Fayne asked.

"It's nothing," I replied, my voice rougher than I intended.

"You're troubled." He reached out to brush a strand of hair from my eyes.

I clasped his hand, arresting his fingers, though I wanted nothing more than to feel them, warm against my cheek. "Stop. Please."

"Why?"

"This is impossible, Fayne."

"This?"

"You. Me ... Us." He didn't answer, twisting his hand to free his fingers from mine. They resumed tracing a path down the side of my neck, feathered against my collarbone, before coming to rest on my brand. The brand's low, purring thrum welled up at the touch.

Did I have to spell it out, again? "I'm a shade, Fayne. You should be with someone real, like Shirra."

"Don't speak to me now of Shirra."

"But you loved her once, didn't you? Some part of you must still—"

"Shirra is—" He glanced away, then back to me, his forehead creased in grief. "Whenever I think of Shirra, I see only Rhinn, and Father, and Errith. My feelings for Shirra brought about their deaths. Perhaps it's too much for a love to bear." He fell silent, gazed down at my brand, then back up into my eyes. "And lately, I sense … something false about Shirra." He shrugged.

Could he really prefer me to Shirra? Even if he did, he was the head of his Clan. His current troubles proved he wasn't at liberty to choose his own match. "If not Shirra, then surely another noblewoman."

He placed a finger to my lips. "Hush."

"I can't. We—"

"Then I shall just have to stopper your mouth." And he leaned in and kissed me.

Despite the rush of desire flooding through me, I pressed my hand to his shoulders and pushed us apart. It pained me to speak the truth. "We have no future, Fayne."

His hand cradled my head, fingers tangled in the hair at my nape, thumb caressing the corner of my mouth. "Do we need one?"

I drew breath to answer, and realized I had no answer.

Fayne stared at me, no mockery in his eyes. "The Clans might lose their livelihood, and split asunder. My entire family is dead, and Iril may yet kill us all. I find myself caring less and less about what others may think of me, and more and more about what's right. And for whatever reason, Umbra, this feels right."

His words nearly undid me. I wanted to hear just those words so badly, to hear him say them again and again, yet how could a mortal loving a shade be right? And this shade in particular. He said my name with such tenderness, yet, was it even my real name? How could anyone love a cipher?

Fayne continued. "You say you're not real, yet you're here, you breathe, you feel, you care." Oh, how I cared. "Perhaps it was chance that led me to find you by the river, or perhaps the Fates made me responsible for you. I don't know. But I do know that I would stand, head unbowed before the Watcher, and proclaim my feelings for you before the Listener, and not fear what the Judge might say in return. If, as you say, I'm doomed to lose you, then I would rather know the joy of what it is I'm losing than forever wonder what might have been."

I'd spent all my time lately doubting myself. Like a drowning swimmer suddenly tossed a lifeline, something in me latched on to his words. If Fayne could believe in me, shouldn't I be able to as well? My breath hitched in my throat, and then I slid my hand up his shoulders, raveled my own fingers in his hair. I pulled him to me, kissed him fast, kissed him hard, before I could change my mind, before the voice in my head could turn me from my path.

Fayne crushed me against his chest. He tilted my head back, then ran his lips down my exposed throat. His tongue circled my brand. The purring exploded in radiating pulses across my body.

The shock of it made me cry out. Fayne grunted and looked up. "What—?"

"You felt that?"

Fayne nodded. "Like tasting lightning. Did I hurt you?"

I shook my head.

Fayne smiled, and lowered his lips to my brand again. "Good, because it's a taste that bears repeating," he murmured against my skin. I arched back against his hands as his tongue seared across my scars and my pores all but erupted with pleasure.

All conscious thought stopped, and my world constricted to one of hands and lips and tongues. Hands that slipped beneath clothing, and tore it away. Lips that fused to lips hard enough to bruise. Tongues that teased trails of fire along skin. And all the while, the brand tingled, resonated, sent pure harmonics up and down my spine.

Fayne slipped his right hand down the front of my breeches and I moaned. With his left, he slid the garment off, caressing my backside, while I worked to untie his laces and free him from his own trousers. I whimpered in complaint when his right hand withdrew, but he gripped my hips and lowered me onto him, and I forgot why I'd protested.

Lips to lips, lips to breast, lips to brand, and all the while we moved and writhed and rocked and thrust until one then the other of our bodies sang with reverberating chords, and the darkness bore witness to our duet.

~*~

After, we washed each other in the small rill that circled the meadow. We sat on a flat rock on the bank and Fayne pressed his lips to my shoulder.

"Fayne—"

"Shh. Whatever it is, we can discuss it during the ride tomorrow."

By tomorrow, we would catch up to the host. No matter how much I wanted him, and how much Iril scared me, it became more and more clear just how much he risked by defending me. If he went to the Elders about the beetles, and they discovered he'd omitted the truth about me … "Are you sure you want to associate with me, Fayne? This … this was …" Perhaps the most beautiful gift I'd ever been given, but … "Maybe you'd be better off without me."

His gaze burned straight through the veil of my self-pity. "Some things a man can never shake off once they're done. I won't abandon you, Umbra. Know it. Believe it. And never mention it again."

My arms, clasped around my knees, trembled. Moisture welled up in the corner of my eyes. I brushed it away. "Thank you," I whispered.

~*~

A half day later the Clan host sprawled in the flat-bottomed valley before us.

"Iril's nearby," I said. At least, the pendant claimed she was.

"In the camp?" Fayne asked.

"Not quite. I think she's shadowing it." The pendant would lead me straight to her but didn't preclude Iril ambushing us if she heard of our arrival.

"What do you suppose she's up to?" Fayne asked.

"She went to Arneth because she mistook me for Murran. To obtain the instrument of my death."

227

"The 'instrument of your death.' It's not what you originally told me, is it? It's what killed you."

"Yes. She's still looking for the way to control me, to use my power as a weapon. She could think it's here somewhere."

Fayne looked perturbed. "Could she have been right about one thing, Umbra? Were you a man, once?"

"No." I answered without a shred of doubt. Searching within me, I didn't *feel* male. Yes, I wore breeches. Yes, I knew the sword. Yes, this spell-woven body I inhabited felt smaller and daintier than it should. But I was a woman. A nameless woman, but a woman still.

"If she has another idea about your identity, what would bring her here?" Fayne asked.

"I wish I knew." And I did. If Iril solved the puzzle of me before I did, I'd be helpless against her.

"What about Lian?" I asked.

"I don't see our banners."

"Shirra's right, though. We can't just leave him be. Who knows what he'll get up to?"

"I can't demand justice before the Elders without proof, Umbra. Do you feel like going before them and telling your story? I wouldn't have believed it myself without everything I've seen. Even if they do give it credence ..." His hand moved to the hilt of his sword.

"... They'll only see a daemon," I finished for him. My hands clenched on the reins and my horse tossed its head.

Fayne continued. "Let's settle in then I'll speak to Braith. Once I've had it out with him we can locate Iril and figure out how best to proceed."

We grabbed a quick dish of braised venison before Fayne's conference with Braith. Sated, I patrolled the rows of tents in the northern edge of the camp, keeping my mental eye on Iril. Clansmen sharpening their swords watched me before they turned in for the night. I doubted Iril would risk any Clansmen seeing her. Why did she keep so close to the host? What was she waiting for?

Most campfires had burned down to their embers in the dark by the time I returned to my tent. I didn't see Fayne. Odd. I wouldn't have expected Braith to keep him that long. Unless the argument had grown heated ...

I crawled into my tent, grateful for the chance to put my head down for a few hours, even just on a wadded up shirt on hard ground. Exhaustion heavied my limbs and sleep overtook me.

The light of the full moon glowing against the roof of my tent woke me. No, not the light—a noise that didn't belong. Someone was fumbling with the fly of the tent. I sat bolt upright. "Who's there?" I challenged.

The scuffling stopped. "You are the woman they call Umbra?" a rough voice asked.

"Yes."

"You are summoned to speak with Lord Dayr."

"Where is Lord Grey?"

"Ask your questions of Lord Dayr. I have no answers for you."

I tugged on my boots and flung the tent flaps out of the way. A scowling Clansman stood waiting for me, his sword unsheathed. Another one held a bow, aiming an arrow at my chest. My pulse raced and I worked to quiet it. If these men had been told anything about me, showing fear to them would make them more nervous. I did my best to project a calm demeanor.

The man with the sword led the way, while the one with the bow marched a few paces behind me. We threaded our way through the rows of tents, until we came upon one flying the silver and green flag of Clan Dayr. The men led me inside.

Fayne and Braith sat facing each other on low camp stools. Fayne's jaw clenched when he saw me.

"So," Braith said. "This is the one the witch wants?"

I stared at Fayne, the betrayal sending a physical pain stabbing through my stomach. He'd said he'd keep quiet! *Did you really believe him? You should know better than to trust a man.*

Fayne answered Braith. "Iril dared to come into the camp with her demands?"

Braith tossed a small roll of parchment into Fayne's lap. "Of course not. She values her head too much. She had this little missive delivered."

Fayne frowned. "Delivered? How?"

"That's what's strange. When questioned, the man claims not to remember how he came into its possession. But he was very clear on whom to deliver the note to."

I glanced at Fayne. Compulsion.

Wait—if Braith knew of Iril's demands directly from her hand that meant ...

Fayne unrolled the parchment, scanned its contents, and looked up at me. His expression completely neutral, he said, "It says she'll call off the beetles if Lord Dayr gives her the woman named Umbra."

My shoulders slumped, despair warring with relief. Fayne

hadn't betrayed me. But now my fate lay in Braith's hands. Unable to get past my allies Fayne and Shirra, Iril had found another way to get her hands on me.

Braith stood up and came to stand before me. He looked me up and down. "Why does the witch want you, girl?"

Had Iril not told him what I was? No, of course not. He'd destroy me before letting something like a shade fall into a witch's hands. I stammered, no good lie coming to my lips. "I—she—"

"Iril plans to take Umbra's life for her own," Fayne said.

Braith spun to look at him. "How do you mean?"

"The witch steals souls. It's how she keeps herself alive beyond her allotted years. We found one such wretch at Perfyd Tower."

"And not just any soul will do?"

Fayne shot a warning glance my way. "Umbra has escaped Iril once already, in the middle of an important ritual. We think it's too far advanced to substitute another."

I stared at Fayne. The lie sounded so plausible on his tongue.

"I must admit, I'm loathe to give Iril anything that she values. But if these insects are as voracious as you say, Fayne, then one life in exchange might be cheap in the bargain. Retrieving the staff is the only thing that will ward off the Fates' wrath." Braith studied me, yet had the grace to look somewhat ashamed of himself.

"And murder won't incur their wrath? She's an innocent in this, Braith. And so are the Gherza. I've seen the staff with my own eyes, in Iril's hands. She intends to keep it. She's behind all these ills, including Rhinn's death, and the deaths of my kin. My own kin, Braith! Do you think I don't want the heads of those responsible just as much as you do? I've lost as much, more even."

"Iril and the Gherza are in league with each other. She stole it to give to them. It's why they're here now."

Fayne snorted. "For Fates' sake, Braith, you stubborn old fool. Listen to yourself. The beetles give us common cause to enlist the Gherza's help in stopping this disaster. Do you suppose the Watcher will view our actions kindly, and intercede with the Judge on your behalf, if you war against the wrong enemy?"

"I have nothing to hide from the Watcher."

"Well, I will, if you force me to lead Clan Grey against the Gherza."

"The Gherza are a scourge who will never rest until they regain the plateau. They did not sufficiently honor the Fates, and what happened? Clan Dayr did, and because of us, the Fates gave the Clans the staff and the plateau. The Gherza brought all their woes upon themselves."

"So the staff is just an excuse, then? You would shame us before the Fates, just to claim that you were the one who finally dealt with the Gherza 'scum?' They are not the enemy, Braith! If you truly wish to honor the Fates, instead of worrying about two-hundred-year-old crimes, go after the right culprit now."

The Elder was silent for a moment, though his nostrils flared and he struggled to contain an angry outburst. He slowly paced the tent. He stopped before a trio of carved wooden Fates that stood near his cot.

Finally, Braith spoke. "The point is moot, at least for the next day. If you believe the witch does not intend to release the staff, then I must consider the possibility. We've had our disagreements but you've never been one for outright deceit." I saw Fayne bite the inside of his cheek, but Braith seemed not to notice. Braith continued. "The witch demands the exchange take place two nights hence. We should at least meet with her then, but I don't wish to give her your friend, here, without conclusive proof that she has dealt with her insects."

"But you do intend to give her Umbra."

"I don't see that we have much choice. But not immediately. Umbra will stay in camp for this first meeting, until we negotiate the proper terms, which, now that I know she has it, may include the staff, if she wants your friend that badly."

Iril would never give up the staff. No point in telling Braith that, though.

Braith summoned the guards, told them to escort me back to my tent. Fayne remained behind with Braith. As I left, I heard Braith speak to Fayne. "Let us pray together to the Listener now, Lord Grey, that we may choose the correct path to retrieving the staff, and that the Watcher may see that even through its loss, we try still to live up to what the Fates originally saw in us so long ago ..."

~*~

I sat in my tent, pondering my new status as hostage of the Clans, when Fayne poked his head inside.

"That could have gone better," he said, pitching his voice so the guard wouldn't hear. "We misjudged Iril. I wouldn't have thought she'd treat with Braith so openly."

"At least I'm still human, as far as Braith's concerned."

"That might not last long, depending on what happens at that meeting. Did you find Iril while you were looking earlier?"

"No luck. So this meeting …"

"Night after next. Between midnight and dawn."

"Fayne, I don't like the timing. What's special about then?"

"It wouldn't surprise me if Lian showed up tomorrow. We left him only a day's ride from Castle Grey."

"So she has no allies now." An idea popped into my head. At first blush it sounded a bit crazy, but even an hour of captivity was starting to wear thin, and Braith would only tighten the noose around me the more time I gave him to get organized. "What if we go tonight instead?"

"Umbra, why are you in such a hurry to give yourself up? Braith wants to stall anyway so he can figure out a safe way of getting the staff away from her."

"That's not what I'm proposing," I said. Although I'd do it if I thought it might spare Fayne any grief. "No. We ambush her."

"But you said she could sense you coming."

"Me, yes. But you? I've been thinking. She took us at Arneth because we used the wrong tactics. We'll split up. Maybe even find some Clansmen to come with us."

"No. We go alone. Less chance of detection. Besides, you saw what she did to the guards at Arneth."

"But I don't think she can handle more than one person at a time. I think that's why she needs me."

"I won't risk it with men I don't know. With Grey men here, so I could explain what we're up against, maybe. But if I rally anyone else to me, word will get around the host. Before you know it, Braith will be wondering what's going on. Where is Iril now?"

"Up in the hills. She must not want to stay too close to the camp. It doesn't matter how long Braith stalls. He intends to hand me over eventually, and in the meantime, Iril has more time to consolidate power and figure out how to control me. We still have a small advantage now, if we can surprise both her and Braith. Going now isn't a great option, but the alternatives are worse if we wait."

Fayne drummed his fingers on his knee. "Then it's decided. We go between midnight and dawn, but tonight, before she's ready. I'll find a way to deal with the guards."

"Going against Braith like this is not going to help you regain Dayr's favor. He'll know I had help getting out."

"I don't give a Watcher's eye what Braith thinks of me. What's good for Dayr's honor is not necessarily what's good for the Clans as a whole. I've suspected that for a long time and Braith didn't say anything tonight to disabuse me. Zealotry won't get us back the staff, or keep you from becoming Iril's tool."

Fayne stood up.

"Where are you going?" I asked.

"I saw Shirra arrive with a few men just before dinner. I think it wiser to let at least one person know where we're going. If we don't come back by morning, she can tell Braith what happened. I can give them that much warning. If she talks to him before Lian does, she might also stand a chance at clearing her name."

Fayne left to find Shirra.

I sat in my tent, arms wrapped around my knees, trying not to fidget. Rest was beyond me. At one point, I heard Fayne's voice outside. He offered the guard a wineskin, chatted with him amiably for a few minutes about keeping an eye on me, then left. About twenty minutes later, something thumped to the ground at the front of the tent. Then, fingers scrabbled at the flap.

"It's time," Fayne said.

When I emerged, I saw the guard slumped over on his side. Fayne grinned. "Poor man can't hold his drink."

We snuck over to the pickets, picking our way through the tents, and trying to avoid fires where Clansmen stayed up late talking. When we couldn't, Fayne simply strolled through, acting every inch the Clan lord he was. Each stray glance directed our way made me grit my teeth and try to look like I belonged out and about at this hour. I expected someone to challenge us, but Fayne's presence lent me legitimacy. By the time we reached the horses, though, we'd racked up quite a few witnesses to our flight.

We saddled our mounts, and Fayne took a few extra minutes to wrap the horses' hooves in hide to muffle any noise. Leaving the pickets, we entered the scrub, following a deer trail that wound through the thickets. The slope rose and the terrain roughened—we'd reached the foothills of the Barrier Range. Moongate Pass still lay a day's ride to the west, but a clever traveler could lose most pursuers in the network of trails, ridges, and valleys hereabouts.

The pendant gave me an advantage. Iril knew I could find her, wanted me to find her, so I could complete the task she had in mind for me. Were we doing the right thing by seeking her out? To my knowledge, she represented my only way out of the mortal realm. I didn't see another choice. I just needed to get to her before she found whatever killed me in my first life. Until then, we still stood a chance of getting the staff away from her.

I signaled Fayne to halt. "She's not far."

We dismounted and crept through the scrub, using the trunks

of large juniper for cover. The moonlight cast deep shadows and I struggled not to trip over roots or snap an unseen twig, giving away our presence. At the edge of a clearing up ahead, the moonbeams silvered the juniper and stunted oak. The sound of voices bounced to us between the boles. Fayne loosened his sword in his scabbard. The pendant tugged insistently at my throat. Fayne squeezed my hand once then slipped off into the darkness.

I crouched behind a large aromatic sage bush at the edge of the clearing, trying to make sense of the scene before me. In the center of the clearing two figures faced off, one hooded, the other dressed in outlandish patchwork garb. A group of a dozen or so Gherza stood behind the strangely dressed man. The hooded figure held out a long rod—Iril, and the staff. How had the Gherza found Iril?

"You are dead to us," the man said.

"Fools!" The staff trembled in Iril's hand. "I'm the only one who can save you now."

"You only ever believed in saving yourself. Once, we could have forgiven you for your original crime. But for what you since became, there is no atonement. No wonder you seek to avoid death. I know how you fear to face the One Who Speaks. You've tried to hide in your tower, but She Who Sees witnesses all."

"You waste my time with speeches. What did you hope to accomplish here? Release me from the binding!"

"Now you truly take me for a fool. Only death can release you. And you refuse to die. We reclaim what is ours by right."

He pulled a small object I couldn't make out from a pouch at his side. Iril took a step back, then froze.

"I see you remember this," the man said. He walked up to Iril, who remained as paralyzed, and tore the staff from her unresisting hands. "Thank you for this gift."

Iril spoke in a strangled voice, the effort costing her. "That won't help you with the beetles, old man."

The Gherza stiffened. "What beetles?"

"The ones I sent to feast on the Aramar trees."

"So the Clan thieves lose their trees. We lost what was important to us long ago."

"Don't you find it interesting that as the Clans take more and more from the Aramar, the Gherza suffer more and more drought? Watching over several lifetimes, I see the pattern of the taint. When the trees go, so does the last of your water, Izir."

Izir. It meant father of the tribe. And how did I know that? I peered more closely at the man, wondering if here stood the man the Fates bade me look for when I made my pilgrimage up Darmid Tor.

The Gherza studied Iril. "You're about to tell me only you can stop these beetles."

"Yes. Give me back the staff and I'll deal with them."

He didn't even take the time to consider. "No. Whatever you unleashed, we will deal with ourselves. I don't doubt you plan worse should we let you back in."

"One day I'll find a way in—and you'll regret spurning me. I'll finish what started in the vale—between that and the beetles I'll see your lands ever blighted."

"Threats won't convince me to lift your exile." The Izir returned to the group of waiting Gherza and they melted into the woods. Throughout, Iril remained still as a stone.

Iril seemed to be under some sort of spell. I didn't trust it though, and hesitated to show myself to her. But Fayne couldn't resist the chance to take her by surprise. He leapt from the trees and rushed at Iril, sword swinging wildly over his head.

For all its speed, his headlong rampage made little noise. Yet Iril roused from her stupor. With the departure of the Gherza, whatever they'd done to her lost its power. She shrieked at the now invisible Gherza. Almost as an afterthought, she flicked out a hand in Fayne's direction just as he closed the gap between them. Fayne dropped like a sack of millet to the ground, insensate. But he wasn't dead. The lack of heat in the brand told me as much.

The hooded head turned to me. I felt her eyes drilling into the shadows where I hid, though the night and the hood cloaked her face.

"Come out," she said. "Now."

I didn't move.

"Come out or I'll kill him."

I stepped out from behind the sage bush. My sword would be useless. I clung to an insane hope that perhaps her protection from me only held while she possessed the object that created me: the staff. I took a deep breath and dug within me for the coldness.

Iril tutted. "You really are stubborn, aren't you? It won't work, but I'm tired of proving it over and over again. Perhaps another incentive will change your ways. If I die, I take him with me," she said, pointing back at Fayne. "We're linked, for the moment."

I didn't know whether to believe her. Iril glided along the ground until she stood less than a pace from me. She stabbed her finger against my brand. I hissed as heat flared out of me into her.

"We're going to come to an arrangement, you and I, since the Izir made off with my prize," Iril said. "I'll keep your friend safe, while you go fetch me that staff."

"Get it yourself."

"There's the little matter of a Gherza curse preventing me from crossing the pass."

"I'm not your dog."

"Oh, but you are. As good as, anyway."

"You have no hold over me."

"Think again." She thrust her finger against the brand again and I flinched. "I can send you into oblivion in a second. True oblivion. That's what will happen if I unmake you outside the middle realm. You *will* do my bidding, become what I brought you here to be, give me my revenge on those who wronged me. Or I'll kill him without a second thought."

"He's nothing to me." *Liar.*

"Really? Better women than you have been tempted by what he has to offer."

"I'm a shade." A shade made flesh and blood. A shade tempted once more by what she'd thought long lost to her. I couldn't let her see that, though.

"Yes. And if I kill him, you'll never see the far planes."

The confusion must have shown on my face.

Iril laughed. "The staff brought you here. It's why you need me too, don't you see? You can't go back to the middle realm without it. And I'm the only one who knows how to use it. You're linked to it. And so is he, through the blood of his line, since they

240

held it last. The staff is useless without their blood."

"Liar. You made me without it."

"Not so. My pet, Lian, bears a small scar to prove it."

I glanced at Fayne, lying so still on the ground. That's why my brand thrummed when Fayne—and even Lian, it seemed— touched it. My secret voice laughed at me. *Undone by a man, yet again.* I shrugged it off.

"You're wasting time. The staff gets farther away the longer you tarry," Iril said.

"It's of no use to you, Iril. I still won't kill for you."

"So sure. So certain."

My skin crawled. She was laughing at me, like a smug child dangling a secret in front of an annoying sibling. "You were wrong about Murran," I said, hoping to draw her out.

"True. I rushed to judgment. I saw what I wanted to see, because it matched my heart's desire. I won't make that mistake again. Stupid of me to think the staff would give me Murran, so long gone. It will take more than luck to get him back.

"No, it stands to reason the staff chose someone newer to the middle realm. If the shades I failed to embody didn't lie—if they are the souls of the unrequited—then it turns out I had what I needed all along."

"Then what's stopping you?"

"Once Lian returns, nothing, really. We'll test my new theory when you bring me the staff."

I could sense her studying me, watching my reaction at this news. I kept my face impassive, willing my hands not to shake. Something Lian possessed—what would that have to do with my death? What did she mean by "unrequited?" I didn't remember ever hearing a shade refer to the term. To cover my confusion, I focused on the question of the staff. "How do you expect me to find it?"

Iril cupped the pendant in her palm. "This should help." If I disappointed her by not rising to the bait, she didn't show it.

The pendant—not linked to her, then, but to the staff. I'd been too preoccupied to pay attention to its westward tug while I dealt with Iril. But since she stood right in front of me, it was the only conclusion.

I glanced one more time at Fayne lying inert on the ground.

"Lord Grey stays with me," Iril said. She flicked her wrist, and Fayne shuddered, then sat up. He got to his feet stiffly, then looked at me.

All the clarity leached from his eyes. His irises swirled a muddy olive. And then I felt it. A thin stream of something foul. I closed my eyes the better to let my shade senses follow it, and—Fates! It tied him and Iril together.

"Find the staff, Umbra," Fayne and Iril said in unison. Fayne's voice sounded hoarse, unnatural.

"What have you done to him?" I shouted at Iril. She laughed, and her dry cackle echoed in Fayne's throat. Then she waved a hand. Fayne's mouth shut with a click.

"He's my eyes and ears, now. And voice."

"How do I know you won't kill him?"

"I have better things for him to do. He's about to change his position regarding the Gherza. That meddler Shirra—sneaking around, putting the wrong thoughts in people's heads. That little trick she pulled to get rid of me at the castle—she possesses a certain item she shouldn't. Without the staff, the Clans grow fractious and unpredictable, even with a Conclave edict. Fayne will keep them united like I need them, for now. Unless I require him for ... other errands."

Fayne stared straight ahead, oblivious. "Is he ..." I could barely speak the words. "Is he still in there? Or have you cursed him like that poor creature in your tower?"

"His essence is still his own. For now. But don't leave it too long. Or there won't be any of him to come back to."

Her meaning crashed in on me. Here in the physical realm, I could only sense dying souls. That I could feel Fayne's meant Iril leached his soul from him. Bit by bit, if she continued for too long, Fayne would die.

"How will I find you again?"

"Perfyd Tower. Even if I'm not there, I'll put wards on to alert me of your return."

Without another word, I abandoned Fayne and set out from the clearing. Here it was, then. The price for indulging myself, allowing even the smallest filament of joy to penetrate my heart. This crushing fear, the anticipation of loss. The terrible, terrible guilt. *What does it matter? It's just one more layer on the palimpsest of your soul.* I should have abandoned him by that roadside long ago. If Fayne died, it would be my fault.

My fault if I left him to his fate with Iril. And my fault if I returned. Because if Iril really would soon possess the instrument of my death, she'd make me kill him. She'd only accept one proof of her power over me: forcing me to murder him. She didn't need to tell me. I knew. And only then would she use me to kill whoever it was upon whom she was so determined to get this so-called vengeance.

243

I slipped into the brush as Iril said to Fayne, "Now, tell me about this Shirra …" I clenched my jaw so tightly I thought I might crack a molar. Iril had brought me to heel but I'd die again before showing it.

THEN

"O, He Who Hears, listen to my prayer. Give my father the ears to heed my pain and annul this betrothal." Jezarel whispered her plea as she approached her father's tent. The incident with the cliff lion had only hardened her resolve. She took a deep breath, and parted the entrance flaps to brave the interior.

She waited as the Izir finished a meeting with one of his shepherds about the grazing location for the flock. At least she hadn't interrupted him discussing arrangements with her future in-laws. The flock seen to, her father gestured her forward.

Jezarel waited until the shepherd exited the tent, and she could no longer hear his footsteps outside. She sank down to the carpet before her father, sitting cross-legged and arranging her skirts. Palms turned inward, she touched her ears, eyelids and lips, then brought her hands to the floor before her in the formal sign of petition. She kept her eyes trained on her lap.

Her father sighed. "Invoking all three Fates, Jezarel? Speak then, daughter," he said. "But if you come for the reason I believe, my answer will likely disappoint you."

Not an auspicious start. "Father, please. Do not insist on marrying me to this man."

"The very survival of the tribe is at stake, Jezarel."

"But we don't know who killed Javeen. What if it was this Murran?"

"The Arneth Izir assures me his Clan does not raid."

"And the barbarians never lie? Father, we should be avenging Javeen and not—"

"Jezarel, your honor is misplaced. Vengeance is not ours to mete out. She Who Sees witnessed Javeen's death and thus we must trust that The One Who Speaks will judge fairly in the end."

"How can you act like you don't care what they did to him?"

Her father leaned toward her, fury in his eyes. Jezarel started back. Then she saw the tear leaking down her father's cheek.

He didn't shout, but his words were all the more terrible for their strained, low tones. "Don't *ever* accuse me of that, Jezarel. I lost my only son. My heir. The boy I loved, chopped down just as he was to become a man. My heart screams its grief every morning the sun rises on this world without him."

Jezarel found she could not answer. Her father continued. "But know this, also, Jezarel. However much I loved him, Javeen was a fool. Yes, the barbarians wielded the swords that ended his life. But he and his friends—all of them, the future of the tribe—died because he refused to listen. And thus the tribe is irreparably weakened."

Jezarel's throat tightened with her own grief. She couldn't bear these recriminations coming from her father's mouth, but she'd come to formally plead her case and now must stay to hear her father out.

"Why do you think the Inarra refused to rally to us last winter, Jezarel? They feared I'd lost control of my own tribe. And so our last chance to present a united front to the barbarians disappeared."

A chill feathered down Jezarel's arms. "You hold Javeen responsible for all the Inarra deaths?" The Inarra had failed to return to their steppe oasis last spring. Jezarel remembered the look of horror on the returning scout's face when he'd brought news of what he'd found at their winter plateau settlement.

"Of course not, Jezarel. That slaughter rests squarely with these Clan men. But they took advantage of a weakness we had an opportunity to correct. An opportunity that died with your brother."

Jezarel gazed down at the carpet between them, its rich reds bringing to mind nothing but the blood of the victims of barbarian marauders.

"*Sha'zara*, daughter of my heart. The barbarians grow stronger and covet the trees of the plateau. We lack the strength in numbers to defeat them in a war. An alliance of mutual understanding preserves our way of life. Otherwise they will take what they want by force, and leave nothing for us."

He took Jezarel's hand, and for the first time she saw entreaty in his eyes. "There must be no more killing, Jezarel. If a fatesbane asked for your hand in marriage in return for keeping you safe and our kin alive, I would accept that bargain. But by all reports this Murran is an honorable man. See the good in him, Jezarel. May She Who Sees open your eyes to how peace honors our people more than vengeance."

Jezarel's teeth hurt, she'd clenched her jaw so hard to keep the tears back. She stood up without a word and left the tent without the formal thanks a petitioner should give the Izir.

He thought he was protecting her—honoring her, even—by giving her over to these savages? As she strode between the tents to her own, Jezarel didn't even hear Lailaz's latest taunt over the turbulence in her own heart. Her father insisted on turning a blind eye to her feelings. She could not see this Murran the way he wanted her to.

If she couldn't convince her father—and she was by no means sure she could count on Kairiya to disgrace Murran—then she'd just have to take matters into her own hands.

~*~

Kairiya found Murran in a dell past the edge of camp. He dug his hole with singular intensity. The cliff lion's corpse lay on the ground nearby. A gust of wind ruffled the long hair of its tail, giving the illusion of life. Kairiya bent down and stroked the soft forehead. A patch of dried blood at the shoulder marked the killing arrow's entry point.

"How could I know?" Murran muttered.

"You couldn't. I should have said something when I let it go."

"It's a waste of a fine pelt to bury it this way."

"The pelt is already wasted. It was of use only to its wearer."

Murran stopped shoveling. "These cats prey on Gherza goats and sheep."

"The Gherza know the cat only takes what it needs to survive. They admire it for this, and for its independent spirit." Kairiya added a sly jab. "The Clansmen also prey on the Gherza. Would you have the Gherza hunt the Clans?"

"You say 'they,' as if you were not also Gherza."

Kairiya let no chagrin at her blunder cross her features. "It's just a manner of speaking. The Izira asked me to educate you in the ways of the Gherza, so you don't offend Jezarel again. She hopes that because I traveled more and know the ways of outsiders, I can reduce the divide between you."

But what of the divide within herself? Kairiya stared at Murran, envying his easy confidence. He knew his place in the world, and his duty. All her life she watched men like him from her position on the outskirts of Clan acceptance. They went about their business, choosing a mate, creating their families and a new circle of warmth and love. But ever they passed Kairiya over, looking on her with suspicion because of her mother's oddness, and Kairiya's own difference. What her father asked of her he ordered in the name of that very difference.

Jezarel begged her to insinuate herself into Murran's good graces because she believed Kairiya's heart just as mercenary as her head. But what if Kairiya wanted Murran for herself? Would Jezarel feel the same way, and hold Kairiya to her word?

Murran buried the lion. Kairiya wished it were as easy to bury her own doubts.

~*~

Kairiya headed back to her tent, but a hand reached out from behind a tree at the edge of the trail and grabbed her. She struggled against a tall, muscular body. She smelled the musky unwashed scent of a Clansman, and upbraided herself for her own carelessness. She should have heard him coming. Or at least smelled him. But she didn't expect a Clansman to try anything funny so near the Gherza camp, not with a treaty at stake.

"Gettin' a bit cozy with the target, are we?" a harsh voice whispered in her ear.

The tension of capture drained from Kairiya's body, replaced by a different sort of caution. Now she understood why he caught her by surprise.

"Hello, Father," she said to the man who taught her everything she knew about approaching an enemy with stealth. Orrith, patriarch of Clan Dayr.

"I didn't send you out here so you could find a pillow to share. Breaking up the marriage won't suffice. Murran's a blood traitor—I won't let him dilute the Clan lines this way. The penalty for treason is death."

Kairiya did not point out her father's hypocrisy. It would earn her a slap, and a bruise she couldn't hide. He had kept Asrar as his mistress for almost twenty years.

Kairiya wondered at her mother's hold over Orrith, and how much the dark arts figured into it. He hated the Gherza, yet she couldn't deny his passion during those long nights when Kairiya huddled in the corner of the shack she and Asrar shared. The desire to remain unnoticed while they coupled warred with Kairiya's longing for a real family, one that didn't view her as a half-breed bastard freak fit only to hurl stones at.

Kairiya had long practice at moving on the edges of any circle, staying out of the way, surviving. When her father first let her handle a sword three years ago, then sent her to his chief armsman to learn, she'd been relieved at finally finding something that might make her useful to him. When he'd taken over her training six months ago, she'd been thrilled, even though he was a harsh taskmaster. Now he'd trusted her with this mission. That made her family, didn't it? Or did it just make her a tool?

"I know the penalty, Father. But the time is not right. I have to be close to Murran to accomplish the task you set me, and this is the perfect excuse. You want maximum impact, don't you?"

"It must happen before the wedding."

"It will."

"The Clans cannot ally with the Gherza."

"I won't let that happen, Father."

"This marriage is filthy. Clan blood must not be diluted. Only if it remains pure will we destroy the Gherza and sweep victorious across the plateau. The trees are the key to our prosperity, and the Gherza will not hand them over simply because they married one of our own."

Kairiya pondered her own diluted blood. Was she not living proof of his own blood treason? Maybe no amount of loyalty would bring her closer to his heart.

Orrith's words that day months ago when he returned from the Clan Conclave with news of the pending alliance with the Gherza reverberated in her thoughts. The day he'd set her upon this path. Kairiya had been helping her mother with the evening roast when he'd flung open the croft's door. "This will debase us in the eyes of the Watcher."

"Orrith—" Asrar had said, ignoring his lack of greeting and using her most placating tone.

He ignored her. "The other Elders would not listen! Said I of all people should understand." He glared at Kairiya. "Illegitimate mongrels are one thing, it's not like you'll ever amount to much. But a legitimate, Elder-sanctioned marriage? I won't have it—the Arneth heir, a half-breed, and eventual Council member? He's smart, that Arneth, I'll give him that. Marrying his son off to the foreign bitch. Oh, he says it's for the good of the Clans now, but when it comes down to it, who'll be keeping the trees, eh?"

"Orrith—" Asrar said.

"Shut up, woman, I need to think on this. I don't care what the Elders say, I won't let Arneth steal what belongs to all of us, just because he's willing to soil his own bloodline."

"What did your allies on the Council say?"

"Cowards all. They won't go against the majority."

Asrar smiled. "What if we could nix this marriage and make the Gherza look guilty in the bargain? Would they back you then?"

"If I could pull that off, they'd back me straight into the position of Eldest. But it must look like I warned them all along, rather than engineered the whole situation. Otherwise it will look too much like tempting the Fates."

"It seems to me you have the perfect weapon right here, then." Asrar stood behind Kairiya and placed her hands on Kairiya's shoulders. Kairiya looked back at her mother in confusion.

Orrith frowned, and stared at Kairiya. Then he threw back his head and laughed. "Ha! I knew there was a reason I let you play at being a swordswoman. Thank the Listener for ignoring my prayer and delaying the flesh trader this year. Maybe you will be of use after all, whelp." He crossed the croft until he loomed before her, then grabbed her chin and turned her face from side to side. "She'll never pass as a Gherza. Her skin and hair betray her."

"She doesn't need to. We can come up with a story to get her in close, and the rest is simple subterfuge." Asrar gripped Kairiya's shoulders more tightly, and whispered in her ear. "It's not like you haven't spent your whole life pretending to be something you're not, now, is it? This will be the same thing, in a different setting."

"I don't understand," Kairiya said.

Orrith's smile frightened Kairiya. "It's simple, really. All you have to do is kill one man, and make it look like the Gherza did it. If you can't kill one man after all the training I've given you, then I might as well bundle you off to the flesh trader right now, because a caravan outrider who can't defend herself is useless to everyone."

"I—" Kairiya swallowed. He wouldn't sell her. He wouldn't! "Who do you want me to kill?"

"Murran of Arneth. Can you do it?"

Kill a man. She was anything but sure she could do it when the time came. But if she did this thing, would her father stop talking of selling her? Would she stop being "mongrel" and start being "daughter?" She couldn't quite bring herself to ask those questions. Instead, "If I do this for you, will you give me a croft?" Because when it came right down to it, the danger of caravan outriding only appealed insofar as it competed against selling her body. But a home ... a real home ...

"If you do this for me, you'll have your croft."

Kairiya nodded. She tucked away the thought of assassination for later scrutiny. There would be plenty of time to harden herself to the idea. The Listener had finally heard her pleas for release from the constant fear of the flesh traders. If she stayed penitent, maybe He would offer up another solution that would still please her father, yet avoid the need for murder.

Orrith reached past Kairiya to lay his palm on Asrar's cheek. "It's brilliant, my sweet. The marriage would have brought the Clans the wrong kind of attention from the Watcher. But I know the Judge will treat me kindly on this in the end—because we'll have punished the blasphemers on both sides."

Now, staring at her father here beneath the Gherza trees he so coveted, Kairiya had reason to question what qualified as blasphemy. Though he cloaked himself in piety, he cared only for riches. Riches that he said flowed freely only to traders, traders that the hardscrabble Clansmen would never become without access to ships.

The western desert caravans were too distant to make transporting Clan grapes and cheese across the mountains worthwhile. Ships, now; ships would open up whole new frontiers. Ships the Clans could not build without trees. Trees that he planned to take from the Gherza whether or not it suited them.

What would happen if he got his hands on the one in the hidden vale? That tree above all—knowing its meaning to the Gherza, her father would use its destruction to break the will of the Gherza. Kairiya imagined its timbers split, its leaves scattered and browning. No. It had given her the one moment of belonging she'd ever experienced.

Kairiya decided not to tell him yet about the Tree.

NOW

Oh, Fates! Fayne! Why didn't I restrain him when I had the chance? Iril couldn't know what I felt for him, but I'd handed her the only lever over me. I stumbled down the hillside and found my horse. I was desperate to put distance between me and Iril. I grabbed the reins of Fayne's horse too. Fayne was Iril's creature for now—anything that hindered her plans helped me. She wanted me haring off after the Gherza. She couldn't know that suited me just fine given that night on Darmid Tor. Still, a little caution might be called for first.

Was Iril just guessing about my identity? What could Lian possibly have that gave Iril control over me? I examined my memories of Garrith Grey's death. My shade self saw Lian. At the time, I'd felt concern for Garrith, a need to calm the victim of a violent death. As for Lian: I'd noticed his presence, tied his threatening manner with the death's cause, but aside from that I'd been indifferent to him. No recognition.

The method of dying only interested shades as regards its effect on the dead. People expecting death were easier to chivvy along in the first critical minutes—the likeliest time for a daemon to sense a new arrival to the middle realm. Murder victims lingered, either shouting recriminations at their killers, moaning with moral outrage at a life cut unfairly short, or simply stunned into frozen shock, unable to believe their fate. Garrith leaned towards the stunned variety.

Did I even have a living link to Lian, or did Iril send him off in search of some other artifact? He couldn't have detoured far from Castle Grey, so whatever she wanted, it must have to do with the Greys. The timing niggled at me. Up until the confrontation at Arneth, Iril believed I was Murran. She couldn't have spoken with Lian to send him on a different quest while he rounded up the Grey troops. So Iril must believe Lian carried the item she needed on his person.

My lurching flight in the darkness felt like a metaphor for my entire situation. If I didn't slow down, I risked breaking an ankle on an unseen root or rock. If I didn't think things through with Iril, I could kill Fayne or lose my free will. Or both. I halted the horses, and took stock. Glimmers of moonlight flashed off the metal bits of the horses' tack. Would that I could snatch a bright idea out of the air like trapping a firefly in a jar.

With every passing moment, the staff got farther away. If I went after it, I'd have to leave Lian to Iril, at the risk of ceding the item controlling my killing power to her. But every day squandered to waylay Lian leached more life from Fayne through Iril's link. I feared he wouldn't last.

Braith would also discover my departure soon. The resulting hue and cry would make my escape that much harder.

I needed help. And I knew only one place to get it.

I reached the outskirts of the Clan encampment just as dawn brushed the valley plain with light. I hurried to a particular tent near the southern edge of the camp, scratching at the tent flap until someone stirred within. Shirra poked her head into the dewy air. I thanked the Fates she'd made haste with her men, allowing Fayne to speak with her last night. Shirra's irritated expression at being woken soured further on seeing me.

"Make it quick, scut," she demanded. "I expected Fayne to come with news himself. I don't have time to waste on his pillow friend of the moment."

I ignored the insult. Fayne needed help, not a cat fight. "I would speak with you in private." I might not like Shirra but she wasn't stupid, and I trusted her concern for Fayne would outweigh her scorn.

She shrugged and held aside the tent flap. The interior was spare. Apart from a large trunk where she must keep the silks she seemed so enamored with, the tent contained a simple pallet for sleeping covered in a heavy bearskin, and a single heating brazier.

"You do not support the Clan stance on the Gherza," I said.

"I don't condone blood treason. But neither do I believe the Gherza gave the Clans cause for a full-scale war."

"Then I have a favor to ask."

"Why should I give any favors to an upstart wench?"

Look who's talking. "Because I saved your life by telling Fayne you didn't kill Errith."

"What do you want of me then?"

"Fayne Grey told you where we went last night?" Shirra nodded. I continued. "He will be returning to the encampment sometime later today. Braith will be deeply suspicious of him because I've gone missing. Have your men intercept Fayne and keep him from the Council. You must find a way to do the same with Lian as he approaches from Castle Grey. Lian still has your dagger. I hope to delay the host. They won't leave without all the Clans."

"Detain Lord Grey? That won't get me back on his good side. And delay the host? Why would I condone any such thing?"

"Fayne's ... not himself." I wondered how much to tell her of Iril. I didn't know Shirra that well, and worried she placed her ambitions higher than Fayne's safety. If she told the Council of Elders Fayne was compromised in order to gain their favor, what would Iril do?

"But Lord Grey shares my views on the Gherza issue."

"He's had a change of heart." There was nothing for it, so I came right out with it. "Iril put him under a spell. He speaks with her voice."

Shirra pressed a hand to her stomach and slumped over the pallet. "Fayne Grey is a good man. He doesn't deserve such treatment at the hands of the Fates." She shook a finger at my raised eyebrow. "Errith considered me a gold-digger but she never bothered to get to know me. Just because I consider an alliance advantageous doesn't mean I can't have feelings for the other party." Shirra *loved* Fayne. I knew he felt for her, but I'd hoped Errith had the right of it regarding Shirra's feelings.

The sandalwood scent she wore cloyed in my nostrils. I repressed a gag. *It's not her smell that bothers you.* Is this what jealousy felt like? An almost physical aversion to one's rival? *Don't act all innocent. You know exactly what jealousy feels like.*

—*So? What does jealousy get me here?* Now I was talking to myself. Mad shade indeed. The greater madness lay in thinking I stood the slimmest chance of happiness with Fayne. It scared me how much our brief intimacy meant to me. How quickly it gained meaning. "Together," Fayne had said. Such a small word to pin so many hopes on.

Shirra got up and paced the tent, her arms hugging her ribs. "All my work, all for nothing?" she muttered. She whipped around to face me. "I can intercept Fayne but Lian is another matter. He'll surround himself with Grey men-at-arms. Detaining Fayne will condemn me in the eye of the Council if Lian produces my dagger. I'd be a fool to help you."

"You're a fool not to." Her grief for Fayne seemed unfeigned. I squelched my own feelings. "You care for Lord Grey."

"More than you."

Are you going to let that slide?

I almost spit out at Shirra the first scathing retort that came to mind, but clamped my lips down hard on my venom instead. Not for the first time, I found myself angry at my inner voice. In my time as a shade, I didn't recall beating myself up like this. Then again, I'd felt little emotion at all beyond the fierce imperative to protect each soul in my charge. I turned the irritation I yearned to direct outward at Shirra back onto myself. I had enough to deal with without fighting myself all the time.

—*Is this what I was like before I died?* I asked my inner foil. — *Mean and spiteful?*

A shade stands up for itself.

—*No. This has nothing to do with shades, and everything to do with Fayne.*

Shirra doesn't deserve Fayne.

—*And I do?* I could never make a life with Fayne. Yet that didn't change anything about what I felt for him. —*Shirra lives. I'm*

259

dead.

So you'll just stand aside then? How big of you.

And then I saw her, for just a moment. Saw the rejected girl, me before I'd died. And shut off her howling wail in a corner of my head. Fayne needed my help, not childish spite.

"I can't release Fayne from Iril's clutches without your aid," I told Shirra.

"I doubt you could regardless. No one easily defeats the witch."

"No. I require the staff to do that, and I can only get it if you buy me some time with the Clans."

"The Gherza possess the staff?" Shirra looked speculative.

"They took it from Iril. They refused to release her from her exile, which means she can't follow them through the pass and needs me to do it." And now Braith had the excuse he needed to hunt the Gherza.

"It's my head if the Council of Elders finds out I delayed pursuit of the staff."

"It's Fayne's head if I don't get to it first."

I had no hope of retrieving the staff in the middle of a pitched battle. I needed it for my own purposes, after which the Clans could have it back as their symbol of unity. I told her a half-truth to sweeten the pot. "If I retrieve the staff myself, I can ensure it finds its way to the people who could most benefit."

I held my breath. I didn't want to give Shirra a firm commitment, but I needed her to see herself as one of those people.

"If Clan Arneth was seen to rescue the staff—wait, I thought you were to bring it to Iril."

"Yes, but with it I think I might be able to foil her as well."
Wishful thinking maybe, but if it got Shirra onside … "After
we've dealt with the beetles," I added for good measure, though I
had no idea how we'd do that.

"Delaying the host …" Shirra said to herself. She stared at me
with a calculating expression, the gleam in her eye less covetous
than I expected. "Maybe you haven't ruined everything after all."

"And if Fayne knows you helped rescue him …"

"What's in it for you?" she asked me.

I didn't owe Shirra anything close to the truth, so I told her
something she'd believe. "I have no memory, no history. No
lineage. Maybe I never will. If the Council hears of my deeds,
maybe they'll elevate me to a Clan. And maybe that will make me
respectable in certain eyes."

Shirra's lip quirked. "You can try to make the fight fairer but I
still like my chances better, chit."

You have no idea how much I agree with you, I thought.

~*~

A rustling at the edge of the clearing warned us of Fayne's
approach. I peered through the shrub we'd hidden behind. Shirra
clutched my arm. One of the scouts she'd sent ahead had located
Fayne and we'd chosen this spot to ambush him. I hoped he'd
forgive me later.

"Remember, he mustn't see me," I said to Shirra. I didn't want
Iril knowing I delayed her mission for me, but I needed to make
sure Shirra remained committed.

Fayne emerged into the meadow, blinking as the sun struck
his face. A lichen-like green still clouded the limpid clarity of his
eyes. He halted as Shirra's guards sprang from the brush, swords

261

pointed at his chest. Shirra stood up and went to confront him.

"What is the meaning of this, bitch?" Iril-as-Fayne asked.

Shirra flinched. "I'm afraid I can't allow you to see the Council," she said.

"You will let me go right now or I will grind you to dust. You and all of Clan Arneth."

"That's not possible, Lord Grey."

"You've crossed me for the last time."

"When have I ever crossed you, Lord Grey? This is but a little delay. I can't have you spreading lies about me before the Council, now, can I? At least not until I hold the means to counter them. Besides, I'm not sure seeing Braith at the moment is in your best interests. He's a little upset with you." I admired Shirra's poise. It couldn't be easy facing him down knowing what controlled him.

Fayne lunged forward, reaching out as if to throttle Shirra. Two guards jumped in front of her to block him. Fayne struggled in their grip. I could swear spittle flew from his lips.

"I'll kill you for this, Shirra. I promise you. I'll see you dead." Then he cocked his head. I recognized Iril in its tilt. Fayne peered closely at Shirra's face. "My, my, what beautiful eyes you have," he said.

Shirra paled.

Fayne continued, muttering to himself. "Some things aren't all they seem. We know all about that, don't we? We know ..." He jerked, his mouth dropping open into a soundless "oh," as if realizing something. "Why that little strumpet! Could it be? Can't ignore the possibility. If only I had that Fates-damned stone ..." He tried to shrug off his guards again, but they held him fast. A crafty look crept across his features. He stared at Shirra again. "I have other resources at my disposal, *Lady* Shirra. They will crush you when I bring them to bear."

Shirra flicked a finger at her men and they hauled Fayne away. I joined her in the clearing when I was sure he was out of sight.

She trembled. "I didn't quite believe you before, but now I do. That wasn't Fayne Grey. He would never threaten me so."

I glimpsed something soft and vulnerable behind her oh-so-confident eyes. "Oh, Fayne," she said. She saw me watching and banished the emotion. But the jealous girl in the corner of my head noticed it too. Shirra's perfume burned the back of my throat as I inhaled. I knew I'd forever associate the taste of sandalwood mixed with bile with impotent envy.

To clear my head, I said, "Do you see? He can't go before the Council in that state."

Shirra looked skeptical. "What have you gotten me into? I still held some hope of righting my fortunes until you turned up."

"I need time, Shirra. You're the only one who can give it to me. Whatever you do, don't let Lian anywhere near Fayne. Can you detain Lian as well?"

She shook her head. "I'd have to catch him away from his men. But you're right—without Fayne to speak for me, I can't let Lian anywhere near the Council with his accusations about Errith. They'll care only about the proof of my dagger."

I left her staring in the direction her men took Fayne and retrieved my horse. I prayed Shirra wouldn't lose heart. Setting out on a trail that led upwards into the mountains, I began my journey to Moongate Pass. My one hope steadied me—with the staff now out of Iril's clutches, if I found it—and that Gherza father—I might figure out how to use it to send myself back to

263

the middle realm. That thought sped my feet on their march up the trail. That, and a new worry: what had changed for Iril?

~*~

According to what I gleaned from Fayne, I rode now through Clan Dayr territory, a swath of land across the river from that of Clan Arneth. The host gathered at the far eastern edge of the Dayr lands. The Dayrs' domain extended all the way to Moongate Pass, giving them the easiest access to the Aramar Plateau. From what I gathered they'd fought intermittent disputes with Arneth over who controlled the pass itself.

The pendant told me the staff and thus the Gherza moved towards the pass. The game trail I followed petered out at a small spring, so when I reached the top of the next hill I studied the terrain.

To my left the river cut a path through the rising moorland, while ahead the great ridges of the Barrier Range loomed in a purple wall. The river road sidled along the water. In the distance, another track left it traveling northward: I presumed this led to the Dayr seat. A couple of log booms floated downriver; I'd need to be careful if I wanted to avoid the log drivers' notice.

Scanning the hills, I thought I saw movement to the west: the Gherza, or just a deer? If the Gherza, they weren't far off the road. I made a snap decision, and nudged my horse downslope towards the road. With speed of the essence, I'd reach the pass more quickly if I dispensed with searching for a clear route across the hills.

I took to the scrub each time a log boom floated past me. The current swept them past my position at a stately pace, but I soon lost them behind curves in the riverbank. I arrived at the

crossroads by midafternoon, a sense of familiarity about the
scene stealing over me. The twisted juniper tree. The cairn
pointing northward up the track.

I stopped the horse and dismounted. A falcon swooped on a
thermal and I heard a rustle in the grass as something small took
cover. A stand of silver birch shivered in the slight breeze.

Yes. I stood in the same spot Lian had when Iril stepped out
of the trees to take the staff from him. The earth remained
slightly discolored where Garrith's blood had spilled upon the
road. Such a beautiful spot to come to such a violent end.

The horse shook its head and tugged at the reins, angling
towards the water, so I let it drink from the river, then hitched the
reins around a branch of the juniper, and entered the birch grove.
A small shrine to the Fates rested at its center, next to a larger
pavilion: a resting place for travelers along the road to the pass. I
walked over to the shrine, ran my fingers across the worn runes.

I spotted another stone I'd missed as I walked in, this one
with fresher carvings. I knelt down in front of it.

Travelers say a mourning prayer
For here was murdered Rhinn of Dayr
Beloved of her Clan, betrothed of Fayne Grey
May she grace the Cycle another day
Fates willing

Fayne Grey. Betrothed to Fayne but loved by Lian. I
wandered back out of the grove, mind racing, and stared
northward up the track. Just thinking about the Dayr family seat
set off murky rumblings in my head. I'd thought Iril the
instigator, and Rhinn in the wrong place at the wrong time. But
Lian's protestations Iril was helping him avenge Rhinn always

rang false. Lian killed Garrith. Rhinn died in the same ambush. If Iril felled Rhinn, Lian should have felt betrayed. Unless ...

I froze. *You know exactly what killed her. Jealousy. You of all people should know what love makes one capable of.*

And a scenario presented itself to me. Garrith and Lian bringing Rhinn back to Castle Grey, honoring her by traveling with the staff. The entire party, perhaps with a few men-at-arms from both Dayr and Grey, stopping at the shrine. Lian and Rhinn arguing sometime in the night, he trying to convince her not to go ahead with the marriage, failing. A blow, perhaps one not meant to kill, but that killed nonetheless. Lian panicking.

And Iril taking advantage. Covetous of the staff, perhaps she watched the Greys, lying in wait an opportunity to seize it. She'd convinced Lian she could bring Rhinn back with her necromancy, and either through compulsion or persuasion wiled him into dispatching his father as cover. I doubted Lian alone could deal with the entire traveling party, so Iril must have helped him somehow. And he'd blamed the whole thing on her and Shirra, making himself out as a martyr in the process.

I thought about it some more, and gave Lian a slight benefit of the doubt. If Iril shadowed the party, she could have used her powers of compulsion to twist Lian's harmless envy into something darker. I wouldn't put it past her. I shuddered.

All speculation. *No. You know. You know very well. Takes one to know one.*

Rhinn, dead at Lian's hands ... I sucked in a breath. Was that the link? Iril thought I was Rhinn? What did she say, back where she'd captured Fayne? Someone more recently dead than Murran, something about "the unrequited."

The word threw off my thoughts for a moment —"Unrequited." Iril implied she'd spoken to other shades, that they imparted information about themselves and why shades remained trapped in the middle realm. Although I'd never faced the Fates, I'd always had the distinct impression my existence was a punishment. But Iril made it sound like she believed shades pined for lost loves. That would explain why she hoped Murran had not passed through the Far Gates. That belief could still be in error, though.

I remembered the searing torture of Iril tearing me from the middle realm. The sudden flaring of excruciating sensation after ages spent in the muffled numbness of the middle realm. Iril might not be able to embody a shade without the staff, but if she'd found a way to pierce the veil to establish contact, however briefly, searching for Murran, most shades would say anything to cut off that pain. Fates, one might even have believed its words. But that didn't make them true.

A strong through line ran through the myriad beliefs surrounding the Fates, but each culture brought something different to the table. Newly dead Clansmen always seemed particularly worried about the Judge, which I never understood given how much they valued their honor. Whereas Gherza always believed they'd failed the Fates for some reason, but approached the Gates without fear. I'd never met anyone who truly claimed they'd untangled the entire mythology.

I could see how the idea of Rhinn made sense to Iril, working on guesses and only the vaguest of clues. She'd stayed near the host waiting for Lian and the weapon he wielded to kill Rhinn— sword or bare hands, it didn't matter. Yet I couldn't be Rhinn, unless time worked differently in the middle realm. I endured years as a shade, escorted thousands of souls to the Gates.

I breathed a sigh of relief. Iril couldn't control me through Lian. I still had a chance to find the instrument of my death first. Unless—I remembered Iril-as-Fayne confronting Shirra. Iril realized something then, a possibility she couldn't ignore. Fates! Out of one stew pot and into another.

I returned to my horse. It tossed its head at my approach and backed away to the full extent its tether allowed. I frowned. What now? I glanced around the clearing but nothing indicated the presence of a predator. I untied the reins, flipped them over the horse's head, but it sidled sideways away from me.

"Fates! Will you just hold still?" We did an idiotic little dance, me hopping with one foot in the stirrup as the horse pranced sideways. I finally mounted again, the inner tug of the pendant telling me the Gherza traveled slightly north and well ahead of me. I wondered how they planned to get through the pass. Were I Braith of Dayr I would set guards to corner the Gherza between the pass and the host.

As the terrain rose, the river narrowed and the water foamed around rocks. I noted a flume paralleling its course. On the far bank, cliffs and jagged peaks precluded the construction of any road, and I saw why Dayr attained supremacy over Arneth in the timber trade.

At sunset, I set the horse free after loosening the saddle girth, slapping the animal's rump and sending it back off down the road. Good riddance. The horse had spent the afternoon balking and shying at nothing. I needed stealth more than speed now anyway to get past any scouts. I trudged about fifty paces off the road then picked my way along the slopes, keeping the trail in sight. I hoped to avoid the gaze of anyone watching the road.

Near midnight, I spotted a guard post, a warm glow of lantern light spilling from within and paradoxically plunging the towering peaks around me even further into darkness. I snuck closer, alert to any movement.

From behind the safety of a boulder, I studied the outpost. At its base, a shadow shifted in the doorway of the small fortified guard hut. One man there. I picked out one lookout on a platform at the top of the building, the man at the base, and one man patrolling the road at ten minute intervals. Not to mention any troops garrisoned inside.

Right about now would be a good time to regain my traditional shade invisibility. Given the impossibility of that, and after a few more minutes of confirming the foot patrol's pattern, I set out just upslope from the road.

I crouched low, using my hands for balance. I set each foot with care so as not to dislodge any loose shale or pebbles. Fortunately, the moon hadn't yet risen.

Each time the foot patrol returned to the post, he conferred with the man there. The most dangerous place for me lay closest to the guard post with the stationary guard.

I began my gauntlet run when the patrol reached the furthest distance from me, then halted as the man started back down the road, moving only after he passed me and faced away from me.

I relaxed the farther away I got from the outpost without the lookouts spotting me in the darkness. Things went well as I crept along, pausing each time the foot patrol drew near. I held as still as a statue of the Fates. He passed not ten paces away from me, then moved off.

I stole along the slope. I approached the limit of his patrol range where he'd turn around.

Fates-be-damned. A huge piece of granite jutted from the slope, blocking my path with a nearly vertical wall.

I fumbled around, blind in the dark, until I found a couple of small seams running across the rock. Not ideal, but enough for a foot and handhold. Below me, I heard the guard's steps crunching in the shale. He moved off to give his report. I edged out onto the rock face, praying the Watcher would for once cast a kind eye toward me.

From behind my back, I heard a soft "All clear" and the answering "Well met." One of the men kicked a pebble up the road, then I heard a shuffling noise, and returning feet.

I needed to get off the rock before he got too close. Almost there.

My foot slipped. My fingers clutched at the seam like a golden eagle's talons in a rabbit. I nudged the rock to find the lower seam again with my toes. I waited for the echo of the gasp I'd been unable to stifle to reach the guard's ears. But the guard's pace didn't alter. I thanked the hiss of the river for masking my mistake.

Except those precious seconds brought him too close to me and I couldn't risk moving again until he turned back. A muscle jumped and cramped in my forearm.

Don't look up. Please don't look up.

The Listener smiled on me, because I heard him head away again. I breathed a small sigh and crept off the face back onto the relative safety of the slope.

And dislodged a rock.

It bounced down the scree in a hail of small pebbles. To my ears, the rattle ricocheted and crescendoed off the cliffs louder than the river. The small avalanche struck the road with a clap and clatter. I held my breath, willing my deep desire for escape into reality.

But no. The sentry's running footsteps echoed up the path, and no amount of wishing would save me now.

I scrambled away but slipped in the shale and skidded downhill, scraping my right arm, calf and hip. I landed in the road just as the sentry reached me. He whipped his sword to my throat.

"Gherza bitch. If you move I'll kill you."

Fayne said I looked vaguely Gherza, and in the dark, I supposed the mistake was easy. I reasoned with my captor.

"I'm a friend of Lord Gr—"

"Shut up." The blade's edge pressed into my skin. Back down the road, the sentry called out to his missing partner. I didn't have much time.

I smacked at the flat of his blade, knocking it away. As he swung it back, I kicked him in the groin. He dropped his sword. I rolled left but he flopped on top of me. I struggled beneath him. He recovered from the shock I'd given him and grasped my throat with both hands. He knocked my head against the road, once, twice, three times.

My vision blurred. I couldn't breathe. In another few seconds I'd be gone. The part of me that didn't think, that acted on pure survival instinct, took over. The cold blasted through me.

The hands at my throat spasmed once then relaxed into

death. The weight of the body pinned me to the earth.

In the ensuing quiet, I heard the man at the guard hut returning up the road towards me. I heaved myself out from beneath the body, placing a rock next to the man's head that I hoped the remaining sentry would think fell down and brained his partner. I scuttled away.

I didn't stand upright again until I rounded a small outcropping and felt safely out of sight of the lookout's gaze. Then I ran, putting as much distance between me and pursuit as possible. With any luck they'd search the immediate area, find no one, and, without a mark on the man's body to prove violence, chalk up their loss to accident.

But it had been no accident. What if each person I killed counted against me with the Fates? Given that they turned me into a shade as punishment, murder would certainly count as a crime worthy of further retribution. Would they see this as murder? I was only defending myself …

I didn't think the Fates would begrudge me the right to save myself. If I'd killed him with that rock, it would be self-defense. His soul would take the normal path to the Far Gates. But when I ripped his essence from him, did he get the chance to return to the Cycle? I couldn't know for sure, but I didn't think so. And that worried me. That the Fates would see using my shade power on humans instead of daemons as a perversion of their will.

I risked a glance back behind me, but no pursuit followed. The Gherza must cross the Barrier Range via a different route—though they still traveled well ahead of me, no alarm had sounded here. It explained how they'd gotten all the way to the Grey holdings without raising any hue and cry.

The peaks rose cliff-like ahead of me, the road and the river at the bottom of a narrow chasm between them. I followed the now-shallow incline of the path, the high walls petering out towards morning. Large fir and pine stubbled the bare, rocky slope.

The road climbed a small ridge while the river curved round it. I crested the ridge, and the Aramar Plateau spread out before me. A large lake glittered like liquid topaz in the dawn.

The strange disjointed sense of the almost remembered filled me once again at the sight—the scene familiar but not. The land rolled away from the lakeshore in a patchwork quilt of thick forest and swatches cut bare. The Clan loggers favored easy terrain, so steeper sections tended to remain treed. On the lake I spotted teams of men preparing log booms for transport to the river mouth. Yet my inner sight rebelled and kept superimposing an infinite carpet of trees over the land.

I scanned the landscape. There. An uneven line clear of trees snaked out of the Barrier Range to the south of the river. It reached the shores of the lake and spread like a blight to either side. I couldn't see the individual trees vanishing, but a shivering at the edge of the forest told me where the beetle incursion ate away at the Clan's treasure.

I stood on the northern bank of the River Grell. Just a bit farther on, it curved northward to meet the lake, which lay on a tilted north-south axis on the plateau. The Gherza had crossed the river, heading farther westward.

Here where it lazily left the lake before becoming a torrent in the chasm, I forded the Grell easily, staying out of sight of the log drivers. Within an hour my track intersected that of the beetles.

Up close, the devastation was total. Here and there they left a tree dead, its needles brown and drooping, trunk gaping open, flesh exposed to the world like a half-eaten apple. But for the most part, the trees were simply gone, erased from the earth as though they'd never existed, little heaps of needles the only sign any living thing ever grew upon the terrain.

I took a little detour to the lakeshore, to find the expanding wave of insects. I could hear them: a sound easily mistaken for the rustle of wind in the branches, except no breeze stirred the day. The high-pitched crunching reminded me of feet walking on dry leaves in autumn.

The trail of destruction ended where the waves teased the rocky shore. Trees shivered to either side of the scarred earth, and the swath widened. I stepped up to the bole of a quivering tree.

A lone beetle crawled on the outside of the tree, although I knew thousands must gnaw within. I speared the insect on the tip of my knife. Grey ichor oozed from its shell, and its legs thrashed as I examined it.

Aside from the iridescence on its shell, it looked like an ordinary beetle. But Iril brought it into this world with the staff, and I wondered if it bore any similarity to the other being she'd used the staff to embody: me. I couldn't remember seeing a creature like it in the middle realm, but strange things stalked the planes, and even during my long stay between the realms, I had yet to meet all of them.

Was it a daemon? Daemons fed on the souls of the newly dead, and I discharged my duty as a shade by fighting them. But

274

daemons exuded power in and of themselves. This creature lay almost helpless without its brethren.

I risked touching it with a finger. I felt nothing until my skin brushed against the glistening ichor, and then I hissed. A faint malevolence jolted the hairs on my arm upright. I speared the insect to the ground and recoiled.

I didn't know how she'd done it, but it was a soul. Transmuted into a hideous shape, bearing no resemblance to its original form, small and shrunken, but still a soul. A human soul.

But where did it come from? The only souls in the middle realm walked it as shades; the recently dead just passed through on their voyage to the far planes. Iril couldn't have found enough of them to drag them back in the numbers now attacking the trees. And a shade should have come back embodied like me, shouldn't it?

And then it hit me. The only kind of soul left: the kind the Fates deemed irredeemable. The souls that would never see the far planes, were never given even the limited existence allowed a shade.

According to shade lore, the Fates trapped these souls, purified them by stripping them of all that made them human, and returned their energy to the Great Cycle to nourish the earth.

I avoided the place in the middle realm where the Fates kept the Irredeemed. It reminded me too much of my own failings.

And now Iril had found a way to exploit the Irredeemed herself. I shuddered at the implications.

What she'd done to me was unnatural, and I still had little inkling of what sort of imbalance she'd created by her meddling with the laws of death. But unleashing thousands of the

Irredeemed in this insect form must have devastating implications. What attracted them to the trees? And when they'd exhausted the trees, what would they feed on next?

I glared at the beetle I'd impaled on my knife. Its legs still thrashed, the knife wound not enough to do it in. I wondered what would happen if I killed it. Theoretically it was already dead, but perhaps I could end its existence in this embodied form. I considered just crushing it under my heel, but hesitated. Iril brought it here with a powerful token—the staff. I had no idea how much power kept it here. A little caution might be warranted.

I drew my sword, and, standing as far away from the beetle as possible, lopped its head from its thorax.

A tremendous soundless blast blew me off my feet. I bounced off a rock, and my head cracked the ground hard on the rebound. I blacked out.

"Unh—" I came to, my head pounding as though crushed beneath a horse's hooves. I spit dirt from my mouth. It took me a few moments to reorient myself.

The tree I'd pulled the beetle from now lay on its side, its trunk split open with beetles pouring out. A small crater scarred the earth where I'd killed my sample insect. There was no sign of my dagger. My sword turned up behind a small boulder, the blade's steel tip sheared off. I touched it, and small pieces of metal crumbled off. The beetle itself had vanished.

Well. So they were killable, but not in any practical sense. And getting rid of them all at once might do irreparable harm to the surroundings.

I didn't want to think of the implications of my little experiment for my own return to the middle realm. I banished the beetle from this plane, but I had no idea where it wound up. Any one of a number of possibilities suggested themselves. It either retook its place in the middle realm waiting for its return to the Great Cycle—with luck, the ordeal I put it through qualified it for re-evaluation before the Judge. Or its unnatural end sent it to oblivion, and I snuffed out its existence for all time.

Nothing in my current meager arsenal would help me combat the beetles, so I concentrated on that which I could do something about first.

Farther to the west, the plateau dropped to flat, golden plain. The Gherza lay that way, and so went I.

~*~

The damn Gherza traveled fast. After crossing the pass and coming down from the Aramar Plateau, I traveled at night to avoid the worst of the heat and the inquisitive eyes of several shepherds trying to eke out an existence. Not that I saw any pasture capable of supporting much of a flock. The long steppe grasses my mind wanted to conjure up didn't exist here—only some scraggly scrub eking out what little moisture it could from the parched earth. I'd expected a rich, fertile land, and instead, found one on the verge of famine.

On the way down from the plateau, where I thought to find large forests of tall polegrass, the slopes were bare. Patches of dried husks creaked in the hot winds. I heard an occasional snap as a segment of dead polegrass broke off. In other spots, burned stubbly stumps attested to large fires scorching their way through. Withered weeds struggled to reclaim the slopes, but the dust my passage raised convinced me that only an extended rainfall could slake the earth's thirst, and that hadn't happened in a while.

I struggled to stay ahead of the Clan host that I knew made its way behind me through the passes. Shirra could buy me a day or two at best. Traveling alone gave me a slight speed advantage, but didn't guarantee I'd get to the staff first. The pendant at least told me where to go, whereas I assumed the host relied on scouts to determine the direction of their hunt.

My tracking led me to a tiny oasis on the edge of the Gherza's drought-scorched lands. The sun hammered down on my head as I crouched behind the shelter of a boulder, surveying the Gherza settlement. Little more than a camp with a few temporary pens for animals, it nevertheless hummed with activity in the searing heat.

I slumped against the boulder. A tiny wildflower clung to life in the shade at its base. I reached out to stroke its creamy petals— a struggling symbol of vitality in this barren wasteland.

My frustration mounted with my thirst as I staked out the settlement. Though the pendant told me the staff lay down there, I couldn't figure out how to infiltrate the place without being seen. In daylight, women bustled among the tents, hand-milling grain, milking goats, or washing laundry. At night, the herding dogs barked at the slightest sound. The tribe posted a guard at the small oasis. A dire drought indeed if the old Gherza tradition of water sharing had fallen by the wayside.

I contemplated my options, with the pendant at my neck pulsing against my brand. The staff lay very near. I peered around the boulder again and searched the camp for activity.

Everything looked normal. No approaching riders. No tribesmen arrayed on the slope looking for me. Except ... a woman rode a galloping horse down the trail leading back towards the plateau. Her golden hair blazed in the sunlight, betraying a lack of Gherza blood. Puzzled, I frowned. Was that Shirra? What was going—

"Ouch!"

I whipped around, pain from whatever jabbed me spreading through my shoulder blade. So absorbed in the camp, I hadn't heard my stalker sneak up on me: the Gherza who'd faced down Iril when she'd lost the staff and taken Fayne. I muttered a silent prayer to the Fates. —*Please let this be the man you told me about.*

His garb differed from the usual dun or black robes of the tribesmen. He wore a colorful linen patchwork robe. Black eyes gazed out at me from his sun-lined face—the tribe Izir. He held the staff pointed at my chest, using it to keep me at bay.

"You will rise," he said. "Slowly."

I did as he said.

"Turn around."

I faced the camp, and he prodded me in the back with the rod. Somehow I expected to feel something from the staff when it touched me, but nothing happened. We marched down the hill to the settlement. I slipped once on the loose shale but my sure-footed captor poked me forward again. Curious Gherza stared at me as I trudged past the tents. We stopped in front of one at the far end and the Izir flipped back the flaps at the entrance with one hand, all the while keeping me at staff's-length. I ducked into the tent.

It took my eyes a few moments to adjust to the sudden dimness. The tent contained no chairs, just a sleeping pad and layers of frayed carpet and faded red and gold cushions.

"Sit," the Izir ordered.

I lowered myself to the floor. He circled around me and sat down cross-legged on the sleeping pallet.

"You are an abomination," he said.

"Do I know you?" I countered. How could he know anything about me?

"No, but the staff does."

"Is everyone a necromancer around here?"

The man hissed. "Don't equate me with that witch. I follow the teachings of my father and his father before him. They deal in life, not death." He shook the staff. "This made you. I can feel it. You do not live."

"I didn't ask for this."

"No, but your very presence endangers the balance between the realms. Death follows you wherever you go."

"So why don't you just kill me?" I asked.

"It's not as simple as that."

"It never is." But this man intrigued me. He seemed to understand quite a bit about death and the far realms. Maybe instead of stealing the staff from him right away, I should take the time to pick his brain. As a shade, I knew only what I needed to perform my function as guide. Here, I was as a blind person feeling her way through a complicated maze.

"What happens if you kill me?"

"For you: most likely oblivion. For this world ... I'm uncertain. I fear one of two things—either the violence of your departure sowing destruction and death, or the opening of a permanent gateway to the realms of death. You will agree, neither is in the interests of the living."

No. Beings worse than me prowled the planes between the

realms. The creatures I was made to kill. After what occurred when I'd exterminated the beetle, the Izir's words rang true. Had Iril's threat to end me been empty, then? Or did she think her powers up to the challenge my death might present?

"Does Iril know this?"

The Izir spat. "Reckless necromancer. She acts without thought for the consequences of her actions."

Reckless, maybe. But she didn't strike me as stupid. Iril must have a few holes in her understanding of what she'd done. Or she'd been bluffing.

"And if I stay?"

"If you stay, I fear Iril will use your power to create more death. I'm not sure how, yet. But she brought you here for a reason, and if I know Iril, it has nothing to do with peace and reconciliation."

"I could kill her." Not with my power, maybe, but any one of a number of more traditional methods would render her just as dead.

"And the spell that keeps you embodied might die with her. With unpredictable consequences, without the staff."

So, this then, was the cost of Iril's sacrilege. Widespread death and destruction. All because of me. I thought of Fayne. How I could never stay with him. He could never hide me from Iril, and I'd never be able to protect him from her. I'd prepared myself for leaving him, but a part of me still daydreamed of defeating Iril and perhaps staying in the mortal realm. That idle fantasy now lay just as dead as I truly was.

Outside, a female voice argued with someone at the entrance of the tent. "… but I must see him." The sure confidence, with a hint of arrogance, confirmed my earlier suspicions: Shirra. Mounted, she'd managed to catch up to my slower hiking pace.

She poked her head inside the tent. Her eyes widened when she saw me.

"Not now, *sha'zara*," the Izir said.

"But the Clan host …" Shirra insisted.

"Not now!"

Shirra ducked out. *Sha'zara*, he'd said. Daughter? Shirra couldn't possibly be his daughter. *You know all about fathers using daughters to further their plans.*

The stray thought tickled at my memories. The Clans and the Gherza. Rhinn caught between Garrith Grey and Braith of Dayr's wishes for an alliance and Lian's love. Errith the victim of another man's plotting. And what of me? Something told me someone used me as pawn as well, long, long ago. But if Shirra was Gherza —I hissed. This explained how the Gherza knew Iril's whereabouts that night. Fayne told Shirra, and Shirra somehow got word to the Gherza.

And also … a Gherza father. My heart hitched. The Fates told me true!

I felt trapped between two peoples, unsure where my loyalties, if any, should lie. The Clans remained hostile to the Gherza, yet Fayne believed they could be allies instead. The Gherza opposed Iril, and that also made us allies. But so far, the Izir didn't act too friendly. I couldn't blame him, given his opinion of the threat, no matter how inadvertent, I represented to his people. All people. Yet I required the staff, and I knew he wouldn't just give it to me.

The Izir's attention remained on the opening where Shirra disappeared. I launched myself at him, knocking the staff from his hands as I flattened him. I picked it up and jabbed it into his sternum. It would be so easy to just kill him and run.

"Why do you need the staff?" I asked instead. "It's not just to keep it from Iril, is it?"

The Izir stared back up at me. "If we can cleanse its taint, perhaps the abundance of the steppe will return."

The scent of tall grasses baking in the sun flickered through my memory. So my imagination didn't betray me—this region once grew fertile.

"But the staff can also send me back. Back to the realms." If it brought me here, it could reverse its own effects.

"Is that what you want?"

The question unnerved me. Since I awoke on the shores of the river, I'd been focused on first remembering, and then finding a way to keep my power out of Iril's hands. She yanked me into the world against my will, and forced me into damaging my own mind to thwart her. Fayne initially agreed to drag me around the countryside only because my goals aligned with his, and he wanted to keep an eye on me. And now because of how I felt for him, because of the thinnest of hints from the Fates, I'd chased the Gherza because I thought it my only play in a game I didn't understand.

So busy focusing on each current predicament, I'd lost myself in the process.

From his position pinned beneath me, the Izir's beady black eyes studied my face. His expression never changed, but I sensed —not a softening within him—an ever so slight a shift in his demeanor. Like I'd passed some test I didn't even know I was taking.

I wanted …

"Forgive me," I whispered.

"That is not for me to do," he replied.

"Then who?"

He shrugged, and against my better judgment I let him sit up. "The Fates? We Gherza believe each of us responsible for cleansing our own souls. If you lay your soul open before She Who Sees, speak the truth in your heart to He Who Hears, only then can you expect mercy from The One Who Speaks. One who hides from herself is not worthy, not ready to complete the Cycle. To face the Fates, you must face your past, face yourself. What do you fear the most?"

That I'll always be a shade. Hovering between life and death. Never again allowed to feel. Never permitted to move on. Enslaved by my own mistakes, and condemned always to watch others complete the natural Cycle.

The Izir correctly interpreted my silence. "Do you know why the Fates create shades?" he asked.

"I must have committed a great crime."

"You don't remember?"

I told him how I'd eluded Iril's grasp.

"Effective," he commented, "but not very practical. The Fates mete out punishment in many ways. Most get the opportunity to redeem themselves in the next Cycle. It is said, even killers may pass beyond the planes, although our lore scrolls tell us the Fates usually return them to the earth. We Gherza believe it takes a special kind of person for the Fates to single out as a shade."

You always were special, my inner voice sneered.

"Tell me something I don't know, old man." I couldn't tear

my eyes from his, even though I dreaded his next words.

"Some say, only one who never truly loved becomes a shade."

His words sank like stones in the fathomless pool of my heart. According to him, its depths unplumbed.

I laughed. "Then the Fates picked a fine punishment," I retorted, thinking of my almost emotionless existence beyond the mortal plane. The solitude that muffled me in a veil of, not loneliness, but a longing for a contact I couldn't define. The infinite time stretching before me punctuated only by my regular forays to the gates of the living.

Each of these encounters deepened my isolation. Performing my duty as guide to the far realms reminded me of what I had lost, my brief contact with each person's essence limited to the time necessary to protect it from the more sinister creatures stalking the middle realms. Each essence hummed with an energy my own lacked, a light I tried to replicate but could not spark to life within me, for want of what, I never understood.

But then, what of Fayne? Was this what drew me to him? Some inner instinct for salvation? And if so, was what I felt really love?

My thoughts turned to Iril and her belief in the "unrequited." How easily could the interpretation become twisted with the telling? A love not reciprocated often turned into something darker. Something that forced the Fates to create a shade.

"A fine theory," I said, "but I don't see how my loving someone helps. Not if that love can never be consecrated."

"I cannot tell you how to change your fate. But I fear there is only one way for you to return to the middle realm without endangering us here. And it is barred to you."

Perfect. "Explain."

"You must reverse Iril's spell. But if the staff made you, then you likely need it to do so. I believe its past taints it too much for you to use in this way. Regardless, I will foul it so badly for you that it will never do your bidding."

He's bluffing. "You said yourself I'm a danger to you if I stay."

"I can't risk the staff falling back into Iril's hands. You are still somewhat of an unknown quantity. But Iril with the staff at her disposal, that is a certainty I fear more."

"I don't intend to let her have it." Though I hadn't quite worked out how to keep it away from her and still save Fayne.

"Why should I believe you? Do you know why Iril wants it?"

"No. All I know is that it's a token of power."

"Yes, but a broken and imperfect one. Iril bears responsibility for the staff's desecration. She will do worse if she's allowed to study it further. She holds fast to old grievances with both the Gherza and the Clans. She'll use the Clans to take out her revenge on us. The staff isn't a weapon. Ignorance and misplaced desire twisted its history and use. Once we cleanse it we can maybe restore the steppe."

"So what's stopping you?"

"Only one deeply tied to the original corruption can remove it. Which means only Iril can do it, and she would do anything but. Our beliefs forbid us from practicing her kind of magic. The cost is too high. So we must settle for keeping it out of her hands, unless, Fates permitting, we find another way."

"Why didn't you take it from the Clans long ago? Why leave it where she could steal it?"

"The Clans guarded it too carefully. After we learned Iril stole it we felt emboldened enough to enter Clan lands to retrieve it."

I pressed the staff into his sternum. "You're not in any position to stop me just leaving with it."

He grabbed the end of the staff. "No? You will need to kill me for it. Iril has done too much harm with it already. We saw the beetles. Your own presence upsets the balance between the planes. We can't leave it with her. She would only do more damage." He stared straight into my eyes. "This also I swear: I will die holding the staff in my hands. I will not let go."

I laughed in his face.

"My death curse will make the staff useless to you and Iril forever," he said.

I yank on the staff. He smiled. And held on.

Kill him. Who knew what the Fates would make of that? Up to now, I'd only killed to defend myself. But if I killed the Izir it would be a cold, intentional murder. Snuffing out the Izir's life surely weighed against me on the scales of redemption. Would I throw away my one chance to ever be more than a shade? But sparing the Izir might sentence Fayne to death at Iril's hands—a poor way to prove my love.

And now this death curse! If I killed the Izir, I could bring the staff back to Iril. How would she know I'd rendered it useless? I'd save Fayne, but at the cost of never getting back to the middle realm. I'd have to spend the rest of my life hiding from Iril's vengeance, but in the end, would that be so bad? Alive, and feeling, but alone? My physical body would die naturally at some point, wouldn't it? And I'd either go back to the middle realm or nowhere. *Or open a daemon gate.*

My hand trembled holding the staff. —*Come on, Umbra, choose, and choose well,* I urged myself. *Because you're so well known for your wise choices,* my inner voice answered. *There's no reason to believe his tale. He's in league with Shirra. He's bluffing.* Maybe the staff itself would spare me the choice, confer protection on the Izir as it did to Iril. Mocking my hope, the brand cooled at my throat. It had already chosen for me. A shard of ice froze my chest beneath the pendant. Smoke leached from my fingertips, reaching for the old man.

The Izir tensed as he felt the tug on his soul. His eyes rolled back in his head. Still he didn't let go of the staff. He sighed out a long breath. In it, I heard the thready vowels of his curse. The whorls on the staff writhed once, twice. The wood jangled against my palms, jolting and crawling, like the staff itself thrust splinters into my skin. Through the pain, I felt at one with its foulness.

Recognized it.

And made my choice.

THEN

"Tell me of this promise ceremony." Murran said to Kairiya. They sat in a small glade. She took him here hoping to avoid prying eyes while she schooled him in Gherza tradition.

Kairiya sighed. "It is where your bride presents you with her finger dance."

"Finger dance?"

"Most Gherza girls live and breathe the art of the finger dance."

"And you don't?"

Kairiya ignored his question. "Gherza women show off their finger dances at all family and ceremonial occasions. It's a language of its own. Jezarel creates hers as her pledge to you. Of love. Loyalty. A bride spends years preparing and developing the unique gestures for her marriage dance. She offers it as her gift to her future husband, performed only once, at the promise ceremony."

"And if I accept it, we're married?"

"Yes."

"Show me."

"I am not your bride."

289

"Not the promise finger dance. You said there are many. Show me an example."

Kairiya felt flustered. She had watched Asrar perform her dances for Orrith countless times. But she always rebuffed Asrar's attempts to teach her. Or acted clumsy when Asrar forced her to practice.

Gherza traditions hindered her acceptance into Orrith's Clan. Kairiya needed to show twice as much loyalty to Clan ways as any Clanswoman, if she hoped to ever find a husband of her own. Except that she spent so much time learning the sword to please her father, that she never mastered the reels the Clan girls danced to draw the eyes of suitors.

At least skill with the sword held value in the eyes of certain Clansmen: the landless who traveled the dangerous roads between Clanholds, eking out a living during the olive and lavender harvests, or those given crofts near the borders between Clanholds—the fractious rival Clans settling claims by raids or the battle rite of the Fates.

What had Asrar's Gherza wiles gotten her? A bastard daughter, a rude shack on the outskirts of the village, and a reputation for witchery.

Murran watched her. For once, Kairiya saw a man looking on her not as the witch's bastard, but with a strange earnestness. It almost undid her. She who had hidden behind her sword and her toughness for almost as long as she could remember. And now he wanted her to finger dance!

Kairiya raised a trembling hand. Summoned the steps her mother showed her so long ago. Closed her eyes. Willed grace into her fingers. Imagined enjoying Murran's fingers dancing across her skin.

Instinct coursing through her, her movement melded the forms she practiced for the sword with the intricate whorls and gestures of the finger dance. She danced without thinking, putting all her raw longing into the movement of her hands and body.

She heard Murran draw in a sharp breath, and stopped. Opened her eyes.

Murran gazed back at her with frightening intensity. Kairiya knew if she was to do what Jezarel wanted of her, it should be now. Every nerve under her skin crawled with the desire to feel his hands on her. But Kairiya didn't want Murran on Jezarel's terms.

She cleared her throat. "So there it is. The finger dance."

Murran didn't take his eyes from her face. Kairiya looked away from his burning stare. Frowned when a shadow moved across the bole of a tree.

She looked back at Murran, and the truth of what she just saw registered in her mind. She launched herself at the sitting Murran. Her tackle bowled him over backwards, but she didn't stop. Gripping his shoulder hard, she rolled and yanked him with her behind the safety of a boulder. She heard the arrow whizzing into the empty space they just vacated.

"It's not every day I get women throwing themselves at me like this," Murran said. His lips tickled her ear. Kairiya would have liked nothing more than to stopper his mouth with her own, but she pushed him off her and directed his attention to the still quivering arrow.

In silence, Kairiya pointed across the glade. Nothing lurked there now, thought she heard the muffled thud of footsteps running away. Murran motioned her to stay put. He crawled away. Kairiya caught sight of him again when he rose from his crouch near a tree. He stared at something on the ground, and waved her over. Kairiya ripped the arrow out of the ground where it had landed before joining him.

"Which of us do you think was the target?" Murran asked as he examined the set of footprints on the ground.

Kairiya hadn't even considered a target other than Murran. As far as she knew, she had no enemies here. "Gherza fletching." The part of her still subservient to her father's will kicked itself. She just prevented what her father sent her here to do: kill Murran and make it look like the Gherza did it. And she could have walked away guilt free, yet still a good daughter in Orrith's eyes. "Someone doesn't want the wedding to go ahead."

Murran caged her against the tree, one of his arms on the trunk to each side of her.

"And what if that person is me?" Murran whispered.

Kairiya felt a tightness in her chest. She couldn't look at him. His breath feathered ever so softly against her cheek.

"You would call it off?" she asked.

"You gave me a gift back there," he said.

"I couldn't let you die."

"I'm talking about the dance." Murran reached down, his fingers searching out hers.

She needed an answer to her question, though. It changed everything. "I don't want to hide … this. Us. Will you make an honorable woman of me?"

"Don't worry, Kairiya."

Then he kissed her, and drew Kairiya into a different kind of dance. One of shed clothing and warm skin against skin. Let Orrith rage. She no longer cared what he thought.

~*~

Jezarel watched the barbarian perform his ritual. The entire tribe arrayed themselves behind her and her parents, facing the shoreline of the lake. The Clansmen also sat in a group facing the lake, to their left. Murran stood on the cropped grass near the water, focused on the ceremony—a Clan custom meant to signal his rejection of all others in favor of her.

Normally she'd chafe at sitting through yet another boring rite. But her father agreed to blend traditions between the two peoples, and without this one Jezarel might be going straight to the promise ceremony. And she was just not ready.

A piper played a lilting melody, accompanied by another man on a drum. Women of Murran's people danced in strange mincing steps in a circle about him. One by one they moved towards him with proffered gifts, each of which he cast aside. She couldn't blame him—none of them looked capable of performing a competent finger dance. Their linen finery hid any inkling of shape or desirability. These hags would tempt no man in his right mind. She wondered if the Clans aimed some slight at her—presented with better specimens, might he go back on his word?

She kept her features neutral. She didn't want anyone to know that the ritual fascinated her despite herself. She had maintained an air of injured outrage since the delegation arrived. She wanted everyone to know she would not enter into this marriage willingly. Yet her initial anger at Kairiya for spoiling her bowshot had turned to relief. It was a stupid idea. Had she succeeded and the truth come out, she would never have lived down the consequences.

Her anger at her father's betrayal, compounded by the slaughter of the cliff lion and her desperation as the promise ceremony drew closer without any visible results from Kairiya pushed her close to the edge. Too close—she saw that now. But as she sighted the arrow at Murran's chest, she felt liberation from her helplessness and grief. She was finally doing something—something to avenge Javeen's death, something to take her future into her own hands.

But with the calm of hindsight, she recognized the cost would have been too high. If Kairiya did manage to seduce Murran—and yesterday's finger dance looked like progress—some blame would fall upon Murran himself, preserving the tribe's honor. Her father already believed Javeen had shamed the tribe through his own rash action. That reminder shifted the tide of anger within her: she would not be the second child of her father to bring shame upon them.

Having escaped one type of shame, she kept herself awake last night contemplating another: her own mortification at being given to the barbarian. She wondered if only she felt this way. The rest of the tribe treated her like some kind of heroine, the women fussing so much over her that she hardly had a moment to herself. Her father thought he did her a great honor by making her the symbol of peace between the Clansmen and the Gherza.

Had she overreacted? Let her anger at Javeen's death cloud her judgment? What other match within the Gherza could be as important to all the tribes' well-being as this one? She still couldn't imagine married life with the barbarian. And yet, as she watched him, the lake water limning him with reflected sunlight, something intrigued her about this Murran. An exotic confidence. A simple honesty. She knew that if he gave of himself to a woman, it would be his all.

Jezarel's thoughts turned again to Javeen. He'd hated the Clansmen's incursions so much that he'd gathered up a small group of like-thinkers and gone after the last raiding party. Against their father's orders. Against all common sense, though what boy didn't believe in his own invulnerability?

Javeen's anger brought him only death, and his family only grief. Her father's words niggled at her. Hadn't she herself feared for Javeen, tried to talk him out of it? She'd known Javeen was making the wrong decision.

Jezarel studied the hard planes of Murran's face, and saw mirrored there the hard walls around her own heart. What if she let Murran in? Jezarel's choice might mean no one else's hotheaded brother would have to die. There was not a little honor in sacrificing one's own happiness for the greater good. And who knew? Perhaps in time Murran's charms would grow on her.

She shifted her gaze to Kairiya, who appeared enthralled with the ritual. Jezarel returned her attention to Murran, and saw him glance at Kairiya. Jezarel sucked in a gasp as it hit her: he *had* given of himself to a woman.

So Kairiya succeeded in her task. Something must have happened after Jezarel fled. Jezarel knew she should be happy. When she made the truth known, it would free her of her obligation under the new treaty. A treaty whose value Jezarel now appreciated better.

A twinge of jealousy shot through her heart. Part of her did not think Kairiya would prevail, hence Jezarel's own misguided attempt on his life. After all, what wiles could a girl like Kairiya— a mongrel bastard—have at her disposal to attract a man to her over Jezarel?

Jezarel had not thought her plan through. The tribe would ridicule her when the truth came out. The Izir's daughter, incapable of securing her man against a half-breed's simple incursion? Jezarel's cheeks went hot. She would force Kairiya to call it off.

NOW

I made my choice, and with a gasp, for the first time found the strength to push the coldness away. The Izir's chest rose and fell, and he looked at me, clear eyed. I couldn't kill him, not on purpose. Not without knowing he'd be returned to the Cycle. Not even to save Fayne. I wanted to cry. Fates, how would I rescue Fayne now?

The Izir smiled. "You felt it."

"Your death curse? That's not what saved you." I'd reeled as the staff invaded me, its foulness seeking out a profane answer within me. As though it wanted to become one with me. But that wasn't what stopped me. He'd done nothing to me, and I couldn't, wouldn't trade his life for Fayne's. Did that mean I didn't love Fayne enough?

"There was no death curse, child." He'd bluffed me! "No, it was the original taint! Didn't you feel the staff respond to you? Don't you see?" the Izir asked. I held my breath. He continued. "Iril blundered when she brought you to the mortal realm, in more ways than one. Of all the shades in the middle realm, why do you suppose the staff chose you?"

I stared at the rod in my hands, not liking the implication of intelligence on its part. The whorled grain and knots drew my eye, the pattern searing itself into my retina. My brand pulsed once. I let the staff go as quickly as if I'd found an uncoiled snake in my palms. "Chose me?"

"The staff—it wouldn't resonate like that unless you were tied to it. My guess: to its original corruption. With a bond of blood, lies, and death. But not a recent one. I must take you to the Blighted Vale."

Not the vale! The word stabbed at my heart. For the first time I wondered if I'd really stolen my memories to keep my identity from Iril, or to avoid facing the pain in my own past.

I took a deep breath and glared at the Izir. "I don't have time to go anywhere with you. A friend needs my help. And I need the staff to give them that help."

"You don't have much choice in the matter. I doubt you can use the staff while it stays fouled. Iril's warped magic gives her some control, but you would need the staff whole and pure to send yourself back to the middle realm. But if you are tied to its defilement, you can cleanse it."

How convenient. The one thing he needs to get his steppe back. I couldn't blame him, though. I felt myself wilting as the oppressive sun squeezed any hint of coolness out of the tent. The Gherza barely subsisted. The Clans kicked them off their winter grazing lands on the Aramar Plateau and the steppe was dying. All because of whatever sullied the staff. *Because you tainted it.*

It would explain too much. My affinity for the staff. Why I knew Iril. But not what Iril planned. If I'd desecrated the staff, if that caused the drought, then I'd caused all this misery. No wonder the Fates made me into a shade. I shook off the thought and latched onto another.

"How do I accomplish this cleansing?"

"I don't know. I think you already do, but you locked the knowledge away from yourself. Now—will you help us?"

"Only if you promise to give me the staff afterward."

"You may take from the vale whatever the vale wishes for you to keep."

Something about his wording bothered me. "I'll take the staff, and you'll let me."

The Izir stared me down. He knew he had me. I couldn't leave without the staff. I couldn't kill him. But he'd give me what I wanted if I performed this task for him. I didn't like it. Every minute I wasted on this chase meant leaving Fayne under Iril's influence that much longer. I feared the damage to his mind. But what if the only way to save Fayne involved fixing the staff?

"Where's this vale?" I asked.

"On the Aramar Plateau."

So be it. I'd go with him to the vale, or at least pretend to. To get back to Fayne, I needed to head for the plateau anyway. I'd abscond with the staff at the first opportunity. I doubted that I'd know what to do with the staff at the vale, anyway. I reached out to help the Izir to his feet. "The beetles. Do you know what they are?" He shook his head. I told him my theory about the Irredeemed. "Do you know of a way to fight them?"

"No, but I came here to consult with the other tribal Izirs. I will leave word for them to gather on the plateau to save what little we can. We cannot leave the beetles unchecked. Perhaps when you unlock the secrets of the staff you will find a way to eradicate them."

The tent flaps rustled and Shirra's head intruded. I became aware of a commotion outside.

"Apologies, Izir," she said. "But the barbarians are upon us and you must strike camp."

I wondered how Fayne would react to a sorry band of goatherds calling the Clans barbarians. The Gherza had fallen far from what I thought I knew about their station. But I didn't have time to ponder further. The Izir grabbed a hip bag, strapping it to his waist, and thrust me outside.

"Shirra, we go to the vale. Find us mounts while I tell the tribe where to rally the Izirs."

He hurried from the tent. We had no time to waste. Clan warriors poured down the rocky hillside.

Women in dusty robes gathered up goats and children alike, abandoning tents and scurrying to find what shelter they could. They would be hard pressed to make it to the distant ravine system I heard them yelling about and lose the Clansmen in the gullies.

I had my own escape to make, and better for me if the Clans didn't notice me. That went double for Shirra, who played a deeper game than I'd given her credit for. I grabbed a dusty tan robe from a pile of unwashed laundry. Wrapping it around me, I did my best to blend in. The Izir stopped another Gherza and spat out orders.

The horde of Clansmen howled down on the encampment in a billowing cloud of dust—their arrival easy to mistake for a sandstorm if not for their raging screams. We would never outflank them on foot, so I searched the camp for mounts. The first horsemen already rampaged through the outer ring of tents.

We'd never reach the horse pickets in time.

"Izir!"

I whirled to the right. Shirra held three mounts. She'd tucked her golden hair under a large hood, to keep it from standing out like a beacon among the fleeing Gherza. The Izir vaulted onto a roan gelding. Shirra held out the reins of a dun-colored mare. I snatched them from her and swung up onto the horse, bareback. Shirra might not be trustworthy but she and the Izir now constituted my best way out of here.

"Follow me," she shouted.

I kicked my horse after her as she galloped away. The Izir tucked the staff under his arm, bringing up the rear. I glanced over my shoulder to check on the attackers. And nearly fell off my horse in surprise. For Fayne burst out of the swirling dust astride a black stallion.

I slowed my horse, wondering if he'd somehow escaped Iril's influence. Surely she couldn't control him at such a distance.

Shirra looked back. Spotting Fayne, she paled and turned her face away. "Hurry, he mustn't see me!" she said, veering her mount between one of the many tents the Gherza had abandoned.

Don't trust the spy. I shook my head. For that's what Shirra must be—a Gherza spy. Or a Clanswoman the Gherza somehow turned to their cause. I twisted once more in my saddle. Fayne had closed to within thirty paces. His eyes held no concern for me. Instead, everything that made his face handsome to me vanished as he glimpsed the staff in the Izir's hands. His features contorted in an ugly look of triumph. And then Lian appeared behind him.

Fates! Iril still controlled events. I feared her reason to send Fayne in after me had something to do with the instrument of my death. I raced after Shirra.

I urged my horse down a dust-filled lane between tents, the Izir trailing. Behind me, Fayne's stallion clattered ever closer. Our own little mares were no match for his well-fed steed—he was gaining. Shirra reached the edge of the camp, her horse leaping over the goat pens. If we could just make it past the low ridge a bit farther, we might lose the Clans in the dry gullies and arroyos that cleft this area before it flattened out into desert.

The Izir gave his mount its head and it caught up to me. Out of the corner of my eye, I saw Fayne's horse's nose bobbing beside the Izir's. Fayne leaned over. The Izir slashed at Fayne's arm with a small leather crop. Fayne, undeterred—a soul that couldn't feel his pain driving him from afar—grabbed the Izir's wrist.

"Here! Take it! It mustn't fall into their hands." The Izir tossed the staff between our two horses. I snatched it out of the air.

With Fayne grasping his wrist, the throw unbalanced the Izir. He hurtled to the ground. In the headlong gallop, I didn't see him land. I flicked a glance behind me, saw him writhing on the earth. Lian reined his mount in sharply, its hooves kicking up dust as it skidded to a halt.

"No!" Shirra screamed, as Lian vaulted to the ground beside the Izir.

I couldn't spare the scene any more of my attention, since I now played the rabbit to Fayne's hawk.

Fayne's horse drew even with mine. He bumped the mare,

who stumbled. Taking advantage of the small hitch in her stride, Fayne reached out and grabbed me. Without a saddle, I toppled sideways off the horse. Fayne gripped me hard. I hung for an instant between the two racing animals, before my mare careened off to the left.

Fayne heaved me away. I hit the ground with a grunt. The stallion's hooves flashed past my head, but Fayne threw me just far enough that the horse didn't trample me. The staff hit me hard in the ribs.

I tumbled away, winded.

Fayne wheeled his horse around. Lying on my side, my lungs hollow, desperately trying to draw a breath, I scrabbled at the desiccated earth. Hooves appeared in my field of view, and booted feet hit the ground with a small puff of dust. Pebbles scattered beneath my frantic fingers, and then I felt it—the staff. I clutched it to me and finally sucked in some air. But Fayne pinned the staff to the ground beneath his boot.

I rolled over onto my back, still gripping the staff. Fayne stared down at me, his lips drawn back around his teeth in something resembling a snarl. A sallow cast mottled his skin, and sickly yellow-grey now tinged the whites of his eyes. "Give it to me," he said.

A broach I'd never seen before, black stone inset into silver, clasped his cloak to his shoulder. Lian, standing over the Izir several paces away, wore a similar broach. Lian kicked the Izir in the ribs, then bent over him and rifled through the Gherza's hip pouch. The Izir resisted but Lian launched another kick at his temple. The Gherza lay still.

"Give it to me," Fayne said again.

"No." For this wasn't Fayne—Iril spoke with his voice, through his body. She still held him under her spell, or perhaps she'd given Lian the power to control him through the broach. I couldn't tell.

"Give it to us. Don't make me kill you again," Lian said. He pocketed something he'd taken from the Izir and mounted his horse.

Again? "What do you think you're doing, Lian?" I shot back with as much authority and contempt as I could muster.

Lian laughed and fingered the broach.

"How could you do this to your own brother?"

"You started it." Iril must have told him her theory about Rhinn. Ominous warnings went off in my head, despite my near certainty I wasn't her. Lian had loved Rhinn, and her betrayal stung him. Lian continued. "He won't remember a thing when it's all said and done. If Iril lets him live. Now let go of the staff." As Lian spoke, Fayne raised his boot above my hand. "I'll just make him crush your fingers if you don't."

"I won't give it to a puppet. I'll deliver it into her hands and no one else's. She and I had a bargain."

"If she's in a good mood, maybe you still do. You'll answer to me first, though. We're here to retrieve something else for Iril, but since you've fallen so conveniently into my hands, I'll avail myself of the opportunity to kill two foxes with one shaft."

A flicker of movement behind Lian was all the signal I got. Fayne's calf muscle tensed and his heel came smashing downwards. I heaved with all my strength, and rolled sideways. The staff rolled under his other heel. He lurched off balance. I whipped the staff behind his knee, and he pivoted over it, smacking down onto his back.

Lian's mount reared up, screaming, Shirra's dagger embedded in its neck. He struggled to control it, but the animal pitched over sideways, tangling itself in one of the tents. Grateful for Shirra's diversion, I didn't wait to see if Lian lay pinned beneath it. Fayne was already getting to his knees. I swung the staff around and cracked him in the temple. He fell back to the dirt, out cold.

I scrambled over to him. I'd reacted without thought, but now I feared I'd killed him. I relaxed as I felt a flutter at his throat. His chest rose and fell evenly, but I feared he would lose his hold on his body.

How much time could he spend sharing it with Iril before he gave up? I reached for the broach, prepared to smash it to bits, then reconsidered. What if breaking the link hurt Fayne? Iril implied something similar about breaking the unadulterated link between them, without the power of the staff. But I held the staff. I just had no idea how to use it.

I withdrew my hand and took a step away from him. In his weakened state, I couldn't risk a mistake loosening his hold on life even more.

Shirra spoke. "Leave him."

"We should help him."

"There's no time. He'll be safe with his own kind."

"And the Izir?"

Shirra's face twisted in grief. "I don't have the strength to lift him to a horse, do you?"

I shook my head.

"His life is in the Fates' hands now. We must fly."

I looked around me. Most of the Clan host followed the mass

of fleeing Gherza, with a few men like Fayne and Lian peeling off to look for stragglers. Clansmen would soon overwhelm the entire camp, and I couldn't let them find me with the staff. I needed time to figure out how to remove its corruption, time to discover how to free Fayne without hurting him in the process. There was nothing for it but to leave Fayne here, and find a spot safe from the Clan host where I could regroup and decide on a course of action.

"You have some explaining to do," I said to Shirra.

"Later."

I grabbed the reins of the dun mare, who'd stopped a short distance from us, and swung up onto her back.

We didn't stick around to find out if the tribe escaped. I followed Shirra into a small gulch. We faced a long trek to the plateau.

~*~

We pushed on all night to get distance between us and the fighting. We'd slunk away from the Gherza tribe, avoiding ululating Gherza defenders and shouting Clansmen alike. She Who Sees watched over us as we narrowly missed colliding with three Clansmen bent on Gherza destruction charging down the slope—our one close call. In the chaos, we managed to slip away.

Or so I'd thought. But towards dawn, with exhaustion setting in after the long night of picking our way half-blind through the darkness, my skin prickled. Unseen eyes watched me in the predawn greyness. I didn't know how I knew, but I could sense them out there, stalking, following. We left the parched steppe behind us, climbing to the plateau, but the feeling got worse.

Ducking into a ravine and doubling back, I watched the

foothills behind me until I spotted a small puff of dust, the telltale sign of a rock tumbling down the hillside.

Someone tracked us. And skillfully at that, since I couldn't pinpoint them no matter how hard I stared. We postponed sleep and pressed on until my yawns gaped wider than my strides.

We progressed into the foothills towards the plateau, but my horse pulled up lame. I dismounted, removed its bridle and abandoned it to its fate. I felt bad for letting it go but suspected it would have an easier time finding its way back to the grassy steppe than climbing farther with us.

The terrain leading to the plateau got steeper, and since we couldn't take the direct route teeming with Clansmen, we avoided the main trading road and clambered across scrub-filled foothills, using goat trails where possible.

I didn't intend to use the staff as a walking stick, but setting my horse loose gave me few options. The staff felt like a regular piece of wood in my hand, although if I gripped it too hard its whorled surface left an imprint in my palm that took longer than normal to fade. Aside from that, nothing else indicated that it was an object of power, or the instrument of my current predicament. Though it was useful to lean on the staff while slogging across the rocks, it felt sacrilegious.

Without the horse, we covered less ground. Shirra suggested I ride behind her, but I declined. I wanted to know what she was up to, but worried such nearness would provoke my snarky inner voice.

I looked back down the slope at her. She let me set the pace while her mount picked its way up the path. "I want you in front of me, where I can see you," she said.

"Fine, but first, we talk." I might not find a better time, and I had a decision to make once we reached the heights of the plateau: vale or pass?

"Just who exactly are you, Shirra?" I never would have guessed an association on Shirra's part with the Gherza, and marveled that she'd risk giving herself away to the Clans by coming to the Izir.

"I don't answer to you."

"You do if the Gherza ever want to see the staff again. The Izir called you *sha'zara*."

"What? 'Barbarian?' He'd call any Clan member that."

I gave her my best "don't take me for a fool" look. "Daughter. You're about the right age, but I've never seen a blonde Gherza. Unless you tint your hair." She did have the blue, blue eyes common to the Gherza. Steppe-sky eyes, they used to call them. Did they call them desert eyes now?

Shirra played coy. "You must have misheard him."

I stopped in the middle of the path and gave her a hard stare. "You didn't kill Errith but that won't stop me from telling Fayne you're playing him. 'Blood traitor' might be as bad as 'murderer' in his eyes. Your idea of marrying into a Clan is as dead as Errith."

Shirra stared up the path towards the high ridge we'd been aiming for. The one that would take us to Moongate Pass. Back to the Clans. A different fork on that same path led to the Blighted Vale. In that direction, my feet didn't want to go.

"Everything I've worked for. And it comes to this …" she whispered. Shirra squared her shoulders. "It's obvious you want Fayne for yourself."

And I'll never have him. Although who knew what was possible if I succeeded in the task the Izir gave me. "Fayne will never marry me. We're not … compatible."

"I doubt you'll intercede in my favor once you know what I have to tell."

"You'll have to take a chance."

Shirra bit her lip. "Fine. You guessed right. I am the Izir's daughter."

"But your hair …"

"Over the years, the Gherza and the Clans mingled. Some legends even claim we were one people, long ago. Every now and then, a Gherza woman bears a child with golden hair. A throwback. I'm one such."

"So you're a spy."

Shirra shook her head. "An emissary. The Gherza believe we can't subsist for much longer here. Not since the Fall turned the steppe into desert. Not with the Clans raiding and harrying us. They've wanted to exterminate us for a long time, and they're getting close. We can't survive without peace. We're not strong enough to take any of their land. Besides, we're too tied to this one. We need to heal it. Nothing less will be acceptable to the Fates.

"My father sent me to marry into one of the powerful Clans. Clan Grey seemed perfect, given Fayne Grey's openness. Once I established a voice within the Clans, I could change perceptions. And maybe get close to the staff."

"But the Izir said the Gherza believed only Iril could fix the staff."

"My father thought perhaps if we could examine it, we'd find

309

another way."

"You told the Gherza where to find Iril that night, didn't you?"

"Yes. The staff—unprotected like that—how could I disappoint my father by passing up such an opportunity?"

"But if you're Gherza, why would you agree to help me chase after the staff?"

"Any delay of the host gave my father more time to escape. I wasn't helping you—I knew he'd never cede the staff to you."

"What went wrong?"

"Lian joined the host and took his accusations about Errith to the Elders before I could waylay him. He set Grey guardsmen around the Arneth camp even before he approached the Council. My scouts warned me of his arrival. I escaped camp unseen, but only just. I left Fayne behind—I couldn't reach the men guarding him in time. Iril saw my eyes. She guessed my secret. With her controlling Fayne, and Fayne no longer in my men's hands ..."

"... Your secret was out anyway. Lian said Iril sent him and Fayne to retrieve something. What did he take from your father?" Fayne and Lian in the Gherza camp didn't quite make sense to me. Iril sent me to get what she wanted. What would she risk letting Fayne go for?

Shirra reached into her belt pouch, and pulled out a small item. She handed it to me. Unlike rock, it gleamed in a translucent warm amber color. "The *copal*," Shirra said.

"The what?"

"The Gherza carved this from the *copal*. It's like amber but not as old. Iril can't be near it." That explained how Shirra saved Fayne and me at Castle Arneth. Shirra went on. "The power in the original piece keeps Iril from crossing the pass. The tribes banished her years ago—our legends say the *copal* enforces her exile. I'd wager my position as head of Arneth that she thinks she can destroy it."

I remembered the object the Izir held out that froze Iril where she stood. I puzzled over why she hadn't ordered me to retrieve it along with the staff. "If she destroys it, will it release her binding?"

Shirra nodded.

"But how can she destroy it if she can't get near it?"

"The spell is not related to her proximity from the *copal*. It protects the Gherza territory. The smaller piece protected me, as its bearer, from her."

"And what happens once she breaks it?" I asked.

"Then she can freely walk anywhere west of Moongate Pass again."

The timing felt off. Again, why not ask me to get this *copal* for her at the same time? The only explanation was that, before, she'd had no need to enter the Gherza's lands if I brought her back the staff. I tapped my knuckle against my lip, thought back to Shirra's confrontation with Iril-as-Fayne. Iril also lacked the instrument of my death. She heard or saw a clue that gave away that I was not Rhinn, but someone who died in these lands, not the Clanholds. But why not send Lian and Fayne straight for that item instead of this *copal*?

Unless ... unless they'd already tried to get Iril's first choice, and failed. Or worse, succeeded, and she required the *copal* for something else.

I couldn't breathe, suddenly. Where would Iril send them?

Where did she think I'd died? I wanted to scream to the hills around me—tell me! Fates damn you, tell me where to go!

Shirra frowned at the hills surrounding us, as though she could hear the echo of the scream I'd suppressed. "This isn't the way to the Blighted Vale."

"I never promised your father I'd go. We're going to Moongate Pass." But a small tremor fluttered through my heart. *I* didn't know the vale, but the me-that-was feared it. I didn't want to look too closely into that corner of my head. I knew it would be horrible. I knew—

"Fates take my future!" I shouted. Shirra jumped, sending gravel skittering down the slope. "Shirra, how far off the road to the pass is the Blighted Vale?"

"Not too far, a morning's ride, maybe?"

Could Fayne and Lian have done it? Split off from the host, gone to the vale, then gotten back in time to thunder down on the Gherza with the host? "We must hurry, Shirra."

"Not to the pass! I won't let you bring the staff back into Clan territory."

"Don't worry, I've changed my mind. Take me to the vale." I couldn't go back to Iril now. Not without knowing if she held the means to control me. Because only one thing could make me fear the vale as much as I did, which despite the gaps in my memory I associated only with pain and loss: I'd died there. And if Iril beat me there, Fayne was a dead man, and I'd already lost.

The ground rose up, and we struggled to find routes through the terrain. To get to the vale, avoiding the Clan horde along the way meant abandoning the traditional Gherza migration paths to the Aramar Plateau. Time and again we circled back and left the

312

shepherd's trail we followed. Landslides blocked our path, the steep sides of the gulches giving way without the stabilizing influence of polegrass.

I buried the thought that the deterioration of the landscape was all my fault. I couldn't be the only reason an entire people faced at best displacement and at worst extinction. *No? Sure you really want your memory back?*

Now, as we approached the Aramar Plateau, I hadn't seen any signs of our pursuers for several days. Maybe we'd lost them. *And maybe you became a shade because the Fates couldn't do without your pretty face.*

Above us, I spied the dark green of tall pines. Only a little farther and we could melt into the forest that crowned the plateau. But right here, we needed to risk the trail to make our last upward push over the final escarpment. I ducked down behind a boulder, signaling Shirra to do the same.

The trail below—clear for now—wound around jutting rocks and cliffs, making it hard to spy its entire length. I wasn't willing to stick my neck out yet. I surveyed the hillside for a good hour, debating whether to make our move during daylight or not. We'd be less visible at night, but the moon tonight could also betray us to any ambusher up above with a crossbow. Plus, any delay gave our trackers time to catch up.

A movement downslope caught my eye. A horseman trotted up the trail as Shirra and I watched from the rocks. Fayne. He disappeared over the escarpment. I sat back and thought hard. Lian must be up to something if Iril ordered him elsewhere. How long until Iril joined him?

I couldn't do anything about it now. Time to risk it.

I motioned Shirra to follow, then I moved up the slope in a crabbed crouch, trying not to knock down any rocks. I thanked my impulse to steal the dun-colored robe. Uncovered, my ebony hair would stand out like a raven against the pale rocks, but hooded, I blended in.

I set foot on the road and paused, scanning the ridges above. Nothing. I proceeded up the road with caution, keeping as close to shelter as possible, and scurrying across open spaces like a rat fleeing a hawk. Shirra mirrored my every move.

I let myself breathe again when I could see over the crest. Once in the trees, our stalkers would have a harder time guessing our destination. I broke into a trot. We gained the trees, and I sank down behind the trunk of a fallen pine, peering back down at where we'd come from.

No movement.

Either our trackers excelled at stealth, or I'd imagined our danger. Time to go.

"Lead the way, Shirra." We snaked through the pines—the bed of needles muffled the noise of our passage, and my shoulders released some of the tension they'd held. My shoulder blades contracted again, however, when we burst from beneath the pines out into a sunlit scene of devastation. Not a single tree stood in the entire expanse right down to the lake, shimmering off in the distance. The beetles continued to wreak havoc, before moving northward. And now they'd taken our cover.

Shirra gaped. "It looks so—so different. I'm not sure I can find the way."

"You have to, Shirra."

"It's not that easy. My father never brought me. I counted on finding the markers from his stories. But now—" She steered her horse eastward.

Now I worried. Shirra appeared tentative and confused, casting her gaze about, looking for clues to the location of the vale. We meandered up and down rolling terrain coated with browning pine needles, an odd carpet given the lack of visible trees. I kept glancing back, worried about pursuit, but the variation in elevation hid us from casual observation. We crested hilltops quickly.

"Over there!" Shirra stabbed a finger to her right. A cairn stood on a rise ahead. On the other side of the hill lay a small valley, its slopes denuded of trees. The farther we went along the floor, the more the valley's sides rose up, until soon we could no longer see the sun. Up ahead, a wall of rock blocked our way.

We could go no farther. "Is this the vale?" I asked.

The dejected slump of Shirra's shoulders gave me my answer. She sat in silence, staring at a large boulder snugged up against the cliff face.

"Shirra, what's the problem?"

"I knew it was a forbidden place, but I didn't realize they'd blocked it off." She pointed at the boulder. "Behind that—there's supposedly a path through the rock."

At twice my height, and three times my girth, the stone presented an immovable obstacle.

"But—your father. He wouldn't bring me here on a useless quest. There must be another way in." Or a trick to moving the stone. For two women alone, the task appeared impossible.

"If so, only the Izirs know it."

The boulder sat there, stolidly fixed, mocking me. Suddenly I found myself laughing back. Hope jangled my nerve endings, heated my cheeks, took my breath away in gasping chortles.

"What's so funny?" Shirra asked.

I wiped tears of relief from my eyes. If we couldn't get in, neither could Fayne and Lian. At least one part of Iril's mission had failed. I was still free. I could still save Fayne. But time grew short with every step Fayne took towards Iril. This boulder might have thwarted Fayne and Lian, but I suspected Iril could deal with it in other ways. I stepped away from the boulder.

SHHHWUUNK.

The arrow, its fletched tail still quivering, pinned the edge of my robe to the soil. I shrugged off the robe, but another missile thunked into the ground at my feet.

"Don't move!" Lian stood barring the way back through the valley. He grinned as he dropped his bow and unsheathed his blade.

I cursed myself for relaxing my vigilance.

"Give it to me," Lian demanded.

I said nothing. Was he alone? Lian dipped his sword blade, pointing it towards my chest. I raised the staff, prepared to use it as a quarterstaff if he forced me to.

Lian hesitated. *That's right you bastard, sure you want to risk breaking the very thing you're after?*

"Iril's not known for keeping her promises," I taunted him, even though I still harbored hope she'd honor hers to me. A little conversation might give me time to work out how to overpower him without killing him. Because Fayne reserved that judgment for himself, and the last thing I needed was another mark against me with the Fates. "Glory? Power? She'll never share any of that with you."

"Don't you think I don't know that? No, it's you I want, Rhinn."

Fates damn Iril for her lies. She wouldn't have sent the brothers after the *copal* if she still thought me Rhinn, but that didn't stop her from stringing Lian along. "Whatever Iril told you, Rhinn of Dayr is dead. You're more gullible than I thought."

"Denying it won't save you. What else makes sense? Your soul was close, closer than anyone's—easy for Iril to snag."

"Rhinn's soul is gone, Lian. It's a one-way trip to the far planes. Then back into the Great Cycle, but not in any way you'd know each other."

"Liar! The unrequited stay behind, mooning over their lost loves. Only I'm not who you pine for, Rhinn, am I?"

"Lian—"

"You denied it then, and I almost believed you. I cried so much after I killed you, nearly took my own life for letting my anger get the best of me. But I see how he looks at you now— how you look at him. It was always Fayne, wasn't it, Rhinn? You never loved me."

I edged towards the side of the road, looking for an opening. Lian lunged, anticipating the move and cutting off any escape. His blade sliced towards my ankle. The awkward length of the staff made me miss the block. I hissed as the blade edge caught my calf. Blood welled from the gash. Lian's eyes widened as smoke curled from the edges of the wound.

Lian continued our discussion. "Did you know Iril's over two hundred years old?"

"Is that what she told you? More likely she stole another

necromancer's name." I knew this for a lie, but I needed to instil doubt into Lian.

Lian flicked his sword at a dissipating wisp of smoke. "I believe her. You're living proof."

"I'm proof of nothing but her own hubris. Whatever she promised, you'd be wise to cut your losses and run."

"You."

The skin at the back of my neck tingled.

"She promised me you. And through you, eternal life like her."

I snorted. "More like eternal death. You're a fool, Lian. You have no idea what you're playing with."

"I know I'll be a hero when I return the staff to the Clans." He glanced at Shirra, who'd circled just to his left. "And bring in a murderess."

Shirra flicked her wrist and a dagger dropped from her sleeve into her palm. Lian pivoted, but instead of using his blade, kicked the knife from Shirra's grip. She cried out, clutching at her wrist. I moved to close the gap between us, but Lian grabbed Shirra, pulling her to his chest. He held his sword to her throat.

"I see my mistake now," Shirra said in a flat, cold voice. "It was thinking you supported anything your brother did in the first place."

Lian punched her temple with his free hand. She fell limp to the ground.

I took advantage of his momentary preoccupation. One quick jab with the staff knocked his sword out of his hand. He stumbled backwards. I lunged left. If I could just make it to Shirra's horse, I could outrun him to the mouth of the valley, and find an untouched stand of trees to lose him in. I'd just need to wait for night again to make my move for the pass. Shirra could fend for herself. The blow hadn't killed her, otherwise I would have seen her leave this plane.

I misjudged his speed, and how much the slash on my calf hobbled me. His tackle slammed me into the ground. I writhed to escape his grip. The sting of steel at my throat stilled my frantic scrambling. Lian pressed Shirra's dagger in just hard enough to break my skin.

I glanced at Shirra's body, only a few paces away. Thought of the Izir, and his warnings. Despite not killing Fayne at the ambush in the meadow, my power remained fickle. If I used it on Lian, too close to Shirra, would she die too? If I used it at all, would I damn myself forever?

"Shall we find out if Iril spoke the truth about shade blood?" Lian drew a finger along my neck, then held its bloodstained tip between our faces. A single wisp of smoke rose from his finger, like that left after blowing out a candle. "That it gives the drinker eternal life?" He smeared the blood on my lower lip, then bent forward to lick it off. His tongue touched my skin. He gasped, then bit me.

I struggled not to move, the dagger still at my throat. My blood? Some new witchery on Iril's part, or yet another lie to attempt to control Lian. I'd promised Fayne I wouldn't kill Lian. Now I might not have a choice.

Lian raised his head. The brand caught his eye. He trailed a bloody finger over it and I gasped at the buzzing jolt. "Iril assumes that I can't take what she promised me for myself. I have the staff now. I have you. What do I need her for?" He bent to ravage my mouth one last time. "It's too bad—I would have liked to show you, Rhinn, what you missed by choosing my brother over me. But I need more blood than just a taste. We've had practice at this, you and I, though. It will only hurt a little."

His arm holding the dagger tensed for the killing slice. He was evil. Evil! And if it damned me to kill him, so be it. I closed my eyes. Prayed to the Fates to give me the control to spare Shirra. Apologized to Fayne for what I had to do.

Infinite cold blasted through me.

~*~

I heaved Lian's inert body off me, and picked up the dagger. Who knew when an extra weapon might come in handy?

Soft footsteps crunched in the loose shale next to me. Shirra. She plopped down beside me, one hand feeling the outlines of a large lump on her forehead.

"Are you a necromancer as well, then?" she asked. "I felt ... I felt your power pulling at me. I thought I was going to die."

I stared at her in horror, one of my fears confirmed. If Lian caught me a few paces closer ... "I'm so sorry, Shirra. I can't ... I don't have as much control over what I do as I'd like."

"Does Fayne know?"

"Yes."

"What are you? My father doesn't tolerate witches, and he wouldn't give the staff to one. Did you kill Errith?"

I laughed, a strange, mirthless sound to my ears. "No." I nudged Lian's body with my toe. "This one did. He framed you, to take down the last objector to any pursuit of the Gherza."

"Convenient that he can no longer dispute the accusation. What proof do you have?"

"Just the word of the victim."

"She told you before she died?"

I needed Shirra's trust, because I required her continued help. And she'd learn the truth about me from her father, if he still lived. "No. She told me after she died. I'm a shade, Shirra. I don't belong in this world. It puts everyone in danger, and I just want to set things right again."

Shirra took the news she traveled in the company of a deadly supernatural being surprisingly well. Her complexion turned a little green, but I chalked that up to queasiness from the bump Lian gave her.

"Listen, Shirra, I'll keep your secret if you explain to Fayne that I didn't simply murder his brother. I won't tell Fayne anything about you being Gherza."

"It might be too late. What if he remembers what he saw while Iril controlled him? He really knows? About you?"

"Yes."

"Now I understand why you said you were incompatible."

"I would have him believe me honorable. For as long as I can." Though Fayne accepted my accusations about Lian, he still wanted to confront Lian himself. And I'd promised. Fayne would not have meted out eternal oblivion to Lian's soul as his final judgment. I dreaded seeing the same look of horror in his eyes I'd glimpsed in Shirra's.

"Shirra, we can't let Iril into the vale. What she finds in there will allow her to control me, and my power to kill."

Shirra swallowed. "There's another reason. My father always worried that if she entered the Blighted Vale, she'd make its corruption permanent."

321

"What does that gain her?"

Shirra shrugged. "Revenge on those she feels slighted her? A base from which she can operate free of enemies? Because we'd have to abandon the plateau—Gherza, Clan, all of us. She'd leave nothing for us."

"Can she do it without the staff?"

"I don't know."

Iril no longer had a reason to wait for me at Perfyd Tower. She would likely rejoin Fayne as close to the pass as she could get. Our diversion to the vale bought Fayne at least a day's head start on me. Plus, he was mounted. "We need to keep Iril as far from the vale as possible. If she comes here I'll lose any chance of confronting her. I'll take the risk, to get Fayne free now, while I still operate under my own volition."

"Leave the staff with me."

"No. It's my only bargaining tool, and maybe my best weapon."

"You can't bring it right to her!"

"I don't have a choice. I think Iril knows who I am. If I can trick her into telling me, maybe I can get back my memories. Without them, I'm pretty sure I can't heal the vale."

"Iril isn't easily tricked."

"I'm willing to entertain better ideas. Waiting here for Iril doesn't seem like one. Even if I leave the staff with you, if she has the *copal*, she'll eventually track you down." Shirra looked unhappy about my assessment, so I distracted her with a task. "You can help, Shirra. Gather up the Gherza and set a guard at Moongate Pass. Ask your father, if he's still alive, or the other Izirs, about any ways in to the vale, and make sure they stay blocked. I'll find a way to get back here ahead of Iril if she doesn't kill me. I don't think she will, though, because she needs my power."

"And if you're dead?"

"Then your people must stop Iril." However slim their chances.

Shirra frowned. "Iril won't use the pass."

"Not even traveling under Fayne's 'protection?'"

"She likes to creep and hide. 'Inhabiting' Fayne is one thing, but I doubt she'd risk a personal encounter with the Clans. Braith planned to leave a sizable garrison at the pass. She'd have seen that when she posed as Fayne. My father crossed the mountains another way, and Iril likely knows it. I can show you."

And if Shirra was wrong? If Iril went for the pass and not this other route? I tried to think like Iril. She'd shown an awareness of my rough position. She knew I had the staff, and would know I'd come to the vale. I could use this fact to lure her to me—I doubted she could resist the triple bait of me, the staff, and the uncertainty of not knowing if I'd found a way into the vale.

I nudged Lian's body with my toe. "What should we do about him?"

"There's no time to dig a grave."

"Lian doesn't deserve a decent burial." I told Shirra my theory about Rhinn. We dragged Lian's corpse to the side of the valley and propped it behind a boulder.

I eyed Shirra's horse. "If I'm to have any hope of waylaying Iril in time for you to gather reinforcements, I need to get to that trail as quickly as possible."

Shirra followed my gaze and nodded. "We can double up. It's only half a day."

We mounted up and took off at a slow canter, making good time around the lake. The horse stumbled as we forded the river, and I challenged Shirra on her pallor, but she insisted she was fine, and pushed on until we reached the steep mountain slopes. Shirra pointed out a goat trail zigging up the mountain side. "Once you reach the top, this will lead you down into Dayr lands, but we've always found his scouts easy to avoid in the terrain."

She sighed, then clasped my hand, a gesture of faith in me that moved me more than I was willing to admit. She then reached into her pouch and pulled out the small piece of amber. "Here, take my piece of the *copal*. It doesn't emit the same the power as my father's, but it may protect you from the worst of Iril's magic."

She headed back to rally the Gherza. I trudged off up the slope, my heart heavy. I prayed to the Fates I made the right choice avoiding the pass, that Shirra's feet would be fleet enough to locate other Gherza, that I would somehow find the strength to confront my past. I climbed, each breath providing less and less air for my lungs. I thought of Fayne, and Iril's link leaving him with less and less of himself.

Fayne wanted hard proof of Lian's crimes. Would he be angry with me for breaking my promise to him? Iril shouldered most of the blame. She set Lian on me. Her lies convinced him to kill me. How many lives did I save by killing him and saving myself?

If it makes you feel better to think that, go ahead.

I squashed my snide conscience back into the box from which it kept escaping. It was either me or Lian, and while I might sacrifice myself for Fayne, Lian deserved no such consideration from me. The Fates could judge me as they would; this was no time for doubts. I needed to intercept Iril and figure out how to free Fayne. I'd deal with what to tell him when the time came. He would hear the news from me. Not from Shirra, or anyone else.

Night overtook me just before I approached the peak, so I made camp underneath a small rocky overhang. A chill breeze teased at edges of my robe, but I took some time to examine the staff before turning in. Inert in my hands, it left me with no special impressions, no burning or tingling sensations. I scrutinized its entire length, studying the gnarled carvings, intricate whorls of wood raised in organic patterns along its length. I felt it was trying to speak to me, but deaf to its language, I couldn't hear the words.

Wincing in anticipated pain, I touched its end to my brand.

Nothing happened. Did I imagine a faint resonance, a slight tingle? If so, it was so minuscule as to be not there at all.

I slumped back against a tree. How could I rescue Fayne if the staff's power required the magic of necromancy? My abilities lay in my connection to the otherworld, the middle realm—my defensive shade power. I knew no magic.

No. Wait. That wasn't true. What of my instinctive explorations of my brand, and the harmonic notes my voice had sung so naturally? I'd been too frightened and confused to explore any further, afraid to face what it meant, but nothing had come as easily to me since awakening on the riverbank except my skill with the sword. Iril used similar vocalizations to draw forth the beetles.

And the spell I'd cast to take my memories: I *had* to have once known magic in order to do that. Before I died and became a shade. I just couldn't remember that training. I'd hidden that knowledge from myself.

Face it. You know things you shouldn't.

I stared at the staff. The Izir said Iril didn't understand the consequences of her actions. How many years had she studied the dark arts? Dabbling in magic blindly seemed the height of folly. But should I not arm myself with every weapon possible? Time to follow my instincts and see where they led.

Hopefully not over a cliff.

THEN

"I've changed my mind." Jezarel sounded like an idiot, even to herself. She held out her hand for Kairiya to pass her one of her earring hoops. Kairiya dropped it into her palm like a person getting rid of quince peelings.

"It's too late for that," Kairiya answered.

Jezarel wrapped herself in her injured dignity. "It's for the good of our peoples."

"I thought you'd die before you'd let a barbarian touch you."

"Don't lecture me."

"I only did as you asked."

"And now I'm asking you to stop. You will see no more of him."

"What if he says differently?"

"Then I will complain to my father. He will not endanger an important treaty over the wishes of a half-breed."

Kairiya flinched, but Jezarel didn't care. Too late to take back the slur.

"He doesn't love you." Kairiya wasn't talking about the Izir.

"We'll see about that." Jezarel made sure Kairiya knew this for a dismissal. After a moment, Kairiya stood and left the room.

Readying herself for dinner, Jezarel took extra care with her hair and jewelry. Just before she crossed the threshold, she made the motion and muttered the words Asrar taught her, calming her thoughts until the energy of the next realm washed over her, adding the desired hint of glamour. She sealed the spell with a short tonal hum. She put a hint of swing into her hips when she entered the dining tent, throwing her scarf over her shoulder with a flourish, so the movement would attract attention.

The interior of the banquet tent glowed from the light of a dozen braziers and bronzed lanterns. Dappled light in the shape of stars and moons circled across the cloth walls of the tent. It crawled across the faces and dresses of the gathered revelers, glinting on Gherza bangles and torcs, Clan medallions, and mail. One of her father's men turned the special pattern caster, so the movement never ceased, always drawing the eye to something or someone new.

Every man in the tent admired her entrance, several of the barbarians leering in appreciation. Every man except Murran. Deep in conversation with the Izir, his gaze stayed locked onto Kairiya, who placed herself so that if Murran faced the Izir, he must also face her. Kairiya acted oblivious to his attentions, but the quirk of her lips as she looked at Jezarel betrayed her awareness of her victory.

Jezarel's lips tightened. *What have I wrought?*

~*~

Throughout dinner, Jezarel seethed. She did everything but throw herself into Murran's lap, and he took no notice. She even went so far as to offer him the choicest slice of lamb from her portion of saffron stew. He took it, but ignored the lingering brush of her fingers against his, and swallowed the morsel whole, too eager to resume the conversation with the man beside him. A conversation that gave him an excuse to stare at the other side of the tent.

She needed some air, and kicked at the cushions that blocked her path to the entrance. Kairiya had not made a sound, but Jezarel heard the half-breed's crowing laughter in her ears nevertheless.

Outside, the cold night air shocked in its piercing freshness, compared to the fragrant miasma of cloves, ginger, and cinnamon she had just left behind. She fought back tears. In the moonlight, the wavelets on the lake glittered—the repository of a million tears shed before hers. The crazy notion to throw herself in came upon her—maybe a rescue would force Murran to notice her. She shook some sense into herself. She couldn't swim. She would drown before anyone even missed her at the banquet.

"Things not going your way tonight, dearie?"

The voice in the darkness startled Jezarel. "Asrar? What are you doing here? I thought it was dangerous for the barbarians to see you."

"I sensed your troubled heart, so I came."

Jezarel spilled out her frustration to Asrar. "Nothing I do matters to him."

Asrar laughed. "We can fix that. Forgotten all your lessons already?"

"Even the glamour didn't work."

"Time for something more powerful, then."

Jezarel's heart thumped faster. "Really?"

"I think you are ready, child. Here, take this." Asrar pressed something into Jezarel's hand—a jet-black piece of cut glass that sucked in the light the moon gave off. Even though it gleamed, it looked darker than the blackest coal.

"What is it?"

"A vessel. And a conduit. Channel the magic of the near realm I taught you through it, and it will focus your power. Use it in just the right way, and you can trap a small piece of your target's essence in it—just enough to direct his thoughts along a path you and you alone control."

Asrar incanted a few words and made Jezarel repeat them until she was satisfied Jezarel understood the technique.

"But be careful," Asrar warned. "Trap too much of the essence and you will leave only an empty shell."

Jezarel nodded, but Asrar already slunk away to the treeline. Jezarel headed back to the banquet tent. The treaty must go forward, she saw that now. Her fault or not, Murran's fixation on Kairiya now forced her hand. She didn't need a vacant, useless husband, though. Just a biddable one. And one just biddable enough so that Kairiya never suspected how she lost him. Just a small application of Asrar's teachings would get Jezarel what she needed. No one need ever be the wiser.

~*~

As the diners awaited the evening's entertainment, Jezarel noticed Kairiya leave the tent, presumably to make water. Jezarel seized the opportunity and sidled up to Murran. She took his hand, and, winking at her mother, led him off into a corner of the tent. One of the many hanging tapestries that served as both decoration and privacy barrier concealed them.

Murran at first seemed to want to look anywhere but at her.

"What is wrong, my betrothed?" Jezarel asked.

"Have you decided then that being my betrothed is not such a hardship?"

"I perhaps came to my conclusions in haste," Jezarel allowed.

Murran hesitated, then came to some decision. "There's something I must tell you."

"Shhhh." Jezarel placed her fingers to his lips. If he mentioned Kairiya, he would give her no choice but to take her offended honor to the Izir. It was her own fault that she'd placed Kairiya in his path.

A small part of her regretted the need for magical interference to make him want her. Maybe one day he'd desire her without it, but for now she couldn't risk losing him … She palmed the jet glass and placed her hand in his, whispering the words that would make him hers. She made the briefest of connections with his essence, as Asrar told her to expect, but Murran reared back and severed the delicate thread between them.

Murran snatched away his hand. "What sorcery is this?"

Flustered, Jezarel dropped the piece of jet. It landed on the carpet with a soft thud. "I'm sorry, I thought you were breaking it off. I only wanted to make sure …"

"Where I come from, you could hang for this."

"Please forgive this foolish girl! I didn't mean … I needed you to love me."

"I felt what you did. Only a powerful necromancer could …"

Jezarel flinched back. "Necromancy? How dare you accuse me of that? Asrar said …"

"Asrar?" Murran picked up the jet. "Did she give you this?"

Jezarel had made a colossal mistake. But Murran's next words surprised her.

"It's not your fault. You were taken in by a witch. She'd do anything to sabotage this wedding."

Murran took her hand with a fierce intensity, his fingers tense with the effort not to hurt her yet hold her fast. "I've been a fool. I let all this talk of trade and treaties blind me to the fact that you're just as real, and human, and scared as I am. And to the fact that others would do anything to tear this union apart. Promise me to never, ever try such madness again. I must trust you if we are to marry."

Jezarel swallowed, and nodded.

"Good. Jezarel—love can't be imposed. It comes from within."

Jezarel stared at Murran's foreign features, and suddenly saw the man beneath, and the truth in her heart. "I don't know how to love."

"Maybe we can learn together."

"It's not too late? Do you think you can ever love me?" Jezarel held her breath, waiting for the answer.

Murran squeezed her hand and then brushed past the tapestry on his way back into the room, bellowing out a name.

"ORRITH!"

NOW

When I first lived, I dabbled with necromancy. My early
confusion as to my identity, and my recent unclear conscience
pointed me at that conclusion. I wasn't just a blunt instrument
capable only of severing souls from their bodies. Buried deep
inside me, I knew more of the subtleties of magic. Maybe in the
same way I'd instinctively retaken to the sword, I could exercise a
long unused skill in the dark arts.

The sword was a physical undertaking. Muscle memory aided
me that day back at Castle Grey. I dredged up what little hard
information I knew about necromancy. While the specific hows
and whys evaded me, necromancy was all about the control of
souls. A fledgling necromancer learned to mesmerize and
glamour by tricking another's essence into subjugating itself to
theirs. As his or her power grew, subjugation and suggestibility
became compulsion, until a truly powerful necromancer
developed the ability to latch onto the other essence completely,
leaving the object of their attention no option but to obey.

The necromancer harnessed the soul like putting a halter on a
horse, then bridle, saddle, and whip. Iril went one step further and
stole souls from their owners whole and complete.

I suspected that my greater yet different power as a shade now subsumed whatever small power I wielded long ago. Here in the physical realm, I could crudely separate a soul from its body. Even though I now had a modicum of control, I'd struggled long and hard to gain even that small measure. I could sense links: the one between Iril and Fayne, between the staff and the pendant. Yet I didn't think I could create or control a link.

But you already did.

I stopped in my tracks and pulled the pendant's chain over my neck. I leaned the staff against a tree and backed away about twenty paces. When I first found the stone at Iril's tower, I thought I used her residual association with it to establish a link between it and her. But had I? The stone wasn't linked to Iril, but to the staff. So what, if anything, did I do back at Perfyd Tower?

I stared deep into the blue stone, probing with my shade sense. I felt its inexorable attraction to the staff. Still I didn't understand. I only sensed linked souls. The staff and the pendant, as inanimate objects both, should be beyond my abilities.

I shut out the extraneous bird noises and shushing of the breeze, until nothing intruded but me and the pendant. Why could I sense this link? Why—

And there it was. So obvious. The soul at the root of the joining: mine. The link dated from when I lived. I could perceive it because I'd died, however long ago.

My awareness snapped away from the stone. I reached my arm back to hurl the pendant down the mountainside, as far away from me as possible. It wasn't fair—the tiny piece of me within the jewel radiated an innocent happiness. The stone held a part of me that no longer existed, might never exist again.

A tear slid down my cheek. I stayed my hand. I should honor that lost girl by keeping this last shard of her as close to my heart as possible.

The Izir claimed a connection between me and what fouled the staff. It would follow that my soul was linked to it in some small way, and thus why I could track the staff using the pendant. For an instant, hope flared within me: if I'd created a link with the pendant, I could deal with the link between Iril and Fayne, no?

I hung the pendant on a juniper branch and backed away, so that the staff lay to my right and the pendant to my left. I closed my eyes and threw my awareness out along the boundaries of myself.

And felt two resonances. No, three. The known one between me and the staff—this one rang with a dark tone. The more joyful one between me and the pendant. And a thin thread of something I recognized as yet another small part of me connecting the pendant and the staff.

Now that I paid close attention, the links shared one thing in common: they all felt old. Familiar even. The link between Iril and Fayne possessed a freshness about it, a sharp quality that as a scent would have tickled the hairs in my nose. These links gave off a sensation more like the lingering finish on a well-aged wine. The one between me and the staff would taste more like vinegar, I suspected.

I sighed, disappointed. This meant I'd only created a focusing mechanism with the pendant, not the actual link itself. Something older tied me to the pendant. Had I created it so long ago? Why did Iril keep a souvenir of me near her for so long? What tied it to the staff?

Discouraged, I closed my eyes again. Now that I knew the pendant had nothing to do with my ability to sense the staff beyond perhaps a mild amplification of the resonance, I could point unerringly at the wooden rod.

Now that you don't need the pendant ...

My eyelids snapped open. I might not be able to create links, but could I break them? At its crudest, didn't I do exactly that to souls in this world? Broke their connection to their physical bodies, tore them away and sent them who knew where? I could practice on the pendant without fear of major consequences.

I concentrated on the faint thrum of resonance between me and the pendant. Gathered the smallest ice flake of cold within my brand possible. Twisted ever so slightly. Though the same action, the resulting sensation differed from pulling souls. The cold splintered against the center of my brand. At the same time something ripped from the core of my being. I cried out; I hadn't thought this through. What if I severed the link between the core of me and this body?

Something popped, and I thought I heard the faintest discordant chime. I couldn't sense the pendant anymore.

The chain still hung from the juniper branch, but the stone no longer sat in its setting. I went over to the tree and knelt down. There.

I picked up and placed in my palm the shattered pieces of the stone, cleaved in two. That last happy piece of me was now well and truly lost. I swallowed. I'd succeeded in breaking the link.

But I'd failed, and a feeling of helplessness threatened to overwhelm me. My shoulders sagged.

I'd also destroyed the object of the link.

That doesn't bode well for Fayne.

~*~

The morning brought a clammy mist that shrouded the peak up above. I clambered carefully along the trail, which grew increasingly treacherous and required careful selection of handholds, until it felt like I spidered up the rock instead of hiked. The trail petered out at a sheer face. Shirra said the way would be obvious but I could go no farther.

I spied a rope dangling off to the left. It disappeared up into the mist. I tugged at it, testing its strength, dubious that something left out in the elements could last very long. The Gherza came this way only recently, though. The rope creaked but held when I jumped up and put my full weight on it. I had to risk it.

My feet slipped several times on the damp rock but the rough strands of the rope gave me purchase as I hauled myself up. Pain fired through my shoulders and arms. I looked down, wondering if I should just slide back, but the ledge I'd started from vanished, lost in the swirling fog. I gritted my teeth, heaved myself up a few more lengths, and suddenly felt no more rope above me. I flopped over the edge of the cliff onto a new ledge and spotted the trail. It disappeared between two tall natural spires. I staggered over to the twin rocks, where the trail began its descent of the flank. I'd reached the peak.

I leaned against the rightmost spire, resting my aching arms. My gaze lingered on the top end of the rope, knotted to a ring set into the ledge. Why make things easy for Iril? With the dagger I'd taken from Lian's body, I hewed at the rope. The strands parted with little difficulty, and I tossed the rope over the cliff. If I'd made a mistake and didn't find Iril, I'd just have to brave Moongate Pass again, but if she came this way, this would force her to go back as well, and maybe give Shirra a little extra time.

I made my way slowly down the Clan side of the mountain, looking for a good spot to lie in wait for Iril. Some place with good footing in case the confrontation got physical. The trail finally crossed a small grassy patch, and I might not find anything better. I sat down on a rock and listened for approaching travelers. Sounds carried strangely in the mist, but I didn't want Iril to surprise me. If only the clouds would lift—then I could use my higher position to scout the trail.

The waiting did nothing for my state of mind, giving me too much time to think. What if Iril slipped through the pass? Sitting here wasted time. Time Fayne didn't have. Time the beetles would use to destroy more of the plateau. Time in which Iril could find the tool to control me. I reviewed my plan.

Knock out Iril but don't kill her first. Get Fayne away. Break the link between the two of them. Don't kill Fayne in the process. Somehow tease my name out of Iril. With the link broken, she'd no longer have any leverage over me. Despite not being able to use my power on her, I could still threaten her physically.

Downslope, small pebbles clattered. I hid behind one of the boulders lining the trail. For a moment the mist made it sound like someone was making their way down the trail from the direction I'd come. The echoes shifted and I heard the soft crunch of footsteps on the grass below me.

Peering around the rock, I hissed at what I saw. Fayne stumbled up the trail, with Iril sauntering behind him, the ax from

Arneth slung across her back. Maybe if I rushed her I could club her unconscious with the staff. I hadn't marshaled my power over death, afraid it would give me away to her. She would know I was near, but maybe not exactly where.

I tensed to spring. Iril turned, a slight smile visible on her face, the hood still half-shrouding her. As she stopped, Fayne slumped to his knees.

"So you brought it," Iril said. "I knew you would. Did you have to kill Shirra to escape with it?"

The pleasure in her voice at the thought of murder chilled me. Yet the part of me that knew the intimacy of escorting an essence across the planes understood. The desire for power over another's essence. The ability to snuff it out, send it on its way. Or in Iril's case, trap it for the strength it conferred. I shook my head. I wasn't here to vindicate Iril.

I stepped towards Fayne. Seeing him as such a husk stoked my rage at Iril. I hoped the link's damage wasn't permanent. The movement got me closer to Iril. I looked for an opening to blindside her; Shirra's piece of the *copal* might do the trick. I reached into my belt pouch and fingered it. I cast outside myself for the link between Fayne and Iril.

Iril tutted and waved an admonishing finger at me. "Don't try it. I'll yank the rest of him to me before you can blink."

She took two quick steps towards me. I pulled my hand out of the pouch and held out my amber talisman like a ward. She froze, then threw back her head and laughed at me. "The changeling gave you her toy! How thoughtful of her, but I'm afraid it's too little, too late."

She unslung the ax from her shoulders, then shook something

into her palm from a pocket in her cloak. The real *copal*. In her hand, it flickered with a darker, copper-tinted light. She laid it on the ground next to Fayne.

"It took me a while—Rhinn was a good guess but seeing Shirra reminded me of someone else. Someone with even more reason to fear me than Rhinn. Once I put the pieces together I knew I had to send someone after this. You see," Iril said, "Your trinket becomes useless slag with its parent destroyed."

"I doubt even you could hurt it that easily, Iril."

"No? Think again. It's quite vulnerable to the weapon that caused the wound that made it." She heaved the ax over her head and arced it downward. I cried out, thinking she meant to behead Fayne. But the ax blade smashed down instead on the *copal*, splitting it in two. Iril leaned her hands on the ax handle, cocking her head as if listening to something. "Somehow, I expected to feel it more—the release, after all this time. Wait … Aah, yes. There … A gate opens. A chain breaks. It will be so nice to visit the vale again. I didn't think it possible or even necessary to go there before. But you changed all that."

She made it sound like going on a casual stroll. I disabused her of that notion, even though I doubted Shirra had rallied any Gherza, if any even survived the Clan incursion. "You can't go this way. I cut the rope. You'll also find your path back through Moongate Pass blocked. Do you really plan to take on a small army?"

"You think you're so clever. Fine, then. It's less than ideal, but you leave me no choice." She picked up one of the halves of the *copal* and laid it like a bowl in her palm. Something like thick sap still pooled in its center.

"What are you doing?" I asked.

"The Staff of Binding and the *copal* are two manifestations of the same thing. And they'll take me to the spot they recognize as home." Iril waved her hand over the shattered *copal* and murmured something I couldn't make out. A curtain of smoke flowed up from the ground. I lost sight of both her and Fayne. Without thinking, I whipped the staff at the last spot I saw her head.

My arm jolted as the staff connected. Did I get her? But then an unseen hand yanked me behind the veil of smoke.

Iril gripped the end of the staff. Her eyes blazed out at me from beneath her hood. She chanted, her voice moving up and down the scale in a way no voice should.

"Whatever power you think I wield is useless to you without the instrument of my death," I said.

"I'll have that soon enough. There's really only one person who would be so afraid of my vengeance they'd erase their own identity. I know exactly where you died."

"The Gherza blocked the way into the vale."

I held my breath, hoping she'd take the bait, say my name.

"You think that will stop me, you little whore? I would move mountains to make you feel the smallest amount of the pain I've lived with for the last two hundred years. And I will make you kill your love—it's the only fitting way to commemorate the day you died. Remember that scene. Remember that day, because that's what's waiting for you." She paused, cocked her head at me, then hissed softly. "You still don't remember, do you? You wouldn't have called me Iril before if you did."

"Tell me ... Please." *Why are you pleading with her?*

"You'd like that, wouldn't you? No. I like you hobbled." She resumed chanting. The smoke around us whirled.

Blood pounded in my temples. I yanked at the staff but Iril held fast. She shot a glance at Fayne and I worried she'd kill him if I hurt her or worked at the link. I castigated myself for not being fast enough or good enough, for failing Fayne.

Iril shoved the *copal* onto the end of the staff, soaking it in the sticky sap. Between us, wisps from the curtain of smoke funneled into a point near the tip of the staff, now covered in a thick, golden coating. The sap flared, not quite flaming, but too bright to look at. I felt a sucking pull towards the smoking vortex. Iril dropped the *copal*, reached out and gripped Fayne's wrist. Their outlines swam before me. They disappeared into the hole, dragging the staff in after them.

Pain sliced across my skin as I clenched the staff in fingers screaming with fiery stabs of heat. I scrabbled at the ground and snatched up the *copal* just before I crossed the threshold.

Don't let go. Whatever you do, don't let go.

If she'd found a way into the vale, I couldn't get left behind.

~*~

I woke to something jabbing me in the ribs. The *copal*—I'd fallen on top of it. I rolled off it and sat up.

Unlike when I first regained consciousness in the physical world, I knew instantly where I was. But I didn't understand. The soft twilight of the middle realm shimmered around me. I was back. But everything felt wrong.

I wasn't in my original shade form, the one given me by the Fates after I died. I still wore the body Iril gave me. I pondered this. According to the Gherza Izir, my return to the middle realm under the wrong circumstances would spell disaster for the physical world. But did he mean in my current, embodied form? Or would my metamorphosis back to my natural shade incarnation wreak havoc?

I'd leapt after Iril without thinking, believing she'd punctured reality and created a hole straight to the Blighted Vale. Never, not even if I spent a thousand years waiting for the Fates to redeem me, would I believe her crazy enough to try this. I couldn't think properly through my growing fear. I never thought I'd long again for a normal shade's muted emotions, but now I craved something, anything, that would allow me to settle my mind and quell the shaking in my hands.

I'd crossed the veil into the middle realm. In the wrong form. Could I even stay here? Could I, should I, try to go back?

If there's anything to go back to.

I shook my head. —*Focus*. Neither the Fates will nor Iril's magic had obliterated me. I needed more information before I jumped to dire conclusions, and I needed it fast.

I stared around me. The Fates created me to walk this land. To escort the newly dead on their journey to the far planes. To protect them from the daemons who craved their essences. They gifted me with an arsenal of weapons for that mission. As a natural shade I should feel in my element. At least, normally I did. I flexed my fingers. Drew on the power required. And met with a thick resistance. Tried again. Same result. A trickle of power flowed through me. Not enough to blast a daemon. Not even enough to stun.

I swore. Here, supposedly in my element, where even as a cursed creature I should be able to do some good, and I was effectively hamstrung? "This isn't funny! Do you hear me, Listener? I'll take your ears myself next time I see you!" Part of me winced at the blasphemy, but I needed to keep my anger fueled or I'd never survive here.

Heart taking off like a startled hare, I panicked, remembering Fayne and Iril. Where were they? Had they arrived in the same spot as me? Recovered and taken off? I hoped so. Otherwise I wouldn't be able to track them.

I tested the ether, searching for the telltale trace of a human essence. When escorting someone across, I always knew their position, regardless of whether we got separated in the event of a nasty brawl. But I'd lost even that. Maybe the ability relied on the other being dead. I examined the loose shale in the vicinity. I saw nothing. My alarm mounted. Maybe they'd perished already. I didn't know what would happen to a living body that materialized in the middle realm.

Then again, as one of the dead, I'd done all right in the physical realm. I had to trust Iril's magic protected them. The staff was gone; unless the journey destroyed it, Iril must have taken it. I scanned the distance. The featureless landscape faded to a false horizon, as though hidden by fog. My shade senses, though dulled by my human body, still provided me with a sense of orientation, but I wondered how Iril would find her way. Where would she go? She couldn't hope to mount an attack on the far realms. Sheer madness.

A disturbance in the random pattern of scattered rock caught my eye. Yes. Fayne and Iril arrived here. A trail of displaced fragments led off to my left. If Iril searched for the far realms, she was headed the wrong way. I tucked away the *copal* and set out in pursuit.

Jogging through the twilight, I calmed my churning thoughts. Iril had no idea what she'd gotten herself into. I suspected her powers lacked potency in the middle realm. She'd find herself defenseless against even the weakest daemon.

I probed against the barrier keeping me from my full power. It felt like slogging through thick mud, instead of the usual quicksilver response. But my tentative attempts soon grew more assured. The sluggish initial link, once established, got me more than that first tiny trickle. It must be this body. The unnaturalness Iril bestowed on me brought about unintended side effects. But I could still defend us. Not as effectively as in my natural form, but maybe well enough to save our souls.

I focused on gaining on Iril, trying not to think about the consequences of our departure from the physical world. What if a wave of destruction *had* engulfed Clan lands? Killed everybody? Would it spread to the Gherza steppe? But unlike the beetle that had exploded so catastrophically when I harmed it, Iril had brought us through intact. That had to make some difference. I chose to assume that everything remained normal. Otherwise, there was no point in going on.

When was there ever?

—*I'm done with despair,* I told myself.

Ahead of me, a flicker of movement attracted my notice. Iril and Fayne. I picked up my pace. Off to the left, a shimmer in the air urged me on. A daemon. Closing in on the oblivious travelers.

My feet tore across the shale. Pebbles skittered away. Even at this breakneck pace, I wouldn't make it in time. I cursed Iril and her blind foolishness. She had no idea ...

I narrowed the gap to the point where I could clearly see Iril and Fayne. He staggered behind her, not looking very steady. She held his arm in a tight grip, dragging him along. The shimmer, now a few paces away from them, coalesced into the form of a fatesbane, a minor daemon. I skidded to a halt and gathered my energy for a strike, however ineffective the distance rendered it.

Iril's head snapped to the left. She'd spotted the fatesbane. Her lips moved. She flung out her arm. No doubt trying a spell. Her body jerked as she noted its failure. The fatesbane sized up the humans. I suspected the unfamiliar wrapping around the essences confused it. It decided the bodies didn't pose a problem and lunged for the humans at lightning speed. I flung my strike, but it bounced off the daemon. The thing didn't even flinch. I prayed to the Listener Iril would flee with Fayne.

Instead, she whipped the staff in a roundhouse at the daemon's head. The wood collided with its neck with a sickening crack. To my extreme surprise, the fatesbane vanished in a shrieking shimmer of nebulous fog. I gaped. The staff must store the power of the Fates themselves.

Seeing me, Iril wrestled Fayne to his feet from where he'd collapsed on the ground, but seeming more alert, Fayne resisted. Iril raised her head to look at me, and I could feel the malevolence in her glare, even though her eyes remained hidden. Iril took a knife from her belt, slashed Fayne's wrist then placed her sleeve over the gout of blood, soaking it. She whirled, and ran off.

I hurried to Fayne. He lifted his head, but I didn't think he truly saw me. His features blurred, as though he wasn't in full possession of his expression.

"Umb'a? Wha' are you doing he'e?" he said.

I knelt down beside him, touched his face. Such a miracle that he still breathed, warm and alive. By any logic, his physical form shouldn't be allowed to exist in the middle realm. Neither should mine. I marveled at Iril's power, even as I cursed it.

"Be still," I said to Fayne. His dopiness indicated to me that Iril's link still held. I needed to break it, otherwise Iril's whims would hold us both hostage. But first I ripped a piece off my own sleeve and staunched the flow of blood at his wrist. I rocked back onto my heels and frowned.

I stared at Fayne. I could still sense his essence, ever so faintly. He was dying, faster now. Not in the next instant, but inexorably, his soul's hold on his body loosened. I couldn't tell how long he had, but I knew the outcome was inevitable.

Did his presence in the middle realm increase the rate at which the link weakened him? What if he died here? Such an abnormal death—the implications for his soul scared me. I didn't know what skipping a step in the Great Cycle meant.

At best, his soul would simply separate from his body, and he'd make the journey to the Far Gates like any other. But would a regular shade find his soul this far from the veil? I doubted I could effectively protect him for the entire trek if one didn't.

At worst, a physical body dying here might disturb the balance of the Cycle—like my effect on the physical realm. That could mean oblivion for Fayne.

I couldn't risk him dying here. I had to get him out, and while I looked for a way to do that, I needed to slow down his deterioration. Assuming his presence here, and his link to Iril, doubly affected that downslide, the one thing I could currently affect was the link. There must be something different I could try that wouldn't break Fayne like I'd broken the stone.

I took his hand in mine, placed the palm of my other hand against his cheek. "Fayne, can you hear me?"

No response. He was fading fast now.

"Fayne. I will not let you die. I love you. Do you hear me? With the Listener as my witness, I love you, and you *will not die*."

I closed my eyes and concentrated on feeling out Fayne's essence. Yes. Right there. A tiny dent in the ephemeral shell that encapsulated him. A kink where Iril inserted the link. It felt different than the one between me and the pendant, or the staff. I probed more deeply.

My breath caught—I also felt Iril. I settled even deeper into my examination. And then it hit me. Her essence was getting weaker, fading slowly. Which meant she was dying as well. What was she up to? She must know she couldn't stay in the middle realm without a plan to return. Unless she hadn't anticipated arriving or an extended stay. That would mesh with the Izir's opinion that she didn't understand all the ramifications of her actions.

I retracted my mental feelers. What did I think I was doing? I didn't understand the ramifications of my own actions, either. I stared at Fayne. His head nodded, and he looked like he was having a harder time drawing breath. I set my jaw. I'd promised him I wouldn't let him die. Which meant I had to try something, anything, no matter how desperate.

I probed around the dent a bit more, to determine if I could somehow prevent damage to Fayne when I severed the link. I told myself that if I could separate an essence from its body, I could break apart two linked essences. Over and over, I whispered it to myself. And over and over, my inner voice contradicted me. *You either wind up killing the body or breaking the shell.* Maybe the duality of this link would help. Or maybe I'd get lucky and the backlash would kill Iril instead. The divot-like feeling gave me an idea. If instead of twisting like I did with souls, I slipped a wedge of the shade power against the link like a pick, just so …

It felt for all the world like a reed piercing the surface of a pond.

Fayne gasped and collapsed to the ground. Fates! I killed him!

Then

Kairiya rose from her squat over the midden, pulled up her breeches and buckled her belt. On her way back to the banquet tent, a dark figure blocked her path.

"You don't have much more time to act, child."

Kairiya sighed. "I know, Asrar. But what if I prevent the marriage another way?"

Asrar stepped forward and peered into Kairiya's eyes. Asrar possessed an uncanny knack for uncovering secrets. Kairiya tried to hold steady but her gaze flickered to the lake. Asrar clutched at Kairiya's tunic. "You let your emotions get in the way of your task."

Kairiya shook her head. "Maybe my way is better. Did you consider that, Mother?"

"Better?"

"No one gets hurt this way. No one gets killed."

Asrar cackled. "Trust me, child, because you can't trust a man. You're fooling yourself. You're the only one who will get hurt."

Kairiya brushed past Asrar. "We'll see."

Kairiya approached the tent, but heard a commotion inside. She hung back in the shadows. Her father stumbled out of the tent, Murran on his heels, sword drawn.

"You thought to poison this treaty? Where is she?" Murran shouted.

Kairiya tensed. How could he have found out? If she ran now, she wouldn't survive for long in the mountains without her gear.

Orrith regained his balance and spun to face Murran. But Murran was upon him, and smashed his jaw with a left hook. Orrith's head whipped sideways. He keeled over, spit blood and a tooth upon the ground. Kairiya felt surprisingly little sympathy for him.

"She's your mistress!" Murran shouted. "Your responsibility. If you don't tell me where to find her, I'll hang you for treason against the Clans."

Kairiya relaxed. Murran was after Asrar. Kairiya glanced towards the midden, but Asrar was nowhere to be seen.

Orrith muttered something and Murran leaned the edge of his sword against the pulsing vein in Orrith's neck. At the entrance to the tent, curious Clansmen and Gherza watched the unfolding drama. Murran continued.

"You will find your witch, and then you will gather your things and leave. Take the rest of Clan Dayr with you. And be glad I don't kill you where you kneel. The Elders will deal with you when the rest of us get home."

Orrith rose from the dirt and jerked his head at the Clansmen gathered near the tent. "Dayr won't stand with blood traitors."

Murran spat at Orrith's feet. "I won't let a bitter old woman and a deluded bigot jeopardize peace and honest trade between our peoples. Get out of my sight."

"Honest trade!" Orrith pitched his words to the Clansmen standing behind Murran. "Do you really believe Arneth will share the bounty with you once this marriage is consummated? They will use their new family ties to cut you all out of the timber harvest. They duped the Elders. You'll see. Align yourselves with Clan Dayr now. I'll guarantee you a piece of the new trade. Mark my words. The Watcher looks not with a kind eye upon mixing our blood with these savages. Arneth will suffer the Judge's wrath."

Several Clansmen jeered, but Kairiya noticed the ones who did wore Arneth colors and would remain loyal to Murran. Orrith had succeeded in planting doubts with the others. Under the glare of the remaining Clansmen and Gherza, he cut his losses and walked away. Kairiya knew Asrar would follow not far behind. Now she was all alone.

~*~

Kairiya met Murran early the next morning for one of their Gherza culture sessions. After the events of last night, she'd worried he wouldn't show up. She still found it odd that she should be the one teaching him Gherza ways, given that Asrar's bitterness filtered her own perception of the Gherza.

She'd avoided Jezarel since Orrith fled from Murran's wrath. No one came to challenge her yet about her own origins, but Jezarel was not stupid. She would soon ask what connected Asrar with Orrith if she so hated the Clansmen. A quick jump linked those suspicions to the question of what exactly Kairiya was doing here herself.

Jezarel performed her finger dance for Murran tomorrow, a simple formality before the evening wedding. Kairiya was running out of time. She could still complete her father's mission if she made Murran break off the wedding. An entirely better way—no one got hurt and she gained a family in the bargain.

Murran arrived, and Kairiya stood on the balls of her feet to brush his cheek with her lips. Murran held up a hand to stop her.

"We mustn't," he said.

"But I thought …"

"I do care for you."

"Then call off the wedding." Orrith would never forgive her for changing the plan in this way, but what did that matter now?

"I wish that were possible."

"It's as possible as you want it to be. Just say the word."

"I can't. Too many factions want to plunge our peoples into a war that will just leave all of us worse off. The Gherza who shot that arrow. Even some of my fellow Clansmen. They can't see how a peace will benefit all of us. They value preserving our differences more than lives. They want to take what belongs to the Gherza by force. It's …"

"Don't say it." The unspoken words rang in Kairiya's ears. *For the greater good.*

"Please understand."

"It's you who doesn't understand! You said you would call off the wedding. I gave myself to you! What am I supposed to do now?"

"I never said I would call it off. I just said I didn't want it."

"You let me think … You let me believe …" It was all just a lie then. He'd used her just like everybody else.

"Kairiya, come back with me. After the wedding. I can give you a croft. We can be discreet."

He might as well have punched her. Here it was—her dream of a small croft of her own, twisted into her worst nightmare. She would be just like Asrar in the end, living on the fringes, muttered about, looked at askance by her respectable neighbors. An object of gossip and ridicule. Always second after Jezarel. Jezarel, who used her like a tool also, then reneged.

Kairiya tried one last argument. "You're just a prize to her. Why would you want to live a lie?"

Murran's face hardened. "You misjudge Jezarel. Besides, it's my duty. I have a responsibility to the Clans, and to the Gherza. Love is just the stuff of dreams."

Kairiya felt the mask of indifference drop over her face. The one she assumed each and every time a new rejection hammered her heart into the ground. It always made it worse if her tormentor knew how much she hurt.

"Without dreams, a people comes to nothing," Kairiya answered as she walked off.

She entered her tent, sensed an intrusive presence.

"You see? Men cannot be trusted. I told you he would betray you."

"Shut up, Asrar. You know nothing."

"He did to you exactly what was done to me. When I refused to give up, and did everything in my power to hold onto the man I love, how did they reward me? Exile."

"I thought you left with Orrith."

"I needed to make sure you would carry out the plan."

Kairiya remained silent. Asrar stirred in the shadows, and Kairiya raised her meager defenses against Asrar's power.

"I won't coerce you into it, my daughter. But he used you

354

sorely. Will you just let him trample on your honor this way?"

The rage that Kairiya held in with such desperation since Murran cast her aside threatened to overwhelm her. He used her, yes. But Kairiya held no illusions about what Asrar did either. Kairiya would forever be the tool, never the hand that wielded it. They all sought to use her; now she'd turn their instrument against them.

Kairiya resolved to be the best tool possible. The hardest knife. The truest arrow.

Now

I screamed with rage and grief. Cursed myself for a fool.

Then realized I could still sense Fayne. And his essence wasn't standing next to his body awaiting an escort to the Gates. His chest rose and fell. Then he blinked. And sat up.

Not twisting at the link worked! Giddy with relief, I cradled his face in my hands.

"Umbra," he said. "Where are we?"

I shook my head. Then I kissed him.

He didn't pull away, and the clean, vital scent of him invaded me. I savored the moment. The warm softness of his lips. His matching hunger for mine. It wouldn't last, couldn't. But Fayne lived, free of Iril's foul influence. Nothing else mattered.

Except getting him out of here. I could still sense his soul fading. I could save him if I returned him to the physical realm.

Fayne's hand reached out and gripped mine. I squeezed his fingers, brushed his closed eyelids with my lips then leaned back. Fayne's pale eyes gazed solemnly into my own, before drifting away and taking in his surroundings. The jagged shale, sharp boulders, and glowing twilight would be like nothing he'd seen before.

"What is this place?" he asked.

"The middle realm," I answered. Fayne didn't understand, so I chose the path of bluntness. "Where you go when you die."

"I don't feel dead."

"That's because you're not."

"But how—"

"Iril."

He nodded as though this explained everything. Then he stared at me, hard. "You did something to me. I felt ... clouded, before. Now I don't."

I told him of Iril's link, how I severed it. I clasped his hand again. I might never get another opportunity. "Fayne, there's something I have to tell you. About Lian." I ploughed on. "I killed him."

Fayne blinked. Once. Twice. "Is he ... here?"

"I don't think so, Fayne. I think he's just gone."

"To the Far Gates already?"

"No. Gone from the Cycle."

At this, he repossessed his hand, and edged away. I sighed. I forced myself to watch him struggle with his grief.

"He deserved a trial, Umbra. No matter what he did, it was for me as the last of the family to punish him in life, and the Fates to judge his soul at death."

"I know, Fayne. But he would have killed both me and Shirra. If I'd had any other way to defend myself, I would have used it."

His jaw quivered. A change of subject might give him time to absorb Lian's death without focusing on me as its cause. "What do you remember of what happened just before I broke Iril's link?"

"I ... I think ... Iril fought a monster."

"*That* was a soul eater. A fatesbane. It would have taken both your souls, but for the staff." I looked more closely at Fayne. So he did have an awareness of events despite Iril's link. "Fayne, do you remember anything else? What Iril made you do before she dragged us here?"

"I—" He cut off and I knew what he'd seen in his mind. "She—we went after that stone."

"Not just you and her."

"No. Lian too. Lian did her bidding. She told him you were Rhinn. He ... he railed at her for that. For undoing the lesson he'd tried to teach Rhinn." Fayne put a hand to his temple. "Fates, Umbra, forget what I said. He moved beyond my judgment long ago. He asked for whatever you gave him." He sighed. "Are you really Rhinn?"

"No."

He smiled wanly. "That eases my mind somewhat. Otherwise, I could have prevented all this by loving you like I was supposed to before you died."

"Then maybe you would have died in that ambush along with your father."

Fayne squeezed my hand. "The Fates had other things in mind for me." He fell silent for a moment. "Umbra, once you obtained the staff, why didn't you just run? Or hole up somewhere and figure out how to heal yourself?"

"I couldn't leave you to Iril. She was draining you, Fayne. It was only a matter of time before she killed you."

"No abandoning each other, eh?"

I shook my head. "Never." Or at least, not until the spell that held me together released me.

"Umbra, if we get out of here, will you consider staying? With me?"

"What are you saying, Fayne?"

"That I would pledge my troth to you now, if you wished it."

I gasped, and for once, in the middle realm, my emotions overwhelmed me. The joy of it, the sheer crazy wonderfulness. "Fayne, it's impossible."

"Why?"

"Besides the fact that I probably can't stay in the physical realm?"

"But if you could ..."

"If I could, it's not fair to you. You're the head of your Clan. What am I? In the eyes of the world, nothing. Worse than nothing. You'll be ostracized."

"If you help reclaim the staff from Iril, no one will gainsay you a honored place among the Clans."

I bit my lip. He made it sound so easy. "What about children, Fayne? You need heirs."

"Who's to say there won't be any?"

"I can't know that I can have children. My body was made, and likely poorly." Just a construct. Not really real.

Fayne caressed my palm with his thumb. "At least think on it. And if not marriage, then, I promise that whatever time you have before you cross over again, I will spend it with you."

Words. Just words.

Instead of being angry with my bitter, inner voice, I felt pity once again for that girl. She would never see beyond the pain someone had caused her, not enough to trust. But I'd come to realize something. I wasn't her. Not anymore.

I lingered for a moment, treasuring the feeling of my hand in his. Despite Lian, despite what I'd done, Fayne still believed in me. He looked past all the things that others would judge me for, and accepted me. For that above all, I loved him. I could never show that love for him by sharing his life, or giving him children, growing old with him, despite what he'd just said. But I would do anything to save him, and see him happy.

"We can't stay here," I said. "If I don't get you back, you'll die for real. I don't know how long we have. Did Iril say anything about where she was headed?"

Fayne's forehead creased as he extracted the memory from his link-fogged brain. "She muttered something about a tree."

Oh Fates. "The Tree of Souls?"

Fayne nodded.

My stomach clenched. I leapt to my feet. "Come on. We have less time than I thought."

~*~

Out from the shimmering gloom, the Tree faded into our awareness like the afterimage left on the inside of one's eyelids after staring at an object too long. It wobbled and coalesced into our vision, its shape not quite discernible if looked at straight on. I suppressed an urge to flee.

I had never felt comfortable near the Tree. According to the lore of the few other shades I'd ever met, daemons would not set foot beneath its branches, which made it one of the few safe havens in the middle realm. But it always induced a nagging unease in my heart.

Its bark, smooth and charcoal black, absorbed the light

around it. Its leaves, rustling even though no breeze ever disturbed the middle realm, gleamed a dark, oily green, so deep as to almost be black themselves.

Shade lore told that the Tree gathered up the essences of those who didn't make it to the far realm—the Irredeemed. It acted as the conduit that broke them down and allowed their pure energy to nourish new souls in the physical world. I didn't know if this was true. But I suspected it explained Iril's interest in the Tree. A necromancer's power lay in his or her ability to command another's essence. She'd view the Tree as the mother lode, and it might account for where all the beetles came from.

The only thing I knew for certain about the Tree was that for a couple of centuries now, it had been dying. An ancient shade I'd once come across told me he'd never seen it shed any leaves until after I entered the middle realm. Now, a thick carpet of foliage lay all around it, and once full branches showed skeletal against the sky. No one knew what would happen when the Tree died. Would it cease to shelter travelers on their journey? What would become of new souls if the Tree died?

Fayne jostled my elbow. "Do you see her?" he asked.

"No. We'll need to get closer."

"Hard to sneak up on anyone in terrain this flat."

Fayne was right. Between where we crouched behind a shard of jet rock, and the Tree, the ground lay bare except for the dead leaves. The eye-tricking gloom obscured Iril, or else she hid behind the trunk.

On our way here to intercept Iril, I'd wracked my brain to come up with some sort of plan to get us out of the middle realm. Fayne already looked ill, the whites of his eyes yellowish, his skin an unhealthy grey.

Iril used the staff to bring us here, somehow opening a gateway between the realms. The staff's power rested in Fayne's world, and Iril claimed the Greys' possession of it tied it to Fayne. I did not possess Iril's strength in powers of necromancy, and I doubted I could cast the same spell as she.

But I did possess some minor ability to break the barrier between the worlds. When a person died, I came across, however briefly, and to the living, however intangible my form. But could I bring a living body back with me from this direction? The question skittered through my skull without an answer.

Shade legend also told that the veil between the worlds thinned where the Tree grew in the middle realm. Some even said the Tree was a reflection of another tree in the world of the living.

There was nothing for it. A faint hope in my untested power to cross the veil as a physical being, and an intuition that the staff's own resonance with the living world would help us across, spurred me on.

"We'll need to ambush her." I outlined my plan to Fayne. I stood up to put it into action, but he gripped my hand. "Distract her if you can," I told him, "but leave the actual fight to me. You're not equipped to face her."

"I'm not afraid to die." He brought my hand to his lips, pressed a kiss against my palm. "But if we don't make it, Umbra …" He left the thought hanging.

But my heart didn't. So many ifs. If I wasn't a shade. If we'd met while I lived. If I really was a good person.

He backed away to circle around and approach the Tree from

a different direction.

Too late. For so many things.

~*~

I walked straight up to the Tree, its outline solidifying as I got closer. Dead leaves susurrated underfoot. The canopy above trembled in an invisible breeze I could not feel. Iril crouched next to a gnarled root. She heard me approach, rising to face me, leaning on the staff. She didn't look healthy, either. I allowed a small flower of hope to blossom.

"Where's Fayne?" Iril asked, looking over my shoulder.

"Dead."

"Liar."

She couldn't know this for sure. Not with the link broken. I pressed on with my little misdirection, letting my face sag into what I hoped looked like grief.

"He's *dead*, Iril! You brought him here, and it killed him," I said. "A living person can't remain so for long in the middle realm. The far planes pull too strongly. I know you can feel it. I can see it in your posture." I stroked her ego. "Your incredible power let you last longer than Fayne. But it won't do you any good here. How long have you honed it?"

"Longer than most."

"Nobody lives forever."

"I will."

"Not if you stay here, you won't."

"I've lived for two hundred years and I have no intention of dying now. The souls of the living are generous to me."

"Generous? You steal their essences." I remembered Perfyd Tower. The skeletal, comatose almost-corpse Fayne and I found there. The one I'd lacked the courage to send on its final journey, in case any chance remained to reunite the essence with its body. The deep, raging horror that swamped me then flooded me again.

I'd suspected but needed to hear it from her own lips. She'd taken the soul to extend her own life. How many more did she suck dry over the years? Only small-time magicians and deluded fools tended to practice the art of necromancy. The goal: always control over death, but no one ever achieved it. Except Iril.

"Steal is a strong word. I prefer to think of it as enhancing the usefulness of a life otherwise wasted."

"And that's not enough for you?"

Iril laughed. "I can only take one soul at a time. I'm tired of having to find a new donor every few years. It takes too much planning, and limits me. Much too hard to keep one's subjects in line when you're hiding a body in the basement. They tend to think they're next. After all this time, I'm tired of living in hiding. I wish to live in the open."

I couldn't fault her logic, warped as it was. Any rival who discovered her weakness would make short work of taking her down. I regretted my earlier mercy. I still didn't understand what any of this had to do with me. But then she added, "With my consort."

"Who would consort with you?"

She leaned into me and I felt the full intensity of her venom. "The one you took from me. Murran."

Her hooded head tilted as she searched my face for a reaction at the name. But I'd dealt with the discomfort of hearing it back at Arneth, even though I still didn't know why it induced so much guilt. My conscience thought me responsible for his death. So did

Iril.

I of all people could understand loneliness, despite the middle realm's muting of mine. Iril benefited from no such dampening of her feelings. She grieved alone, and plotted alone, for two hundred years. But what Iril wanted was twisted. Not to mention impossible.

"I can't bring him back for you. Lian implied you thought I could. But Murran's passed the Far Gates. Only the Fates can return him to the Cycle, and when they do, you won't recognize him as Murran."

"Your lack of faith hurts me. I found a way. If it works, I need you for something else. You are a guide—a conduit. Not all roads lead to the Far Gates."

She reached beneath her cloak and pulled out a jagged shard of the jet rock that littered the middle realm. I tensed, thinking she might stab me with it. But I guessed wrong: she whipped around and scored a deep gouge in the bark of the Tree.

Oily black sap welled from the scar. The sap burst into what I could only call a lightless flame. Shapes and figures flickered into brief existence before burning off into nothingness. I thought I heard faint, hissing screams.

"You're not the first shade I've played with, only the first I managed to fully embody. Before you, I trapped a few, forced them to tell me secrets the Fates would rather we mortals not know. You're a young shade, so you might not be privy to these yet. There's a Tree like this in each of the planes. You could even say the same Tree spans all the planes. The Middle Tree here is a vessel for the Irredeemed, whose souls nourish the roots of the Tree in our world. The Far Tree controls how most souls get

365

returned to the Cycle. Since they're connected, if the Fates haven't already given Murran back to the world, I can find him by communing with the Tree."

What she planned didn't sound anything like "communing" to me. Iril wiped the sleeve soaked in Fayne's blood over the staff. She held out the staff before her, and touched its tip to the wound in the Tree. Preternatural fire licked the entire length of the staff. Iril laughed as the inky flames caressed her skin.

A laugh that cut off with a violent gasp as Fayne slammed into her torso. Their tumbling bodies whacked the ground. The staff cartwheeled through the space between us, jarred loose from Iril's grip by Fayne's flying tackle.

Severed from the Tree's sap, the flames consuming the staff snuffed out. But they still lapped at the gash in the Tree's bark. Fearing Iril released something she couldn't control, I placed my hand over the opening to staunch the flow.

And screamed.

Screamed as the cold fire seared my palm. Howled as its necrotic blast scoured through my flesh.

Huddled mute as the firestorm of the Tree's power breached the last defenses around my heart.

As I remembered.

THEN

Kairiya waited in late afternoon in front of the cleft in the rock. The sun dipped low over the trees and dusk would inveigle her too quickly. Jezarel came soon to overcome her wedding night jitters here. Kairiya had run out of time. What if Murran didn't show?

A shuffling of leaves around a bend in the path altered the quality of the tension she felt. Murran strode towards her. "Why are we here?" he asked as he reached the opening.

"I told you. You need to understand one last thing about the Gherza before you marry into the tribe."

Kairiya slipped between the looming rocks, pausing to make sure Murran followed. They entered the clearing. Murran gasped.

"Is this … ?"

"Yes," she replied. "It is the Tree." Just as she told Jezarel what seemed so long ago, Asrar did tell her of this Tree. But she also told Orrith—without knowing its location—and Kairiya wondered how much he divulged to other Clansmen about it. Asrar always claimed that if the Clans gained dominion over this Tree, then nothing could prevent them from controlling the entire Aramar Plateau. Kairiya searched Murran's eyes for any sign of covetousness, but saw only wonder. The blood in her own veins thrummed in recognition.

Murran moved to touch the Tree.

"Wait." Kairiya inserted her body into his path. "We must do this right. When Gherza marry into this tribe, the elders show them the Tree and perform a special ceremony." Kairiya lied through her teeth but Murran had no way of knowing. "I worried they might not do this with you because of your foreign roots. There's no harm in sanctifying it tonight. My final gift to you. Let there be no bad blood between us."

Kairiya unslung the waterskin she carried. She uncorked it, pulled from her pouch a carved wooden cup she stole from the banquet tent.

"The cup came from a fallen branch of the Tree. The wine symbolizes the sap. The Gherza believe the Tree nurtures all life on the steppe." Kairiya poured the garnet wine into the cup. "Drink."

Murran took the cup from her hand. He downed the wine in three swallows. He tilted his head back for the dregs, and Kairiya struck. Her throat formed a deep resonant hum that moved up and down a quick atonal scale. She hurled all the energy she'd hoarded from the next realm at him, using every technique Asrar ever taught her in a single, focused onslaught. The black tide ripped through her and it was all she could do to hold on and not go down with it.

Murran slumped to the ground. Kairiya touched his forehead. Yes. She'd trapped his essence for now. If she had for once in her life succeeded in Asrar's teachings, he would stay out just long enough. Just before she released the magic, she focused once more deep inside herself and planted a thought in his head.

Kairiya reached behind her for the ax hidden against her back underneath her cloak. Daughter, friend, and lover no more—this would seal it. They'd all thought to use her for their own desires. And now none of them would get what they wanted. She stared at the Tree. Took a deep breath. Swung the ax.

The blade flayed open the trunk. Kairiya shrieked in pain.

Jezarel lowered her eyes as her father kissed her on each cheek. The sun set an hour ago. Her mother watched from behind the formal veil she donned for tonight's vigil. Jezarel could barely make out her mother's high cheekbones behind the gauze, meant to separate them visually, a preparating before she left one family to enter another. A final consignment of her daughter's fate to She Who Sees. The Izir placed his hand on Jezarel's shoulders and turned her towards the cleft in the rock.

"Go. Fast and meditate, and heed the wisdom of the Fates that the Tree places in your heart."

Jezarel left her parents behind at the entrance. She had much to think on tonight. She tried to take away his will, yet Murran still forgave her. There hadn't been enough forgiveness in her life. How could she expect to face the Fates at the end of her life if she'd gained her love through dishonesty?

She held her anger at the Clan raiders who murdered her brother close to her heart, warming it and nurturing it like the seed of a black prickly thorn bush. Maybe she resorted to tricks and deception to find love because the boys and men surrounding her could somehow sense the hardness within her. What if her father was right, and only love could heal all the rifts between the

Gherza and the Clansmen?

She resolved to work on the rifts in her own heart first. Murran was a good man—he put his people's honor above his own, saving the treaty after her stupid foolishness nearly destroyed it. Despite Asrar's influence, he could easily have blamed Jezarel for what she'd done, but he'd seen past that. Seen her.

Already her breath quickened at the thought of performing her finger dance for him. She would dance until he could feel her very soul moving for him, to prove to him that she was his and his alone. He'd be unable to take his eyes from her. Even the Fates would have to take notice of her flashing fingers and swinging hips. Jezarel smiled as she saw the end of the passage, the opening to the vale glimmering in the last of the dusky light.

Jezarel could make no sense of the sight that assailed her as she emerged into the hollow. The carnage was too much to grasp. The splintered tree, lying on its side, branches askew, spilled amber sap staining the earth. Murran, slumped against a rock, ax in hand. Kairiya, pale and panting, leaning against the fallen trunk.

Jezarel moaned. Kairiya just looked at her.

"Fates. Oh, Fates … Oh, Fates." No other words sprang to Jezarel's mind. She didn't want to look. Couldn't look. Had to look.

The Tree splayed like a broken bird. Already its leaves lacked luster, hung withering from the cracked branches. Even the quality of light in the vale had dimmed, more than the deepening dusk warranted. Jezarel strove not to picture the Tree's eventual skeletal decay, but her imagination betrayed her and images of burrowing beetles and flaccid mushrooms eating at the Tree's flesh crawled through her mind.

Still Kairiya just stood there. Languid, almost. How could she be so calm? All Jezarel's father's teachings flashed through her mind. The implications smashed into her soul just like Murran's ax. The Tree—dead. The Tree of the Fates. And Jezarel bore the responsibility. She'd shown Kairiya the vale. Trusted her. Trusted Murran.

Jezarel quailed. The Fates would punish the tribe. Mete out a terrible retribution to those who'd failed in their sacred duty.

They'd punish her. She was Fates damned now. She half expected the One Who Speaks to reach out this instant from the beyond and drag her into eternal penance in the middle realm.

Murran stirred, opened his eyes, raised his head in a daze.

"I couldn't stop him," Kairiya said.

Jezarel couldn't stem the keening that arose from somewhere deep within her.

"I thought if I showed him the Tree, he might choose me," Kairiya continued. "But he went berserk, and attacked it instead. I knocked him out, but it was too late."

"LIAR!" Murran shouted. "I didn't do this. I couldn't!"

Kairiya spoke to him as if to a child. "But you did, Murran, I saw you."

Murran's eyes zagged wildly back and forth. Jezarel could tell he did not see the scene before him, but scoured within himself for the truth. "Did I?" he asked, voice small and frightened. "I did. No. Yes."

He pounced on Kairiya, bludgeoning her with his fists. "Witch! Are you all witches?" Her lithe warrior's body couldn't shake off the sheer weight of him. Jezarel didn't move, even when she realized he was no longer punching, but had pulled out a knife and stabbed Kairiya with fierce, frightening intensity.

Finally he stopped, kneeling beside Kairiya's inert body, holding his head in his hands and rocking back and forth. Jezarel shook herself out of her own stupor. She sat down next to him.

"Murran."

"I'm sorry. So sorry. I've betrayed you, betrayed my people."

"Shh." Jezarel placed a quiet hand on his arm.

Murran stared at the Tree. "It will grow back, won't it?"

Jezarel shook her head. It would never grow back. Not without intervention from the Fates.

"The marriage … The marriage will make up for it, no? We can still join our people together."

"Together?" Regardless of whether she married Murran, Jezarel was forever sundered from the tribe. There would be no healing. No peace.

"You forgive me, don't you? I'll plant you a new tree, no—ten, fifty trees."

Jezarel smiled sadly. Murran leaned his head on her shoulder and sobbed. "Shhhh," she whispered again. She fingered the dagger she was to have used to extract the sacred sap for her cleansing ceremony. Plunged it into his heart.

Murran's head slid off her shoulder. He hit the ground like a sack of steppe grain. Beside her, Jezarel heard a gurgling cough, a harsh, desperate intake of breath. Kairiya.

"He really thought he did it," Kairiya said.

Jezarel looked around, took in the churned earth, the hacked roots of the Tree. Not a berserk attack, but a methodical, planned killing.

Jezarel saw Kairiya as if for the first time. The defiant tilt to her battered head. The small upwards quirk of her swollen lips. This wasn't contrition. It was triumph. And Jezarel brought Kairiya here, showed her the Tree, made her a blood sister.

"Ironic ... isn't it?" Kairiya could barely get the words past the blood welling in her mouth "That I should ... do the most damage with your best weapon, the arts ... and you with mine, the knife. I didn't think you would kill him. Now neither of us will have him. Murran ..." Kairiya's voice trailed off.

Jezarel shrieked. But it was too late. Jezarel killed the wrong person. Killed her love for no good reason. And by trusting Kairiya, brought about the destruction of the Tree. Jezarel reached out and ripped the pendant from Kairiya's neck.

She turned at a small sound behind her. Asrar crept from the opening in the vale wall. Jezarel's breath hitched and lurched against her ribs. She remembered Murran's words when he'd confronted Orrith. Preoccupied with her reprieve with Murran— coming to terms with her newly found understanding of the trust and respect around which one built true regard for another— she'd only half-heard his words. "*Old woman ... Witch ... Mistress.*"

Kairiya gulled her right from the beginning. She was a scion of the Clan faction opposed to anything Gherza. Jezarel's self-absorption played straight into their hands.

Asrar cackled when she saw the felled Tree. She shuffled over to it and picked up the ax. Jezarel reached out to stop her, but Asrar flicked a hand in Jezarel's direction, screeching out two notes like an annoyed raven. Jezarel found herself wrapped in numbness, wanting only to please Asrar. She watched with an almost comforting detachment as Asrar hacked off a straight branch from the Tree, set it aside, then collected kindling. But something within Jezarel snapped when Asrar struck her flint to the kindling. Merciful darkness overcame Jezarel as the warm flames snapped at the Tree.

She woke to the smell of woodsmoke. Saw her horror-struck parents stumble from the cleft. Felt the first small glimmer of fear as she noted the rage and despair in her father's eyes.

NOW

The torrent of remembrance ebbed, leaving me stunned but aware of my surroundings once again. Fayne and Iril still grappled on the ground next to the Tree. I took advantage of Iril's distraction and picked up the staff from the ground. I reached deep within myself and searched for the memory of the pull I always felt at a death in the physical realm—the call that compelled a shade to respond. Gripping the staff, I willed it to respond to its resonance with the world of the living. Because now I suspected what it was. I knew who I was. With every remaining drop of my tattered inner strength, I stabbed at the veil between worlds.

Nothing happened.

"Fool."

Iril's voice. Harsher with the years, but a voice I now recognized.

Fayne sprawled on the ground next to her. My heart quailed —I could not detect his essence within him, even though his chest still rose and fell.

"You stole his soul," I whispered.

"It only took one moment. For the Tree to gift me with its

power. The power to draw from more than one soul."

I gathered myself to strike, but hesitated.

"Good," Iril said. "I see you understand. You can't break this link, because we are truly one now. He'll die if you kill me. Move away from the Tree."

"Murran's gone. Gone! Nothing you do will bring him back." What I'd perceived when I'd touched the Tree—a churning morass of souls, not an identifiable personality among them … And all of them, small, shrunken: Irredeemed. No possibility of communion with anyone past the Far Gates. "Didn't you feel it too? You'll never find him. He's lost to you." *To both of us.*

"Murran," she whispered. For a moment, in the sag of her shoulders, the trembling of her fingertips, I saw the girl from long ago—why she wanted to make me kill my lover, because I'd tricked her into killing hers—the terrible grief that drove her. I thought that perhaps she could let it go. Instead she flung her arms wide, her cape billowing over Fayne's body. "Then this one is lost to you." She and Fayne disappeared behind a cloud of that infernal smoke she conjured so easily. One part of me tensed to leap after her. The other part screamed *NO! She wants you to follow. You're safe here.*

—*Really? Can I survive all the middle realm will throw at me as an embodied shade?*

What does survival matter?

—*Fayne's survival matters. Loving Fayne matters. Facing what I've done matters.*

I took out the broken *copal*, dipped my fingers into its remaining half shell. I scooped up the last traces of sticky amber, the last sap from that once-beautiful Tree that had given me my pendant. Swabbed them across the end of the staff, like I'd seen Iril do to get us here. Prayed to the Fates that I'd got it right. And dove after Iril, through the gap I wrenched open between the planes, my memories shrouding me in my own veil of grief.

You killed him.

I didn't know whether I meant Murran or Fayne. I hadn't delivered the fatal blow to Murran, but I bore the blame for his death. Just like I bore the blame for Fayne's predicament. The Fates seemed determined to rob me of the men I desired.

You robbed yourself.

Do you even know what love is?

My conscience mocked me. I knew it for truth.

I wouldn't have committed my crime if I truly loved Murran. Because I couldn't have what I wanted most, I'd chopped down the Tree out of spite. Not out of love, as I'd told myself at the time. Regardless of his flaws, he never deserved what I did to him.

And if I loved Fayne, I would have kept him out of this mess. Instead, he was as good as dead.

The Fates showed me mercy by turning me into a shade. The numbness of existence in the middle realm masked my guilt, keeping true feelings at bay. Now, with a real body and memories intact, my chest ached and tears stung my cheeks. Nothing dammed the flood of self-hatred that threatened to drown me. I'd told myself I wasn't that girl anymore, but now I knew it was wrong to try to separate myself from her deeds. They were mine, and I needed to own them if I was ever to atone for them.

"You don't give up, do you?" Iril said, but she smiled as if in victory. I took in the high cliffs, the narrow strip of stars overhead. Recognized the hidden meadow. Noted Fayne's body off to the side. Stopped my gaze before it could find the now-rotten stump. Then steeled myself. I had to look. I would only get one chance to beat Iril to it. If it was here, it would lie near the stump. But it wasn't.

"Fine," Iril continued. "You can help me teach these people their final lesson."

I thought she spoke in the abstract until a movement in my peripheral vision caught my attention. Near the cleft in the rocks stood a knot of people: Shirra, her father the Izir, Braith of Dayr, and a dozen or so Gherza and Clansmen. Shirra's distraught expression told me she'd spotted Fayne's body.

"Shirra, stay back! You can't beat her," I shouted.

Iril glanced at me. "Did you think to ambush me? You've condemned them to death."

She was right. Though I blamed myself, I lashed out anyway. "Are you Fates blinded, Shirra? I asked you to keep the ways in blocked, not enter yourself!" I could hear their upcoming demise in my aching words. "Run!" Instead, the Izir and Lord Dayr stepped forward together, and I truly looked at the scene before me. "Wait—why aren't you fighting?"

Braith spoke first. "Shirra found me near the pass, assessing the beetles. She explained the atrocity committed upon Lord Grey. She also told me of Lian Grey's vile betrayal of my daughter. I didn't want to believe her."

I marveled at what it might take for Braith of Dayr to swallow his pride and admit he'd been wrong. He must have seen the doubt on my face.

"The Council doesn't take kindly to being played for fools,

nor to one of our own being … compromised in such a manner. I, personally, could not face the Judge had I let stand Iril's desecration of all the Fates hold dear. We agreed to set aside our differences with the Gherza to fight our true enemy. Once we released the Izir from Lian's chains, he suggested we come in just in case you found an alternate path." He smiled wryly. "Which it seems you did."

"Enough from you!" Iril said. Braith clamped his lips together. She strode up to me. I swept the staff in front of me in a slow weaving motion, to keep her at a distance.

"Jezarel," I said. "They don't deserve your hatred. It's me you want."

Echoes of the two-hundred-year-old name resonated across the years between us. Iril quivered. I wondered when she'd last heard it. The harshness that so infected her voice before vanished when she finally spoke, shades of the young, lively girl she'd been rippling across its surface. "Kairiya."

Her hand shook as she swept back her hood. The face beneath was as beautiful as I remembered, if etched with a hardness I'd never seen when I lived. Darkness now subsumed her steppe-sky eyes. They looked more like the louring sky before a storm. Shadowy glints of madness or some worse evil swam in the irises. Maybe the souls of the people whose lives she'd stolen.

"I chopped down the Tree, Jezarel. I let you believe Murran did because I thought there was no way you'd marry him after that." I stared down at the starlight-silvered grass, almost expecting to see it still steeped in Murran's blood. "I didn't think you'd kill him."

"The honor of the tribe …" Iril's voice trailed off.

"You need to forgive yourself, Jezarel. Forgive them."

"Do you know what they did? Even after I avenged the sacrilege? They cast me out of the tribe. Said it was my fault for leading you to the Tree in the first place. That I'd abdicated the tribe's responsibility to the Fates."

"Nothing good comes from the dark arts. Let them go. Asrar misled you. Only grief comes from meddling with others' souls."

"Asrar! That bitch. She's the one who kept your little souvenir," Iril waved at the staff—with the *copal* and its amber sap, one of the last remnants of the Tree of Souls in the physical plane, "when she fled back to the Clanholds with Orrith."

I glanced at Braith, whose eyes widened at the mention of his ancestor. He looked disconcerted at Iril's characterization of the arrival of the Staff of Binding within the Clans. I supposed I should consider Braith my step-step-stepsomething or other.

Iril choked back a sob. "The barbarians left us nothing. Without the Tree to shade our lives, the steppe dried up. It took me years to get strong enough, and then find her. But when I did, she was my first. The first soul I took. Asrar gave that father of yours everything he wanted." Iril's glare should have withered Braith in his boots. "Just look at his get. So smug. Rich and powerful. It gave me endless pleasure to watch Lian take his whelp from him when I claimed the staff."

Braith flinched at Iril's mention of Rhinn. I shuddered. I hadn't liked my mother much but she didn't merit that fate. Never to cross to the middle realm, never given the chance to traverse the Far Gates and perhaps return to the Great Cycle. Surely she didn't deserve that.

But you do.

I couldn't save Fayne. I didn't know how to stop Iril. But maybe if I killed her, that would be enough to undo the taint Shirra's father spoke of. Rid the world of the last casualty of my sin. Then use the staff to send myself to oblivion.

Iril intruded on my thoughts. "… take even more. I feel your pull. I can take more than one, and now you'll bring them to me. With you as my conduit, they'll never stop me."

"I won't let you use me like that."

Iril smiled. "Won't you, Kairiya?" She walked over to her right, dragging my reluctant gaze after her. Stopped, bent down. Over the stump. The stump of the Tree I'd chopped down those long years past. She slipped her fingers into splits within the cracked and rotted wood, looking for something. Then, straightening up, she shrieked. "Where? Where have you hidden it?" She took a threatening step towards Shirra's group.

The Izir shrugged. "I don't know what you mean."

Iril lunged for him and clutched his face between both her hands. Shirra stiffened, and looked from the Izir, to me, and then, of all places to her hip pouch. "The dagger," Iril demanded. "I know you took it. Give it to me."

The Izir grimaced at the pressure of her fingers on his jaw. "I do not have it."

"Then you will tell me who does." Instead of questioning him, she clenched her fingers into talons. The Izir's eyes rolled back into his head. He sagged, and Iril tossed him away like an empty water skin. Shirra took off like a flushed rabbit. Iril, the questing hound, turned. In the same instant, I figured out what Shirra tried to tell me with her eyes. I darted towards her.

My position and Shirra's charge gave me several steps'

advantage over Iril. Shirra shouted, "In the main pouch!" and tossed me the bag. I dropped the staff to catch the bag. I fumbled with the buckle. Iril's footsteps smacked the earth like a headsman's ax.

Fates, Fates, Fates! Do I have time to destroy it? But how?

I clutched the bag to me, scrabbling at the flap, and plunged my hand inside.

Iril's tackle clobbered me in the ribs. I tumbled, sprawling. The hit knocked the bag flying, strewing its contents across the ground. I whipped my fist at Iril's temple, but she rolled away— unnaturally spry for a two-hundred-year-old. My knuckles crunched against a rock, splitting open. I kicked at her ribs instead. Heard a satisfying crack.

Where is it? Find it, find it!

I scanned the ground. Hardtack, feminine rags, several coins, two stoppered vials, a flint—there! I leapt towards it.

Iril's hand came down on a dagger that lay propped against the flint, as if on display. She pushed herself into a crouch, an ugly smile twisting her face. "Look what I found," she said. "Look familiar? Do you feel the burn in your chest? The pain from a dozen stabs from this 'instrument?' Do you hear its song of death, the one it sings only to you?"

Murran's dagger. The one he'd killed me with.

"That's the advantage of a new body, Jezarel. No old wounds." *Liar.* The pain still seared. Fresh as if it was yesterday. A worse hurt pierced into the core of my heart: knowing how I'd driven Murran to do it.

"Then maybe you'll feel this." Iril backed up a step, picked up the staff, and scored it with the dagger, carving a deep ridge down half its length. Her lips moved soundlessly. They enunciated my name, the syllables unmistakable.

I froze as the chill formed within me. I couldn't stop it. It built in a wave of freezing death all around me. Frost silvered beneath my feet. A column of icy darkness welled up into the sky, spread out until it dimmed the stars. They glimmered behind a veil of hoarfrost.

Several tugs plucked at me. Shirra and Braith of Dayr collapsed to the ground next to the Izir, the group of soldiers a breath behind them. Their souls impacted mine with a brief and sudden flicker of horror before Iril wrenched them from me, snuffing out everything that made them human.

I moaned. If I'd grabbed the knife just a few instants faster

. . .

A thin icicle of frost formed between me and the staff. Iril threw her head back in ecstasy, as life funneled through me to her.

The wave of death intensified to an avalanche. I had no control. The power of the staff amplified my shade ability beyond anything I'd imagined.

Far away, a shepherd's soul, unable to resist my pull, separated from his body and winged towards me. Too distant to see, the truth still hammered at me—people keeled over, dead, everywhere, the Clan host, the Gherza, mothers in the middle of going about their daily routine, children playing Fates' Bluff, everyone. I pulled essences from farther beyond, souls coming to me from across the mountains and barren sands. My reach encroached into the Clanholds and out into the desert-dry steppe.

From a trickle of essences to a torrent so fast. The effect fed on itself. Soon I might explode into a million shards of ice, but still Iril laughed. What did she expect would remain to lord over when she was done?

The Izir was right. I had become the end of all things.

~*~

I can't let this happen.

Within the flood of death, I felt a swarm of stunted souls. The beetles.

Maybe I can do one good thing, I thought. *But who will be left to see it?*

Since they were still nominally human, I focused a minute portion of my attention towards the insects, and gathered them up with a flick of thought. I wondered what effect they might have on Iril. Did absorbing the Irredeemed make one irredeemable as well? I spit their souls at Iril.

She didn't even flinch.

Fates! It was a plea, not an oath this time. Surely the Fates wouldn't let this happen. Surely they'd intervene at this distortion of their intent.

But the Fates remained silent, and still Iril consumed.

I have to die.

But what if the Izir was right? What if my death caused more destruction anyway?

I had to risk it. I couldn't cut off the flow to Iril any other way.

My gaze fell on the staff, the only physical weapon around. Iril held me in a psychic lock but I could still move.

Impale yourself on the staff.

Yes, I decided. And Iril too, if I could manage it.

Embrace death.

I grabbed the end of the staff. Iril, sensing something wrong, jerked it away. The tip of the staff brushed against my brand. A trickle of fire burned at my throat, so faint against the freezing torrent rushing the other way.

I don't want to die.

And I knew. The searing truth blazed incandescent in my heart. After two centuries of escorting the dead, shepherding them along their journey, wondering when the Fates might release me, aching for any kind of oblivion, I knew.

I wanted to live. I had never truly lived. Never truly loved.

And the answer blossomed within me as well. I wrenched the staff from Iril's hands. Slashed my hand against a jagged rock, wrapped my bleeding palm around the staff and drove it into the ground. My blood linking me to the power of the last branch from the Tree of Souls, more than enough to counter Iril's compulsion.

Iril shrieked when the link between us severed. But still the currents of death raged within me.

Iril cackled. "You can't stop it! They'll all die anyway!"

"You forget. I touched the sap of the Middle Tree too."

And I used its gift. Gathered the power of all the souls rushing to me, stored them inside me, instead of passing them on to Iril. All their lives coursed through me. The joy. The sadness. The sheer vibrancy them all.

Beneath my palm, their energy poured into the staff, my blood feeding its wood, the grain becoming engorged with sap. I grabbed Iril's wrist. Yanked it up and bit her hard. She cried out with pain, her blood hot and salty on my tongue. I shifted my grip so my bleeding hand covered the wound.

"Blood sisters," I whispered.

And all the essences she'd just stolen flowed back through her into me. Into the staff. Which now pushed out roots into the meadow's soil. Shoots wriggled out from its side, branches reaching out to the sky.

The roots spread, and my limbs warmed. I'd stemmed the tide. I charged the Irredeemed with nourishing those roots, then sent each life back to its owner, shared each person's joy as they became one with the new Tree. Its buds sprouted and its shade spread over the land.

Iril jerked her arm, trying to escape me. The reverse flow between us picked up strength, and she fought me harder. My hold never slackened.

Suddenly, her frantic efforts ceased. "I can give it to you," Iril said. "Everything you've ever wanted."

"And what would that be?"

Iril pointed to Fayne. "Him."

"I've already taken him back." I'd felt the Tree restore his essence.

"Not his soul. A life with him. I can make you mortal. Or not mortal, even. You could go on, even after he dies. As long as I don't die, you live."

Did I believe her offer of mortality? I looked at Fayne, let Iril's offer tempt me, imagined it all: Fayne and I together, loving each other, living as couples are meant to live. "And in return, I give you … ?"

"Let me go. I promise to leave here, and never come back."

"That's not what I meant. There's always a price—in lives or souls. Who dies so I can stay?"

"Anyone you like. I can get her," Iril indicated Shirra's limp form, "out of your way, so that no distractions tempt your lover."

Fayne—all to myself. For however long we lived.

I shook my head. It didn't matter if Iril told the truth. If I gave in, let Iril do this, I could never face Fayne. Even if I didn't choose Shirra as the sacrifice, he'd always know—I'd always know—that an innocent died to keep us together. That people continued to die to keep Iril alive, to keep her from facing the Fates' judgment. I wanted Fayne so much. Just not on Iril's terms.

So I gave them all back. Every single soul I'd taken. I laughed, a clear, joyous belly laugh the likes of which I couldn't remember ever consuming me.

And then it was done.

Beside me, Iril moaned. Without the sustenance of the essences she'd ravished, her smooth skin parched and split, her fingers gnarling like the branches of some twisted shrub. Farther away, I saw Fayne stir, and I smiled.

But my own hold on this world loosened. I didn't have much time. With the Tree restored, and Iril dying, Iril's spell lacked the power to keep me embodied.

I knelt beside Fayne.

He lifted his head. "I always knew you weren't a monster."

I stroked his cheek, thought of what I'd done to Murran and Jezarel, of the death within me. "You're wrong. I used to be."

"No longer, then."

"True. You saved me." I caught a glimpse of the grey world behind the veil. "Fayne, I have to go."

"Stay. Please stay."

"I can't. We knew we might not have much time. I only wish

it could have been longer."

"Then take me with you."

"Oh, Fayne, no. You don't mean that. You need to live."

"For what? It's my fault they're all dead. Father, Rhinn. Even Errith. I let it happen. Through my own selfishness, my own blindness."

"No, Fayne. Don't let your grief blind you. Lian killed them. And Iril put him up to it. There are still people here who love you. Live for them."

"It's you I want, Umbra."

"Where I'm going, you can't follow. Yet. But I promise, when the time comes, I'll be the one waiting to show you to the Gates." I put a finger to his lips as he interrupted. "When you leave here, you must seal up the cleft. Shirra will explain. The Tree must thrive in peace."

"You'll help me."

"No, Fayne. The Fates have another plan for me." I stroked his hair, but already the silky feel of it was lost to my deadened fingers.

"Umbra, don't …"

"I'd have one thing from you before I go, Fayne. Will you say it? Just once? My real name? Kairiya."

"Kairiya … I love you, Kairiya."

I drank in his sea-green eyes one last time. "Go, there's a lot of work to do. Unite the Clans. You should reconsider Shirra's offer. She's not what you think. But she's an honorable woman. Make peace with the Gherza. Heal the rift between you now that we've healed the steppe."

My lips brushed his in a final kiss. My body dissolved,

wrapping him in an embrace of smoke, and I gave him the only gift I had left. "I love you."

And I went to accompany Jezarel to the Far Gates.

ACKNOWLEDGMENTS

There are so many people to thank for their help over the years in getting this book into your hands.

First and always, thanks to my husband Guylain for supporting me during the ups and downs of this book.

To the folks at KidCrit who had a first look, even though it's not a kids' book, thanks for your thoughts on a very rough draft: Mahtab Narsimhan, Ellen C. Oh, Marsha Skrypuch, Hélène Boudreau, Carmen Wright, Eric E. Wood, Sharon Jones., Niki G. Elias, Suzanne, and Sheryl Prowse.

To the Viable Paradise staff and alumni: thanks for accepting me into your tribe, and particularly for feedback and encouragement: Elizabeth Bear, Debra Doyle, Jim MacDonald, Theresa Neilsen-Hayden, John Scalzi, Athena Andreadis, F. J. Bergmann, Carolyn Burke, Marko Kloos, Steve Kopka, Grant Simmons, Chang Terhune, and Alberto Yañez. Also thanks to Tiffani Angus for critiquing *that* scene.

For page critiques and encouragement that they may or may not remember, thanks to Robert J. Sawyer, Don McQuinn, and

James McCann.

Thanks to Bev Katz Rosenbaum for a zippy developmental edit.

To all my beta readers: your feedback and friendship helped make this book better. Eric Griffith, Janice Hardy, Marko Kloos, Steve Kopka, kc dyer, Mike Walsh, Juliane Knoll, and Beth Morris Tanner: you all rock.

To cover artist extraordinaire, Heather McDougal: you make my books beautiful.

And to you, reader, thanks for taking the time to share Umbra's world with me.

If you enjoyed this book, please consider leaving a review on Amazon, Goodreads, or your favorite book site.

Reviews and word of mouth are an independent author's life blood.

This independent author thanks you!

ganache
media

For more books by Ganache Media
visit
www.ganachemedia.com

Follow us on social media:

FB: www.facebook.com/ganachemedia
Twitter: @ganachemedia

Follow Katrina Archer online at
www.katrinaarcher.com

Social Media
FB: www.facebook.com/katrinaarcherauthor
Twitter: @katrinaarcher

Katrina Archer lives and writes on her sailboat in Vancouver, BC, Canada. She has worked in aerospace, video games, and film, and has been known to copy edit for fun. She is the author of the dark fantasy *The Tree of Souls*, the young adult fantasy *Untalented*, and the nature photography book *Shorescapes of Southern British Columbia*. She owns 500 books, four vehicles (none of which is a helicopter), one dog, too many Apple devices, and is tolerated by her cat, who is more famous in Germany than she is.

www.ingramcontent.com/pod-product-compliance
Lightning Source LLC
Chambersburg PA
CBHW022032120726
47899CB00001BB/80